Praise for *The*

"Riveting. . . . *The Last Goo[d]* [—] f work, a brash, big-strokes boo[k] f rich material here."   —*New York Times Book Review*

"Buzzing with emotional conflict and humming with worthwhile ideas about our times, Barbash knows how to bring the gravitas of literature and the romp of entertainment to bear on a single story. The nuances of character are unfailingly well established. . . . Approaches the scope of a work by Richard Russo, John Irving, Walker Percy, or T.C. Boyle."
          —*Plain Dealer* (Cleveland)

"Redolent of the atmosphere of small-town culture and wise in the ways of how real estate development can send towns on a fool's errand."   —*Pittsburgh Post-Gazette*

"A captivating debut."   —*Seattle Post-Intelligencer*

"Characterization soars to new heights. . . . *The Last Good Chance* insightfully explores why individuals and their communities depend upon creating hopeful images of the future in order to figure out how to experience life in the present."
          —*Press-Citizen* (Iowa City)

"There are memorable turns of phrase, smartly crafted vignettes of description . . . and flashes of outright brilliance in stretches of prose. . . . [A] well and tautly conceived story."
          —*Readerville Journal*

"Barbash brings fresh seriousness and sympathy and wit to bear on the ancient problem of loyalty. This is an ambitious, deftly plotted, multifariously satisfying piece of genuine American realism."   —Jonathan Franzen, author of *Purity*

"Here is a wonderful book. Humorous, poignant, filled with people we either know or have been, we watch, spellbound, as characters and a town struggle to invent and reinvent themselves, and to ultimately save themselves as well."
　　　　—Elizabeth Strout, author of *My Name Is Lucy Barton*

"This is a terrific book! If you can imagine a land that lies somewhere between the Coen Brothers and Richard Russo, then you have some idea of the territory occupied by Tom Barbash's hilarious, suspenseful, captivating novel."
　　　　—Dan Chaon, author of *Ill Will*

"Rich in plot and characters, *The Last Good Chance* is an old-fashioned novel that manages to embrace an entire world while, amazingly enough, deftly exploring the relationships between friends and lovers."　　　—Akhil Sharma, author of *Family Life*

"Tom Barbash has imbued his first novel with a strong and evocative sense of place, which infuses the entire book and reminds me of Russell Banks's writing. *The Last Good Chance* is heady, lyrical—and darkly funny in small, offhand moments. It's a pleasure to read." —Meg Wolitzer, author of *The Female Persuasion*

"A first novel with extraordinary empathic reach. . . . This is a taut, intricate vision of ambition, corruption, and love."
　　　　—*Publishers Weekly* (starred review)

"A winning debut. . . . A nice mixture of narrative, history, setting, and character: an amiable story drawn by a sure hand."
　　　　—*Kirkus Reviews*

"A well-paced drama with strong characters . . . suitable for reading in a rocking chair close to your woodstove. Highly recommended."　　　　—*Library Journal*

THE LAST GOOD CHANCE

ALSO BY TOM BARBASH

The Dakota Winters

On Top of the World

Stay Up with Me

THE LAST GOOD CHANCE

TOM BARBASH

ccc

An Imprint of HarperCollinsPublishers

THE LAST GOOD CHANCE. Copyright © 2002 by Tom Barbash. All rights reserved. Printed in the United States of America. No part of this book may be used or reproduced in any manner whatsoever without written permission except in the case of brief quotations embodied in critical articles and reviews. For information, address HarperCollins Publishers, 195 Broadway, New York, NY 10007.

HarperCollins books may be purchased for educational, business, or sales promotional use. For information, please email the Special Markets Department at SPsales@harpercollins.com.

A hardcover edition of this book was published in 2002 by Picador.

FIRST ECCO PAPERBACK EDITION PUBLISHED 2018.

Designed by Michelle Crowe

Title page and part opener photograph by debra millet/Shutterstock, Inc.

Library of Congress Cataloging-in-Publication Data has been applied for.

ISBN 978-0-06-235531-7

18 19 20 21 22   LSC   10 9 8 7 6 5 4 3 2 1

FOR HILARY

PART I

HOMECOMING

CHAPTER 1

Dusk set on the sidewalks of Lakeland, New York, and the children roamed free, gathering around parked cars, or squirting water pistols under the Lakeland Theater's gold art-deco marquee. A trio of girls gathered at a pay phone while one talked urgently. On his walk home from the Lakeland bureau of the *Syracuse Times Chronicle*, Steven Turner watched them with both the affection of nostalgia and a little pity, all made up, same blue eyeliner and lipstick; fourteen-year-old cheekbones hollowed with rouge. Turner wondered what it would be like to grow up here rather than downstate, a dozen blocks from the Brooklyn Bridge. If he'd been one of those boys across the street, strutting beneath a backward baseball cap, high-tops unlaced, baggy Orangeman T-shirt hanging to the knees. He might be more resolved now, he thought. He might be married, for instance, to one of those small-town sirens, and he might repair bridges or command a respectable road crew for a living instead of churning out news stories people glanced over at breakfast and then dropped in the trash, or under a dog.

Turner remembered the first time he actually saw this, a Doberman puppy at a friend's apartment shitting right over one of his Sunday features. "That-a-boy," Turner had said. "Don't hold back. Show me what you really think."

He could convince himself sometimes—because Turner needed to believe this—that what he did was imperative, and that his life up here was as well. He was twenty-eight years old. He was reasonably healthy, though prone to colds in winter because of his bad hours. He was liked and esteemed by most of the people he interviewed and worked with, if invisible to the newspaper's decision makers. He'd managed to make an enemy out of his immediate supervisor (not without cause: Turner told him once to go fuck himself), and while they decided not to fire him, they'd passed him up for the last three promotions. He was an energetic observer, he'd been told, but jealous editors complained he overwrote his articles and lost the purpose (and any news) along the way. "Well, I guess we know about his screwed-up childhood now, but who cares? He's a housing inspector, right? Wasn't this going to be about housing codes?"

But tonight, more than for his career, Turner had begun to have concern for his emaciated social life, because it was Friday and there had been a time not so long ago that he'd had company on his Friday nights. He didn't even have a decent beer-drinking partner now that Jack Lambeau had gone into premarital retirement. Turner was on his own.

He walked now across the Elm Street Bridge, to the town's thornier east side, where he lived in a peeling-paint rental house that listed noticeably on its flawed foundation. Turner's apartment had two bedrooms, one large and one tiny, a living room, and even a small sunken dining area. The floors slanted slightly. And the amenities were a trifle archaic—the bathroom had only a shallow tub, no shower, and a toilet that tilted worse than the floor. At night the street drummed with sounds from the corner bar. Turner had his window pinged once with a BB-gun, and several times he'd watched fistfights break out in the street. There was an edginess to this part of Lakeland that both disturbed and intrigued him. It wasn't unheard of to spot a syringe along with the crumpled beer cans at the basketball courts near the old armory where he played pickup games, or to find kids with primary-colored hair, nose rings, and a few tattoos.

His furniture was either dilapidated or bohemian, depending

on your perspective. Turner took pride in the fact that nothing, not the lavender couch (which came with two stuffed pillows) nor his brass framed bed nor the swollen chartreuse armchair, which he settled peaceably into now, had cost him more than $75. To cut down on clutter he'd recycled a roomful of newspapers and kept only his own stories, which he sorted into loose categories: Rural Crime (there were strange ones—Satanic Possessions, Animal Sacrifices, Shotgun Accidents Involving Grade-Schoolers), Tearjerkers, Governmental Dirt, and Profiles—puffs and slams.

He smoked a joint and then read for a while, Gogol's *Dead Souls*. Friday evening and again this was his date—a dead Russian. After a half hour Turner's phone rang. It was his landlady, Mrs. Willhillen.

"Hello, Steven?" She was the only person outside his family who called him by his first name. "You know on Friday afternoons at the Captain's Quarter they have a lovely Polynesian buffet."

Her voice was high-pitched and saccharine. The first time she'd called, Turner had thought a friend was playing a joke. He'd responded with a sexual suggestion that Mrs. Willhillen fortunately hadn't comprehended.

"Thank you, Mrs. Willhillen."

"It's very authentic. Do you like roast pork?"

"Very much."

"Did you get the pie I left for you?"

"I did. It was delicious."

"I've made better, to be honest. Well, bye then, Steven."

She'd been calling once or twice a week with suggestions: a garage sale, or a church dinner a single boy could take advantage of. They were designed to cheer him, but they had the opposite effect.

He decided to go for a walk.

He entered a bar. He drank a beer and played a game of pool, which he won on dumb luck. His opponent sunk the eight and then angrily watched the cue ball drop too before glowering at Turner as if it had been his fault.

Outside, the street was bathed in fluorescent light that shined off the trucks and souped-up Camaros and Mustangs that swept by. Turner stared at the cars in a slit-eyed rendition of the redneck cool faces that hung out the windows, and he imagined riding that way through the night, spitting Skoal, revving his muscled-up engine at intersections, stopping every once in a while for a tall boy and a few shots of Jägermeister (the third one of which he'd get on the house), being hauled outside at a quarter past two by a cop he'd know from high school, who'd make him walk a straight line for his freedom.

Turner had had only a passing fondness for Bruce Springsteen until he lived in Lakeland, and now all his songs seemed heart-breakingly perceptive.

HE DECIDED TO CALL a secretary from the college whom he'd met at a bar once. He read her number from a napkin he'd left folded in his wallet.

"Kathy?"

"Yes?"

"It's Turner."

Her silence was disheartening.

"Turner?"

"The reporter. We met at the Saw Mill?"

"The Saw Mill? Oh, Turner. Yeah, I remember you. You were supposed to call a while ago." He pictured her doing something else while she spoke to him, cleaning out a drawer perhaps.

"Yeah, well, I was wondering, if you weren't doing anything, if you'd want to maybe get a drink later?"

"I don't think so. I've got plans."

"Well, I just thought I'd take a chance," he said. "How about some time next week?"

"Maybe. Give me a call."

Of course she had plans, he thought. Friday night for Chrissakes. Who calls someone out of the blue to make plans at eight o'clock on a Friday evening?

HE THOUGHT HE'D TREAT himself to a decent dinner in order to pick up his mood. No fast food. Hardees or Burger King would do him in right now. He'd see a wizened old man in the corner, talking to himself over a ketchupy cheeseburger, and imagine that as his future. He chose Giovanni's Fine Italian Food, where he could eat at the bar and talk to the bartender, Serena, a rough-edged, perpetually tanned woman of twenty-two who lived with a wealthy sporting-goods store owner twice her age, and occasionally, when the sporting-goods store owner was away, had sex with Turner, and shared with him some of her boyfriend's pot.

She brought him his plate of spaghetti and his beer.

"Nice story about the dog," she said.

"You liked it?"

He hadn't entirely. A dog had burned its paw on a tarlike substance that had found its way onto on old stretch of farmland. A neighbor had found the dog stumbling up the road and had had the prudence to call the newspaper along with the veterinarian. Turner thought it might eventually be a good story, because there was no reason chemicals should be left out on a farm. He hadn't been able to reach the vet or the owner of the land, however, and the state DEC said it would be a while before they could send anyone out to check up on it. So for now it was, as his editor, Clark, said, "just a dog and a fucked-up foot."

"Absolutely," Serena said. "That's really disgusting, someone leaving stuff like that around."

She walked down to the other end of the bar where a couple of men had just sat down. She took their orders, began measuring and pouring. Turner loved to watch people who were good at their work, whether they were athletes or dancers or concert pianists. Serena was an exquisite bartender. She sprayed vermouth into a martini glass with what looked like a tiny plant sprayer, and poured a perfect pint of lager without glancing at the glass. She handed them their drinks, listening dutifully while one of them told a joke about lawyers.

"Someone's paying those farmers, I'd bet," she said when she returned. "Exxon or someone like that."

AS HE ATE his plate of spaghetti, Turner glanced across the restaurant floor at the diners and saw a disconcertingly attractive woman smoothing the veins on the forearm of his friend, Jack Lambeau. Even if he hadn't known who it was—and he knew it was Lambeau's fiancée—he would have known she was from somewhere else, a land where people met on the front steps of museums, or at flea markets, or in bagel lines. She wore a charcoal V-neck sweater with something black and lacy beneath and with the sleeves rolled up near her elbows. Her arms were slender and pale; she'd pulled her auburn hair back from her face in a barrette. A strand or two fell over her eyes and she tossed her head back from time to time to clear them away.

He hoped that up close she'd have an unpardonable flaw he couldn't spot from that distance: crossed eyes, gray teeth, an emptiness of expression, something that would enable him to escape his envy. But when they'd finished their meal and walked toward him that hope collapsed.

Lambeau spotted him and waved.

"Hey, Turner. I told you we'd go public. Anne, this is Turner."

She smiled at him. She had a long neck and an elegant collarbone. He wanted to run his finger along it.

He couldn't think of what to say. He looked away from her as one would from a bright light. Then he thought that was rude, so he looked her in the eyes. They were warm and intelligent.

"Nice to finally meet you," Turner said.

"Likewise," Anne said. The locks of hair descended again.

"You've had quite the buildup."

"It's all true, you know," Anne said.

"The boxing career and all," Turner said, randomly.

"Absolutely," she said, fists raised.

She and Lambeau smiled at one another then in a way that made Turner think of the moment after sex. Perhaps they'd done it at the table without him seeing.

"Actually, Turner, I tried to call you earlier. We're going to find a place to do some dancing. You want to go make fools of ourselves?"

He pictured himself in a corner watching Lambeau wheel his dream woman around the dance floor. There'd be only one fool.

"Thanks. But I gotta get up early tomorrow," he said, then added, "I'll take a rain check."

"You're working on a Saturday?"

"Well, yes—got a few things going on."

WHEN THEY LEFT he felt discourteous, because the invitation had been genuine—Lambeau was trying to include him—and because he wanted to be happy for them. He would be at some point, but for the moment he was absurdly forlorn. He looked at his reflection in the mirrored side wall. He took off his glasses, messed his hair up a bit. It was pointless. He put his glasses back on. He looked over again and he saw that Serena had been watching him.

"No date tonight?" she said.

"No, in fact, the women of the world got together, took a vote, and decided I could go another ten years without one. You were there, weren't you?"

She smiled at him.

"No, I think I was working then."

There was no one else at the bar. She was drying glasses with a rag.

"Nice-looking woman, huh?" she said.

"She's all right."

"All right? She's a total babe, Turner."

"I guess she's a babe."

Serena cleared the bottles and glasses from the other side of the bar, then stacked her checks next to the cash register before returning.

"I get off at eleven," she said. "You want to come back and pick me up? Garrett's away for the weekend."

"Was it written on my face?"

"Nah," she said. "But I'm a good reader."

CHAPTER 2

When he was a year out of graduate school, Jack Lambeau
published his graduate thesis as a book, a thin, hundred-page
rant on all that had gone foul in urban design and town planning, and what he might do in its stead. That it would gather
so much attention had never been in his plans; that it would
be excerpted in two national magazines, appear on a New
England bestseller list, and that he'd have a short life on the
lecture circuit and on public television and radio talk shows
was beyond proper proportion. He didn't think there was anything earthshaking in what he'd written (entitled *Death by
Landscape—How America Lost Its Soul*). It was all common
sense. He'd ripped into easy targets: suburban shopping plazas
and housing subdivisions, zoning, cars, cul-de-sacs, television,
fast food, parking lots, crass consumerism, the disposability
and accompanying ugliness of everything built in the last
twenty years, and he made the prediction that at the dawn of
the new century there'd be a countrywide yearning for the sort
of communities that had been banished to the historic waste
bin: a return of small-town life. It was a sound and sensible
piece of work, he believed, but it was nothing more than luck
and good timing, and possibly his youth and height (6'3") and
purportedly passable looks (and a jacket photo that made him
look, according to a friend, "like a bookish water-polo player")
that had made him, for a short while, the new and ubiquitous
voice on urban design.

If he was liked and revered by a sector of the reading public, he did not see his standing within the New York City Planning Commission—where he'd been working—improve. Rather, there was an element that clearly resented Jack his minor celebrity, though he never trumpeted his accomplishments and was for his own part unconvinced by them. They buried him in paperwork, silenced him at meetings, and ignored him at city functions. He had begun to see his early success as less of a stepping stone to greatness and more a roadblock to it.

Typical in its futility was his effort to create a health park in western Harlem. Within the first month Jack found himself mired knee-deep in something called the Uniform Land Use Review Procedure, preparing cumbersome documents, sending forms out to twenty public agencies, and then waiting for signatures to come back while the project died and the main hospital went under. And there were other frustrations—a section of city with no traffic and still a two-month wait for approval from the Department of Traffic, or someone finding an arrowhead on a building site and demanding it closed so that a team of archaeologists could scour it for a year. It got so that his biggest triumphs were securing permits for a street fair, or helping ensure that a group of buildings in Park Slope didn't block the lunchtime sun for a bunch of families in three-story brownstones.

The Lakeland project came about on one of Jack's visits home. He'd been recruited by the mayor to give a talk on waterfront development and the re-imagining of small towns, subjects on which he had a lot to say. When he finished he'd won everyone over, with the possible exception of the town planner, Karl Farnach, who'd been heading the project up to that point and whom Jack eventually supplanted.

He declined initially, for a hundred reasons, but each week the mayor sweetened the pot (more pay and more say, and finally a turn-of-the-century farmhouse he and his fiancée, Anne Marks, could live in). Within a month Jack had decided to take the project on. He was thirty-two, and thirty-two was as good an age as any to build something lasting, to leave a mark, to show he could do more than just talk the talk, and why shouldn't he begin with the town where he was born?

OUTSIDE THE FRONT DOOR of the Octopus's Garden, three employees did the bump to Madonna's "Lucky Star."

The doorman, who wore Wayfarer-type sunglasses and dressed as an octopus with wiry tentacles squirming from his back, called out, "Jack Lambeau, am I right?"

"Yes?"

The octopus took his sunglasses off. Jack searched the muscular face. It belonged to the younger brother of a boy from his high school track team.

"How you doing, Ronny?" Jack said.

"Must be kind of pathetic being back here after New York, huh?"

Ronny's tentacles bobbed as he moved to the beat. Jack glanced at Anne to gauge her reaction.

"This is New York, Ronny," he said.

THE DECOR INSIDE was like a cruise ship lounge—thickly perfumed air, flashing colored squares on a dance floor flooded with strobe lights. Two couples danced mirthlessly in opposite corners.

Jack began imagining how he might transform the place if he were a club owner: an antique bar, oak booths rather than the Formica conference tables, speakers hidden from view or at least less obtrusive. This was time-warp decor, and there was plenty of it in Lakeland.

"You know, don't you, that I invented the bus stop right here," he said. "Travolta got it from me. It's not a well-known fact."

"I knew that."

"You want to dance?" he asked.

"Sure," she said. "But take it easy on me, killer. I'm new in these parts."

Through the fat white disks of light, they twisted and swooned. They danced ten straight songs until Jack was exhausted. Anne didn't want to quit. She'd spent all day stretching canvases and painting and it hadn't tired her. She walked onto the floor and began dancing to another Madonna song—by herself this time. She rolled her shoulders, swirled her head around so that her hair brushed back and forth across her face. She smiled at him then. It was all in fun. She was a good dancer, and she knew it.

So did the men in the place. A couple of weight-lifter types raised their eyebrows. The bartender, who wore Day-Glo green suspenders over a white T-shirt, paused between drinks to stare.

It was just a woman dancing, for Chrissakes, and not even their sort; no cleavage showing and no heavy-duty makeup, no stiletto heels. Still, they stared. He joined her on the dance floor.

"People don't do that here," he heard himself tell her.

"They don't do what?"

She had no comprehension of what she'd done to the room.

"They don't have as much fun as we're having," he said.

Loosen up, he told himself.

AS THEY DROVE BACK to the farmhouse, Jack thought of how contented they'd been in their sequestered little world, away from the town, among the cows and corn. He'd feared that Anne would last a week, that she'd find it dreary and isolating and then give up on it and on him, for all the reasons he'd left here fifteen years earlier. But right off she saw it for what it could be, quiet and green, and agreeably slow; *regenerative* was the word she used, a good place to become an artist, which was what she'd wanted to be since college, when her paintings had won the undergraduate prize and covered the walls of the campus coffee shop. She'd postponed that dream the last six years while she did marketing research, focus groups and the like, for a large

Manhattan advertising agency. Now she was having a go at it, waking early in the morning and setting up a still life, or walking down to the lake with her brushes and easel (Jack loved that image: Anne in shorts and a loose-fitting tank top, hair pulled back in a band, heading to the lake to paint). And if it was hard to make the adjustment to having all that free time, and living in a strange place where she knew no one, Anne had yet to complain. Even the dinner with his parents had been tolerable, despite his father telling her how much respect he had for "the Jewish people," and his mother trying to commandeer their wedding, and both of them staring at Anne like she was a museum piece they appreciated but didn't entirely understand.

Mostly they were alone together, in exquisite privacy. They fished for their dinner and barbecued out back. One time they set up a card table in the empty grain silo. They drank Stolichnaya and sang to each other in the cavelike acoustics. Another night they put paint on each other's bodies and made angels on a wide white canvas, which they hung in the dining room. When they slept, their dreams were softened by the breeze that crept through the tiny cracks in the bedroom walls, and by the summer sounds of crickets and owls. And while he could imagine what that breeze might become in winter, Jack didn't let that thought occupy him for long these warm days and nights. It was summer now, green and warm and awash with promise, and this was where he wanted to be.

THE FARMHOUSE UNDER A NEW MOON seemed almost too perfect as they pulled down the dirt driveway: the weather vane on the roof, the troughs that still stood from when the owners raised horses, the unused grain silo out back, the split-rail fencing. They'd spent their weekends buying furniture from antiques stores, and the house he'd taken over empty was beginning to look like a home.

A foot apart from Anne on the front steps, he asked, "Would you think me forward if I asked you to stay over?"

She smiled. "Only if you'll tie me to the bed."

He clasped his hands around her waist.

"That was fun tonight, huh?"

"Yes," she said. "But I feel like I've landed in someone else's life."

"You landed in my backwater adolescence."

She laughed.

"It feels so wonderfully random. Other than you, of course. But it feels like we could be anywhere." She pulled him close. "Kansas. Switzerland. You're the only familiar thing. My one landmark."

He didn't remind her that they were only an afternoon's drive from Manhattan. He pushed her hair out of her face, then kissed each eyelid. They'd been together a year and a half in New York, but up here, away from their old friends and old lives, everything felt new. They were right to do this, as crazy as it had sounded to everyone else.

He took a deep breath, and took stock of where he was.

"Sometimes I just can't believe we're here, you know. Either of us, really, in this town, in this old house."

"I believe it," she said. "It's all I've ever wanted."

He lifted her sweater, began rubbing her pale, soft stomach. The unfamiliar woman from the dance floor.

Wife, he said softly, loving that word.

HE SAW A NOTE on the door, written in a penciled scrawl:

What the hell, Jacker? Thought you guys never left.
   Got your message. As to why I'm tough to locate—
   I've been working my tail off. Didn't know I had one,
   eh? Now it's your turn to visit, big brother.
   Don't say I don't love you.
   Harris.

CHAPTER 3

Money was starting to trickle in. The city put out a request for proposals, and largely due to Jack's campaigning, and perhaps his name, downstate developers responded. A full twenty-two of them paid five hundred each just to pick up the request. The banks bought in, offering cheap seed money for preliminary plans, borings, and environmental assessments.

After that it was like dominoes. The merchants' association signed on, and then the churches and clubs, the Masons, Elks, Knights of Columbus, the Moose Lodge, and the Rotarians. Even the unions were eager and were talking about waiving some of the work rules to get the jobs. Jack seized the momentum. He worked closely with a consulting firm to figure out how much the city should charge for the land, how much financing they should provide, if any. He convened a panel of social scientists and academic advisors for their suggestions, making sure the newspapers were there to capture the discussions. There were questions about Lakeland's main (and badly ailing) commercial center, Pine Street, and whether a waterfront marketplace would kill those businesses. Jack assured the merchants they'd be linked easily to the waterfront, some could even move there, and that they'd get more in overflow business than they currently got without competition—everyone will benefit, he said, and most were convinced.

The crowds at the meetings doubled, and then doubled again. A small confederation of naysayers nitpicked and whined about increased traffic and higher rents, but now the supporters drowned them out. The winds were in their favor. Development schemes were tricky, sensitive to market factors, the economy, demand, fads, interest rates. They had to be timed right, not six months late nor six months early, and it appeared in this case they had hit all the numbers. What he'd like, Jack said at one public hearing (which the paper said had the feel of "a football pep rally with a genius coach"), was to reclaim not just the water-front but the relevance and self-confidence of the entire region, and to start a ripple effect, whereby over the next decade, dozens of these old down-in-the-mouth factory towns east of the Mo-hawk Valley and down the Hudson might *find* themselves again, following Lakeland's lead.

It was a waste to let these great places rot and die, he said. And who could argue with that?

Jack put together a marketing scheme and began pitching it to downstate developers. He sent deftly tailored proposals to busi-ness and historic preservation groups, the state, private founda-tions, and federal agencies. He was pitching it two ways: it was regeneration and it was smart business. It wasn't simply a bailout.

Planning all this by conventional means took years. What Jack had done was collapse the first year and a half into three months. There was something happening nearly every night, a town workshop or another expert panel, which meant there was always a story in the paper, and more often than not on the nightly news.

A Rochester reporter called Jack "supremely bright, and perhaps a touch cocky." It was meant as a compliment, and he took it as such. In truth he was more than a little apprehen-sive (though he was careful to hide this, to reinvent himself as the world-beater they imagined him to be). He worried someone would point out he'd never actually *built* anything in New York, and that he was out of his depth here. But maybe that was what this was about.

Great acts began with leaps of faith, he was coming to believe, and the ability to convince others to see what you see.

DURING THESE DAYS, Jack and Steven Turner had an ongoing lunchtime competition, begun when Jack first returned to Lakeland. They'd race the trails and potholed backroads along the lake, play basketball behind the armory or, on Turner's insistence, miniature golf, and whoever lost bought the drinks the next time they went out. In basketball, Turner gave up a few inches to Jack, and more in the way of athletic ability, but he managed to steal the occasional game because he played street ball—constant hand checks and bumps—and because he had an odd running left-handed hook shot he hoisted from his hip, a shot that was nearly unguardable, and on some days, like this one, went down in bunches.

"You're missing some pretty awesome evenings down at the Three Corners," Turner said as they took a water break at ten all. "Two fights on Saturday night."

"Only two?"

The Three Corners was a combustible section of town where one street angled into another and formed three corners with three shoulder-to-shoulder taverns, with loud dance music and lethal drink specials. Jack and Turner had gone there a few times and once Turner had met a girl from the college who'd told him that he looked like Eddie Vedder with glasses, and had run her hand through his hair a few times before eventually leaving with someone else.

"I saw a guy get his head smashed with a bottle," Turner said. "You really ought to bring Anne down there."

Turner liked to conquer his loneliness, Jack thought, by immersing himself in alienating settings and proving to himself he could fit in.

"Sorry, I've been so busy lately," Jack said.

"It's all right. I'm making new friends."

"Really?"

"No. But I'm getting close to my goal."

Jack looked at him. He was supposed to ask, Which goal? He didn't.

". . . of winning a bonus game on every pinball machine in town."

"I think you're setting your sights a little high there, Turner."

"Everyone's gotta have a dream."

Jack had called Turner his first week back in town, on the urging of a mutual friend, a woman he'd dated briefly, who had gone to college with Turner and described him as funny and bright, if at times a bit aloof, or tediously distrustful of anyone making more money than him. "He's got *issues*," she'd said, and left it at that. The two men played on now; Turner hit a couple of hooks and then, abruptly but predictably, his shot went cold. Jack tied the game, and then hit four straight jump shots to finish Turner off. He didn't mind a close game, but he couldn't stand to lose to someone who looked as unorthodox on a basketball court as Turner. He beat him for the sake of the sport.

"I wish they could see this side of you," Turner said.

"Which side is that?"

"The cutthroat son of a bitch."

"I'm not hiding it," Jack said, smiling.

As was their ritual, they would end with a game of H-O-R-S-E, the contest where a player has to match the other's shot from wherever on the court, or whatever crazy method the shooter decided.

Turner heaved up a shot from the top of the key and it splashed through without touching the rim.

Jack tried to match the shot and missed.

"It's just kind of strange to watch them listen to you," Turner said, as he gathered the rebound. "You speak of re-zoning and it might as well be scripture. They *quote* you."

"Who?"

"Lots of people. Old Marcia at the Chamber of Commerce, most of the councilmen, even people I overhear in bars. They've read your book. They speak in little Lambeauisms. Those meetings of yours are starting to feel like church revivals."

"Praise the Lawd," Jack said.

Turner took another shot, a reverse lay-up preceded by an awful-looking double pump. The ball swirled around the rim twice and then tumbled in.

Jack shook his head in disgust. "You *didn't* just make that crap."

"It's not crap if *you* can't do it."

Jack mimicked Turner's double pump as best he could and managed to sink the shot.

They played on, Turner using his reborn hook shot to take a two-letter lead.

"You know what I think it is," Turner said when Jack had reached H-O-R-S. "You give them a vision of themselves. A scrubbed-up, more cultivated vision, and they like that."

"I'm a salesman is what I am," Jack said.

"Maybe," Turner said. "But if you are you're good at hiding it. You're one of them. And you're not. And I think they like the Ivy League pedigree, so long as you don't breathe it in their faces."

"I'm not the first Ivy Leaguer to grow up here, Turner."

"No, just the first to move back."

AMIDST THE GROWING BELIEF in Jack's plan, there were, of course, some small battles with the city council and with Mayor Bill Hickey. Hickey had an unyielding and indiscriminate affection for chain stores and restaurants, for one thing; if something was well known, it was worth knowing. And they had other differences, over matters like land acquisition, and over word choice. When asked at a press conference if the city could put aside its failures over the last thirty years, Hickey came up with the concept of *re-remembering*.

"You mean like lying?" Turner's colleague, Stewart Dix, had asked.

"Not lying. We're re-remembering. The past is a *flexible* thing," Hickey'd said.

That ended up being the lead in the paper the next day:

Lakeland's Mayor William Hickey says the past is a "flexible thing."

AT THE CLOSE OF the mid-August Common Council meeting, he watched the mayor whip himself into a near evangelical pitch, cleaving the air, sermonizing about the harborfront project, comparing it at one point to, of all things, the Statue of Liberty. From his seat in the front row, Jack motioned the mayor to settle down. Hickey glanced skyward, then continued.

"I don't want to get overly elated on you here, but I think this all goes to show that good things come to those who wait, and those who deserve it. We're talking about a whole new Lakeland here," he said, his red face beaming cartoonishly. "If this doesn't excite you then your circuits must have fizzed out a decade ago."

The crowd applauded the mayor's histrionics. Five or six people whistled. After years of dwindling galleries—and deservedly so—the meeting was packed to standing room. Two Syracuse television stations and one from Utica hoisted cameras. The faces around the vast old meeting hall were hopeful, expectant. The end of their social and economic winter was nearly at hand.

"No longer will we have to make excuses or apologies about anything. We'll be the envy of the Ontario coast."

LATER THAT NIGHT, when they'd been served their second beers at the Holiday Inn, Jack began ribbing Hickey about the Statue of Liberty reference.

"Means we're not apologizing to the pricks of the world. That's liberty in my book."

Hickey owned the back left-hand corner table of the Holiday

Inn dining room. It had been his idea to bring the Holiday Inn to Lakeland as the city's first chain hotel, and when business was slow he'd almost single-handedly kept it afloat. Having a Holiday Inn was the first step in becoming a great American city, the mayor once said. "Name me a great city without one."

Hickey took off his Kelly blazer now and rolled his sleeves up. He was a burly man with almost no discernible neck, a squat though not unappealing face, red from days spent on his boat, and a flattop of brittle white hair. His wife called him Whitey, an address he permitted no one else.

"Remember that charter I took out with those banker boys you sent me from your college?"

"Pawkins and Dial and them?"

Hickey winced. "Yeah, those are the ones."

"I thought that went well. Dial's got a picture of you and him holding up a chest-high steelhead."

"That's nice."

"So why does that stick in your mind?"

"This is what I'm talking about, Jack. First off they ignore me almost the whole way, like I was the maid or something. Not that I need or even want constant conversation. Far from it. It's just something I felt from them, that kind of blue-blood frostiness, you know what I'm talking about, I know you do. Finally the blond guy, Pawkins, asks, 'Do you live here year-round, captain, or do you take this gal down to Florida?' I think more to impress the others that he can talk the way we do up here. I tell him I need to be around town all year. I've got responsibilities.

"He asks what kind of responsibilities a fisherman would have in the winter. 'Your responsibility is to fish, am I right?' he says.

"I tell him what I thought you'd told him, that I'm mayor of Lakeland. He looks at me like a guy who thinks he's with a woman and finds out it's a fruit in drag.

"'You're kidding,' he says.

"'No. I'm not kidding,' I tell him. 'I've been mayor for six years now.'

"'Mayor,' the other one says, 'that's so cool. That's how it is up here, isn't it? I bet you're fire chief too?'

"All right. So it was a joke, and I can take a joke, Jack, you know I can as well as anyone. But something in the way he says this makes me want to smack him and toss him off the boat—I swear I'm this close." He held his thumb and forefinger an inch apart.

"But I don't, because they're friends of yours. But I'm thinking, Jack's buddies with these guys? I have to tell you, it didn't make me feel so very fond of you right there. It was the complete lack of respect and their sense of, how would you say it . . ."

"Entitlement?"

"That's it. It's what you'd call a *metaphor* for how people shit on upstate. They make fun and we take it. They send their criminals and their trash up here, and we take it. They come up and buy up the Adirondacks—they're doing that right now, Jackie, subdividing that big beautiful forest. And then they make us keep land empty to solve their water problems. Now I know we stand to make some money in these situations. But it's the attitude I mind. It makes my skin crawl."

He sized Jack up with his stare. Hickey had bushy white eyebrows that knitted together in one long line.

"You weren't like that. Even when they had you on all those talk shows, and in that magazine."

"Thanks," Jack said. But from the age of twelve, he'd had an attitude. He remembered wishing he was from anywhere else, from California, or Alaska, or Boston, or even Albany, just not central New York with the flat accents, folks having "birbecues," cans of "soda paap," joining bowling leagues and 4-H clubs. When he'd opened his college acceptances Jack had leapt around town like a convict given his release.

"You always had a strong character. That's why they all worship you."

"Hey, Bill, got some business to ask you about."

"Hmmm. Sounds serious. Go ahead, Jackrabbit."

"What's up with us canceling the site inspections at the old factory yards?"

"We didn't cancel. We just moved them back a couple weeks."

"Why'd we do that?"

"Had a few last things to clear."

"Barrels."

Hickey nodded. "Yeah. I told you about 'em."

"That was back a while."

A month ago, Hickey told Jack that the cleanup crews had removed four 55-gallon barrels of chemical waste and carted them to a waste treatment site in Buffalo.

They agreed then not to call the state about it, because it was only four barrels, and because calling attention to them would have meant a far more protracted inspection period, and missing out on a one-shot grant to expand the sewers. And besides, Hickey had assured him, the barrels would soon be disposed of properly, if not publicly.

"No big deal, Jack. Ten total and that's it. Really."

The waitress came by then with two new beers.

"Woman of my dreams . . ." Hickey said.

Jack stewed.

"Come on, Jackie. It's nothing. You want to report them? We'll do it tomorrow. We'll call the state DEC."

They should, but they couldn't now, Jack knew. They had meetings the next week with the banks.

"I just don't like new information. I need to know what's going on."

"You're one hundred percent right, Jacker. I'm sorry. It's your baby and you call the shots. But everything's taken care of. The sites are ready next week. That's what we wanted and that's what's happening."

Jack felt mollified if not entirely reassured.

"Tell me we've got nothing to worry about here, Bill."

"We've got nothing to worry about. We're going great guns. No snags."

Jack looked across the empty dining room and Hickey finished the last of his beer.

"How's our Annie settling in?" Hickey said finally.

"Great."

"It's just that we'd love to see her. Sarah tried to phone her a few times to take her down to Syracuse for some shopping—a ladies' day. The one time she got her on the phone, Anne said she can't now, but maybe next month. Not next week, next month."

Jack could hear Anne saying that. He knew she hadn't meant it as a snub. She was trying to establish a work routine.

"She's a little absorbed in her work right now. I'm sure she'd love to go."

"No big thing. She's adjusting. Why don't we plan a dinner, though? Just the four of us. That'd be nice, wouldn't it?"

BEFORE DRIVING HOME, JACK thought of those extra barrels. They could indeed be a snag. He imagined someone complaining—and legitimately—that they hadn't followed protocol. Still, he'd seen too many projects die on the vine while lawyers argued about something that ultimately amounted to nothing. If there was more to this, they'd act, and he would need to keep an eye on it, but for now they needed to forge ahead. If he'd learned anything in his early stumblings as a planner it was not to squander momentum. You could lose it, and once you did it was nearly impossible to get it back.

As he made his way through town, he moved his thoughts to Anne, to just how absorbed she'd been with her work. He was proud of her, and maybe even a little jealous. She already had concrete results from her efforts, after all.

If he had a complaint—and maybe it wasn't a complaint so much as a concern—it was about the tendency of her workspace to wander about the house. That morning he'd noticed a tube of paint next to the bagels on the kitchen counter, and he'd stumbled in the dark over a bicycle wheel and a headless mannequin she'd been using as subjects in the living room. But it wasn't a big deal, really. She was still figuring out where she worked best, he thought. Eventually she'd designate a single room as a studio and she could make whatever kind of mess she wanted.

WHEN HE REACHED HIS brother's street, Jack saw his pregnant sister-in-law sitting on their porch, next to Harris's ancient huge bloodhound, Samson. In the moonlight Marla looked pale and spectral.

"Is he home?"

"Oh, great. This time he said he was with you."

Jack wondered if waiting up every night for someone aged you. In her daisy-print nightgown and her violet cardigan, her hair tied back so that it pinched her young face, Marla looked like a girl made up as an old lady in a school play.

He petted Samson. The dog's mouth foamed. Gobs of sleep ringed his sad eyes.

"It's not what you think it is."

"Is that so? What do I think it is, Jack?"

"It's not that. He's not screwing around," he said, and when he said it he believed it.

"Well, what is it at this hour of night, and why's he lying to me? You're not supposed to lie like that to the mother of your child. That's not supposed to happen. This isn't how it's supposed to be."

"I guess not. Listen, we've been missing each other. You want to tell him I stopped by?"

"Sure will," she said absently.

Jack turned and started for the car.

"You know what I did today?" she asked. He braced himself. Marla didn't have enough people to talk to.

"What'd you do?" He stepped back onto the porch.

"Well, on Monday I hid a few boxes of lemon pudding under cushions under that crappy couch in the basement, the one from Harris's old place? You know why I did that?"

"Why?"

"I don't know why I'm telling you this."

Jack shrugged.

"I just wanted to see if I had the discipline, if I could make it through a week without making pudding. You know how many days I lasted?"

Samson pushed his behemoth nose against the door. Marla let him inside.

"Take a guess," she said.

"One?"

"Two. I lasted two days. This morning I find myself walking down the basement steps, like one of those zombies in the movies." She laughed a sad laugh. "Then I stopped. No, I said to myself, and then I thought, The heck with that. I can eat whatever I want."

"Absolutely, Marla," Jack said. "And the kid probably loved the pudding." He hoped this was the end of her confession.

"Hold on. I'm not done. Everyone wants to finish my stories for me."

"Go ahead. I'm interested," he said.

"I don't like it when people do that," she said.

"I'm sorry, Marla. I really want to hear this."

She composed herself, ran her hand over her hair.

"I'm just a little sensitive these days," she said. "You can't talk to a dog all day, 'specially one that's going deaf."

"I understand."

"You're a lot better than Harris."

"I'm not so sure," Jack said, "but thanks."

In his years away Jack had seen Harris only sparingly, once or twice a year, and to say they'd drifted apart did not adequately describe the distance between them. As kids they were always together, attached at the hip, his father used to say. Pictures at the old house testified to that, the two brothers in baseball uniforms, or swinging from the same tire in the backyard. Lean and guileful, Jack wasn't always the better child. He just got away with more than his brother. His mother recognized it, if his father never did. Jack cut the occasional class, got high from time to time, broke a store window once with his BB gun. But he knew how to work the system, whatever it was. Harris was the opposite. Harris might do the work all semester in a class and then not study for the final or hand in the final paper. Even their bodies bore this inequity. While Jack had reached his full height in college, Harris, who, at twelve had been taller than his brother, stopped growing after his fourteenth birthday and never made it above a muscle-bound five-foot-ten. And while Jack's face took on the lines and expressions of the worlds he moved through, Harris's stayed unfledged and youthful, his shoulder-length hair resolutely thick, as though he was caught in a biological holding pattern.

If Harris harbored any resentment toward his brother, it never showed. Harris bragged about Jack's success as if it were his own. Conversely, Jack had failed to introduce Harris to any of his close friends the first time Harris visited him in New York. Jack felt disgusted with himself later, and interpreted the slighting as a form of self-loathing. The next and only other time Harris came down, Jack threw a party for his brother and invited everyone. They all liked Harris (who unfortunately got rather wasted)—in the superior way they'd perhaps liked *The Dukes of Hazzard* as kids. "Must have been *wild* growing up in a world like that," one of his friends had said.

"Well, I brought the boxes out," Marla explained. "I was going to make one box. That's all. I hid the other one again. Then I think: That's the wrong move. Make them both at once, get it all over with, Marla. I mixed together both boxes. I made two large bowls of that goopy yellow pudding. I let them sit. I said, 'Will power, will power.'" She winced. "Then I ate a whole bowl in about ten minutes."

"Well, it must have been good."

"Don't you get it? It's *love*. I'm eating all that pudding 'cause I want him to love me and the baby."

"He does, Marla."

"He's got a funny way of showing it. Listen, I don't really care anymore, to tell you the truth."

She talked a while longer about her back pains and her nausea, how she saw the baby as a tiny general giving orders. She pictured him pointing at diagrams on a blackboard. When she felt a kick, it was his hand pointing out things he wanted her to do. The baby was taking over her consciousness, she said. Did Jack know what she meant by that?

He didn't, he said.

She said she hadn't been able to tell Harris any of this.

Jack looked at Marla's stomach and he thought of how he was in no hurry to have kids, none at all.

"What time does he usually get in?" he asked.

"One or so. He acts disgusted around me when he gets in bed, like he can't stand the sight of me, when it's part of him that's making me look like this."

"You look great."

"That's just it. I mean the least he could do is lie a little, like you."

CHAPTER 4

Lakeland, Anne wrote in a letter to her sister, was bowling alleys and *Charlie's Angels* hair. Slipcovered sofas and flannel shirts and Old Glory hanging from the roof of the portico. It was a town of churches and bars, and bars that played the role of churches. If not as ascetic or inspirational as the Aix of Cezanne, it was a perfectly good town for an artist to inhabit for a year or two. She explained how the river divided the town into distinct sections, poor and not so poor; how the further east you strayed the worse the homes became; how the west side had the country club, the nicer churches, the better homes and restaurants; how, according to Jack, eight or nine families ran the city, and they all lived on the west side.

Anne and Jack's farmhouse—the rustic, postcard red farmhouse—was outside it all, in a land of rolling pasture and deep woods so quiet you could hear a door shutting a quarter mile away.

If I don't become a painter, she said signing off, I won't be able to blame it on my surroundings.

Right away, she loved the farmhouse. It was exactly as she'd imagined—several of the rooms offered terrific light, especially at the end of the day, between seven or so and the sunset. She found herself liking best the empty room on the second floor, the one with a southwest exposure. For a couple of evenings she sat on a rocking chair in the center of the wood floor, looked through the window at the purpling dusk, and thought to herself that this is what it should feel like.

By the second weekend Anne brought her paints and sketch-pads out, and began playing around in a rudimentary way. She sketched a milk carton, a wine bottle, one of Jack's haggard old running shoes. She painted a shirtless old man sleeping under a tree. She'd looked at the house across the road, and there he was—his crooked concave nose, his creased skin, a smirk beneath his closed eyes. She felt good when she finished these.

She painted more, and while doing so she tried to study the world around her. There were tons of trees in Lakeland, and Anne studied how the greens varied, and the size of the leaves too, that on the maple in the backyard, the longer and lovelier leaves were found on the uppermost branches. And she noticed how the wind didn't simply twist the leaves and thin branches wrong side up, like a million drawings she'd seen, but that it swirled dust and dirt into the air, and that this union was a chaotic one.

She tried to capture this in simple quick paintings. She'd see, make an image in her mind or on a sketchpad or in her memory, and then she'd paint and try not to think about how isolated she felt some days or about the gulf between what she wanted and what she ended up with on the canvas.

At night she was with Jack and she could forget about her work and try and ease him out of his, which could also be difficult. His hours were long and the demands on him endless. He was a pop icon here. People flocked to him after meetings, and murmured about him in reverent tones at the supermarket. Jack pretended not to notice, but the difference was pronounced: In New York he'd been hers, now she was sharing him with eighteen thousand others.

She imagined how they saw him, tall and angular with those keen gray eyes and that high heroic forehead. The thin light brown hair parted just left of center, and falling gracefully for-

ward. He had a seducer's compassionate face, her sister had said.
"He makes you want to please him," she'd said, and Anne could
see that. He had a palpable and inclusive charisma, an unas-
suming speaking style. He leaned in when he spoke to people,
made eye contact, remembered names. He took his time before
speaking, as though reluctant to step on the toes of the previous speaker, but the pause he allowed had the effect of making
people listen closer. Still there was something self-protective, she
knew, about his charm; a face that elicited, and concealed, more
than it gave. She'd gleaned this from their first dates together.
And it was in his non-public moments, when she saw an unprac-
ticed curl of his lips, or an off-color thought play in his eyes, that
Anne felt closest to him.

"Listen," he said when she'd mentioned his popularity, "it's
us together, right? We're *both* going to make a splash before we
leave, right?"

He'd already made one, of course. She wasn't so confident.

"Perhaps I can rob a bank," she joked. But she agreed; it was
an opportunity for them, and she liked that he was putting her
work on a line with his.

When she first arrived here he'd poked fun at his town, maybe
to keep her from starting in, which she might very well have
done. He took her on a guided tour of the coastal decay and deterioration, dormant lakeside factories where grandparents and
uncles and his father once worked. He introduced her to upstate
kitsch and bad taste, all the ornaments on people's lawns, the
swans and plastic Jesuses, Betty Boops, and Wile E. Coyotes,
and also meaner-looking lawns with old car parts scattered about
amongst the thistles. Then he took her out to eat some classic
Lakeland fried food: haddock, chicken, and steak. "Everything's
fried here," he explained, "even the ketchup." But she began to
see that after a few months of speaking at meetings about the
town's subtler virtues and endless maritime possibilities, Jack
had started to believe them. He'd repeat his script at home (the

story of America, of what was, what had happened, and what could be), and though he might laugh afterward, and say something like, *It's coming out of my ears, isn't it?*, she knew he didn't think it was. It was his skill to see always what could be, to see a vacant briar-filled space and picture it filled with shops and restaurants, to see a broken warehouse and imagine it packed with fresh food stalls, to see scarred ground and imagine a boardwalk.

She liked seeing through his eyes; it made her see her own life differently, made her want more from it than she'd been getting.

SHE TRIED AS SHE PAINTED to believe in herself the way he believed in himself, and to value her own judgment. She tried not to place importance on his responses, good or bad (his praise was so immediate lately it had the disturbing ring of reassurance), and she tried not to call him at work more than twice a day. She'd work hard and she'd improve, and in doing so she would answer her own doubts.

She began sealing herself off from any intrusions, turning the phone off sometimes. And she started to work through lunch because she saw how it broke her momentum and might cost her a painting. She started to appreciate quiet so much that it irked her to hear the sound of a lawn mower in the distance or of someone hammering. In silence, her mind might wander to the right places. She wanted it quiet enough to hear wind in the trees. She took walks out into the nearby fields of wildflowers and along the marshes. She met a naturalist there one day, who showed her what to look for, showed her Virginia creepers and bittersweet nightshade, snakeroot and wood sorrel and large flowered trilliums, blue-eyed grass.

Occasionally she'd have a sense of neglecting someone. She'd think of all the people in New York she'd left behind.

ON A DAY SHE'D PAINTED (albeit unremarkably) all morning, she then prepared herself a good lunch—salad and bread, soft Brie, a yellow apple, and a glass of wine. And before she could finish eating, she'd begun sketching her lunch. She hadn't noticed for a few minutes that she was doing this. She took cuts of the cheese and then made another sketch. She poured wine on her plate and sketched the tipped glass, the red pool.

She liked that painting was no longer a decision.

On the bottom of one of the sketches she began a note to her former boss, Sonja, telling her how she'd somehow managed to find peace in the land of salmon and algae. She drew a salmon slurping a thin layer of algae.

I've got a little too much time on my hands, she thought, and she laughed.

While she was folding the sheet carefully, placing it into a cream-colored envelope, and putting a stamp on it, her sister called.

"You know what I just did?" Anne said. "I painted my lunch. Nice, huh? Leave me alone enough and I start to lose my marbles."

Lauren didn't laugh.

"Actually, I still have most of my marbles."

"That's good," she said.

"Describe your lunch and I'll paint it too. So long as it isn't soup. I'm a hack with soup."

"Anne, I've got some bad news."

"Oh God."

"It's about Grandpa."

CHAPTER 5

"Are we bending over far enough for you, Mr. Lambeau?" Olin Ambrose said. He pronounced the last name with the Texas accent of his birthplace, so that it sounded like Layambah.

"What do you mean?"

They were in Jack's storefront office, in the four-story brick Walker Building directly across the street from City Hall. The sign in front read DREAMS ALONG THE LAKESIDE.

"I mean every time something happens in this town we end up getting the shaft. How's it going to happen this time?"

Twenty years earlier, Olin had managed to slip his way onto the Lakeland City Council. During his brief time there he'd so alienated everyone else they'd passed a measure to eliminate his position. Redistricting, they called it. Teachers told their students Olin Ambrose was the reason the city had six council members and not seven.

He wasn't pleasing to look at. He had a large, potatoey nose and the gaunt, demented appearance of a man who spent his life pacing and quietly ranting.

"That's why I want your opinion, Olin. I've set up community workshops every week to talk about what's going on here."

"You don't think I'm seeing through that bullshit. It's lip service stuff, right? You let me rant about for an hour or two, take a lot of notes, and then you throw away the notes. I'm not an idiot, you know."

This was exactly what Jack had done. Olin grunted three times. He got up from his seat and paced the room.

"You're big on growth, right? You're always talking about growth."

Jack could see where this was heading.

"Well, a lot of us around here aren't so big on growth. We're here because it's not New York City. Not much crime, not too many drugs, not too much of what you like to call *variety*. We've got about as much variety as we care to have."

"That simply isn't true, Olin. The look of this place will change, and maybe the population some as well. I haven't hidden that."

"We've had a nice clean place here, Mr. Lambeau."

"And we'll still have a nice clean place."

Olin shifted his head about in thought.

"You know what it was like living near that trash burner? You have any idea? We woke up every morning and our cars were covered with the stuff, soot—that place was a first-class disaster."

It was the seventh time Olin had mentioned this. And it hadn't been a trash burner. It had been worse, a liquid-waste incinerator that had been a massive failure and had left the land and the spirit of the town scarred.

Jack stopped near the door.

"Yes. I know."

"Pavio, he paid for our laundry and a car wash a few times. That was responsible. Too bad he didn't pay the doctor costs for all the folks dropping dead around here."

Jack stood near the door.

"What I want to know is who's gonna clean off the human soot that drops on us?"

"I don't really want to think about what you mean, Olin."

"You don't, huh." He nodded and smiled. "You know what an enforced relationship is?"

"No, I don't."

"You think about it."

"Thanks for the tip."

Olin extended his hand.

"Listen, thanks for indulging me. I know you're busy."

Olin always tried to end on a positive note, like a nasty waiter trying to make nice for his gratuity.

JACK SPENT THE REST of the morning trying to work on the master plan (Hickey called it his *War and Peace*, as in "Anybody ever gonna read that *War and Peace?*"), but he kept getting interrupted. First by a friend of Councilman McHale who wanted to talk about building a studio lot to attract film people from Hollywood; then by Clem Mullen of the merchants' association, who wanted to know if it was true the city would be permitting X-rated movie theaters in the new harborfront. Were they crazy? Then by Stewart Dix of the *Times Chronicle*, who apologized for the article he'd written implying the city would be allowing porno at the harborfront, when the fact was simply that a group from Syracuse hoped that was true. Then by Betsy Simmons, the intern from Cornell, who recognized how busy Jack was and volunteered to bring him back a sandwich.

The afternoon started smoothly enough, but everyone on Jack's staff seemed to need his help. And there was Hickey calling him for advice and a decent joke or two for a speech in front of the Lion's Club. Later his sister-in-law called to say his brother hadn't made it home until five in the morning, and his mother, who was head of the volunteer ambulance corps, stopped by to tell him she just rescued Mrs. Collingworth down the street from choking on a baseball-sized hunk of lamb.

"She shot it straight across the kitchen—*bafoooom!*" she said. "Nailed the family portrait."

Finally he could get back to the master plan. The key to Lakeland's transformation was all about making it a Great Lakes town again, both literally, by extending the town down to the lake, and psychologically, by re-creating—without *Disneyfying*—elements of the old port. Borrowing a page from Ghiradelli Square and Faneuil Hall, they'd retrofit some of the old brick and iron warehouses and fill them with trendy new shops and ethnic restaurants, and perhaps some loft apartments for artists (artists being the first inhabitants of the purest neighborhood renaissances), exposing the old wooden beams, stone pillars, worn bricks, and paving stones. And they'd keep a watch over new construction to make sure it was contextual, and tasteful, and not slipshod or hokey. *Walk around the Lakeland waterfront,* he wrote, *and you'll be transported to an appealing hybrid of the late eighteen and nineteen hundreds.* No more dreary lots of trash and weeds or crappy box-style buildings with convenience stores. A boardwalk will open up to waterfront berths filled with yachts and sailboats, rebuilt wharves with chowder houses and boutique shops, and maybe a dozen or so of those wooden pushcarts that had worked so well in Boston. For inspiration, Jack drew from old photographs and drawings he'd dug up in the Lakeland Public Library. He tried to imagine not just the look of the old port but the mood of it, with stevedores jostling about, and boats everywhere, and the lake a governing aspect of everyone's life.

Just outside of town is a bucolic world of nature preserves and rolling farmland.

It was a bit like theater, planning like this; like creating an elaborate set. And that was the fun of it. He'd loved that aspect of theater, the set design, since he first traveled to Manhattan as a boy and went to two Broadway shows—*A Christmas Carol* and *The Phantom of the Opera*—in one weekend. That feeling when the curtain rose and you joined a completely different world. That's what he wanted to do here, along the neglected northern edge of America, create a place—albeit a real working one, and not a collapsible facade—that made you feel something, made you want to take a walk, sit down on a bench, and look at the water. Made you want to fall in love, or if you were in love, made you experience it more intensely. He'd felt this way in Grand Central Station. Always had. And when he lived in New York he'd sometimes spend his lunch hour walking around that glorious space, noticing what it was that made it so. It was what the suburbs lacked. A sense of authenticity and history. A past. Meaning and context.

These towns had lost their sense of who they were when they lost their industry. Someone needed to remind them.

THERE WERE TWO MORE phone calls, the longer of which was from a man who wanted to know if he could open a vivarium along the waterfront, and kept on talking even after Jack had told him he wasn't the one to ask.

At six, Jack could leave work and have a little peace. The sky had blackened and in the wind he could feel a storm percolating. He stretched his arms out. He took several deep breaths. It would all work out fine, he thought. Everything. It was good that people kept calling, wanting this and that. People depended on him.

He thought of calling Anne and asking her to meet him in town for dinner. He didn't want to go home just yet, where Anne was unlikely to have prepared anything, and might still be painting, with her supplies left about.

As he made his way to his car he felt a finger tapping his shoulder. He turned and saw him, his broken face wet from the rain, shirt untucked, his eyes screwed up.

"Niggers and Jews, am I right? That's what's in the forecast."

He wasn't so much offended by the comment as he was repulsed by the closeness of this dripping human gargoyle. Their eyelids were almost touching. Jack stepped back.

"I don't know how to respond to that, Olin, except to say I hope so."

"I got nothing against it. But you've got a history here you need to pay attention to. Irish, Italian, and French-Canadian folks like your grandparents. That's what we're built on here."

His voice was raspy in the growing wind.

"Somewhere down the line you're gonna sell your soul, or ours. There'll be something you really want; always is with guys like you. And you'll give something of ours away."

It was an interesting prediction. Jack wondered if he'd gotten it off the radio, a warning from a radio preacher.

"What will I give away?"

"I don't know yet. I just know you'll do it. It's all part of your *slickness*."

Out in the cold, wet, darkening air, Olin seemed tragic, almost heroic. Jack wondered if he had any place to go.

"Are you okay, Olin? Where'd you come here from?"

"Psshhht," he said, and waved his hand at Jack's concern. "Live right across the street." He pointed to a red brick apartment complex that sat above a patchy lawn. "Saw you out here and I thought you and I could finish our business."

CHAPTER 6

The week before Anne moved to Lakeland, she went to lunch
with her grandfather at a minipark between two buildings on
Fifty-third Street in Manhattan. The minipark had a small concrete waterfall with some rocks and a few lonely looking trees.
This was nature in New York. He gave her his antique Leica
camera for a going-away present—"It's got a slow speed thing so
you can take pictures at night—no flash," he said. They ate hot
dogs, and her grandfather twice called her Annie Bananny, the
name he'd called her as a child. He was worried about the rash-
ness of her decision to move upstate.

"This is a big opportunity for him," she said. "He's doing what
he's always wanted to do, and he's doing it for his hometown. It's
going to be like Baltimore."

"Like who?"

"Baltimore. Not a who. Are you wearing your hearing aid?"

"Yes. I suppose I'll turn it up. I just don't like the way it
doesn't discriminate. I get you and the taxicabs eating with me
at the same time."

He fingered the tiny device.

"Good?"

He nodded. "He's all wrapped up in his little kingdom up
there, isn't he? I know. Needs to think it's the only thing worth
thinking about. Just make sure you're happy too. Don't let him
lock you up somewhere; we men like to do that, you know.
Lock our women in, throw away the key. Makes us feel virile.

I saw this thing in the *Post,* a man from Islip, broke his wife's legs . . ."

"Jack's not this thing in the *Post,*" Anne said. "I want to go. The decision was mine."

"Yes. Of course. I just can't see who in the world could become an artist in a place with no art. It's all gift-shoppy up there, isn't it? This is where it's at, Annie. You'll be cut off up there in Lakeworld. Out to sea. No paddles."

"I'm a good swimmer. Let's get off this, huh?"

"Well, okay then. But I'm coming up the first week to visit you. Help you get the place in gear."

Anne took his hands, liver-spotted and dry as paper, in hers. She squeezed them and then let them go. Behind him a boy and girl wrestled over a popcorn bag.

"Listen. I want very much for you to come up and stay with us, but I'm going to need time to get settled."

Sauerkraut stuck to his chin. She pointed to her own chin and he wiped his clean.

"All right, then. How 'bout August?"

"How about October, Poppa? You can come up for Halloween. We'll go trick-or-treating together."

She turned her hands upside down and made them into a mask. He feigned fright.

"Maybe I'll move up there too," he said. "Rents must be pretty cheap. We'll bait the hooks together or whatever you do up there."

"What about Trudy?" Anne asked.

"It's a free country. She can do what she likes," he said, referring to his wife of ten years. "C'mon, Annie. There's not a lot of time left. Pretty soon you'll be scattering my ashes over that waterfall."

He must have read her face.

"I'm sorry." He lifted the camera. "Take a picture of me whining and keep it on your mantelpiece."

NOW ANNE WAITED FOR JACK to arrive home to tell him that her exasperating grandfather, whom she'd so adamantly kept from visiting, had had his third stroke, and likely his last. She'd felt drained and unhinged all afternoon. At one point she saw spots and almost blacked out.

She was splayed on the couch when he walked in.

"Hi," he said. His hair was wet.

He leaned down to pick up a sketchbook and a pencil box from the floor, then placed them on the mail stand.

"I have this fantasy," he said quietly, as he pulled off his tie, "of having a few feet to myself, of having just one empty place in the house to sit down."

"What . . ." she said.

He shook his head and chuckled softly.

"Can you clean up some of this crap?"

He was looking at the rest of her art materials as though they were discarded clothes.

"Yes, of course," she said, and she grabbed what she could get her arms around—a canvas, some pallet knives and paints—and moved it all into a corner. He went to the bedroom to change.

He called from the bedroom, "I don't know how anyone could work like that."

Heat gathered in her head. You callous shit, she thought.

She walked out the front door and out to the road, where the wind blew strong and the sky was gathering for another downpour. She wore only jeans and a thin T-shirt, but his unkindness had shifted her sadness into a defensive rage, and she wanted to walk it off.

She barely noticed the half hour it took her to get into town. It started drizzling again. The houses began to duplicate, clapboard after clapboard, each with peeling paint and a square plot of lawn, like a depressing wallpaper pattern. When she made it to the stores on First Street, it was raining hard.

She knew she should find shelter, but nowhere seemed obliging. She passed a shoe store, a pharmacy, a laundromat that looked like it had recently survived a fire. The linoleum was charred brown. A girl waited for her clothes. She seemed too young to be doing her laundry in a public place. Anne walked on, her arms folded in front for warmth. A car stopped to offer her a ride. But where would you take me? she wondered. The car was already crowded. *I'm fine*, she said. But she was cold and very wet.

THE DAY HAD DEGENERATED into frigid rain by the time Turner made it back to the bureau. Winter in Central New York was a nightmare houseguest, arriving too early, and unwilling to leave at a decent hour. The way he'd get through it was to plunge himself into work.

The office was dark. When he flicked on the light he saw gray wool pant legs, white socks, and heavy loafers protruding from below his bureaumate's gray metal desk.

It was just the two of them in a rectangular beige room with two desks, two phones, and two computers, and when Turner was away, Stewart, a heavy, dispirited man, often liked to lie flat on his back in the dark.

"Hey, Turner, did you do your Sunday story?" his glum voice asked.

"I'm halfway done," Turner said.

"Clark is asking for our Sunday stories."

It was like being nagged by a corpse.

Turner settled into his desk. For a while he could concentrate and get his stories done, and then he found himself staring out into the dismal day. He watched a man in a brown ski hat lean against the wind, and a delivery man carrying tan boxes, his hair blowing straight up from his head. He began to cluster words on the bottom of his screen to match the mood of the moment.

Lakeland, he wrote, *a fallow, windswept, depleted, unyielding, unfruitful place.*

He added *dolorous.* Then *lachrymose.* Nice word, he thought, like something you'd put on ice cream.

He looked out the window again. Some miserable fool was standing over a smoking engine. Turner identified with him. Something dreadful was always happening to his old green Honda—the brake calipers had shredded, the clutch had failed. It was like a kidnapper gouging him for ransom. He couldn't afford a new one; he had too many debts. And then he saw her on the other side of the street, coatless now, walking with her arms folded, head down. Lambeau's fiancée, Anne. She stopped, clutched her arms tight around herself, changed directions, walking a few yards, then changed directions again. She ran a block and then she stopped and stood. He watched her. She shook her head in futility.

He shook his own head in sympathy, then he turned off his computer screen.

"Give me your coat," he said, his eyes out the window.

Stewart walked over and looked out next to him.

"You gallant knight, you," he said. "Trying to get a little boom-boom?"

Turner pulled Stewart's coat on. He grabbed his own to give to Anne.

"You like the ones with the screws loose, huh?" Stewart said.

Turner chased after her.

"Hey, are you okay?"

He held the coat out. She didn't take it.

"Yes," she said. Rain fell in sheets.

"Can I buy you a cup of coffee?"

"No. I can't . . . I can't really talk right now."

She shivered. Her hair was loose and fell in wet thickets across her face.

"At least take the coat."

She took it from his hands and wrapped herself inside.

"Thanks," he said, weirdly. Then she left him there. He watched her until she turned a corner out of vision. He was beginning to get thoroughly soaked now.

JACK STOOD AT THE foot of the muddy driveway holding a blanket out. The wind whipped the bottom about. "Your sister called again," he said. "You should have said something, Anne. It's crazy just running out like that."

He folded the blanket to keep it from getting wet.

"Do you want me to go home? I can pack my things up now and move back to New York, if you want."

He started to say something, closed his mouth, and then began again.

"I don't want you to," he said.

The swollen sky cracked above them. She stood there a while regaining her breath, which had been racing. He held the blanket out again. This time she took shelter inside it.

CHAPTER 7

Jack ran a hot bubble bath for Anne. Before she lay in it he helped her clean paint from her skin with a cleanser called Goop, which closely resembled animal lard. He liked seeing ticks of paint on her skin, and on her jeans and T-shirts. It was sexy and just a little rugged, he thought, and he liked that quality in her. He brought her the transistor radio and turned it to the college's jazz hour, and then he brought her a glass of wine. Only her face, wet with steam, peeked out from the bubbles. He thought of the pictures he'd seen of her as a child from her family photo albums.

"Getting cozy?"

"Almost," she said. "I overreacted, didn't I?"

Yes, he thought, but he said, "It was me. I shouldn't have started in like that."

He looked at the gray full-length raincoat that lay on the floor near the tub.

"Hey, where'd you get this coat, anyhow?"

"Coat?"

"The one you were wearing."

"A man gave it to me."

"A man."

"Uh-huh."

"Did he give you his name?"

"I don't think so."

"That's pretty odd. I guess we've got ourselves a new coat, then."

He went downstairs to the kitchen then to start boiling water for spaghetti. It *was* him, he thought. So what if his things were moved around? So what if her paintings and supplies were left out from time to time? Wasn't this part of the deal when he convinced her to move up with him and start painting again?

He replayed Anne's voice in his head. *I can pack my things up now and move back to New York, if you want.* He pictured himself a bitter old bachelor with a dull but immaculate apartment. Maybe he'd live in Olin's building.

He walked back upstairs. For a moment, he watched her unseen from the bathroom doorway. Seeing her this way, alone in a soapy tub, or standing naked in the kitchen, drinking a glass of water she'd fetched for herself in the middle of the night, was as unsettling to him as watching her dance in a room of men. She was comfortable in her body, unabashed, and dazzlingly natural, and he wondered if it came from the year she'd spent in college modeling for art classes. He thought of something she'd made for him after their first trip away together, a small collage of photographs (two of her nude, one of just her back, that he'd taken while she was sleeping), and she'd painted between the photographs, and there were things from the trip, a piece of bark, a label from a bottle of beer, a clasp of hay, and a pear stem, like something he'd seen by Jasper Johns. A map painted over, their route faintly visible, a story to it, and when he looked at it even a month later, he could recover the entire weekend. It was the single most exquisite gift he'd ever received. Now, as he walked over and bent down to hug her, and as he felt her desperation—so soon after she had threatened to leave—he questioned how well he actually *knew* this person with whom he planned to spend his life; how well you could ever know another.

She pulled him closer, as if reading his thoughts.

"I'm here. I'm right here for you, sweetpea. I'm not going anywhere," he said in her soapy ear.

And right then it occurred to him it would be different if they were married. It was this trial period that was making them look too closely, making him wonder. They hadn't set the date yet, not because they weren't certain about each other, but because they didn't know where to have it, up here and upset Anne's family, or down there and see the hurt expressions on his parents' faces. "I don't want to be engaged anymore," he heard himself say.

Her face went ghost white.

"What do you mean?"

"There's a place we can go and get this done. It's beautiful. It's in the Adirondacks. It'll just be the two of us, and then sometime next spring my mother and your mother or whoever can throw whatever party they want."

"Are you serious?"

She started crying then. His chest stabbed. He could hardly believe how simple and perfect this was.

"Let's go tonight."

The loveliest of smiles spread over her. She threw her arms around him again and covered him in soap.

"Can we just do that?" she said. "Just like that?"

"Just like that."

CHAPTER 8

They drove east in a spell. The air through the open windows was clean and damp, though the rain had long since stopped. They said little, overcome with what they were doing. The word tickled his mind—*elope*. They were eloping. Did people elope outside the movies? They drove through farmland and loamy marshes, passing one-street villages and a few somber mill towns, their contents melding as in a dream. The clouds were separating and then sinking into the distant hills. He imagined their decision had cleansed the sky. He could not pretend to know what Anne was thinking now—of her grandfather, sure, of the two of them, sure, and he hoped she was experiencing something like the peace and assuredness he was.

The road narrowed, then snaked and climbed; it felt as though they might keep driving and never stop. They'd end up somewhere far away, in Canada maybe, Quebec, where no one expected anything of them, where no one spoke English, or even wanted to. He thought of Harris, how unlikely it was that Harris had had the big church wedding and now Jack was running off to get hitched in the middle of the night. Who would have guessed Jack would be the one to let the family down?

They would understand, he thought. He just wouldn't tell them right away. This would be his and Anne's moment. That was the best solution. Why did they have to tell anyone else?

His fears and doubts were gone now, like the clouds. Her head was on his shoulder, though she wasn't sleeping; her eyes were open, gazing ahead. His headlights caught two tall antlered bucks running on the side of the road. For an instant they halted in their tracks and seemed to look into the car as it passed.

"Deer," she said softly, after they'd slipped away.

"Yes dear," he said.

She laughed.

They'd arrive around midnight, check into a bed and breakfast, and then early in the morning they'd go first for the blood tests, and then to the justice of the peace. He wondered, will all this feel different in the light of day? No, he decided, it'll be just right because it's us. Still, he wanted to keep driving. His ears popped from the climb. He did this trick he learned as a child, held his nose and swallowed.

"How are you?" he asked.

"I don't know," she said and then in a few minutes added, "It feels as though we're floating, doesn't it? It's strange."

He picked up her hand and kissed it.

They hit a straight stretch of road with hills all around them. He could smell the hills, the wet grass and loam and some sort of flower. He had never been this happy. And then he felt her trembling next to him. He brushed her face with his hand. Her cheek was wet.

"Oh sweetie, what's wrong?"

"You're sure they'll be there?" she said.

"Who?"

"The people who are going to marry us. They'll be there when we get there?"

She was still shaking.

"They'll be there."

"I keep thinking they won't. Is that silly?"

"Yes, it is. By this time tomorrow we'll be married."

She closed her eyes, as if searching her mind for this imaginary world. She stayed that way a while.

"I'm so *happy*," she said when she finally opened her eyes again.

PART II

THE EXTRA ONE

CHAPTER 9

For the last four months, Harris Lambeau and his crew had been clearing barrels of toxic waste from the old warehouse yards and factory sites along the lake, and dumping them later a mile inland on dormant farmland. Each night at about eleven, the seven of them would wash down a hot meal with a beer at Tuck's Diner, and then head to the sites where the city was building the new harborfront. Once there, they'd put on thick rubber gloves and face masks that made Harris feel like a surgeon, or a welder, and they'd follow an old hand-drawn map that indicated where the barrels had been stockpiled or buried a decade before.

They were paid by the hour to dig, and they were paid double-shift wages, more than the farmers were making for taking the stuff. It was a racket, quite simply, and the best one Harris had found in a long time. He'd started lately to think about what he would buy with all the cash. He'd buy a new car, for one thing; his friend Shawn was selling a cherry red 1980 Triumph convertible that Harris had done the work on. And then some things for Marla and the baby on the way. To make it through the long hours, Harris tweaked some nights on Benzedrine, just enough to help him focus, keep him sharp.

He was always on time, always regardful and energetic, the best worker of the bunch, and yet he had no clue at all what to do when, on a warm fall night, three hundred pounds of Dieter Parkhurst dropped dead in a trench he'd dug on a vacant onion farm.

At first they'd thought he was sleeping, because with the hours they kept, someone was often nodding off. But his face was buried in the oily dirt. When he found him, Harris thought maybe Parkhurst had had a heart attack. Harris knew basic CPR from his mother. Parkhurst wasn't breathing. He had no pulse and his lips were blue. There was a trail of something like vomit on his shirt. Harris tried pounding the big man's chest and blowing air into his mouth, but he was deader than a rock. They couldn't call for a second opinion because what they were doing wasn't legal, and Harris had the wherewithal to recognize that.

It was a terrible thought to have, but it struck Harris that all the rest of them had wives or girlfriends—whether or not they wanted them—and children, or children on the way, and something big they were saving up for, like that Triumph and the extra room for the baby, all except Parkhurst, who lived by himself—if you could call the way Parkhurst lived, living. There was no one to inform or comfort, no best friend who'd be worried.

He was a nice enough guy, and a pretty good hauler, and a good person to back you up in a fight. It was wretched, Harris thought, but if it was going to happen to someone, better Parkhurst than one of the others—than Harris, for example.

The group of them stood over the body.

"What the fuck. What the fuck, what the fuck do we do here?" the smallest, a jittery, thin-faced man named Jameson, kept saying.

Harris knew that you were supposed to call a hospital at this point, or the police.

"Call the cops," Sorento said.

"No fucking way. And say what, we were out burying barrels and one of us croaked?"

"We should take him to a hospital," Sorento said.

"A hospital? It's a little late for that. I think I smell the rigor mortis," Terry Miller said.

"We can't just leave him here, that's for sure," Harris said.

"On the bright side," Bazorcik said, grinning a mildewed grin, "one less mouth to feed."

"That's not so bright," Harris said.

THEY LOADED PARKHURST onto the back of the truck. Sat him there as if he were sleeping. And they started making jokes on the way back.

"Hey Dieter," Terry Miller said. "Penny for your thoughts."

"If you're done with that Deere cap, Dieter, you mind if I take it home for the kids?"

They snickered and then began laughing hysterically. There'd been seven of them two hours ago, and now, without warning or explanation, there were six. How were you supposed to react?

OUTSIDE OF TUCK'S, HARRIS CALLED Harlan Stanyan, head of the Lakeland Department of Public Works, and woke him out of a deep sleep, to which Stanyan said the call had better be life or death.

Harris explained.

"You're sure he's dead?"

"Trust me."

"Heart attack, huh? Dieter was no Carl Lewis. He just never took care of himself, too many scoops of chocolate-chocolate."

"That was no heart attack. That was a guy choked in poison. He dropped one of the barrels. It leaked, and he keeled right there onto the dirt. End of story."

"Was he carrying it by himself?"

"I think he was rolling it. What difference does it make?"

"You're supposed to be damn careful. There's a reason I gave those instructions."

Bazorcik and Terry Miller were tossing a rubber ball back and forth.

"I'll be sure to give them to him."

"He was rolling it? What an idiot. He deserved to die, the fatass."

Harris didn't know what to say.

"I'm sorry. I didn't mean that."

"Yes." Harris was losing patience. "Don't we got to report this?"

"Report this? My God, you're worse than him. You want to see your butt in a sling?"

"I didn't call nine-one-one or nothing. I called you."

"It's a good thing you did. You did right, Harris. Now you're absolutely sure he's dead?"

"Hold on." He called out to the back of the truck, "Are you dead?"

More silence.

"We're bringing him over."

"Here? No, you're not. We can't have him showing up here."

It occurred to Harris that something positive could be made from all this. "We got to take him somewhere," he said. "Maybe a funeral home?"

"You may as well be signing our jail notices."

"What do you want us to do?" Harris asked, though he knew the answer. "You want us just to bury him?"

"It'll be getting light out soon. Just hold on to him overnight. Then take him out tomorrow and yes, give him a decent burial. Think of something nice to say."

"How do we hold on to him? He's not exactly pocket-sized."

"One of you guys must have a shed or something."

"A shed?" he said incredulously, though he'd thought of this too. There was an old industrial freezer in his basement from when the house had been a fraternity.

"We do this . . ." Harris said.

He gathered his resolve. Stick it to him, he thought. Now or never. "We do this and we want two grand in return."

"For one night?"

Harris steeled himself. You couldn't push Harlan too far. Rumor had it he had mob ties.

"Make it two and a half," Harris said.

CHAPTER 10

What was eeriest about the death of upstate was the lack of any marked insurgency, of the appropriate fury. Perhaps that was because it had been coming on for forty years.

The factory closings themselves never happened the way they did in movies, with drama, a door slamming shut and everyone out in the cold. The ones in charge were too wise. They laid people off a few at a time. They even followed production sometimes. When the last piece of merchandise came down the line the last worker followed it out the door. It reminded Jack Lambeau of the story about frogs and boiling water. Put a frog in a pot of boiling water and the frog leaps out. Put the frog in tepid water and then bring it to a boil, and the frog never manages to escape, doesn't even struggle.

By every measure it was a wrecked part of the country. Work was scarce, home prices low as the ground. Hundreds of family farms closed down every year. There'd been until now a shortage of hope you could read on people's faces, in their posture, in the way they dressed and kept their ailing homes. The Republicans blamed Mario Cuomo; the Democrats blamed the corporations, and the smokestack-chasing southern states. It was a different America here. A spiritually lost America. An America of closed factories, and pregnant teenagers, and boarded-up community centers and storefronts.

The deterioration was psychological as well as physical, Jack told a reporter from the Associated Press. By losing their source of employment, these towns had lost their meaning, their context. And like a person who loses his life's work, the task before them was to find a new definition. A postindustrial identity, a new reason to be. It meant drawing on the past, while not being defeated by it. It meant reinvention. And on these matters Jack counted himself an expert.

There was no more profound challenge at the dawn of the century, Jack said.

IT STAYED WARM THROUGH OCTOBER, an oddity in Lakeland, and people commented on how late the falling of the leaves was occurring, how brilliant the colors were. A real fall, a New England fall, with pumpkin festivals, and touch football, and long cold walks.

Jack and Turner ran now along the curling whitecaps, by red and yellow oak trees, by the golden-hued cigar stacks of the steam plant, and by the now-cleared warehouse and factory sites. Men in orange helmets were carting the last of the construction debris. A few brick buildings were left, waiting for their makeovers. There'd be a long esplanade built, and plenty of activity. Soon, Jack thought, the whole thing would be covered in white, great sheaths of it, and he was even looking forward to that, to winter's cold beauty.

He wore his Brown University sweatshirt; Turner, a thermal underwear top and a navy wool Davis watchman's cap that put Jack in mind of Randle McMurphy in *One Flew Over the Cuckoo's Nest*. It had been a month now since their last time out, and Turner was breathing hard.

Jack slowed the pace so they could talk. He'd been asking about Stewart Dix's coverage of the harbor.

After a season of reprinting Jack's and Hickey's press releases, Stewart had taken to interviewing and misquoting. Today he'd said Jack had called the harbor "another South Street Seaport," when Jack had said it was what he didn't want.

"It's sort of fascinating," Jack said. "I have no idea what I'm going to say each day in the newspaper. I might have declared war on Finland."

"I guess he's losing his edge. He used to be good. I've seen his old stuff. He's really pretty smart."

"It'd be nice if you covered us. At least people would know what was going on."

"Maybe not."

Jack ran ahead now to try out some speed, and then circled back, grinning, which he knew pissed Turner off. Turner ran like an old man, hunched and wheezing, and complaining often about his aching feet.

"When you did it you did a good job. I didn't have to run around correcting misinformation."

"It's because I essentially wrote PR for you."

"You were fair."

"Don't sweat it," Turner said. "No one reads us anyhow. And don't mess with Finland. That's a bad, bad mistake. Those are some ornery cold-blooded fuckers."

Jack ran ahead again. Light dwindled, smudging the border between lake and sky. He'd thought that afternoon that he might tell Turner on this run how he and Anne had gotten married; he'd thought he'd feel compelled, that it would be all over his face.

How strange, he thought, that it evidently wasn't.

WHEN THEY'D FINISHED their burgers at a back table at Tuck's, Turner asked him, "How was New York, anyhow?"

"Well, we weren't doing the town up. Anne's grandfather died. We went to the memorial."

He told Turner about how close Anne had been with her grandfather, how they hadn't spoken much recently, and how Anne felt guilty about that. How it made her think of her father, who'd been hit by a car and killed when Anne was in high school.

"Anne's taking it hard," Jack said. "But she's resilient. She'll bounce back."

Tuck came by with a pint bottle of Jim Beam and three glasses. He poured jumbo-sized shots, then cleared their plates.

Turner downed his. "Sure beats Gatorade," he said.

The counter was empty except for a gaunt unshaven man with pasty slept-on hair who seemed irritated with the cup of coffee before him. Tuck gave coffee and sometimes a sandwich to what he called the No-lucks, though he asked that the No-lucks come in the off hours and not during breakfast and lunch, or after 10:30 at night when the late-shift power-plant workers filled up the room.

Tuck pulled up a chair. He sat on it backward, leaning over the backrest. A filterless Camel hung from his mouth.

Decades of smoke had painted the walls sepia.

"That part of your plan, Indian summer right through Christmas?" he said.

"Absolutely."

"And it'll be like this every year, won't it, Mr. Lambeau?"

"Every year, Tuck. You want warm, I'll give you warm."

A serious look crossed Tuck's face.

"Now I know you didn't say that about the Seaport," he said.

Jack grimaced. "And how do you know that?"

"Can't believe the papers," he said, and raised an eye at Turner.

"Distortion is our long suit," Turner said. He unlaced his sneakers and pulled his feet out.

"Just doesn't sound like you, Jack."

"No, it doesn't, does it?" Jack said.

"Personally, I don't care much for the South Street Seaport," Tuck said.

"There's some good things about it," Jack said.

"Goddamn bullshit, corporate bunch of stuff to buy. It's a piece of garbage and you know it. Went down there last summer with Bernice. Know what it is? It's like what you were talking about in one of those round tables of yours. People peddling history. Everything seems like its all historical, right? But it's all artificial. I don't like it."

His nostrils flared.

"You notice the people making money from history are the ones that know shit about it—corporate types—saying how great it was in the old days, then cleaning your pockets. Well, it wasn't so great. Not here, anyway."

Turner nodded like an acolyte.

"I'm with you," he said. "It's like those colonial villages in the South, and those trading posts in Oregon: Lewis and Clark come back to life before your very eyes. Or Deadwood, South Dakota. Come see the death of Wild Bill Hickok. Am I right, Tuck?"

Tuck's nostrils flared again. He sniffed the air. "Something die in here?"

"Sorry. My feet are sore," Turner said.

"That's crap, Tuck," the man called over from the counter. "This was one helluva town."

"When, Curtis? Not in your miserable lifetime, that's for sure," Tuck growled.

"How 'bout during the nuke plant? A whole lot of money flying around." He sounded almost wistful.

"Did you see any of it?"

"Guess not," Curtis said and went back to looking at his coffee. It was sad, Jack thought, how quickly nostalgia could be eviscerated.

"It is a helluva town," Jack said, trying out the sound of it.

"It's nice in the summer," Tuck said. "That's about all I'm gonna say."

"It's a terrific town, and it's going to get a whole lot better very soon. You'll see when we're done, Tuck. It'll surprise you. We're going to raise some eyebrows. Not just in the summer, and not just around here. It'll be a real waterfront Main Street. We're going to take the town right up to the lake. No more chain-link fences. No more peering through the ruins for a glimpse of blue."

Turner applauded. "Go girl!" he said.

Jack resisted the temptation to smirk, to indicate to Turner he'd been imitating Hickey. He stuck his ground.

"Places change or they die. You been to Thomasville lately? The whole downtown's boarded up; there's some desperate religious message on the movie marquee. It's like a war's torn through. Even the rats want out."

"And they take your forty bucks too," Curtis said. "Crooks. Murderers."

Tuck tilted his head inscrutably. The door swung open, letting the wind cut in, and slapped shut—*thwack!*—then did it again. The noise startled them, but no one moved.

"On top of everything it's jobs," Jack said.

"Whose jobs?" Tuck asked.

"People here. The ones picking the trash for bottles, for one thing."

Curtis mumbled, "Shut up . . . shut up. . . ."

"And it's a stronger tax base," Jack said.

". . . shut up, shut up, shut up, *shut up!*" Curtis stomped over and closed the door properly, then tested it to make sure it wouldn't open.

"It's closed, Curtis," Tuck said.

Curtis tested it once more. "Damn . . . thing . . . d-drives . . . me . . . c-c-crazy," he said, his lips trembling as though that might be true, as though the door by itself could push him over the edge.

He sat down again at the counter and began mumbling into his coffee.

Tuck pulled on his cigarette, then whispered out of earshot of Curtis, "Neighbor of his, owed him forty bucks, hasn't showed his face around. Curtis thinks he willed him dead. Says he saw his body riding around town in a truck."

Tuck raised his eyebrows. "I get the charmers," he said.

Turner was wrong, Jack thought. People were reading the papers, and they'd renew their apprehensions given the slightest opportunity. Why was everything a fight? Every single project in every single city. It was a fact of local government: People wanted to think you were screwing them even when you were saving their lives.

"I didn't come back here to screw things up," Jack said, "If everyone could . . ." He didn't finish because his voice sounded too defensive.

Tuck rose from his chair.

"Relax, Jack. I believe you," he said. "Just make sure you don't crowd me out with another corporate crap seaport, okay? That's all I'm saying. I kind of like this little hole in the wall."

He put his apron back on.

"We're counting on you, Jack. Not Captain Mayor," he said, and walked into the back room.

Jack and Turner got up to leave.

"Thanks for stopping that banging, Curtis," Turner said on their way out.

Curtis turned and squinted suspiciously.

"Who the hell are you?" he said. "You don't know me."

WITH A WARM BUZZ in his head Jack left Turner and headed toward the old harbor parking lot where he'd left his car. New York had been greener, and more beautiful than it had the right to, but he'd willfully focused on what he hadn't liked there, the sardined streets, the rank smells, the thin ribbons of sky, and wondered how you could expect to live on that. The temperature had dropped while they were inside Tuck's, but it was still fine to run in. He didn't want a corporate-crap seaport any more than Tuck did. That was one of his fears, his pet peeves, the towns Turner was referring to and the cheesy stunts they came up with to bring in tourists—waterworlds, wax museums, the biggest ball

of twine, but most of all some conspicuously contrived historical section, filled with fake history, some slightly sad depiction
of historical ambiance, shop and restaurant employees dressed
like escapees from old musicals at the community playhouse and
speaking in bad brogues and fake regional dialects, treating all
who come before them like children. When you tried to preserve
a town's history, you always ran the risk of missing your mark
and preserving merely the history of kitsch and bad taste. It was
everywhere.

It was part of what he'd written about in *Death by Landscape*.
But there were worse sins. There was the demolition, or simply
the neglect, of every great old building, ones with cornices and
dormer windows and fabulous sloping roofs—places with *character*, and the tendency to supplant them all with tin boxes, with
convenience stores, or with fast food, or parking lots, or with
nothing at all, leaving formerly attractive streets with the tawdry look of a highway truck stop. It was an American disease.
And it was festering up here, like the Dutch Elm sickness forty
years ago.

He thought of Anne now. He wanted her to be as happy as
she'd been when she got here, but he worried for her now. In her
first days back from the funeral she'd worked hard at her painting, starting before he awoke and still going when he arrived
home. But she seemed dissatisfied with everything lately, and
several times she blotted out what looked like a terrific start with
white paint. Self-doubt had crept in, like an insidious illness, and
she was distant from him. He didn't think it was deliberate, or
a reason to worry, but it hadn't felt much like a honeymoon. He
was worried that she might be regretting what they'd done, and it
was a little crazy, wasn't it? *Just like that.* He didn't think he was
regretting it. It was right. They were right. It was just a hard time
for now, and they'd get through it.

Before he stepped into his car, he looked out at the sites again.
No longer was it a ruined industrial necropolis. They could start

building tonight if they had to. He imagined it a year from now, shops open and people strolling about even at this hour, someone playing a clarinet and maybe another plucking at a stand-up bass, a couple of youthful, clove-cigarette-smoking portrait artists, a vendor selling souvlaki (Anne loved souvlaki), another flipping crepes; a vegetable and fruit stand with local vegetables and fruit. It wouldn't be some cheesy historical rip-off. God, he hoped it wouldn't. It would revitalize the town, maybe even pull a few people away from the TV.

He realized how deeply within his conceptions lay Anne's urbanity, how often he asked himself what she'd think, where she'd shop, and eat, and browse. And he wondered for a moment for whom he was doing all this.

CHAPTER 11

Peering out the window of the bureau office made Turner think of a fish tank, the people outside the indifferent owners and he and Stewart within, the circling fish. So many times he'd looked up at the window and seen Stewart there as lively as one of those oscar fish you could buy for five dollars at the pet store. If you tapped the glass would he inch forward, poking a puckered mouth against the pane? Would he swim to the surface in search of floating food? Whenever things got bad, Turner thought to himself: At least I'm not Stewart.

He banged out his daily like a good soldier and then his Sunday feature, a fluff-puff about a family in the woods who farmed maple syrup for a living. He'd learned everything you could find out about tree sap in the morning and "tapped" it out that evening. This was his life.

Six P.M. and Steven Turner wasn't famous yet. He hadn't made it to the *New York Times*, hadn't sold his first screenplay, hadn't dated a starlet, hadn't won the lottery, hadn't committed a bleak post-modern crime that would cause talk-show hosts to interview his ex-girlfriends, hadn't crossed the country on a unicycle, hadn't spotted a UFO, hadn't even gotten himself promoted to the downtown frigging office of the Syracuse Newspapers.

But that would soon change.

What he needed was a few solid stories that would strip themselves across the top of the front page. He needed to go after someone or something. His predecessor downtown had published a series on the mob's involvement in the building of the nuclear power plants. Now *there* was a beauty. It had everything—sleaze, money, power, and some juicy characters. People had objected to the way the union was being led, and one guy had actually gotten his leg broken. Hollywood stuff.

The weather was awful, his social life sucked, his salary was miserable, and his career stalled. And while he could see how one might be distraught under the weight of these circumstances, Turner found himself often surprisingly, and almost secretly, hopeful. He'd more than adapted. He was learning resolve. He'd taken a risk, giving up a job as a production assistant for documentaries at Channel 13 that had played well at loft parties but was a dead end and had become mind-numbingly rote.

He would be rewarded for his gumption, he believed. If not next week, then down the line. It could all begin with something like the story he'd written the day before.

Two puppies, about four months old, had been found, one sickened and the other burned, on the same stretch of road where the older dog had been found. One had rubbed its eyes and was blind now. The other had nearly died from whatever it had ingested. The night before Clark had given it a decent-sized header, and some people had been calling in to ask about the puppies' progress.

He had no luck reaching the farmer on the phone, and when he drove by he found no one there, only an imposing barbed-wire fence. So he had little to go on, for now. But there was a significant story here. He was farsighted enough to know that.

He left the office into the early evening, the sun at the angle he liked best, reddening the dusty storefronts of Pine and First Streets and the sagging Colonial Hotel. This part of Lakeland had a faded grandeur to it, the look of the port town that had boomed in the heyday of the St. Lawrence Seaway. In the clear morning light it could look sad and desiccated, but in the evenings Turner liked the rococo feel of the buildings and the old street lamps, the warped wood and muraled walls of the restaurants, the antique jukeboxes that raved old love songs. Often he felt as if they hadn't simply stationed him in a regional bureau, they'd stationed him in another era. He pictured a kid on the corner screaming, "Extra! Extra!" the way they always did in black-and-white movies: "Collins Family Taps Delicious Syrup!"

He stopped by Giovanni's. Serena was seated behind the bar reading Sidney Sheldon. Turner settled onto a stool and waited to catch her attention, but Serena was focusing fiercely, as though lost in its richness. Beneath her blond, freshly shampooed hair, Turner thought he could see a furrowed brow. What was she reading? he wondered. Was an overtanned lovely cheating on her fat-cat older boyfriend? Was the boyfriend plotting revenge, serving her paramour's balls to his pit bull?

"He writes those in about a week, you know," Turner said.

She glanced up at him.

"Hmmm . . . that's a pretty good week, then, don't you think?"

"I read that he recites those things into a tape recorder. 'Helen stood magnificently in the Grecian moonlight, her willowy legs extending all the way to the floor. . . .' His secretary types it up and he's got a hit."

"You're jealous, Turner."

"You think so? You think I'd want to be a bestselling writer, my picture in *People*, that kind of crap? That kind of life leads to vanity and vacuity. I'm a truth teller. I affect lives."

He said it in jest, but Turner still believed it was true.

"Really?"

"Yes, I'm jealous. But you don't have to encourage that crap."

She smiled at him, then leaned across the bar, concern in her eyes.

"So, puppies this time? What's going on?"

"I guess someone's done a little polluting out there."

"It's criminal, people destroying a nice big farm like that," Serena said.

She sat back down on her stool.

Turner had searched through the old clips on farms and dumping. There'd been a lot of it, not just in farms but in backyards, public creeks, ravines, and sinkholes, mostly because there hadn't been any regulations until a few years ago. All you needed to do to haul waste legally was fill out a form at the county office. No troubling questions about what you were carrying and where you were going to put it.

A guy at the other end of the bar was motioning now, arms waving like he was bringing a plane in.

"Be right there, Henry," she said. "Don't get your panties in a bunch."

She whispered to Turner, "He's out of town again. Ten o'clock sound good?"

"Very good. I'm going to the store to get some dinner. I'll pick up some beer."

"Don't be a cheapskate this time, Turner. No Genesee, okay? Something German, or Japanese."

TURNER WAS ONLY A foot or two inside the Price Chopper when he saw Lambeau's fiancée, Anne, alone in aisle two. He watched her consult a list, then place things into her cart. She wore paint-specked blue sweatpants and a stretched-out, rust-colored sweater he'd seen on Lambeau. He imagined the two in matching sweaters, curled up on a couch as they watched an old movie on TV. He planned to talk to her in produce. But he wouldn't be caught empty-handed. He wanted to show her he was purposeful—the sort of man who knew the difference between parsley and basil, who soaked his beans overnight—so he grabbed a red plastic basket from near the checkout line and he walked over to where she was standing. A Lionel Richie song played overhead.

She was at the turnips when he began his approach. He hovered, then stopped and feigned interest in an eggplant. Then he glanced over again but she'd traveled to the fruit stand. He followed, but an overfilled cart, wielded by a hassled young mother, her two children punching each other's shoulders, cut him off. The smaller of the children, five perhaps, reeled around in a fit of kindergarten anger and punched Turner's leg. She was baffled and then frightened when she realized what she'd done, and she hid behind her mother.

"Molly. What do you say? What do you say to someone you hit for no good reason?"

Turner didn't want an apology. He wanted to catch up to Anne, who was now slipping down an aisle.

Molly shook her head side to side and then hid it behind her mother's thigh.

"What do you say?" the mother said. She looked about twenty-one, Turner thought, her face still doughy with youth. Turner had recently written a Sunday story on teen mothers in Lakeland County, headlined BABIES MAKING BABIES. All of them had dropped out of high school and were on the dole. None had thought of having an abortion—perhaps because the lone doctor who'd performed them in the county had had his windows blown out by a shotgun.

"It's really all right," Turner said now. "No blood drawn. No major injuries."

He wanted to run down the aisle. The young woman pulled her daughter away from her. She held her forward, then forced her to face Turner.

"What do you say?" the woman asked again.

"Nothing . . . poopy!" Molly said.

Her mother slapped her face hard. The girl started to cry. Other people watched them now.

"What do you say to the man, Molly? You say 'I'm sorry,' right? Isn't that what you say?"

"No," she said.

Her mother shook her.

Molly screamed. And her mother slapped her again.

"Say 'I'm sorry,' you little shit!"

"It's really all right," Turner said.

"*Sorreee*," Molly said, her little voice defeated. The older girl seemed now to commiserate with her sister. They looked at Turner as if it was he who had humiliated them.

"Apology accepted," Turner said.

They walked away, and Turner felt the collective stare of a dozen shoppers who wondered why a five-year-old had been forced to apologize to him.

TURNER FINALLY CAUGHT UP to Anne in the parking lot. He began walking beside her.

"How are you liking our little town so far?" he said. He was breathing too hard, still shaken from his fruit stand run-in.

"Fine. It's a nice change."

"From New York City? Yes, it's a change all right."

She looked him over.

"Turner," he said.

"Yes, I didn't forget. You're from the city too."

"Brooklyn Heights."

"How'd you end up here?"

He sighed. "Jail sentence. Two counts of armed robbery. Cleaned out a couple of sporting-goods stores."

She seemed puzzled.

"Actually, it was the only place that had an opening and wanted to hire a guy with no journalism experience."

"Well, a job is a job."

They stood there in silence. Turner stumbled around for something trenchant to say, but what came out of his mouth was, "That's for sure."

"What?"

"What you said about a job."

"Being a job, yes, well, and a nose is a nose, I suppose. I'll see you around," she said.

She opened her car door and piled in her groceries. He wasn't usually this awkward. This felt like high school.

"Anne," he said.

"Yes."

"The other day in the rain. You looked upset."

"I was upset," she said, eyes trained to the ground.

"Things any better?"

"A little. Thanks."

"No rush on the coat, by the way."

She put her hand to her mouth. "Oh, that's right. I completely forgot about that. Of course I'll get it back to you."

"Really, no rush."

"I can bring it by your office. Where's your office?"

He told her.

"I'll bring it by."

He felt jumbled when she left. His arms were empty, he realized, and he tried to remember where it was he'd left his briefcase and bags of groceries.

"HE WANTS TO GET MARRIED," Serena said as she climbed atop Turner to begin round two. Their first times together Turner had actually liked hearing Serena talk about Garrett while they were screwing. It seemed quirky, maybe even a little twisted. Now, like anything overindulged, it had become tedious. They'd each had a joint and three beers, and Serena had mixed hers with a speedy diet pill called a Christmas Tree, which made her even more talkative than usual.

Turner was having trouble concentrating tonight. He'd been thinking about the farms and the puppies. And then regretting his bungled conversation with Anne.

"I just think he's too old, too possessive, and he's got no real passion, other than for his damn cars."

They were doing it in Garrett's oak-paneled living room, which was filled with expensive toys: a high-tech stereo, huge-screen

TV, a padded corner with workout equipment, lacquered shelves of New Age-y lifestyle and self-improvement books. There was a legitimate hot tub out back. Garrett belonged to the parochial tribe of Lakelanders that had more money and liked to live near one another on the far west side, where the houses were larger, the paint fresher, the lawns more manicured, and the people a good deal more self-satisfied—the fifteen or twenty lawyers and doctors, and a few moderately successful business owners like Garrett. There was even a tiny Lakeland Country Club that tried to be stuffy but didn't quite get it right, where members could sit by a small pool hidden from the multitudes, wearing straw hats and sunglasses, with thick navy blue country club towels, or playing golf on a patchy nine-hole course while their kids signed chits for drinks.

Of all the Lakelanders, these, smug in their distance from the masses, were the saddest, Turner thought. Still, the house was a whole lot nicer than anything he had lived in, and he was often jealous of the deal Serena had here. Sex for lifestyle; he'd certainly consider it.

"Know what I mean?" she asked.

"Hunnh," Turner said, which was his fallback when he hadn't been listening. He kissed Serena absently. She kissed him back twice, then pulled her face away.

"He's not like you. I mean, even when you're writing about a dog, you can see that you're passionate about what you're doing."

She bounced up and down now, a kid on a rocking horse.

"Take that article you did on the old man who built that miniature Christmas village for his wife. I liked that. I mean, it doesn't have to be a Nobel Prize. They seemed like real people. I could never go around writing about who got caught for drunk driving, though, and who shoplifted and all that other stuff."

She moved her hands to his shoulders and gripped them tight.

"You've been here what? Two years?"

She gripped tighter. He was losing circulation.

"One," he gasped, and she eased up.

"Garrett goes through the motions. Except when it's about his cars. He's forty-nine years old, but sometimes I think he's just filling up time before he dies."

His mind ran film of Anne stumbling through the rain in just a T-shirt and jeans, hair soaked, teeth shivering, shirt clinging.

"He'll be sixty-five when I'm just getting into my forties. Christ, I'll be cleaning his dentures for him . . ."

He wanted to disappear from Serena's lament, from Serena altogether. He heard Anne's voice. In most instances it was a terrible thing to do, but with Serena complaining away about Garrett, he felt somewhat justified.

He held her waist and began thrusting.

"The bottom line, I guess," Serena said, "is that we love each other. I want to have a family with him." *Ssshhh*, Turner thought.

"I want to have a bigger backyard, and a big oak tree, and three dogs, two of them Newfoundlands, one of them something a lot smaller, maybe a lab or a Swiss Pomeranian, or whatever you call those dogs that look like people."

And then she groaned and began vaulting above him in a protracted frenzy of carnality that engendered admiration in Turner though she'd done this each time. There was something fascinating about the extent to which they'd isolated the process from any complicated sentiments—they were playing racquetball, or doing aerobics.

"Oh yeah, oh yeah. Fuck me harder!" she said, though she might just as well have yelled, *Swivel, leap, swivel, leap, and again group!*

He dug in. Went for broke. Pounded harder, his face hot as steam. On and on they went.

Leap, swivel.

Everything inside him, all his stress and itches and unfed hungers converged, and then left through the pores of his skin.

She gasped at the end, back arched, eyes closed, then collapsed theatrically, warm and sweaty, on top of him. He was happy for these nights; they smoothed his rough edges, and if he and Serena weren't exactly amorous, they genuinely liked one another, and what was the harm in that?

He held her to him like a girlfriend, kissed her cheek.

"What about you?" she asked.

"Me?"

He wondered for a moment if this was as close to love as he would get. He was in the weather-beaten end of his twenties, after all, and stuck in this small, gawky town. Was there more you could demand, he wondered, than that the world provide for you air to breathe, food to eat, a story to write, a decent bed to sleep on, and every once in a while, a woman like Serena? Maybe he was content. Maybe this was it.

"Me?" he asked again fondly.

"Well, yes . . . Do you think he's too old for me to marry?"

CHAPTER 12

"Harris, did you read the paper?"

It was Harlan Stanyan, his boss, on the phone.

"No. Not yet."

"There's an article about dogs that stepped in some kind of black gunk out on McBride's farm."

"So?"

"So. It's gonna have people wondering why there's gunk out where there should be onions."

"I see. So we don't go near McBride's for a while."

"Yes. And I think we've got to hold off on burying old Parkhurst for a while longer."

"No way."

"Just a few more days, say until Tuesday. Let this thing blow over."

"No way. I'm not running a hotel."

"We got no choice."

This was the line Harris was waiting for.

"Then it's gonna cost, Harlan."

"You're in this just like I am. You're the one with the body right now, Harris, and if I go down, you go down harder."

"Is that a threat, Harlan?"

"No, it's not a threat. It's the fucked-up truth. I'm not crazy about this either. But no one has to know anything. It's just a couple of days, that's all."

"I hear you. It's still gonna cost."

When he'd gotten Harlan to consent once again, it occurred to Harris he was a pretty fair negotiator, because this was starting to add up to some very nice numbers, and what did it matter when they went back and buried Parkhurst—up to a point, of course. Keeping the freezer going had made them blow fuses a couple of times, and he was having trouble explaining to Marla why she couldn't run the stereo and the TV at the same time. But he wasn't only seeing that Triumph now and the room for the baby. He was thinking about a nice 700-horsepower motorcycle, with saddle bags, and an extra TV so he didn't always have to watch Marla's shows, and maybe a swing set with a little tire the kid could swing on. All and all, he was feeling not half bad.

He would not go back to how it had been a year and a half ago, when he was out of work and had to live back home with Belle and Frank, when he'd had to bum change to take a girl out or even buy himself a few drinks, and when he couldn't afford to fix his car and had to walk to get anywhere.

The fact was he needed to make money, and now he was making it in bundles.

HIS THINKING ON THIS MATTER changed the following night when he called his high school friend Claude.

"Next week?" Claude asked him. Claude studied mortuary science and had worked at the city morgue for a summer.

"Until this thing about the dog and the tar dies down."

"And you're blowing fuses? Do you know what happens to a dead body, Harris?"

"A little rigor mortis, right?"

"Well, first off, Harris, you have your livor mortis—not rigor mortis, although you'll have that too. The blood settles, and all those vessels? They pop. And the skin gets these awful splotches all over it—they call it purpura. And yeah, the muscles can't contract, and everything stiffens on account of there's no more of the phosphate that makes them moveable. Then the enzymes break down your cells and organs. And then, Harris—you start to putrefy."

"Putrefy?"

"Yup. The body starts turning green and it stinks. First around your abdomen, then around the head and neck, and your face starts swelling up 'cause of all the bacterial gas. Then your blood vessels get that nasty blackish-green color you can see through the skin. They call that marbling, 'cause it looks like marble. And it's worse with a fat guy like Parkhurst 'cause all that blubber brings his temperature up."

"Thanks for the lesson, Claude."

"I'm not done yet. Then the gnarly stuff happens, Harris, if you can't keep it constantly refrigerated."

"The gnarly stuff?"

It was clear Claude was relishing this.

"Yeah, the hair starts to slip off the head like a wig and the skin on the hands loosens. Comes right off, like Isotoners. And don't let the birds near 'cause they steal the hair."

"What the hell for?"

"For their nests. Oh, and speaking of flying things, the flies start coming in and hatching their eggs in any open wounds they see, or in your mouth or ears, or in your butt, Harris. In a week you've got a tribe of maggots to make you really retch."

The image lodged in Harris's esophagus.

"So what do I do?"

"I asked my old boss, hypothetically. He says keep him cold and then dump him. If you can't, you best embalm him. Take the fluids out and replace 'em with formaldehyde."

"You're joking."

"No, and Harris, what do you think the law makes of you holding a body in your basement?"

"What? S'not like we killed him."

"There'll be a time when people start looking for him, Harris. I'd get rid of him before your whole house starts to stink."

This was more than Harris had bargained for. He actually got Claude to say he'd help with the embalming if needed. Five years before, after the feds closed the unlicensed snack bars at the nuke site and banned the snack wagons, Harris got paid a bonus to commandeer the cesspool truck that traveled to the site and cleaned out the Port-O-Potty. At two A.M., four of them drained the water tank, then loaded cans of Coke, Pepsi, Mountain Dew, orange Slice, and root beer into the tank, one by one. By hand, twenty-four hundred cans! A few beers while they were at it. At seven, Harris waved to the front guards, they waved back, opened the gate, and he was in. Drinks for a week. This and burying barrels were the craziest things Harris had done for money in his life.

They didn't hold a flashlight to keeping a decomposing fat guy in his basement.

He walked downstairs to see how Parkhurst was making out—to see if he was marbling. He opened the freezer door, pulled the canvas cover up. His cheek had turned brown-purple and his chin was the color of a plum.

He washed his hands at the sink and then washed them again.

As he walked upstairs he started to think about—of all things—Parkhurst as a kid. Playing catcher or something on a Little League team somewhere. Waddling his fat ass up to the plate. No matter how messed up you were, you were a nice kid once.

While he was thinking about this Marla motioned him over. "He's kicking. Come feel him kick."

He didn't want to touch her stomach. Didn't want to spread onto his child whatever it was that was vulturing Parkhurst's body.

"Listen. Don't go down to the basement, all right? It isn't safe."

"How so?"

"What difference does it make? There're things falling from the ceiling, okay? Is this twenty questions?"

Marla rolled her hand across her stomach, her shoulders arched back as if to say, All this has happened to me and what do you have to show for it?

"You know, I can tell. This is going to happen very soon, Harris."

"But you're not due for a month."

"It feels sooner."

He felt trapped in the thick, heated air; trapped inside his skin.

"We'll see. It'll come when it wants to, right?"

He couldn't think about a baby now, about being a father. How many new fathers had a body in their basement?

HE WENT TO THE YMCA and lifted. He started with squats and lunges, then did dead lifts, wide-grip pull-downs, and finished with one-armed barbell rows until his arms burned and sweat flooded his face. Whatever was happening in Harris's life could usually be made better with an hour or two in the weight room. This he'd discovered in his junior year of high school, and it had stayed with him ever since.

He thought often of Arnold's line in *Pumping Iron:* "When I'm leefting weights sometimes I feel like I'm caahming."

Maybe not quite, but it was pretty darn good.

He took a scalding shower after that and rubbed his skin hard until the symbolism of it dawned on him, and he thought: Death isn't contagious.

His skin tingled, and his head felt as though it might be clearing. He'd make sense of this all; he'd get through. He held his head under the hand dryer, then pulled his jeans on, his T-shirt and sweat top. He realized he hadn't brought a change of socks.

He hated putting on dirty, sweaty socks. He'd done that before and it had given him a moldy case of athlete's foot; nor did he want to wear his boots without anything on beneath. When he'd done that he'd given himself a marble-sized blood blister. He didn't need that.

Down the aisle from him a green nylon shoulder bag lay open.

Harris walked over and peered inside. Red flannel shirt, dark pants, a newspaper, light blue boxer shorts, and a clean pair of gray socks.

He looked both ways and then took the socks out. He unrolled them and put them on. He wriggled his toes. The socks felt wonderful, in a way that only thick clean socks can feel.

He heard the shower turn off, and then a whistling man heading his way.

He rifled inside his locker for his boots. He jammed his feet in, and then as he closed the locker door he managed to bang his finger.

"Motherfucker!" he yelled.

The whistler, a short, stocky man in his sixties, walked into the aisle and smiled at him.

"Clean it up, will you, son?"

He recognized the face of his father-in-law.

"Got to be careful these days, don't you, Harris?"

His finger throbbed.

"I guess so, Maynard."

"Now that you got that extra one waiting for you back home." He chuckled.

The *extra* one. A jolt of panic traveled Harris's body—how in the world had Maynard found out about Parkhurst?

"You look spooked, Harris. Did I say something wrong?"

And then he remembered. The baby. His father-in-law was talking about his grandchild. He tried stretching his finger and couldn't.

"No. Not at all. Nothing's wrong."

Maynard regarded him with concern. Harris explained, "I mean, I'm just thrilled about this happening. Really and truly thrilled."

Now Maynard looked disturbed.

"You damn well should be," he said.

Maynard dried himself. His hair stood straight up, even his white chest hair. It was strange for Harris to see Maynard out of his clothes, nothing more than a boy with a few more corns and wrinkles and white hair.

Harris's finger was probably broken. He could barely tie his boots. Before he could get away Maynard began pulling his clothes out of the bag, the shirt, the pants, the newspaper. Then he spread open the empty bag. He searched it for hidden pockets.

Then he sank onto the bench, crestfallen.

"Oh Harris, Harris," he said, shaking his head in defeat. "Don't ever grow old. You grow old and you'd forget your dick if it wasn't attached."

CHAPTER 13

At the diners and donut shops people were talking about the toxic sludge. The rumors were wild. One had it that one of the puppy's legs had been amputated. Another claimed that cows had been maimed and several children had been hospitalized from breathing toxic fumes.

"What's this about explosives being set out on a farm?" a woman asked Turner on the phone.

So far as Turner could tell, all of these variations were false.

Clark wanted a follow-up, then added he still didn't think it was much of a story.

"Why do you want a follow, then?"

"The Big Man wants one. His mother lives somewhere out there."

Turner decided to take one more drive out to McBride's farm before filing. The worst thing that could happen was he could be booted off the land. He'd been booted out of places before. Whatever McBride was doing, Turner thought it made sense. The farmers were broke. He'd done stories on this too. It was all the new technology. Agribusiness. Prices had dropped through the ground.

THIS TIME WHEN TURNER PULLED UP, he saw a man in a red thermal underwear top and jeans standing on the porch.

He started walking toward the front door of the house.

"What do you want?" the man asked.

"My name's Turner. I'm from the *Times Chronicle*. I've been trying to reach you."

"Paperboy. Well, I've got nothing to say."

"Can I ask you about the sludge on your land?"

"You can ask."

"All right, I'm asking."

"I got nothing to say."

"You mind if I look around?"

"Being that it's private property, and being that I don't know you from a cow's ass, I suppose I do mind."

"State's going to do an inspection," Turner said, although he wasn't at all sure they would.

"That'll happen when it happens."

"You're aware you've got some dangerous toxins on your farm?"

"That's what you're saying."

"Guess it's been hard times trying to farm lately."

McBride gave him a look that said he wasn't falling for this one.

"I'll be seeing you," Turner said and started walking away.

"You're barking up the wrong tree here."

Turner thought of a joke—about the last things that had gone barking on McBride's property—but kept it to himself.

"Yeah, maybe so. I've done it before."

"There's a lot of good going on around here without you trying to dig up trouble where there isn't any."

He looked at the new fence. There'd be no more dogs sneaking in.

When he returned to the office, Turner called the police department and asked them whether they could enforce anything.

"That's not really our place," said the sergeant on duty. "You get the state pissed off and then maybe we can jump in, but not until then, Turner."

AS HE WALKED AROUND Lakeland, Turner found himself occasionally pausing to inspect the faces of passing women, hoping to meet up with Anne again, though he didn't know what he'd say if he did.

Back at the office Stewart was eating Oreos and fielding calls.

"They think we know something about it. Probably think we started it."

A representative from the state DEC said he'd come out within the next two weeks.

"People are concerned, huh?" Turner said.

"Got a couple calls from farmers too, Turner."

"What'd they say?"

"One guy called. Wouldn't give his name but he said you should mind your own fucking business, and I do believe that's a direct quote."

Another caller, a middle-aged woman, said it wasn't news because the farms were nothing but trash dumps anyhow. ("They been doing that since you were in diapers.")

Maybe it wasn't news out here. It was a place that had gotten used to being dumped on all winter and in the summer too, he was seeing.

His first month in Lakeland, Turner had awoken one night to what sounded like a boat's foghorn. After a while it stopped and he fell asleep thinking of sailing ships, whales, and hook-handed pirates.

He heard it again from time to time and loved it, thought of it as an elemental song of the Great Lake life. Once when he commented on it to a source, a naturalist he'd been quoting about the mercury level in local salmon, the man broke out laughing.

"*Ship?*" he said. He couldn't control himself. "That's rich."

Turner looked at him with incomprehension.

"That's no ship, Turner. That's the end of the world. It's the power plant testing its sirens."

This was Lakeland, he thought now: farms that weren't farms, foghorns that weren't foghorns, fish you caught but couldn't eat.

TURNER CALLED the veterinarian's emergency number and got Dr. Sharma at his house.

There was a story here. It was just a question of how to get to it.

"This is my weekend, Mr. Turner. Hold on one moment. I will be talking with you in a moment."

He placed the phone down. "Punita," he said. "There are other places to hopscotch."

He told Turner the puppies had second-degree burns on their paws and that some skin and fur had flaked off. They'd been treating them with a restorative cream. One of them would be permanently blind.

"What was it they ran through?"

"I'm not an environmental scientist, Mr. Turner, but I'd say it was a combination of some solvents and other toxins."

"Not a good thing to run around in?"

"Not a good thing to run around in."

That was his lead.

Lakeland—An onion farm on Old Taylor Road is "not a good thing to run around in," said Dr. Ravinder Sharma of the Green Hills Animal Hospital on Tuesday. The farm may be contaminated with toxic chemicals. Three Doberman puppies . . .

Clark ran it small, but the next day he received five more phone calls about the farms. People were starting to pay attention.

At the end of the day his phone rang.

"Mr. Turner?"

He didn't recognize the voice, which was loud and coarse.

"This is Turner. Can I help you?"

"Maybe."

"Maybe?"

"Not now."

"When, then?"

"I'll tell you this, Turner. You're just scraping the tip of the iceberg on this. There's shit going on you wouldn't dream."

"Who is this?"

"I can't say. Not yet. I'll just tell you you're only scraping the tip."

He hung up the phone.

Turner called over to Jack's house to ask him what he made of all this. Anne answered, and Turner froze. He couldn't say anything, so he hung up.

CHAPTER 14

Parkhurst's trailer moldered on a paved lot on the far east side, next to other trailers and peeling pastel clapboards. The sign that used to say SPIKE's on the corner store had two letters missing so it spelled s ik 's. Rust froze the pumps at the old Esso station down the block.

The trailer door and front windows were locked, but one of the windows in the back was open a crack. Harris pried it ajar. He crawled inside and walked the length of the trailer, head bent under the low ceiling. The air smelled rank. The main room was a turbulence of moldy bowls and plates, yellowed newspapers, a lumpy armchair, old milk and juice cartons, junk mail, old car and truck magazines, and a *Playboy* from 1975. Harris felt very uncomfortable, as though he were looking inside someone's screwed-up head. What was he doing? The couch was sunken; the TV an old color Zenith, no cable; there were crushed beer cans near the couch.

It was a sty. Harris cleaned a few things up. He looked for something personal. He found two pictures of Parkhurst and some other guys drinking beer at a picnic, their shirts off, skin bright red. There were some papers with union business. But he found no personal letters. There were three water-curled books: an Ian Fleming, a King James Bible, a book on model boats. There was an unopened kit for a Boston Whaler.

The idea of Parkhurst embarking in his forties on a new hobby touched and then sickened Harris.

The kitchen had a minirefrigerator and a rusty toaster oven but no stove. There was a moldy grilled cheese sandwich on the counter. Harris nudged it with a fork and a dozen roaches ran for cover.

There was no address book. No phone numbers.

Written on the wall—he could not believe or get away from it—was *Mom:* 518-555-6543.

He walked into the other room, but the fact followed him: Parkhurst had a mother. And there was no mother in the world who'd be pleased about her son fossilizing in the basement of someone's house. Someone had to tell her. You couldn't have an old woman living on like that, roaming about town, shopping for dinner, thinking her son was fine when he was stone dead.

He wrote the number down and put it in his pocket. He began to have a terrible feeling. Coming here was a bad idea. The clothes lying around were a dead man's clothes, the grilled cheese sandwich had a dead man's bites in it, and he kept thinking stupid things like, Maybe that's the last bite Parkhurst ever took. Or the indentation on the couch: Maybe that's the last time he ever sat down.

It was so sad to think of a life in this awful place. He wouldn't call what he and Marla had luxury, but how did someone live like this?

A mouse ran across the floor. Harris was so startled he hurled the bottle in his hand and it smacked the mouse and rolled along the floor without breaking.

MARLA WAS AT THE window when Harris arrived at six. She threw the door open. She kissed him and held him tight.

"How was it? How was work?"

"Good. Listen," Harris said. "You got to calm down a little. I was here this morning. Remember? You remember, we had toast and cereal together this morning?"

She pulled back from him. "Why do you do this? I missed

you is all. I'm your wife. I'm happy you're home. There's nothing wrong with that."

"You're right. Just let me figure myself out here a minute."

He walked into the living room and she followed. He slipped into the kitchen. When she arrived there he headed back into the living room, as if squeezing away from a crowd.

"Everyone's got a soul, right? Everyone's got something crucial inside of them."

"Of course."

"No one should just, I don't know, just die and not have anyone care about it."

"What are you saying? Are you all right?"

"Yeah. I think so."

Harris waited for her to walk into the kitchen. Then he walked down the stairs again, where he wouldn't allow her to go.

He could hear the freezer humming and knew it was working, but this couldn't go on. Claude was right. He couldn't just keep a body in his house. But he couldn't just report the death, either. What would he say?

If he did nothing, they could find the body and book him for murder. This suddenly seemed very likely.

Think, he said to himself. *Think of something.*

The dog was lying in the corner like one of those shag throw rugs no one had anymore. Harris thought about getting old; he thought of himself growing old like Sammy. Dying. Samson would die soon. It was another sad fact. It gave Harris an idea.

"Here boy, here boy," he said. But the dog was going deaf now as well as blind. He rolled a tennis ball over.

Sammy picked his head up, then waddled over to Harris and drowsily licked his hand.

"Come on, boy," he said, and yelled, "Going out for a while!"

Marla stood blocking the door.

"You just got here. Why don't you just relax and spend some time with me for a change?"

He spoke slowly and calmly. "Why don't you get the fuck out of my way, you whiny bitch?"

She looked as sad as anyone he'd ever seen. She let him go. He hadn't wanted to be mean, but it was the fastest way he could think of to get out of there.

CHAPTER 15

Night closed in around Harris Lambeau, headlights flashing by. Every other car he imagined to be a cop who would stop him and ask about the *extra one* back home. He kept thinking about Parkhurst's mother. He imagined her looking like Parkhurst, knitting a sweater somewhere for Parkhurst's niece or nephew, and thinking that Parkhurst might have a niece or nephew made matters worse. Maybe he'd been building the model boat for his nephew.

He shouldn't have broken into the trailer. When they found the body, would they search the trailer for clues and find Harris's fingerprints?

This wasn't such a hot deal anymore. Harris wanted out. The only thing he could think of doing was getting Parkhurst out of his basement and into the cool earth.

Then he would face whatever he had to face. He swallowed a couple of bennies to stay alert.

Samson had woken up and was getting restless. He whined and then began barking.

"Just hold out a little longer," Harris said. "We'll go for a run in just a little while longer."

He did not look away from the straight line of the road again until he was five miles outside of Syracuse and saw the dirty lights of that city multiplying around him. His friend Eddy lived in Vestal, a small town outside of Binghamton. Harris called him from a gas station to make sure he could take the dog.

"Sure," he said. "I'm gonna need some money, though."

"For what?"

"For food, for one thing. And for the inconvenience. I'm just talking fifty bucks a month or so, that's all. Whad'ja expect?"

Next he called Bazorcik.

"What's up, Harris?"

"I need you tomorrow night," he said.

"Don't they all."

"And we're gonna need that big green crate from your garage."

He had a few beers with Eddy, and then Harris said a quick goodbye to Samson in the fenced-in area behind Eddy's house. It was an ugly, poorly kept yard full of gangly weeds. He could see that even at night. In the back were the rusted shell of Eddy's old Mustang and a couple of cheap wicker tiki torches.

"You be a good dog," he said. "Stay out of trouble. I'll be back for you real soon. Okay?"

Samson gazed at his hand eagerly, fat black nose in the air, as if Harris were throwing a stick.

"It's a beer bottle," Harris said.

He walked back toward the house but Samson managed to block his way. He couldn't get through the door.

"Great. Now you decide to have a little life in you," he said.

The dog licked his hand, nuzzled his thigh.

"Aw, Sammy. I got to go, boy. I'll come back for you before you know it."

But the dog wouldn't budge.

Then Harris did something truly deceitful. He made a throwing motion with his beer hand, and as Samson stumbled into the dark, weedy yard, he sneaked into the house and pulled the door closed.

"I'm sorry old boy," he whispered. "I really am."

He didn't look back, didn't make eye contact. He gathered his things and pretended not to hear the whimpering.

Cold, cold, cold.

You lie once, you lie to everyone, he thought.

THE SKY WAS A BLUISH BLACK on Harris's drive home, morning creeping up. Everyone, everywhere, was in their house, sleeping, Harris imagined. They'd gone to sleep at ten or eleven, like normal people, after a filling meal, an episode of *NYPD Blue* or *Seinfield*, maybe the news.

He felt exhausted. When you tweaked, the posthigh fatigue hit with torrential force. It wasn't like being tired, it was like a vacuum had sucked up your brains and muscles.

As he passed through Phoenix and Fulton he saw no lights on in the houses, not a one. He drove in darkness, past closed stores, bars, and gas stations, up the narrowing empty road. Along with right and wrong, Harris wondered, when had he lost the distinctions of night and day?

He remembered something someone told him once: that only the tortured were awake at this hour.

The first house light he saw on was at his own house. A long red fire truck was parked outside. A fire truck? What in God's sake for? There was no fire he could see, no smoke even. Through the bedroom window he could hear his mother's coaching voice yelling, "That's it, that's it, that's the girl, *push*, that's it," and then, "Right here, Harris. Your child's almost here," but she couldn't have seen him. He ran in the front door, and through the house to the bedroom. Marla was staring straight ahead, his mother's foster kid behind her, and his mother waiting, urging. He stood in Marla's eyes, which were glazed over, and everything in her was pushing into this. Her face was red with straining. The baby was happening, right now, right here—how could he have known? No way he could have known. The baby wasn't due. Not even close. He wanted to say something now to Marla to let her know he was there, to let her know he was sorry he'd fucked up, and that he'd never do it again. That what was important was him seeing this, him being here for this moment, and that he was ready now to be a father, or almost ready anyhow, and that he was sorry he'd been so rude to her, that he'd said *get the fuck out of my way* or called her a whiny bitch; it was a terrible thing to call anyone, much less the mother of his child. He wanted to explain all that, but all he could do was stand there helpless, saying, "Jeeeezus, jeeeezus, jeeeeezus . . ."

CHAPTER 16

Jack and Anne spent the afternoon at the hospital. Nothing serious, but Marla had some dizziness, and since the baby was a month early and weighed only four and a half pounds, the doctors were keeping her in an incubator for her first few weeks until she reached a normal size and healthier color.

The day had been strenuous. Something was wrong between Harris and Marla, and it threw Jack off. Harris had left the hospital after about an hour, saying he'd return later when there were fewer people, to which no one seemed particularly enthusiastic. He'd been out drinking during the labor, Belle said. Marla seemed much happier once Harris was gone.

Something was also off with Anne. She barely looked at the baby initially, and then she seemed transfixed.

Jack's father said to her, "You guys are next."

It was a skill of his father's to always misread the moment.

Anne looked at him a bit more aghast than Jack would have liked, then seemed to realize that. She smiled over at Jack. But it was a plaintive smile.

Belle was describing the delivery. She and Casey had delivered the child together, she said. Casey had sat behind Marla as a support, and Belle had coaxed her own granddaughter into the world.

"And why wasn't Harris there?" Anne asked.

"Good question," Marla's mother said.

Belle took Mrs. Hacker's hand in hers and patted it.

"At about three A.M.," Belle said, "two calls come in within seconds of each other, car accident out on the lake drive and then a call from the police station wanting an ambulance sent to Collins Road. I knew what it was. I sent Clint and Charlie to the accident. I wanted the boy to help me here. That girl needs us, I said. And on the way over I'm running through the list: *surgical scissors, cord clamps, bulb syringe, towels, receiving blankets.* I knew we'd have no time to figure that out at the house. When we get there I can see the black hair of that baby's head. There was no time even to boil water."

Marla was dreamy from the whole experience. Still, she wanted to put in her version of it.

She said they'd been telling her in her Lamaze class she should find a focal point during the birth that would "relax and center" her. She'd decided to give it a whirl. She focused on a snow-covered mountain from a large black-and-white photograph of the Adirondacks Jack had given them.

She entered into it, she said. It kept her from thinking about Harris not being there. She said there were people swimming around that mountain, or maybe climbing toward it. Someone was piling pillows under her. She tried to slow her breathing down, but she couldn't. Her body was being run by a force, she said.

"What kind?" Anne asked her.

"You know, sort of violent. But I didn't want to think of it like that. I just went into that photograph again, into the snow."

"You know what she said?" Belle was beaming. "'I'm bearing my baby in clean, beautiful snow.'"

"Isn't that a goof?" Marla said.

Anne's eyes went glassy. "That's amazing," she said. "That's where you were."

"She did just great," Frank said.

"Wonderfully great," Belle said.

The doctors came in. They asked some questions. So did

Marla and Belle. They said she'd be fine. The baby's lungs weren't fully developed, they're HDS, he said. Which means she's having a little difficulty breathing right now. Not to worry. The nurses would give her medication to help the branches in her trachea grow.

Jack watched Anne stare at the baby, at the tiny hands and fuzzy tufts of black hair, at the way the skin creased beneath the knees, at the little mouth and the closed eyelids the size of dimes, until the doctors took her away again.

"You'll see, Anne," Marla said. "It's really *incredible*. You can't really think about what it's like."

ANNE'S PAINTINGS AND DRAWINGS were leaning against the front hallway wall when Jack and Anne returned home. Before moving them Jack flipped through a couple of sketchpads.

He held up one of the canvases, a series of green and red swirls around a fruit bowl. Two thirds of the canvas had been used. Other paintings were given up on. Promising beginnings, blotted over with white paint.

When he turned, she was standing in the doorway behind him.

"Oh, don't look at those," she said.

"They're very good, Anne. They just long for completion, a little confidence."

"You can say it. They stink," she said.

She seemed lost. Jack thought it might have to do with seeing Marla with the baby.

"It's like what Marla was saying. You just need to focus."

He flipped through the canvases. He stopped at one with a nude woman resting on a couch, another one of the lake with boats on it but no sky as of yet. "These two are great. I really like them," he said.

"Really?"

"Absolutely."

He spoke more, reassuring her and making suggestions. She needed a plan, he said. A framework for her days. He said everyone did. He certainly did; he wouldn't get a damn thing done without a framework, without making lists. He'd been talking to Turner about that the other day at lunch.

"You told him about me?"

"No. I was just talking in general," he said, which wasn't true, he had been talking about her.

He started to tell her a story about an unfocused period he'd had down in New York, but Anne wasn't listening. She was facing him, but Jack could tell that her mind was far away.

He waited until her glance met his again.

"Where'd you go just then, sweetpea?"

Her cheeks flushed in embarrassment.

"Oh, it's sort of silly, really, I mean with the magnitude of what happened today. A birth." She took a deep breath. "It doesn't matter all that much when you think about a *life* being made."

She'd been ruffled by the day in the hospital, Jack thought, and maybe enkindled. Maybe this was making her think about the future and kids. He tried to imagine Anne pregnant and he now liked the image. He was looking forward to their having children. He hoped they'd look like Anne, but with his mother's dimples, and maybe his determination. He'd like being a father, he thought. He'd like showing his kids off, taking them into the office or on trips.

"Tell me. I'm sure it isn't silly."

"I'll tell you what I was thinking. I was thinking how wonderful it would be to have taken that picture she was staring at. To reach someone like that. With your art. That's what I was thinking."

JACK WAS TALKING TO Anne in bed about her painting and how much he believed in her, how it was just a matter of time and endurance, how anything worthwhile took a lot of patience

and effort, when Harris came knocking. It was close to midnight. A yellow moon hung low in the sky. "It's late," Jack said
when he answered the door.

"Something awful's happened."

"Oh no. The baby?"

"No, not that," Harris said. "It's Sammy. . . . He died."

"Sammy?"

"Uh huh."

It should have happened years ago, Jack thought, and still this
was sad. Harris loved that dog. Jack thought of death and birth,
how often they arrived in tandem.

"I'm very sorry, Harris. When did it happen?"

"Last night. He must have sneaked out the back in all the
commotion. A car nailed him."

"One of those frat boys on your street, I bet. You get the guy?"

"No. Hit-and-run, I guess. I found him two blocks up."

"Assholes, little peckerheads," he said. "Bet Samson took
a chunk out of the car. We ought to check for the right dent
tomorrow—"

"Maybe. Anyhow Jackie, look, I want to bury him special.
Private. Place where I can say good-bye."

"Good enough," Jack said.

"What I mean is, I was wondering about the back of the
house. He'd like it there, with all those pine trees and stuff."

Jack glanced over Harris's shoulder to the red El Camino
parked in the driveway.

"Oh Harris. . . . You didn't bring him with you."

"Sorta."

"You ever hear of a phone, Harris?"

"Well, lots of times you aren't here."

"What would you have done if I wasn't here, leave him on the
porch?" He saw Harris's friend Bazorcik poking his head out of
the El Camino.

"I don't know. I guess we'd have waited," Harris said.

"There's no other place to do this?"

"You've got space back there."

"I'm sorry," Jack said. "Listen. I know he was important to you and he was special to all of us. But this is a little strange, coming by in the middle of the night with a dead dog. Can we admit it's a little strange?"

Harris put on a hurt expression, then a prideful one.

"Forget it then. We'll go somewhere else," he said. He turned and began walking away. It was a technique they used on each other, and more often than not it worked.

"Aw c'mon, Harris. That's not what I'm saying."

"No, you're right, Jack. I can't just expect you to help when I need it. He wasn't your dog."

He left Jack shaking his head in wonderment. It wasn't all that much to ask, he guessed. And Harris was having a day of it.

"Yeah, yeah," Jack called out. "Go ahead. But not near the house."

Harris walked over to check his face.

"You sure now?"

"In ten minutes I might not be."

"Jack. You need me for anything. Repair work. Some Sheetrocking. Let me know."

Anne walked to the door. "Hi Harris," she said, then walked away.

"Listen, we're gonna turn in. If you could keep it down that would be great," Jack said.

"I understand. No problem. This means a lot to me. It really does, Jacker."

"I know. It always does."

CHAPTER 17

People loved to talk to Anne about Jack. Not simply before and after meetings, but anytime they ran across her in town. They told her how he'd brought enthusiasm and energy to a place that had lacked both, how in the town there was a new sense of purpose, direction, and hope (their words), and how it had made them think better of themselves, their prospects, and their children's prospects, et cetera, et cetera—they seemed to be giving him credit for everything short of the air they breathed and the garish Lake Ontario sunsets ("Come to think of it we sure can see them better since he cleared those lakeside lots"). Some told her stories of what Jack had been like as a child and a teenager, stories of the *even back then you could see he was special* variety.

"It's the big fish in the small pond syndrome. Times thirty," she wrote in another letter to her sister. "Jack is pretty much a whale in the bathtub here," she said. "And a blue one at that."

The people who talked of Jack to her—and they talked to her *everywhere*: at the store, in the bank lines, on the street, once out a car window when she was stopped at a traffic light—intended, she supposed, to make her feel good and suitably proud. But increasingly they made her feel invisible, as though they couldn't imagine her having an identity outside of Jack.

She was a painter now, she could say. But then, they might ask, where were her paintings? Had she ever had a show, ever sold a painting anywhere, and did she have a particular style she could describe? She didn't really, and that was the problem. She was absolutely and depressingly competent, which was fine in any other field, but a death knell in hers.

"It's not a competition," Jack would say. "You're going through a slow period but you'll pick it up again. I'm not worried in the slightest."

Anne, however, was worried. It had never occurred to her that she couldn't do this, that she couldn't simply set down to paint again, like in college, and through hard work, and the development of her already good brush skills, become a painter. Before, she could convince herself it was a lack of time that was keeping her from being an artist. Now with all the time in the world she worried that she might not have anything to say.

She stated at the end of her letter to her sister that perhaps she was feeling the "tyranny of Jack's example." She meant it to be offhand, or funny, but as she looked at the words she realized how true they were. He was succeeding, and she wasn't holding up her end of the bargain. He'd never said it, but she'd seen it in his eyes. A talent of his was his ability to mask his disappointment, often with vague praise and encouragement or a list of helpful instructions. But he was clearly disappointed, and it had started to piss her off.

She overheard him once talking about her to an older couple at a party, people he didn't even know very well, and describing her, she thought, like a trinket. He was talking with affection about how outlandish she sometimes looked when she painted, her hair tied back under a baseball cap (she'd done this once), paint everywhere on her clothes, canvases and pallets strewn around, and he laughed as though it wasn't something they'd been getting into spats about.

"I wish I had half her imagination," he said then, a remark so full of false modesty and calculated tenderness, she thought it might be a put-on.

SARAH HICKEY AND ANNE drove down to Syracuse on a cold November morning, and they stopped along the way at the Great Northern Mall in North Syracuse. Anne bought two shirts and a skirt for herself and a gray Shetland sweater for Jack.

They had cappuccinos later at a place called Nancy's Coffee Cafe. Sarah had been asking Anne about her time in Lakeland, whether it was all she'd wanted it to be.

"I've found it kind of hard to fit in so far."

Sarah looked her over. "Well, you know, Anne, people are a little intimidated by you."

"By me? That's ridiculous," Anne said, and indeed intimidating was the last thing she could imagine being.

"This is it. They see you as everything they're not, but wish they were, and rather than admit they're jealous, they go ahead and *judge* you. You're the woman in the fashion magazines they read, the thin, impossibly glamorous one who always knows just what to wear and what to say."

"I never know what to wear."

"They see you as aloof."

It was what they always said about shy, frightened people. "Do I seem aloof?"

"C'mon, Anne. How long did it take you to agree to this trip?"

"I just like keeping to myself."

"And then there's the artist thing."

"The *artist thing*?"

"Yes. They don't really get that. They think, She's an artist. Where's her art? Can we see some?"

"It's not ready for public consumption."

"They're just curious about the kind of girl who'd end up with Jack Lambeau, that's all."

Now it all came together for Anne. A whole town of women were jealous of her, resentful that she'd landed *their* prize, the top dog, the big blue whale. It was a bit alarming she'd been such a prominent topic of conversation among people she didn't know.

"I hope I'm not disappointing them."

"I'm sure you won't," Sarah said, but the way she said it sounded like a suggestion.

ANNE BEGAN TO SEE Turner on her wanderings about town, in the cigar shop where she browsed magazines, at the diner where she bought her coffee, by the little park where she liked to sit and watch the kids jump benches on their skateboards. He'd stop and talk for a minute. She'd promise to bring him his coat. He always seemed awkward and he made her nervous in a way she thought she'd outgrown.

She began expecting to run into him. Once, when she hadn't seen him in a few days, he located her in her dreams. She was at a restaurant in New York and he was her waiter. He kept bringing her what she wanted, even when she hadn't ordered anything. It was an unnerving dream. It was the coat that was making her think of him, she decided. She'd simply have to give the coat back. Then she wouldn't owe him anything.

But when she walked into his office to return it, she realized it wasn't in her backpack. She'd left it at home.

She began to walk out.

"Hey, where are you going?" Turner called.

"I don't have it," she said.

"The coat?"

She nodded.

"That's no big deal."

There were small paragraphs on his screen. Files all around him; he had a pencil behind his ear.

"But I haven't forgotten about it."

"I'm glad to know that."

She liked the office, so much cozier than that cold farmhouse. No dust motes, no spiders. It was a place where work got done. A warm place that made you want to stay. She took another step forward.

"What are you writing about?"

"You really want to know?"

"Sure."

"I'm writing a profile on a couple who make doormats out of tires they find in junkyards."

"Doormats."

"It's a scoop."

He wore a denim shirt and a dark tweed jacket that made him look more put-together than usual. Ordinarily, Turner had the sort of rumpled good looks that she imagined made women want to straighten his tie or tuck his shirt tail in for him. It was the opposite of Jack, who looked neat getting up from bed. Turner's dark eyes were attentive, and there were appealing and expressive lines around them and around his mouth. His wavy brown hair was unabashedly uncombed, like someone who'd just come in from the wind and avoided all mirrors. There were thin black glasses on the desk in front of him, which he'd taken off when she entered the room.

"Are they attractive doormats?"

"Actually, they're pretty terrific. Handwoven. You'd never know how many raccoons they'd run over."

Anne laughed.

"I guess it's kind of strange, my coming by to tell you I didn't bring your coat."

"Not strange at all. I'm done in about an hour . . ."

"I didn't want you to think I was just keeping it."

"Do you want to get a drink?"

"Because I'm usually good at bringing things back. I used to be anyhow," she said, then paused. "A drink. Yes. That would be nice."

"Give me two hours," he said.

"I'll come by," she said.

THEY PICKED A SPOT near the lake that Anne had liked because it had porthole windows and an absurdly pretentious name, La Riviera. Turner pulled her chair out for her. They sat in silence for a minute studying the menu, though they hadn't planned to eat together. The waitress came by wearing a French beret tipped to one side and a knit T-shirt with blue and white horizontal stripes. She read a list of the chef's specials. The chef's name was Jean-Claude, she said, a fact dropped to inspire confidence in his cooking.

Turner ordered a gimlet, and Anne, unthinking, asked for the same.

"Listen. I like talking to you. I just wanted to say that."

"Oh yes?" Anne asked.

"Yeah."

"But we've barely had a conversation. How do you know you like talking to me?"

"I have a sense," he said.

She shrugged. Then she looked the room over. There were viney hanging plants and relics from old vessels: steering wheels, anchors, and scrimshaw, but the waitresses and waiters dressed in what they must have thought was French Riviera style, and the framed posters by the bar held paintings of the beaches of Cannes and St. Tropez.

"What do you think?" he asked.

"A cross between Nice and Nantucket, I guess."

"Cannes or Connecticut. This is the new Lakeland. Too many influences, but they'll get it down."

At the tables people were dressed nattily. Men wore sports jackets, the women new-looking dresses. In her jeans and a lavender rayon shirt, Anne tried not to think about how much she stood out.

"Early this summer, Judd Jewett, owner of the Colt 45 Bar and Restaurant, builds a thick wall and splits his place in half. One side stays the Colt. This side he names La Riviera so he can be part of the French Quarter they're putting together. He moves the cashew and hot tamale dispensers, the stuffed animal crane, and the pinball machines to the Colt side, and replaces them on this side with these plants and anchors, and all that bric-a-brac. Buys a Baldwin piano at an auction, and hires a few cocktail singers from Syracuse. And Jean-Claude."

"Very classy."

"Yes. They're all going exclusive now with the harbor development on its way. Lucky's on the waterfront, they had a little hygiene problem; owners jazzed things up a bit, built a terrace, and now they're Lucille's. Octopus's Garden on Lucas thatched its ceiling and now it's El Tropicana." He raised his arm like a Cuban band leader.

"I liked the Octopus's Garden."

"Really. You went there? Hmmm. It's ancient history now. Upward mobility. Lakeland reinvents itself. Redefines the American small town. You've heard Hickey's speeches."

"I hear Jack's all the time."

"It's great stuff."

Turner imitated Hickey's raspy voice and folksy diction. "Look at the ocean—I mean, lake. Did I say ocean?"

"Can we talk about something else?"

But nothing came to mind. They both sat fidgeting with their drink glasses. The couple at the next table was talking about what had happened at their church. The cocktail singer walked out and introduced herself, Beryl Hynes. She wore a silky plum-colored dress that hugged her narrow hips. She began singing a love song Anne remembered hearing on the radio as a child.

"It's all so Republican around here," Anne said finally.

"Actually, most Lakelanders are Democrats. We haven't voted for a Democratic president since Truman, but we call ourselves Democrats. We came close to liking Kennedy."

"It's your town, isn't it?" she said, though she knew it wasn't. He was as far from home as she was.

"We've got the state's third-best wrestling team, the region's last drive-in movie theater, and its largest nuclear power plant—too bad it can't stay on-line for a few straight hours. Want more?"

"Fire away."

"The fort on the lake. We harbored Jewish refugees there during World War Two. We're proud of that. We were abolitionists during slavery too. Lakeland families were running slaves up to Canada."

"And . . ."

"People belong to the Knights of Columbus, the Masons, the Elks, the Moose Lodge, and the Shriners, and if someone loses their house to a fire or needs money for an operation, someone else will throw a spaghetti dinner or a bake sale. We even burned everyone else's toxic waste until they shut us down."

She laughed, but now he looked embarrassed. "I'm sorry. I'm rambling."

"I'm having a good time," Anne said. She was. She was also getting drunk.

"Excuse me. I'm gonna flag down the waitress," Turner said.

He returned carrying a big plate of steamers.

"They all died right after World War Two, these places. Look at Niagara Falls. Used to be a kingdom, not just honeymooners, they had a bunch of steel and chemical plants, Nabisco Shredded Wheat, you name it, then it all went to rot. Families moved out, housing started crumbling. The mayor built a big convention center to bring business in, and now it sits around like one of those giant Calder sculptures."

"And that's what's happened here."

"Not completely. They're on to something here, as silly as this place looks. They've accepted the truth."

"And what's that?"

"You know. Like Jack always says, the end of the Industrial Age, the end of giant factories where everyone's got a job for life: your children, your grandchildren, your cousin Ed, your uncle

Willie. That's all over with, they know that. Those jobs are gone. And they're not coming back."

He placed a few steamers on a plate for her. He opened one for himself.

"So they change the economy. The new focus is tourism, and high-tech. Lakeland goes Silicon. In this age of Internet technology you can work anywhere, right, that's the thinking, why not work where the living's cheap and the Budweiser's plentiful?" He lowered his glance.

She smiled.

"Who knows if it'll sail, but at least they're doing something."

For a while they ate and said nothing. Turner waved to a familiar face across the room. The man waved back.

"How did someone like you become so comfortable here?" Anne said.

He looked at her from the corner of his eye.

"Comfortable? Hmmmm. I really don't know. Comfortable, huh?"

"Yes."

"Maybe I'm born again."

"I can't believe that."

"It's not like I'm going to tent meetings, but I did hit the depths, you know. I wallowed around in them for a while."

"Really?"

"Oh, yes."

"Describe them to me."

"What?"

"The depths. What were the depths like?"

He guided streams of condensation down the side of his glass. "You really want to know?"

She nodded. She did. She wanted to know what someone else's depths were like.

"Well, it got real cold last winter. I'm talking cold where your face stings and your eyelids freeze. You'll see soon enough. My car door was always frozen shut and I had to kick the ice off each time. Work was uninspiring." He spoke slowly, and looked slightly away from her. "And it snowed for twenty-seven straight days, not all day but for part of it. Every . . . single . . . day. I kept having to write about how cold it was, how no one could remember it being so cold. They ran the headline once, 'It's Snowhere.' I thought that was perfect. That's just where I was. I didn't even want to wake up for about a month. I didn't know what the point was. I smoked a lot of pot. Just say *yes*, I'd say. Then when I was crunching around town one day, something happened. I stepped right out of my body. I'm not shitting you. I looked down at this shabby guy roaming through the snow to the city courts and the police department, stopping to wolf down some coffee and a donut, and I felt this almost romantic fondness. Weird, huh?"

"Sort of like Whitney Houston? The greatest love was inside of you?"

"It wore off by the next morning."

He took his glasses off and placed them on the table.

"It's the swashbuckling scenarios that used to kill me. The visions I carried around of who I should be and what I should be doing. I should be Sydney Schanberg in Cambodia, or Hunter Thompson traveling with the Hell's Angels, or Hemingway driving an Italian ambulance, dropping by Gertrude Stein's for tea, and I should have a nice wife, maybe a kid, maybe a house, maybe a dog, maybe a camel, whatever. Instead I had all these bottled up, unfulfilled dreams."

He was better looking than she'd originally thought.

"So you've accepted this. This is all you want. Is that right?"

"Not at all. It's just what is right now. You do the best with what you got. Like Jack. He's making something of this place, of his time here."

She was surprised to hear Jack's name mentioned so often. She'd managed somehow to forget they were friends.

"You're really fond of him."

"Yes, and I respect him. He's a visionary, he really is."

"And you don't want those other things, Cambodia and the Hell's Angels?"

"Oh, I'd like to be a Hell's Angel. Stomp a puppy or two."

Anne laughed. She told him about her art, the starts and stops. The moments in which she felt full of purpose and the others, more frequent lately, when she felt lost, or like a hackneyed technician.

"Is Jack hip to all this?"

"He's disappointed, I can tell. He keeps saying if I want to be happy, I can be happy. The sadder I am, the more disappointed he is with me. He makes lists of things I can do with myself."

"He just wants to help, that's all."

"Yes, yes, I know."

She saw she'd been ripping apart her napkin. She stopped and dropped the shreds to the floor.

"Maybe that's it. It's strange to go to a meeting and hear everyone talk about him, about what a genius he is. I've stopped going to most of them. I know it's a good thing that they all love him, and that he wants to help them. But sometimes, when I watch him around other people, it spooks me."

She hadn't known this until she now put it into words. "It's like he could have ended up with *anyone* and been happy."

Outside the sun had dipped. Dusk set in. The waitress came by with a bottle of red wine.

"Dig in," he said.

"We can't drink that."

He poured them both glasses. "Have as much or as little as you want."

She drank her glass down in two long sips. "He always wants me to say the right thing, tell him I'm doing just fine when I'm not. I guess it's what he does."

"That's the way it is with optimism, right?" Turner said.

"What?"

"In small doses, it carries you over the rough spots. When it's constant, it makes you feel alone."

She thought about that while she poured herself another glass of wine. She didn't feel alone here. She felt at ease. Calm, almost. Lately, for weeks actually, she'd been stranded from clarity, in a wilderness of questions, noise, and renunciations she couldn't shake or understand. Everything seemed suspect. Even the sunsets lately had looked like bad watercolors.

Now as they sat in a silence both charged and comfortable she was aware of everything around her, the way the glass felt in her hand, the din of conversations, the grapey smell of Turner's breath across the table. She was leaning just a little bit toward him. She held the lime slice from her drained gimlet glass in her mouth and grinned at Turner, a childishly sexy and, as of late, uncharacteristic gesture.

When she sipped her wine again, she did so too quickly. The wine hit the wrong pipe and made her cough. She was suddenly dizzy. There'd always been—in college, at happy hours after work, at family gatherings—a thin barrier in Anne's bloodstream between the desirable amount of alcohol and too much. That last poorly placed sip tipped the balance. Heat gathered in her cheeks. She closed her eyes. It was as though they really were at sea, on high stormy seas, and when she opened her eyes again the porthole windows and anchors and the fake stuffed marlin were bobbing.

Turner had been saying something, for a minute or maybe five, something about hip directors filming upstate, and greasy-spoon diners popping up in the West Village. "Upstate is cool now, according to *New York* magazine." He smiled. "Can't you see it: tube socks and halter tops on the Paris runways."

Anne tried to form words for a reply, to say that she could, but a second wave of dizziness fell over her.

"Excuse me a moment," she said.

"You all right?"

"Yes, I'm fine," she said.

But she wasn't. She was drunk, and something more. She felt drugged, and later she would remember the Valium she'd taken in the afternoon for her nerves. Now her eyesight was filmy. As she crossed the room, she had the sensation of crossing a cruise ship—the club room of the Love Boat. She lost her footing and banged a table. The people there looked annoyed. A goblet of water tumbled onto a woman's lap. There were bits of glass. Anne apologized. The woman was irate. They all glared at her. *Slut*, she thought she heard someone say. But that would be extreme, wouldn't it? She reached the bar and then she couldn't find the ladies' room. She asked the pug-faced bartender, who pointed toward the back of the room, the opposite corner from her table. In the dimly lit ladies' room she washed her face with cold water. She drank from the tap in an effort to dilute the alcohol. There was an awful roaring in her ears.

She must have passed out for a while, because when she awoke she was lying on the white tiled floor.

As she walked from the ladies' room the music had changed to loud rock'n'roll. Someone knocked into her and she stumbled forward into the room, which seemed darker than before. She was standing at the side of a dance floor by herself. Was it Bob Seger playing? Was he still alive? The room reeked of spilled beer and charred beef. People had changed their clothes. And she couldn't find Turner. She walked around the room peering into faces.

Everything had changed. The tablecloths were gone, the nice blue dinner plates, the wineglasses. People ate burgers in waxed paper or bowls of tortilla chips. A big-screen TV showed a car race. There were no portholes; no marlins.

"Have a seat, little honey," a guy in a cowboy hat said.

She realized then she'd gotten herself lost on the wrong side. She was in the Colt 45.

It took Anne another ten minutes to find her table. The waitress pointed out the way. "I'll bring some water," she said.

When Anne found Turner it was like finally finding her car in a darkened parking lot.

"What happened to you?" he said, looking concerned. "Are you all right?"

Her wineglass was full again. How long had she been gone?

"I've got to go home," she said.

"Well, sure," he said. "Let's go."

She reached into her wallet for money, but Turner held her hand. He placed down a pile of bills.

"I'll drive you," he said.

THEY WALKED TOGETHER out of the restaurant. If her legs were still shaky, Anne's headache felt better in the cold air; the worst was over. Several couples passed them on their way in. She dropped her hand when she realized she had been using Turner's arm for support. Night had fallen. Her heart raced ahead, and it confused her. Turner stopped and stood in her eyes. He was not much taller than she was, not exceptionally handsome, certainly not as handsome as Jack, but she realized of all insane things she wanted him to go ahead and kiss her in front of this absurd place.

She said, "I can't do this."

"Can't do what?"

She'd misconstrued him. He hadn't wanted to kiss her. He simply had some other funny story, something else to cheer her up.

"This," she said, trying to steady herself. "I need to get home."

"I know. I'm taking you."

"I want to walk."

"You can't walk, Anne. It's too far. You've had too much to drink. And look."

She glanced at the sky where Turner was pointing but saw nothing.

"Wait a second," he said.

They stared up, side by side.

And then it started, first lightly, a few fat flakes, then harder. In late October.

"My God," she said. She felt like a child.

Snow fell on their hair and faces.

"It's *gorgeous*," she said.

And it was. No moon, no stars, just falling white. The ground sparkled, as if bottom-lit.

He smiled broadly at her as if he'd been responsible for it.

CHAPTER 18

Over those weeks, Jack had been sending up trial balloons, talking to hotel, restaurant, and department store owners to see what it would take to get them to set up on the Lakeland waterfront. From these interviews he continued to tailor his approach. He was unwilling to promise them the moon. He was simply making a case that this would get done, it would be an exciting place, and ultimately they would make money.

The goal was to create a community symbol, and a showcase for tourists; a place you could put on postcards, like say Tivoli Gardens in Denmark, the seaport in Mystic, or Las Ramblas in Barcelona, with people living there so it wouldn't simply be a faux historic novelty block—like Walt Disney's cartoon re-creation of his childhood Merceline, Missouri. There'd be aspects of the festival marketplace, but it would adhere to the principles of good neighborhood planning, which along the John Nolen model meant well-defined edges and a focused center. You couldn't just rehaul a whole town, the thinking went, but if you vastly improved the center, the heart of a town, the rest might follow along. Already the waterfront was noticeably less dreary. In the last weeks, workers—including Harris—had torn down the ugly old grain elevators that had sat empty since the forties, and a few cheap metal storage buildings, and they had already built most of the wooden esplanade. Four of the old warehouses and two old countinghouses had been cleaned out and refurbished, and several of the nearby Victorians had been restored and repainted. What they needed next was something concrete and dramatic to show people who came to town. And so Jack was pushing the idea of making a single street, Lake Street, the centerpiece of the lakefront overhaul, specifically the old brick market buildings, which they would fix up and call the Lake Street Marketplace.

Jack continued to give everyday citizens a voice at all the meetings. It's *your* lakefront, he kept saying. Because it was, ultimately, and because he wanted to deflect the inevitable skepticism about an outsider—and some still saw him that way—coming in and imposing his aesthetic. He *was* imposing his aesthetic (it was part of why they'd brought him here, after all), but he was getting people to see that what he wanted was what they wanted too. He showed slides of the old days, the great old buildings, the intimate streets lined with small-scale facades, the fish and vegetable markets with vendors everywhere hawking their goods. People working and living on a vibrant, briny waterfront. He read aloud a description of a walk along the harborfront taken from the journal of a woman who lived in the 1890s. She described walking from shop to shop all day and then sitting outside with an egg cream and a book, writing letters to a young man in Boston whom she would marry two years later, and "watching the ships come in and leave, and then that lovely sun melting blood orange into the lake."

He felt at times like an actor, night after night reciting from essentially the same script. It was a one-man show about the great Shipping Age and the great Industrial Age, about small-town life, what had happened and what was ahead.

The problem was it wasn't *his* story yet, and that had begun to concern him.

To make anything worthwhile you had to make it personal, a teacher had said in graduate school, and he believed it. You had to figure out what it was a place meant to you, and what it could mean. Jack's feelings about Lakeland were as complicated as those of anyone else who'd rejected his hometown and never looked back. He had hated it and all its citizens; and he had certainly loved it too, though that was long ago. The task, as Hickey had said, was to re-remember. To pick out what you needed, and leave alone what you didn't. At night, walking home on his own, old and unwanted feelings welled up in him; and more than once he broke into a run, and kept running in his dress shoes until he'd reached the town's outskirts. For so long he'd believed that succeeding in life meant leaving this place. He wanted to hide from the feeling that to have returned was to have failed.

HE DISCUSSED NONE OF this with Anne, in part because he feared fueling her dissatisfaction (he wouldn't become one of those complaining couples he'd hated in New York), and partly because he knew it would be lost on her. Anne was in her own distracted continent these days, self-critical and self-absorbed. He watched her some nights, watched her open a magazine, read it for a while, pour herself a drink, a soda maybe, carry it over to the bookshelf, open a book, read that for a while. Forget about her drink and pour herself another, then glance at a newspaper, and soon there was a book, a newspaper, a magazine, a few drinks, and the pint container of ice cream out on various surfaces.

It was like living with an adolescent. He found himself cleaning up after her, and wondering if she even noticed.

He'd ask her how her painting was going. "Lousy," she'd say. But she wouldn't want to talk about it. He tried to make suggestions, to help her look at things a different way.

She'd begun to answer him sarcastically.

"Gee, thanks," she'd say. "If only I'd thought of that before."

He in turn had begun to lose patience.

"What if I can't do this?" she said several times.

"You just can't think that way," he'd say.

"But I do think that way. What's wrong with facing the truth? Why does every question boil down to disposition?"

He knew not to answer her, but in truth he believed that a

lot of matters (in one's work, at least), did boil down to disposition. He sensed she was somehow holding him responsible for her shortcomings, and he hoped there was no truth to that. He wished she were happier. But he couldn't paint her paintings for her, or organize her workspace. He couldn't lead her by the hand through her day. He had so much going on right now, so many people relying on him, demanding things from him. She had no one else to answer to. If there were disadvantages to that, the isolation and lack of structure, there were certainly an equal number of advantages, and he was getting a little sick of her inability to recognize them. What, when it all came down to it, was so wretchedly bad about free rent, and an empty house to paint in?

She should get out of the house more, he thought. She should have some friends. Or at least one good friend. Someone to take the pressure off him.

If she had no interest in her own work, she had even less interest in his. He'd tell her about something he was struggling with, and he'd watch her eyes sink back, her thoughts travel far away.

"And then a woman in a string bikini jumped out and sat on my lap," he'd say to test her.

But she only scowled then.

"I hear everything you say," she said. "I just don't always have a response."

He wanted her to share in what he was doing, to offer advice maybe, to take pride in his accomplishments. She told him one night that she'd stopped going to meetings because "they make me feel artificial. I feel like everyone's waiting for my facial reaction, like they wait for the First Lady's nods and smiles at a State of the Union address. I mean, God forbid I fall asleep. They'd have me hanged."

It was a flimsy excuse, he thought, but she seemed convinced of it. And in truth he wouldn't like it at all if she went and looked bored, or fell asleep, or simply appeared indifferent. It was bad enough at home; no need to drag it all out in front of everyone else.

CHAPTER 19

Harris soon began dreaming about his baby. In his dreams he was swinging through the jungle like Tarzan with his baby girl under his arm, and beneath their dangling feet were piles and piles of what first looked like trash, but were on closer inspection decomposing corpses.

Marla had told him to stay elsewhere for a while, so Harris had been sleeping at Bazorcik's on his foldout couch.

When he called Marla she was short with him.

"I need to be with you," he said more than once. "I'm the father."

"Yeah?" She laughed. "Since when?"

"Since always," he said.

"You never gave me any real respect, Harris, and I don't think you ever will."

"I married you, didn't I?"

She hung up on that one.

Day in, day out, he thought of the baby, thought of her under those lamps, sleeping, growing, drinking the light. He thought of his high school science classes when they learned about photosynthesis, but he also began to think of Marla. Something about her standing up for herself made her seem more attractive— gave her some corners—and Harris began to believe it wasn't such a bad stroke of fate to have married her. But what did it matter now that she hated him and didn't want him around?

It occurred to him he was being punished for what he'd done

with old Parkhurst—not by Marla, though, by someone with more influence.

HE BEGAN TO DRIVE past the house hoping to catch a glimpse of the Baby. He didn't even know if Marla had named her yet. He thought of her simply as the Baby. The jerks next door were having parties, with loud guitar noises and yelling. Keeping the Baby up, he thought.

"Turn it down," he said to one of them through the open window.

They turned it down, but not enough.

He called his buddy Lancatta at the sheriff's department. Lancatta said they'd close it down.

He asked, Could a wife keep a mortgage-paying man out of his house? And Lancatta told him so long as he wasn't beating Marla, she would have to let him in.

"Fine," she said on that one. "I'll go home to my parents."

He thought of Maynard and Alice listening to Marla's complaints for a while—all of them agreeing what a loser Harris was. He didn't want that happening.

"We'll talk on the weekend. All right?"

About a year and a half ago, before Harris and Marla met, a guy Harris worked with told him how to get into the movies free. He said if the movie theater girl liked you, you could go in without paying. He said a lot of guys did it and some got more than a free movie. He smiled basely at that last part. Harris didn't believe it. The girl looked like someone's kid sister. Still, the story got him curious, got him a little hot. He started hanging around the booth and he got to know her. She began to look different to him, sexy, bed-able maybe. And she started letting Harris, and only Harris, into the movies free. In mid-summer, the night manager began leaving early, and when the concessions staff left it was just Harris and Marla and the night janitor, who was often drunk by then and nowhere to be found. Marla would lock the booth and join Harris in the rear of the balcony under the gilt-laced ceiling. When the last of the moviegoers had gone, Marla began taking Harris through the red-and-black-walled corridors covered with oil paintings of Revolutionary War battles to the third-floor mop closet where they'd stash a candle, a blanket, and a bottle of wine. Before they finished the wine, Harris would douse the candle. When they finished once and lay together, hot and wet and exhausted in that mop closet, Marla said to him, "Sometime it'd be nice to go on a real date."

"Of course," Harris said, though he'd liked the relationship fine the way it was.

Who wouldn't? He could do what he wanted, show up or not show up, and whenever he got there and whatever state he was in, she was ready for action, no hassles. So many women wanted you to dress a certain way, act a certain way, talk a certain way. Marla was low maintenance.

And then she got pregnant.

He was only religious on holidays, and he knew people who'd had abortions. But it was difficult in Lakeland. You had to leave the county to get one. And anyhow, it was up to Marla, he felt.

She wanted the baby.

They married a month before Marla began to show. No one forced Harris into it. Belle told him not to do it if it wasn't what he wanted. He thought there were worse women to marry than Marla. It bothered him that she laughed too often and too soon at his jokes or that she might stay inside all day or all weekend even with the sun warm and strong, watching television or reading magazines if no one suggested otherwise, but she loved him, and she was pretty, and he figured that could be enough.

She was there, always, and always in love with him, always waiting for him. It was something he'd grown to bank on, that he'd be the independent one. It wasn't in the deal for her not to need him.

Bazorcik said what Harris needed was a decent porno. So

they rented Bazorcik's favorite. One where all the women were carpenters and plumbers for this rich guy. And while the women were doing the work, they got busy with each other. "I love that they don't take off their tool belts," Bazorcik said.

It was all of Bazorcik's fantasies—someone to watch and someone to do his work for him.

Harris kind of liked it too. The women were better looking than in a lot of those films where they looked like they'd been maltreated backstage. These women looked like lingerie models rather than hookers. But when it was a half-hour old, he started thinking of his little baby girl again and feeling guilty and sick. He looked at Bazorcik, only a foot away from the TV. Eyes fastened to this fake scene. A woman pounding in a nail while the man's doing the same from behind. Harris walked out of the house.

"I'm gonna get some air," he said.

He drove by his old apartment. There was music next door, of course, a thumping bass. It wasn't too loud, but it was loud enough. And it was only nine. He walked around the back. Marla was watching television. His little girl was sleeping, he supposed. He wondered if infants had dreams. What would they dream of? Toys, and colors, and stuffed bears? Maybe the same thing Bazorcik dreamed of, a nice big nipple.

He stood outside a while watching Marla watch her shows. Then she walked into the other room. When she came out again she was carrying the baby.

The sight of her holding their child was startling. Marla looked nothing like the girl at the ticket counter, the girl in the mop closet. She was divine; she was Mary. She was utterly and completely perfect.

As he watched Marla now, any aversion he'd had to her simply softened. He could love her, he knew, if she'd give him the opportunity. And with this knowledge Harris felt a surge of righteousness building within him, which though far from desire was every bit as powerful, and a good deal more significant. *You will be a good husband and father or you will be nothing at all*, he said to himself.

He held his arms in a cradling position. He felt his child in his arms, actually felt her weight. He was glad they'd had a girl. He'd thought he'd wanted a boy to throw a football to, or take to the Syracuse Chiefs games, but he didn't think he could love anything more than this nameless daughter so bent on seeing the world that she'd jumped out a month early.

"It's Daddy," he whispered toward where her little ear would have been. "Don't cry, precious. I'm right here."

The music next door got moved up a notch.

Harris heard a siren wailing.

Good, he thought. They were busting the neighbors. Close the whole house down for good, he thought. Kick the little shits out. Find some other block to torture. Or give them their own street to puke and break bottles on. But then the flashlights the cops held were being shined in his direction. They passed over Harris's chest and then moved back into his face.

"Put your hands in the air!" the cops said.

All he could see was that bright, blinding light.

"What?" Harris said. "I live here. This is *my* house."

The cops moved closer. Harris knew most of the cops but he didn't know either of these guys.

"Got any ID?"

Harris reached into his pockets. He'd left his wallet at Bazorcik's.

"Call Lancatta back at the station. He'll tell you who I am."

The light had stained his retina so that he saw it wherever he looked. He wondered what the light had done to his daughter.

"Lancatta's off tonight," the younger cop said. He looked like he wanted trouble. Like he needed an arrest to make his promotion.

"I want you to put your hands behind your head."

He patted Harris down for weapons, front and back.

"Marla!" Harris called.

No one answered.

"People are trying to sleep around here," the cop said.

"Just ask the woman inside," Harris said. "She's my wife."

"Then what were you doing staring through the window?"

"What business is it of yours?"

"Don't be a wiseass. We got word there was a pervert out here. And here you are looking a little like a pervert. No?"

The cop brought Harris over to the front of the house. He knocked on the door.

Marla came out, wrapped in a red blanket, a poncho sort of thing.

"I'm sorry to bother, ma'am, but do you know this gentleman?" the cop asked.

She looked him over as if trying to place the face.

Don't do this to me, Harris said with his eyes. Don't hang me out to dry.

"Let's go, buddy," the younger cop said, and he took Harris's arm.

"Yes," Marla said before they went any farther. "I know him."

"You want him around?"

She kept her eyes on Harris.

"If he's polite."

The younger cop released Harris and gave him a nasty look.

"You have any problems, you let us know," he said. Then they sat in the car for a bit, talking into their walkie-talkies.

Harris hated them.

When the police car pulled away, Marla said, "We have to pick a name."

"Yes, of course."

It filled Harris with hope.

"The ones I've narrowed it down to are Jamie, Corrine, and Charlotte," she said.

"Charlotte?"

"It's my great-aunt's name."

"I like it," Harris said. "Charlotte."

"Then that's it," Marla said.

"Charlotte," Harris said. "I love it."

"Now I'm gonna turn in," Marla said.

"Charlotte Lambeau."

"Bye, Harris."

"Aren't you gonna let me in?"

"Not right now."

"When, then?"

"I don't know. Not for a while. We'll talk about it. I know you want to see her. We'll figure something."

He seethed. "Jesus, Marla—"

She interrupted him, "See this porch, Harris? You know how many nights I spent out here waiting for you to get home while you were doing who-knows-what? No word. No call. No damn respect. I hate this porch now. It's why I wanted us to move into the house, and now I hate it. You try sitting out here a while."

He sat down on the swinging bench. She stepped inside. Then she came out again.

"And Harris . . ."

"Yes."

"Call next time. This whole thing with the police was kind of scary."

CHAPTER 20

For Thanksgiving, Belle cooked the largest turkey anyone had seen. Hormones, Frank said. Enough tryptophan to last two winters, Jack said.

Marla didn't come, and no one knew whether to talk about the baby or not. Harris had fucked up again, was the general consensus, but at least for the beginning of the day no one brought that up in front of him.

Jack invited Steven Turner, who had to work most of the day. Turner took pictures and wrote down a couple of quotes, then he left. He would go to two other dinners, he said, and write about them. A little feature about turkey day.

Harris and Frank watched football. Harris talked a lot toward the television set. "Good thing they fired that lardass," he kept saying of the Lions' previous coach.

"Doesn't make a bit of difference," Frank said.

"Sure it does. Their attitude's better."

Jack sat down with the two of them for a while and rooted for the Vikings, whom he'd liked since the days of Fran Tarkenton and Alan Page.

His father looked old, Jack thought. His skin was an unhealthy pallor, and his eyes looked tired. Some of this was simply an early winter cold. He kept sneezing into the same gray handkerchief and then putting it back in his shirt pocket.

His father had been a line foreman at the woolen mill before it closed in 1978. He'd been one of the luckier ones. A year after he lost his job, he resurfaced from a funk, took his savings, and bought two old Victorians that the banks had foreclosed on. He made six apartments out of them and began renting them out. Soon he had enough saved to buy another house.

There still wasn't a heap of money coming in, but there was enough to keep afloat. And there wasn't all that much work to do other than to make sure the trash was picked up and the rent collected.

Jack had been trying to spend time with his father since he'd arrived back, but he'd been so busy, and there were times when he wondered sadly if they had anything to say to one another. His father kept saying he was proud of Jack, proud of what he was doing, especially within earshot of Harris. Then he'd tell someone what a brilliant architect his son was. And Jack would say he wasn't an architect.

"But you studied to be an architect. You always wanted to be an architect."

"I guess I must be one then," Jack said once. "My mistake."

The easiest thing to do most visits was to watch sports on television, or an action movie with Nick Nolte or Danny Glover.

"Go, go, go!" Harris yelled now.

A wide receiver for the Lions with the unlikely first name of Herman streaked across the field to catch a forty-yard pass, then faked the cornerback covering him out of his shorts.

Harris smirked at Jack as though he'd caught the pass, and Jack had been the burned Viking. Harris took his victories where he could find them.

AFTER DINNER THEY LINGERED at the table, talking of snowstorms, gossip, and skunk attacks, and then his mother talked about the ambulance team, how the tough new recertification rules meant fewer people were volunteering.

"They don't want some three-day test just so they can save someone's life," she said, though she'd had no trouble passing it.

And then all the long jokes started (the twelve-inch pianist, the three pieces of string who walk into a bar, Pierre the Pig Porker), and they continued and continued.

Anne had a stomachache and wanted to leave early. Jack accused her later of leaving because she was bored of his family's conversations, and then apologized and admitted he had been mad because she'd left for the bathroom in the middle of his best joke.

"I liked it the last five times," she said. "And I'm sure I would have liked it this time but I felt sick. I feel a little sick still."

They decided holidays with families were stressful, picked the evening apart together (can you believe all those skunk stories?), and made up. It was like a clumsily applied patch that was likely to give way again before long.

UNTIL THE SUMMER he was twelve, the summer the Davis family shut down the woolen mill, Jack was a quietly popular boy, uncomplicated, and unaware of any significant hardship around him. He was captain and the wiry, sling-armed third baseman of his Little League team, one on which Harris was a part-time right fielder. Belle worked some, and Frank worked all the time, and Jack remembered the men his father worked with: rough-faced ones who'd come over with their wives for Sunday barbecues, and replenish his supply of dirty jokes, or in the winter would take Jack and Harris ice fishing or to basketball games in Syracuse. All that changed when the mill closed. Suddenly his father was around the house when he got home from school. Jack liked it for a week or so, and they'd gone bowling twice and once to an early movie, but then it felt wrong, and a little troubling, as though the family's balance had been thrown off. His father watched television, took naps, went out late and then slept in the next morning—often still in his clothes. That was when Jack's mother started taking odd jobs filing or answering phones in insurance offices and at the hospital, along with her ambulance work, and had no energy left to make supper. It was when he realized parents could be undependable, and maybe his world had a few holes in it. He began to reevaluate things. He started studying harder in all his subjects, doing whatever he could to distance himself from where his father had ended up. It wasn't difficult for him. He was sharp, and his teachers liked him.

Late one night, Jack woke to the sound of crying coming from the living room. He walked down and saw his father in his armchair. He'd never heard his father cry before. Jack recalled hating him then, because he thought he was weak and frightened and incapable of figuring a way out of the rut he was in. Jack didn't feel like understanding his father. He wanted him to stop what he was doing and be like he used to be.

A FEW MONTHS BEFORE he found his way into those rental houses and got his life back on track, his father showed up drunk to a Little League playoff game. The game was the county title and Jack could tell by the volume of his cheering that his father was lit. Ordinarily he was encouraging and not fanatical, and having played a year of Single A in the minors way back when, he gave decent advice on how to hit a curve or how to trick a runner into going for home when he hadn't a prayer. *"Ma boys!"* he had yelled this time. *"Go-go Lambeaus. Kick their pansy butts."* Never mind that he'd sat in the wrong section, and the other team's parents were two rows above him; never mind that Jack's team was losing. He got even louder, of course, in the third when Jack hit a triple and eventually scored. *"Go-go Lambeau!"* he said. *"M-V-goddamned-P!"* Jack felt embarrassed and hoped his mother would show up soon and take his father home.

In the top of the fifth, the Lakeland pitcher, a streaky player prone to disastrous middle innings, got into a jam. After a strike-out, he gave up a walk and a base hit, putting runners on first and third. Another mistake would be the end of him, Jack knew. He could see it in his eyes. On a two-and-zero count to the next batter he served up a curve that didn't curve, and the batter drove a shot toward left field. Jack leapt for the line, arms and legs fully extended, but he was an inch short of making a miraculous catch. The ball nicked the dirt before caroming into the soft webbing of his glove. A run would score, and there was little chance he could throw the batter out at first. The other team would bat through the lineup and drive up the score. Jack understood this as he rolled his shoulder and fell forward into a somersault. But as he made it to his knees, dirt in his eyes and mouth, the ball snug in his glove, it simply didn't *feel* like a base hit. It felt like the play of an all-star, the third baseman who could bail out his team in times of trouble, who could carry the whole crowd on his back. And so Jack rose to his feet and held the ball aloft like an egg whose delicate shell he'd protected.

The crowd cheered wildly, and the other team's third base coach, fearing a double play, yelled to the runner to get back to the bag. Jack won that race. The umpire seemed confused for a moment. He then pulled his arm back over his shoulder in an "out" sign.

Inning over, unassisted double play.

The other team trudged back onto the field, no big inning, no runs scored. Cheers poured down from the stands. The argument that followed was about whether or not the runner had beaten Jack to the base. No one questioned the catch. And Jack began to wonder if he hadn't actually caught the ball cleanly, it had landed so solidly in his glove. Would it have been right to let everyone down for the sake of something no one saw, or could prove?

"MVP!" his father yelled. "Brooksie Goddamned Robinson!"

LATE IN THE GAME Harris came in as a pinch hitter and knocked in two runs, his first RBIs of the season. It might have been because of that—because a ten-year-old had tied the game—that made the pitcher go inside on Jack two batters later, or more likely the ball just got away from him. Jack turned to move away and the ball hit him in the meat of his back, knocking him to the ground where he flailed in pain for a minute or two while the grown-ups all gathered around him.

"He tried to kill him," one of the mothers said.

"I'm okay," Jack said. And the pitcher said something about the Academy Awards.

"Coulda broken a rib," someone else said.

There was nothing special about the incident, as Jack remembered it. These things happened. And if it had to do with the catch, well then, that would have to be okay. It was the risk he'd taken by playing hard, and playing to win. He'd have a bruise for a couple days. There was nothing out of the ordinary here. What happened after the inning was a different matter. It was why Jack quit baseball and started running cross-country. And it was likely the beginning of his wanting to leave Lakeland, to make a life far away, and far different from all he'd seen up until then. At first Jack thought it was a fight between teammates, or maybe it was the other team's coach who was slamming the kid against the outside wall of the dugout; then, to his bewilderment and shame, he saw that it was his father.

YEARS LATER HE WOULD come to understand what this was about, that it was about his father's frustrations and lack of direction, about how his world had collapsed, how he had no shape for his days, no idea who he was anymore; and maybe it was the rage of a town, a whole sad, lost part of the world, and in his own fucked-up way it might have been an act of love, but right then it was simply a forty-two-year-old man going nuts on a thirteen-year-old kid. There was no conceivable excuse for something like that. It took six players, the two coaches, and a few other parents to pull him away. The kid's nose was bloodied and he had bruises on his cheekbones. Frank entered AA the next day. Miraculously, the parents didn't press charges. And it wasn't anything that was ever repeated. It was simply a pathetic moment and they all wanted to put it behind them. Jack never spoke of it with his father, not once, and his father, to his knowledge, never struck anyone again.

Forgotten in all of this was Harris's double—a ten-year-old doubling in a game of twelve-and thirteen-year-olds. It was the start of a commendable two years in Little League that no one saw, that Harris never much mentioned, even the following season when the team made the finals of a regional tournament, and Harris finished fifth in the voting for league MVP.

NIGHTS AT BAZORCIK'S, Harris was reading an infant-care book the woman at the bookstore had recommended. *What to Do the First Year.*

He read the sections on Your Newborn's Reflexes, and Sterilizing Techniques.

The point of the book seemed to be to let you know your kid wasn't fucked up. That pointy head, those puffy eyes? Don't panic. Skin the color of a banana? A little epilepsy when she's crying? Enjoy it now, you'll miss it tomorrow. That gagging and choking, normal too, the book said. "Remember," the author said, "your baby spent the last nine months, more or less, living in a liquid environment. She didn't breathe air, but she sucked in a lot of fluid. Though a nurse or doctor probably suctioned her airways clean at birth [Harris pictured little Charlotte with a pint-sized vacuum down her tiny throat], there may have been additional mucus and fluid in her lungs." "That's real nice," Harris said aloud, while Bazorcik watched the Monday night game next to him. He read on and on until he got to the section which said: Don't try to do it all yourself. And that made him sad, then a little pissed off.

"You call her today?" Bazorcik asked.

"No. She doesn't want to speak to me."

"You can't put up with that shit. Since when was it her house anyhow?"

Since her father took out the loan, Harris could have said. If he was angry, it was mostly with himself.

LATER THAT NIGHT, when the game was over, Harris and Bazorcik watched a nature show on exotic frogs. The first thing Harris saw was a huge pale mama frog giving birth to dozens of tadpoles, who swam to life through wide pores in her back.

Harris pictured Charlotte swimming like that. Babies could learn to swim, couldn't they? They could swim before they talked. His could, anyway. Harris was in love, he recognized, a frustrated, held-back sort of love you might have in prison. He couldn't wait to see his daughter again—to kiss her little nose, to hold her. His empty hands felt sticky and thick, useless.

He wanted to make more money for her. He wanted Harlan to pay him all the money he owed him for burying barrels and burying Dieter Parkhurst.

He had a purpose now.

Bazorcik started in again.

"The woman's doggin' you big time, Harris. That's absolutely unacceptable. Woman does something like that to me . . ." He shook his head. "I'd break the fucking door down is what I'd do. I just never seen anything like it. That's your house, Harris. That's your kid, and here you are watching frogs."

"Ssshhh," Harris said.

The narrator was showing a type of Australian frog that retained large amounts of water in a balloonlike belly so that it could survive underground.

"That's some frog," Harris said.

A black, nearly naked man poked the ground with a stick until he found one of the frogs. Improbably, he lifted the frog to his mouth and drank from its bloated gray bladder.

"That's disgusting," Bazorcik said. "But kind of ingenious."

"It's goddamn unfair," Harris said.

They both kept watching.

The screen showed other gatherers digging up frogs and drinking from them.

Then it showed a group of men in lab coats talking about frogs.

"Want another beer?" Bazorcik said.

Harris said nothing. Bazorcik went to the fridge.

SHE'D COME AROUND, HARRIS THOUGHT. He needed to show her he was different now. He *was* different. Then he thought about how he still hadn't been paid, and he looked around Bazorcik's squalid living room.

When he returned, Bazorcik held up his beer and sucked it down.

"Rrrribit," he said.

Harris nodded. He thought again of the shit-boy neighbors calling the police on him. That's who'd done it, he knew. That's who called the cops and humiliated him. He thought of them keeping Marla and little Charlotte awake with their music, the constant bass. "That'd fuck with them, huh, Harris? You could go to those deserts, pull up all the frogs, and leave a few frosties in their place."

Bazorcik smiled at his joke. "Or you could fill up the froggies with beer, and then suck their butts."

Harris nodded. He had to get out of here, he realized, or he would become a moron.

"I'm a lot funnier with you around, Harris," Bazorcik said.

BEFORE HE WENT TO sleep Harris went by to see Marla and the baby again. The shades were drawn. He tried his key in the front door.

At least she hadn't changed the locks. He went to the refrigerator for another beer, but there were none. There was healthy food, and baby stuff. There was a box of tea on the counter.

He decided to boil some water and make himself a cup of tea.

Sleepytime. The box had a picture of a drowsy bear in a white nightgown on a recliner, a smile on his face. There was a nice fire in the fireplace and a cat sleeping at his feet, a pair of well-worn boots next to a long bristled broom and a small wooden pickax. An old-style radio sat on a table, and behind the bear, ready for sleep, was a bonneted mother bear, with a little girl bear in tow and a baby boy bear over her shoulder.

What he needed now was a drink, or fifteen. And he needed to find Jim DelMonico or Terry Miller so he could get very high and forget about how fucked-up things were right now. High enough he'd stop wanting the lives he saw on tea boxes.

He drank his tea, then tiptoed to the bedroom. The door was open a crack. He opened it a little more. He could see them both sleeping.

He whispered, "I'm not an asshole anymore."

He watched them for a while, mother and child.

He wanted her to wake up and see him, see the expression on his face. She'd see what was inside him now.

She'd know then. She'd know exactly what he was.

When he walked outside the sky was bluing, and it was all quiet next door. No thumping. It gave him an idea. He tried first the front door and then the back. The back door opened with the turn of a knob. Harris walked in. The house was dark, and landscaped with dead beer cans. A hallway wall had a hole in it the size of a fist. He found the living room and then the stereo. It was shockingly unimposing for all that sound. Harris could barely believe it, that something no bigger than a toaster could shake a whole street. He took a half-filled beer and poured it into the receiver. He ripped out a lot of wires. He heard a sound upstairs but no one came down to see what he was doing. Quietly as possible he kicked in the speakers. Then he walked out to his car. Easy as pie. You do what you can, he thought. And he drove off.

PART III

LAKE EFFECT

CHAPTER 21

December and darkness shrank their days. At four the sky through the clouds was a dissolving scarlet; at four-thirty it was night again.

At lunch Turner wrote in his notebook:

Winter hits Lakeland like a ten-mile-wide anvil. It is a no-parole sentence from which your solace is to carve passing days into the wall. There are colder places, for sure, but only a handful of snowier ones, and in those regions there are at least mountains to give the snow purpose. In Lakeland, snow falls cruelly, then sleet, and ice, and bone-cold winds that whip off the lake and through your skin.

Now wind and sleet whipped the town in concert, lashing storefronts, tearing away the flag atop the Old Colonial Restaurant on Walnut Street. Turner saw a green woolen glove fly by his car window, then that royal blue flag of the Old Colonial, then fast-food wrappings and a newspaper—as he waited at a stoplight, he watched his stories festoon a tree. He wondered about light children; could you lose one to the heavens, like a balloon? He wondered too about his car. Would it tip over if he stayed too long at this stoplight? Snow blew horizontally before him. Before Christmas you could think of snow as a prelude to the holidays. Afterward it was just a prelude to itself.

AS TURNER ENTERED the office, Stewart mumbled, without looking over, "Clark's on the warpath."

"Why?"

"That guy you interviewed Friday. Williamson. I guess you said something about his face."

"His face?"

Williamson. It had been an innocuous feature. There'd been quotes from critics insinuating his ineffectiveness, but Turner couldn't recall what he'd said about the man's face.

"You said he had a weak chin."

Turner waited for the rest. There wasn't a rest.

"Clark says weak chins aren't news."

The line was, *Williamson, a tall, heavy man with silver hair, ruddy complexion, and a weak chin . . .*

"It's a profile. Aren't I allowed a little leeway here?"

"You've insulted him."

"So, I could have said he had a strong chin."

"Right."

"This is ridiculous."

"Clark says call him pronto."

"Your header's all ready to go, Turner," Clark said, when Turner reached him. "Lawmaker Has Weak Chin. County to Allocate Relief Funds."

Turner laughed.

"It's not funny, mister. If I'd been working Sunday you wouldn't have tried this crap."

"I would have."

Turner could picture Clark fuming on the other end. He simply couldn't resist infuriating him. Call it professional suicide.

"How's a weak chin important, Turner? You tell me that."

"I said he was heavy, too."

"It's obvious he's heavy. Everyone could see he's heavy. But it takes a weirdness like yours to say he's got a weak chin."

"Look at that picture, Clark. What would you say?"

"I'd let the picture talk. The point is, Turner, you're a newspaper reporter, not a face critic. Got it? If he's a movie star, then maybe, just maybe, I'd want to hear about his chin. Actually, even then I wouldn't give a shit."

Turner kept silent though he thought in this case the weak chin was the right detail. It was telling of a more central weakness: The man had no cojones.

"We can publish a retraction."

"Don't yank my chain, all right, Turner? We'll let this one slide. Just stick to news, okay? That's what you're paid for. You work for a *news*paper—at least for now."

Truth was, Clark was right.

"Stick around for the storm. I mean, stay by the phone. We may need you."

Stewart shambled over when Turner hung up.

"Bad timing," he said.

"How's that?"

"Rathaman got picked up by the Orlando *Sentinel*. They shuffled the deck and northern suburbs is open now."

"An opening?"

There hadn't been a downtown opening for four months, and that one had been filled from the outside.

"An opening," Stewart said. "You better start sucking up. That wasn't much of a start."

WHEN THE ROAD OPENED Turner thought of Rathaman leaving for Florida. Trading in his mukluks for flip-flops, covering Disney World, maybe. Or immigration. Or crazy crackers with guns. He pictured Rathaman scribbling notes outside his cabana. "Point is, it's an opening," he said to himself with some hope. Northern suburbs. Not a glamour job, but downtown. Downtown was editors and reporters to talk to, rows of padded cubicles, the buzz of purposeful activity. A real newsroom. You weren't so cast out on your own.

The trees were swaying. There was lake effect on the way. All they'd be writing about soon was snow.

AN HOUR AFTER HE'D ARRIVED HOME and settled into his absurdly long book, Dickens's *Bleak House*, Turner began an unproductive routine of thinking about Anne Marks. In the weeks since their talk at La Riviera, she'd become the focus of his romantic life—a woman he barely knew, and who was marrying his closest friend up here. Whether here or out drinking, he'd spend a portion of each night imagining she lived not with Jack, but with him. She'd be back soon, snow sparkling in her hair, the way it had outside the restaurant. She'd cozy next to him in bed. He couldn't afford these thoughts, so he pulled himself out of bed and walked around.

He hadn't so much as spoken to her in weeks. He'd seen her walking around town a few times, but he'd kept his distance. It wasn't his nerve abandoning him, or even his conscience rearing itself, but an unsettling premonition that he could fall, and quickly, and once he did it would be impossible to climb out again.

He replayed words they'd said to each other. Atoms of promise and possibility were haunting him. He smoked the end of the large joint he'd started two nights before and listened to a tape a friend made for him of Brazilian drum music.

No sooner had he fallen asleep to a fading syncopation of drums and sleet than the wind struck up an awful volume. It stopped for a moment and then pounded his window again. "Quiet down," Turner said, and it did.

Like the wolf it huffed and puffed.

"Take a hike," Turner said.

It shattered the window.

Glass rained onto the floor. And then sleet. A frigid wind ripped through.

HE CALLED MRS. WILLHILLEN.

"My God, Steven, that's awful," she said. "That's terrible. What's a window for if it won't keep out the wind?"

"It tried," he said.

"Nothing's safe anymore," she said. "A window jumping in at you like that."

Still, it would take her three days to send someone over.

For now, Turner closed the bedroom door and slept near the heat vent in the kitchen. When he woke up he was disoriented. He thought for a moment someone had transported the stove and refrigerator into his bedroom. And then he wondered if he'd done it himself for convenience, so he wouldn't have to walk through the house to get a midnight snack.

"IT'S GOT TO BE YOU OR ME," Stewart said. "That's all I'll say. I mean if it's you, I'm happy. You paid your dues. Not as much as me, but you paid."

"Well, you know old Clarkie."

"If they hire one of the new dudes," Stewart said, "I'm gonna smash his car."

"That's nice. I'll come visit you in the pen."

"They might think it was you, Turner."

He considered that Stewart might be serious.

"Just apply to another paper."

"I did that already. No one ever wrote back. I called up an editor at the *Boston Globe* I wrote to."

Turner was supposed to ask what came of it. He didn't. There was a limit to how many Unfair World stories he could listen to from Stewart.

"He said, 'Correspond by letter next time.' I said I would.

Then he asked me if I'd been drinking." Stewart let out a puffy breath that blew a strand of hair up.

"I think that's a veiled sign of interest," Turner said.

Turner needed some new clips before he interviewed. Snow and the frozen ground had killed his environmental stories.

Like a drifter through a Dumpster, he'd been scouring the police blotter for his daily rations. The blotter was fertile ground from Thanksgiving through June. People went odd in these months (Mrs. Willhillen, for one, had been phoning at odd hours with odder suggestions). They lost their wits, which, though bad for them, was compelling for a reporter. It wasn't quite the *New York Post*, but there were stories: the kid in Thomasville who shot his father because of an Ozzy Osbourne song; the priest who locked up four altar boys for a week; the mailman who stole an expensive parrot from a house on his route; the woman who froze surrounded by twelve feet of newspapers (including hundreds of Turner's stories); the cheerleaders who Saran-wrapped an unpopular girl to a chair.

If he hadn't been just a quick-shot artist, Turner would have made some larger observations (editors hated larger observations. *You're not a columnist. Right? Do we have this straight?*). He would say the whole town (him included) was a little deranged in the winter, some more than a little, and that this had to do with all the cloud cover altering neurochemicals. He would say that liver and brain cells were dying at record highs in the endless nights, that ten-year-old kids ran households while their parents tried to come to. That there were more suicides. That this stuff on the farms was part of a deeper infirmity which was an economic wretchedness. That with all the dressing up and primping you did, all the face-lifts the harbor would bring, beneath it all would be this sad, creaky, decaying place beset by the worst weather known to earth. He would say that road salt was eating away their lives.

But it wasn't his place to do this. His place was to write the church goings and the misdemeanor arrests.

Clark said opinions were like assholes, and on that issue Clark would know.

One of the television stations had done a four-part series on Seasonal Affective Disorder, and now everyone in town was talking about SAD. SAD was why things happened. It was the new excuse, like the guy who ate Twinkies and shot that gay city official in San Francisco.

Clarence Easterman, who gave the lectures, said to avoid SAD, you had to get out and play in the snow like the Inuits did. "It's a war," he said. "Your body wants to sleep, but society won't let you."

Rather than plug harder than ever, businesses should do what Eskimos do, he said. Slow down in winter. Ease up on hours. Sleep in if you need it.

Then get outside for a bit in whatever passes for daylight.

Have a winter festival, with ice sculptures and a softball game in the snow.

There were rooms where people spent a half hour beneath a light panel that dispensed ten thousand lux. He said researchers were making a visor you could wear indoors that would give you the needed medicinal rays. You could wear it on a long plane trip, he said. Or while you sit in an office doing work.

TURNER WORRIED he wasn't getting enough light. He was getting sick. He tended to the shit part of the job, the school lunches, church events. Two obits.

When he was done, Stewart called him over.

"Take a look at this. See what you think of this."

He looked. It made no sense. It had something to do with county subsidies for the elderly, or maybe it was a felled traffic light.

"What are you trying to say here?"

Stewart told him. They went over the story together, then through Stewart's notes.

When Turner was done, the story was readable. They sent it in. Solidarity. Thick and thin, brothers in combat.

He went back to his own piece. Stewart actually left before him. Halfway through, his phone rang.

"YOU WANT A LITTLE MORE of the iceberg?" the gravelly voice said.

"I think I do."

"Tomorrow at the fish-fry stands."

"All right. How will I know you?"

"It's gonna be cold out. Won't be too many suntanners is my guess."

CHAPTER 22

"You on this, Turner, or do I have to give it to someone else?"

"I'm on it," he said. "I'm on it as much as a guy can be when it's four feet under outside."

"You look at your files. Your old stories on the waste incinerator."

They were seated on a wooden bench outside the boarded-up fish-fry stand along the lake. In summer this spot was packed with families. Turner had done a feature on how people came from Syracuse and Rochester to eat fish shipped in from Boston. Deep Throat was wearing a Cleveland Indians baseball hat tipped low and dark sunglasses.

"I did."

"Good stuff, huh?"

It was good stuff.

For six years, from 1975 to 1981, a company named Northern Waste Alleviation operated waste incinerators on the east side of town. Dozens of Fortune 500 companies, many of them multinationals, sent thousands of barrels of waste to Lakeland. A large work force was hired, and the money rolled in. But the burners didn't burn properly. Management was corrupt. Workers stockpiled drums, or poured them into lagoons and the lake. Around five thousand gallons of oils and chemicals made their way into swamps and creeks around there, and eventually into Lake Ontario. The owner, Dante Pavio, said they'd get some oil-eating bacteria and drop them into the spill areas, but he never did.

Deep Throat sipped from a covered plastic container of coffee.

"When it starts, Dante's a star. Local development company gives him fourteen acres of lakeside and helps him push through a loan from the fed at low interest. And when it's built, it's a smash success. Four hundred thousand gallons of hazardous industrial waste a month."

"Got that," Turner said.

"So then. People who would have dumped on a farm somewhere, or in their backyards, are sending it now to Dante and his 'assured-decomposition hazardous-waste incinerator.' It burns quietly."

"No odors, no soot, state-of-the-art."

"They feel good, he feels good. It's a win-win. Right?"

"Right."

"But keeping the burners at the proper high temperatures for all those barrels of chemicals and waste sludge is costly, and Dante begins to cut corners here and there to keep in the black."

"I got all that."

"He forgets how to say no. He lets them send him things he can't burn cleanly. And once he lets the pig in, it runs amok."

"He can't turn them away."

"Yes. Exactly."

"How much of this was solid waste?"

"Out of eighty drums, three or four maybe."

"All right. So since he can't pay for workers to sift through the drums one by one, he starts stockpiling them."

"And burning, Turner. Stockpiling and burning and stockpiling and burying. Some of them got dumped in that giant lagoon behind the plant. Trucks keep coming in along with the cash, and he tries to ignore the fact he's become a criminal."

He looked around as he said this. There were only three other people in the vicinity and no one seemed to be listening. An old woman was scouring the paper, and a teenage guy was nibbling his girlfriend's ear.

"He's a good man, a family man, and a regular attendee of town meetings and church."

"A contributor to charities."

"Yes. Good bio stuff. Where'd you get that?"

"One of our fluff features. Goodwill. Cancer Society."

"There's an irony, huh? And he suddenly finds himself getting angry phone calls and letters, and being skewered by you media types. A sad story."

The teenage boy and girl were playing tonsil hockey now.

"Only with all that said, there was very little follow-up. Dante begins to break the law. *While the rest of Lakeland sleeps* . . . Use that line, Turner."

"While the rest of Lakeland sleeps," Turner said, "Dante turns his burners on again."

"Yes. For just a couple of hours each night, and he hires night work crews to find places for his barrels."

"Got it."

"Now here's your job, Scooper."

"Yeah?"

"Find out who took those barrels. It's not just the farmers, I'll bet."

"Who then?"

"Exactly."

Turner nodded.

"It's the story of the times, Turner. There were no rules. None. Every factory dumped right out their back door. They dug pits and lagoons. Sometimes they dumped right into the lake. Solvents. Cancerous stuff. You're gonna see high cancer rates here. I guarantee you. A whole lot of people and kids coming down with the big C, and all breathing the same portion of air, drinking the same water, or running around in the same fucked-up field. Dante's not the only one. The thing is, he was supposed to be the hero. That incinerator was supposed to rid the region of a century's worth of toxic waste, so they could rebuild the way they're trying to do. But it's all still here, Turner. That's the legacy of the old age. Now that stuff is buried all over town, and people are so starved for work, they don't care."

Turner furiously wrote all this down. Then he wondered about his good luck.

"Who are you? Why are you telling me this?"

"Let's say I got a reason and leave it at that."

It was a huge story, yes. But for now there was nothing to go on, Turner thought on his way back to the office. Nothing on record anyhow. Nothing proved. He couldn't reach Pavio. And he had an editor unlikely to stand behind him. He needed this ironclad in order to get it in the paper.

Especially with a downtown job open, he could see Clark killing his story just to spite him. As it was, he had an incinerator owner dumping barrels of toxic waste on farms, with the farmer's cooperation.

There was always talk of shadiness, money laundering, contracts given for favors, houses torched for insurance, judges taking bribes—but you needed proof, or on-the-record testimony. You needed time. And Turner would never get the time. He'd always have his dailies to file, and his Sunday story, and his fluff. The snow was knee-deep right now; there was no way there'd be an inspection. And if there was no inspection, then all Turner had to go on was the word of an unnamed, possibly insane, sunglasses-wearing man on a crumbling bench.

CHAPTER 23

It snowed and snowed through Christmas and New Year's. Kids skated on ponds and hurled snowballs at passing cars, the schools were shut down for two days, but life in Lakeland went on pretty much the same. Plows tunneled down the quilted roads each dawn, clearing the new and leaving the old, spraying road salt everywhere.

The Lakeland High School basketball team won its first five games of the season, then lost to Fayetteville-Manlius by twenty. The auditorium had been packed. The Lakeland center, a rail-thin, pimply boy named Erik Alston, was called for three fouls in the first five minutes of the game. After the game a security guard had to escort out the referee who'd made the calls.

With no work, Harris and the others had been getting wasted almost every night. A few of them had begun to worry about their health in connection to the dumping. Sorento and Terry Miller were conducting research in the Lakeland Library and over the Internet on Terry Miller's wife's Macintosh. Terry Miller sent Harris a computer printout "info-letter" that said certain toxic chemicals screwed with your memory and could give you acne as well. Solvents like toluene and xylene could even cause cancer. He was feeling sick, he said, and would never go out on another dumping mission. Chris Porterhouse had become sedentary, and barely left his house, though he still called Harris to ask if there was any more work out on the farms, as did

Bazorcik, who said he'd lost brain cells, and added that he'd been having trouble maintaining an erection.

"Like you've got a use for one," Harris said.

"Never know," he said. "Miracles happen."

HARLAN STANYAN CALLED to tell them that when the ground thawed, as it always did for a few days in January, they needed to do one more drop; then they could collect all their money.

Harris capitulated. He had no choice. He needed the money. But he wondered, not for the first time, what sort of a person he'd be if he didn't. He tried to take solace in the fact that he was helping his brother get his waterfront marketplace built, and when it was a national success, on the scale of that book he'd written, Harris could say he'd done the trench work, he'd been there from the start.

Sure enough, the thaw came on the second Wednesday of January. A freak southern front shot the temperatures up near sixty. People thought it was summer arrived, or that it was the ozone cracking and bringing on that blessed global warming (in January, Lakelanders would pay a week's wages for a little global warming, scorched equator or not), so long were the weeks between even an inch of sun, a moment above freezing. Anyhow, they overreacted, running feverishly around in shorts and T-shirts, throwing footballs and Frisbees. The Lakeland High School band played an outdoor concert and someone set up a grill and sold hamburgers. You'd have thought it was July.

The snow melted into dirty slush. The river ran high. The ice in the lake loosened into massive floes that drifted like lost islands.

The ground was soft and oozed around their shoes.

It was little more than a cruel tease. Someone would always say, Well, we got through the worst of it—and thereby bring on the mother of all snowstorms, followed by more ice and sleet.

Those who spent any time in Lakeland took the January thaw for what it was, a momentary respite from a season of bone-numbing bleakness. When it thawed you could see where the snow had weighed down. The world looked indented, leaves and garbage tamped into the ground.

Flaws showed.

AT THE FARMHOUSE, for example, everything felt wet. The floors, the walls, the air.

After dinner, Jack went upstairs to bring down a few suits he'd stored in a closet. When he opened the door, cold, filthy water dripped from the ceiling. The roof had a leak the size of a baseball, and widening. His suits and some of Anne's summer dresses were drenched. A shard of something both powdery and wet dropped on his shoulder. Soon enough cold air would rush through. His lay diagnosis was that ice had worked its way under the shingles and had melted in the thaw. Some of the ceiling boards had rotted out. They couldn't have an open roof, not when the storms hit. The room would fill with snow and sleet and the floor would warp.

As he carried the wet clothes downstairs, it occurred to Jack that Harris might want a crack at this. He'd offered again and again to do work on the house, hadn't he? Absolutely. Now might be the time to take him up on it.

He went to the bedroom and changed into his sweats and running shoes.

Harris could drive him back, he thought, but he wanted to get a run in. He needed the fresh air.

This would certainly be cheaper than hiring a carpenter, he thought, and in a broader sense it might be nice to make a night or two of it: the Lambeau boys fixing the roof together, the way they'd built tree houses and cardboard forts and igloos together as kids. He'd actually had a picture like that in his mind when he'd decided to move back up to Lakeland—a beer-commercial sort of image with the two of them working and sweating side by side, toasting one another—*This roof's for you, brother.*

"I'm going to get a run in," Jack said on his way out the door.

"All right. I'm going to sleep. I'm bushed," Anne said. They kissed good night.

It was nine-thirty.

"CHARLOTTE'S JUST WAKING UP," Marla said, ushering Jack inside. "Come have a peek at your niece."

The party boys were going at it again next door, with what now sounded like live music: a guitar, drums, and someone's awful voice.

"I'll get mud all over," Jack said.

"Take your shoes off, then."

He followed Marla in his wet socks. He gazed at his little niece in her crib. While she looked more like a Marla, there was a little Harris in her yawn. She smiled at him, or else at the drool hanging from her chin.

"That's a good girl. You're hungry," Marla said.

"She's so pretty."

Marla looked at him skeptically. "Do you have one of those little tapes in you?"

"Tapes?"

"You know, the ones in dolls. They say something sappy when you pull a string. She's a cutie-pie, but she isn't *pretty*. Not yet. She will be. Babies are pretty funny looking, aren't they?"

She said the last words to Charlotte in a baby voice.

"I think *she's* the little doll."

She ignored him. "They got those big heads, don't you sweetie, don't you have a big old noggin. If he's not at Carl's, try Terry Miller's."

"Huh?"

"You're looking for Harris, right?"

She lifted Charlotte, then her blouse. Charlotte began feeding. Jack was a little bewildered. Mothers did this, he supposed, there was nothing unusual here. What was different was Marla. Motherhood befitted her. She didn't look pinched or helpless anymore.

While she nursed, she gave him directions to the two houses. At least, Jack thought, she knew where Harris *might* be.

She said to him on his way out, "I didn't think I could do this."

"Oh, c'mon. You're a natural."

"I mean, close the door on Harris. I didn't plan on it. The words just fell out my mouth, and then once they were out there I stuck to them. I thought I'd cave in. I've always caved in, 'specially with boys. But this time I said, 'Will power,' and it worked."

"Will power can take you down the wrong paths sometimes," Jack said.

She stood and thought about that. He did too. Her face grew pensive.

"I still love him, if that's what you want to know."

"He wants to change."

"Everyone does," she said.

BAZORCIK'S PLACE WAS A TRAILER with two rooms added on. There was a small oak deck adjoining one of the rooms, and beyond that piles of rotting boards, intended perhaps for the next appendage. This was the way Jack's parents lived; when they needed more space, they didn't move, they just added on.

Jack knocked. The neighbor's dog barked and pulled homicidally at a long chain. There was no one home at Bazorcik's.

Terry Miller, another work friend of Harris's, lived close by, so Jack walked on. He wanted to pass through this part of town open-mindedly. But he simply couldn't. He was embarrassed. He kept seeing through the eyes of a prospective investor. The houses—these dejected, pastel clapboards weren't just rundown, he thought, they were swaggeringly so, paint waving and peeling under the early moonlight, storm clouds of pink insulation protruding, car and motorcycle parts spread proudly out on lawns alongside stacks of tires, broken lawn furniture and Christmas displays—plastic Santas and reindeer, colored lights and nativity scenes. Some windows were broken, then hidden in plastic; others were armored in plastic to save on heat. He wasn't mad at the families inside. He was ticked at the cynical pricks who'd built all this crap with cheap materials. What had they told the people, the landlords and carpenters, when they were building it? Did they fess up? We've got lousy stuff here. Last you through the summer and that's about it. Cheap paint. Cheap wood. Cheap foundations—did you have to teach someone what happens then? Everything looked about ready to fall over. They would build differently under his sway. He would see to that.

Terry Miller lived five blocks away in an almost cheerful yellow board-and-batten cottage. It was no mansion, but here at least there was some care taken. The paint was near new. In addition he'd wrapped his shrubs in burlap against the weather and put metal domes over his bird feeders to keep the squirrels out. In the back he'd built a small greenhouse, where he grew flowers and ferns.

At the door he gave Jack a surprised smile. What in the world was he doing in this neck of the woods?

"I'm looking for Harris. Sorry to disturb you."

"Sure. I can tell you where Harris is. But come on in and let me take a look at you." He looked him up and down. "You're looking good, Jackie. Thinning a little on the hairline, but on you it's kind of distinctive."

"Thanks."

"And you're out jogging. Healthy. You want a snack or anything? Glass of pop?"

He rooted his stubby hand in the cupboards for glasses.

"No thanks. Just trying to find Harris so he can give me a hand with some things."

"What's the matter?"

"House stuff. Leaking roof. Cracks in the walls."

"College boys can't do any of that stuff, can they? Too busy looking up notes."

"You're right on that one."

"I think he's tied up tonight."

"Can you tell me whereabouts?"

"I can."

"Where?"

"Oh, you want me to tell you where. I just thought you wanted to know *could* I tell you." He laughed at his own genius.

"Would you tell me where Harris is?"

"I would. They got a nice night. He's out on the farms. I quit that shit for good. Harris should too. I told him. Screws with your memory. Your potency too. Anyhow your brother's doing the Enola Gay thing out on McBride's farms."

"Old Taylor Road?" He felt a tug at the pit of his stomach.

"That's the one."

"Enola Gay?"

Terry Miller made his hand move like a plane, then made a noise like bombs dropping. *Babooom. Babooom.*

"Thanks, then. I'm gonna get going."

"Jack. I've been wondering something," Terry Miller said. "What went wrong with New York?"

"Nothing went wrong."

"We just figured you'd stay there. Run the city."

"I wanted to come back."

"My guess is they didn't give you the asslicking you get here. It's nice having your ass licked, isn't it? Not that I would know."

"Thanks for your help." He buttoned his coat.

"I went to New York few years ago. Saw *Cats.* My God those were some getups. Couldn't tell what was who." Terry Miller shook his head.

Jack was supposed to respond.

"Broadway's quite a spectacle," he said.

Terry Miller studied Jack's face. "Doesn't it shame you knowing what they're doing for that harbor of yours, Jack?"

"I don't know what you're talking about," he said.

"No?" he said. "Ask Captain Mayor. I told Harris I'm out of this. I'm washing my hands of it, what's left of 'em anyhow."

CHAPTER 24

The air was damp and cooling. Jack had an inclination to simply go home and call it a strange night. He didn't like the way Terry Miller had talked to him. Things had somehow taken a bad turn. It was as if he were seeing a movie with himself onscreen, and the deeper in trouble he got the more he needed to keep watching. He wanted to find out what Harris was up to. And he wanted the roof fixed. His legs felt stronger the longer he went. This was the way with distance runners. The farther they went, the less they wanted to stop. He ran by the harbor sites, his sneakers making loud sucking noises as he moved through the melting slush and mud. He looked out at the lake, white caps curling, then at the small clusters of scaffolding and cement. He saw a truck pull out from one of the lots onto the road. It looked like a city truck, only painted a dull green. Jack followed along. The roads were mottled with potholes, wrecked like everything else by the winter. This was muck and wetlands, loamy salt beds and sandy marshes. Cattails and bulrushes, earth with a good deal of lake to it.

The driver sped by him. Jack ran in the same direction until a police car pulled alongside.

"You lose your way?"

"I haven't, thanks."

"Do you live near here?"

"Do I need to?"

The cop stared in recognition.

"You're Jack Lambeau."

"I am."

"What are you doing, jogging out here in the middle of nowhere?"

"Getting some exercise."

"That's right. Weren't you a track star way back when?"

"Way back when."

"All right, then."

Before the cop drove off, Jack asked, "You didn't just see a truck blaze by at around seventy?"

"Sure didn't," the cop said.

JACK RAN AND RAN, and soon he wasn't sure where he was anymore, or why he was still running and not back in bed by now. The land had countrified: no businesses, no homes along the road. Woods, salt beds, quite a few small lakes and creeks, and potato, onion, and apple farms. When spring came you could grow anything in these dark, sleepy fields. It took being outside of town, away from human design, to see this place anew, he thought, to see beyond the gray plains of sky, the dreary buildings and cars and taverns, and find what it was and still might be, a place of quiet beauty.

He was thinking of a night when he was seventeen and headed soon for college. Harris was sixteen, and they'd taken out a motorized rowboat, along with a bottle of Wild Turkey Harris had clipped from a friend's father's liquor cabinet. They had heard since they were boys about a spot the fishermen called the thermal bar, the moment in the lake where cold and warm waters joined to form a vortex that drew in thousands of fish, but for only two unspecified weeks a year. They had heard of it, but never believed it until that night. They caught fifteen fish— walleye, carp, and bass. It was like fishing in a bathtub. Harris kept passing Jack the bottle and telling him it was his duty to drink, that with all the studying he'd been doing he deserved to get toasted—that that's what the fish were telling him.

"Listen," Harris said. Jack would take another long sip, and then something would find its way onto his line.

"See what I mean," Harris said, and he'd pull the net out. "Get the hell in here, you little rascal."

And so Jack listened some more.

He had planned to do a twelve-mile run in the morning, and had wanted to get to sleep early, but the more he stayed out on the lake, the warm blue night all around them, the less he wanted to do anything other than bob around with Harris, catching everything that swam.

They were out until three, and Jack had loved how reckless he felt. And how he wasn't worried about what he'd have to do the next day, the next month, the next four years, or whether they'd had too much to drink.

He almost killed the two of them later that night. He lost sight of the road somehow (he might have been singing shut-eyed to the radio) and drove them into a ditch. Harris cut his leg. A police car drove by a short while afterward and stopped on the other side of the road.

What Jack wanted more than anything then was to disappear. It was Harris's fault, he thought then, for bringing the bottle, and getting Jack to drink so much of it. It wasn't true, but in that moment he believed it, because these things happened to Harris.

"I'm fucked," Jack yelled. "I'm so fucking fucked. I'm going to be like everyone else in our goddamned family. *Goddammit.*"

"Switch places with me," Harris said.

The car was covered in brush, and it might have been possible.

"Quickly," Harris yelled, looking sad and stricken, "do it," and started to climb over Jack before Jack pushed him back down.

A flashlight was in his face then.

"Are you hurt?" the officer asked.

"I don't think so," Jack said, and then he added, "There was a deer out there. We almost hit it."

The officer asked more questions and Jack did the world's best impression of a sober high school senior. There was no arrest.

The cop even helped them push their car out of the ditch.

Jack wanted now not to have to think about the end of that night, and the ugly silence he had afterward with Harris. He wanted to think about everything before: the vision of his brother holding out that net, the burn of the whiskey in his mouth, the damp cool of his sneakers, the sense that time didn't matter.

But what he was feeling was the loss of all that, and the panicked sense that his brother was in trouble once again and he was accountable somehow.

JACK HAD FINALLY LOCATED the truck at an abandoned onion farm a mile later. He'd peered through the dark, unable to see what was taking place out there in the loam. He'd called Harris's name and a man on the porch told him to get the hell off his property, like he'd told him that last time.

Before Jack could answer that there hadn't been a last time the man fired two rounds over his head.

Now he'd made it to William Hickey's front steps, aware it was far too late for a polite visit but needing answers. The mayor stood inside the door in his green plaid pajamas, his arms folded over his chest for warmth.

"What's happening out on McBride's farms?" Jack asked.

"What time is it?" Hickey said and cleared his throat. He looked at Jack's mud-flecked sweats and sneakers. "No no no. Can't bring that stuff inside, okay? Sarah'll murder you."

"Why's there tar out there?"

"I don't know. Maybe they're building a road. What're you doing mucking around in the middle of the night?"

"I just got shot at."

"Shot at? That's not good," Hickey said. His face soured. "Why do I feel like you've got more to say about that?"

"That's not our tar out there?"

"Not mine. Is it yours?"

"Tell me we've got nothing to do with it," Jack said, "and I'll let you go back to sleep."

"All right. We don't. Good night."

"And that's the truth."

"That's the truth. The big question is what you're doing for the Super Bowl. We've got the gang coming over. I'm gonna make my four-alarm nachos."

"I don't believe you, Bill."

"Then why'd you ask me?"

"I wanted to see how much of a liar you were. Now I know."

"I wouldn't talk to my paycheck like that, Jack, if I were you."

"I got shot at. Plus you got my brother involved."

"Who did? You or me? You approved this, remember?"

"I can't believe this," Jack said.

"We're storing a few of the barrels there, that's all. No big deal."

"What about that waste treatment plant in Buffalo?"

"They're going to Buffalo."

"When? Next week, next year?"

"Soon."

"And the inspections?"

"The sites are ready to go."

"How?"

Hickey didn't answer.

"Terrific. So we clean up one place and dump it on the other."

"Storing, not dumping. Storing means temporary. Dumping means permanent. Don't go saying dumping."

"Ah, shit."

"This is the real world, Jack."

"What does that mean?"

"It means we aren't Mayberry, RFD. We get the same road-blocks you had in New York. We have to be creative—isn't that your motto? We have to use our resources."

"We have to break the law."

"Whose law? It's our town, for Christ's sake."

"Whitey," Sarah's voice called out. "Are you okay? Who is that? Who's shouting like that?"

"Can we talk about this in the morning?"

"I'm quitting, Bill."

"Get some sleep. We'll talk on this in the morning."

"I'm not gonna change my mind."

"Everything's going great, Jack. Better than you know. Get some sleep."

"Whitey . . ."

"Don't get yourself worked up here. You just keep doing your thing, and let the behind-the-scenes stuff take care of itself," he said, then to his wife, who was now approaching, "It's just Jack, Sarah."

She stood at the door cinching the belt on a peach-colored robe.

"Oh, hi Jack. Thank heavens. I was worried. It sounded like a fight was happening."

HE TURNED A LIGHT on in the kitchen and sat for a while, waiting for his head to clear.

The house was cold. His clothes and skin were cold and damp. His legs were sore now; his lungs ached.

He would have to quit. If Hickey was lying this time, there had to have been others. And why was he so cocksure? Why wasn't he taking Jack's quitting seriously? He'd have to soon. Without Jack there was no harborfront, no town renaissance. The whole deal would collapse.

Jack's mind kept spitting out the wrong thoughts, negative, pessimistic ones. He saw them all behind desktop microphones at a televised hearing, Olin Ambrose interrogating them.

"Did we bend over far enough for you, Mr. Layambah?"

He felt swindled, sold a counterfeit future he should have spotted a mile away.

Regroup, he told himself. Come up with a plan. There's a path here, there always is.

But where the fuck was it?

HE FOUND ANNE ASLEEP in the bedroom. He leaned over to kiss her.

"Sweetpea?" he said.

She turned. Moved her fist in her eyes. Her breaths were labored, like someone surfacing from underwater.

"Your hands are freezing," she said.

"What if we left here, just packed up and left all this behind. What would you think of that?"

"What are you talking about?" she asked, her voice still pitched in sleep. He looked around at her things cluttering the room.

"Getting out of here."

"Why?"

Her eyes were still closed.

"I'm not saying we will. But what if we wanted to?"

"I don't know. What about the harborfront? That's a big thing for you. What time is it?"

"There'd be other big things."

"This is kind of sudden."

There was an empty drink glass on her night table. He brought it to his nose. Scotch. She didn't even like scotch as far as he knew.

"I'm just thinking of the two of us."

"You are, huh?"

"As a matter of fact I am."

"Hmmm. Maybe you should have done that a while back." She rolled her head into the pillow.

"Thanks for understanding."

She sat straight up now.

"And just what am I supposed to understand?"

"I'm weighing things, Anne."

"Weighing what? We screwed up our lives to move up here and now you want to leave. Maybe I don't want to just yet."

"You think we screwed up our lives?"

"No . . ." She sighed. "I mean, I don't know. I was asleep and you hit me with this out of nowhere. . . . Maybe you haven't noticed, but I'm not sleeping all that well lately and I was finally asleep."

He reached over for her and she moved aside.

"You resent me, don't you?"

She rolled her head into her pillow again. "Please . . . leave . . . me . . . *alone*," she said, a thread above a whisper.

"It's all my fault, right? It's my fault you can't get anything done, my fault you sit around here all day doing absolutely nothing with all that talent. Finishing nothing, or changing around a *perfectly good* picture of a *perfectly fine* bowl of fruit, because it's all my fault, right?" His voice grew louder. "I'm the bad guy who dragged you up here from the job you loved so much into this backwards town of unwashed illiterates, because I'm so selfish and insensitive. And here I am trying to turn this shithole into Martha's Vineyard. It's *pathetic*, isn't it, that I could have thought we could pull this off?"

She looked at him dispassionately. "You through?"

He was.

She wasn't angry. She was something else, and it worried him. He shouldn't have woken her.

He kissed her. She let him. She was crying.

"I'm sorry. I'm so sorry, Anne. I didn't mean any of that," he said.

She reached for a tissue and blew her nose. "You're a classist, did you know that? Who made you better than anyone here?"

"I've had a weird night. I didn't mean the things I said."

"Go to bed, Jack. Whatever you decide will be good. It doesn't make any difference to me anymore. It really doesn't."

CHAPTER 25

Lake Ontario is the runt of the Great Lakes, but it's far from small. One hundred and ninety-three miles long, and fifty-three across, which means even with the best binoculars you can't see the other side. On rough days the waves can look almost surfable, but they're far too erratic for that—no clean swells, too much rancor. Over the years more than a few boats have gone down, and many good swimmers have drowned. The lake begs to be anthropomorphized, or deified, because it's always butting into everyone's life. It's prone to caprice and mood—now serene, now snarling. It is inscrutable, seductive, and staggeringly vast. That it doesn't taste of salt is astonishing.

The French. The British. The Dutch, William Hickey was saying. The five nations of the Iroquois: Senecas, Cayugas, Oneidas, Onondagas, and Mohawks, all fought tooth and nail for the chance to live along the lake. "And here you are volunteering to leave it all over again. This storage thing is no big deal, Jack. You understand that. We're cutting some corners. That's all."

They were seated in the stern of Hickey's boat, the *Sea Queen*. In high school Jack and Harris had crewed on some of Hickey's charters. Most of what Jack knew about the lake and fishing he'd learned from Hickey.

"You gotta think ahead, to six months from now," the mayor said. "This July, when we have a big-name performer in the amphitheater and fireworks you can see from Canada. Ten thousand packed in, oohing and aahhing. The boardwalk will be done, we'll have the Lake Street Marketplace open with all those wooden carts and the magicians and artists, and there will be Jack and Annie, Bill and Sarah strolling arm-in-arm while those antique street lamps dance their little diamonds on the water. A few stores'll be open late, a little jazz sax playing from somewhere—maybe from one of those Mark Twain Mississippi ferry boats."

Jack had pictured the scene Hickey was describing so many times it had taken on the quality of a remembrance. "And you're getting all the kudos. Believe me, you won't be saying, I shoulda quit back then, Bill. Now will you?"

Hickey finished his beer. The sky was a vaulted powder-blue, the clouds fat and dense. A single seagull swayed over them like a shabby paper plane.

"I know you. You can't just chuck all this—not while it's rolling so strong."

Hickey allowed a silence. Jack really didn't want to chuck all this. Being on the lake was a reminder of all that was left undone.

Hickey leaned in again, sensing an opportunity. "And there's another little reason you might want to stay."

"What's that?"

"Wasn't gonna tell you yet. Has to do with your ego."

Hickey poured the rest of Jack's beer into his glass.

"Beneath it all, you're a chowhound for fame, like everyone else, Jackie."

He raised the glass.

"Chowhound?" Jack muttered.

"You didn't get your mail today, did you?"

"Didn't go in."

"I was gonna save the celebration until we were all together, with the girls, I mean."

"Lay it on me. Then I'll decide if I want to celebrate."

"All right." Hickey leaned into him, eyes afire. "We won. Or more precisely *you* won, you brilliant son of a bitch."

"What are you talking about?"

He stepped off the boat and walked into his boathouse. When he reemerged a minute later he was carrying a letter.

"You. We just got word. They want to make us an example. A prototype—Lakeland. That thing you wrote—that *War and Peace* I kept needling you about—won everyone over. *Everyone.*"

Jack read the letter. It was from the American Planning Association, and it said the harbor plan had won two gold medals. They'd be asked to do a presentation at the meeting in Chicago, and the APA was picking up the cost of the trip.

He inspected it closely to make sure that he understood completely, or that it wasn't something Hickey had thrown together as a gag. It wasn't.

They mentioned the projects that won silver and bronze medals. One in south Florida, the other in Madison, Wisconsin. They said that while the Lakeland plan had elements of Baltimore's Inner Harbor and Boston's Quincy Market, it was "not a mere simulacrum, but a blueprint for bringing prosperity back to the working-class towns of the Great Lakes."

Jack read the last few words quietly aloud. Then he looked at Hickey.

"I still need a few answers," he said.

"And you'll get them. What's been done has been done, Jack. It was a small matter and it's been taken care of. I can give you all the verification you need."

"I'll require it."

Hickey beamed at him. "Just read that end part, will you?"

In conclusion, the judges said the plan was both dynamic and achievable, and in addition, "brilliantly presented."

"Brilliant and obtainable—nice words," Hickey said. "After all those years of getting crapped on, we're making the big time, Jackie. Thanks to you, we finally won."

Jack kept staring at the letter. If nothing else the honor was nice, very nice. He felt just a bit exhilarated.

"'Course, we can write them back and say we're bagging it after all. Sorry for the trouble."

OVER THE NEXT DAYS, Jack's stubbornness began to dwindle. There was a phone call the next morning from a *New York Times* reporter wanting to do a story for the real estate section. *The New York Times.*

Another, from *Fortune*, wanted to do a small feature story when they got back from Chicago. He called the work Jack and Hickey had done "a breath of life in a dying region."

"Commerce, jobs, and a nice harbor, and all thrown together by a local boy come home. The urban myth in reverse," he said.

Investors read *Fortune*, and everyone read the *New York Times*. And so Jack couldn't find it in himself to say, I'm not on that project anymore.

HICKEY STOPPED OVER to discuss travel plans. They would need a lot of things fast if they wanted to capitalize on all this exposure ("and life is nothing but an opportunity to seize," he said). Full-scale models and engineering maps, a finished topographical.

Jack found himself, against his better judgment, making suggestions. There he was, pulling together chart plans of all the private financiers, banks, and law firms behind the project, exaggerating a little, just enough to convince a brand-name developer or two that all this would happen. He was gathering historic photos of the skyline, then recent ones, writing up expenditures for expanding sewers and drainage. His staff worked overtime. He found himself buying Hickey's logic.

"No work, no business, towns die. That's not rocket science."

Or: "Can you take a town's jobs and future away, its chance for growth, and tell them you're doing right by them?"

NO, HE THOUGHT, and beyond that he tried to picture him and Anne leaving Lakeland in the next weeks, which they'd have to do. Just where would they go? And what do? They wouldn't go back to New York. Europe, maybe? California? Anywhere they went, they'd be starting again at ground zero. He didn't like feeling unsettled, mailing résumés, searching for a place to live. He was too old to try and find himself all over again.

He would fix whatever problems came up regarding the harbor sites and the farms, and his brother's legitimate or illegitimate activities. He would see to it himself, he thought. If worse came to worse, he could still quit down the line. Only not this instant. It was a timing issue more than a moral one.

"Just don't go pulling a Marlon Brando, Jack," Hickey said. "At least let's go to Chicago and grab those awards."

THE HEADLINE IN THE Sunday real estate section of the *Rochester Gazette* read, A DYING PORT TOWN REINVENTS ITSELF.

Maybe not the headline he would have written, but the story was essentially a rave.

Then the *New York Times* article appeared, with the headline: PRESCRIPTION FOR THE GREAT LAKES: LAKELAND'S HARBOR.

It was a small article, but Jack liked the way it felt to read something so complimentary about his hometown—and in truth, *himself*—in a place like the *Times*. People were seeing this for what it could be, and they weren't saying that it couldn't work because it was upstate after all and upstate had died. They saw the opportunity for a rebirth just as he had spun it out for them. It would work because it *should* work.

If a town was going to get the attention, and some legitimate development interest, why shouldn't it be Lakeland, he thought? And if someone was to get the credit, why shouldn't it be him?

"You still planning on quitting?" Hickey asked.

The answer was he couldn't.

CHAPTER 26

Anne wasn't being productive. She began her days determined, but then too often inspiration would fade to mistrust. She'd foul up her colors, wouldn't wash the brush off, or she'd use too much black or brown and everything would look like mud. She wasn't able to see solutions. She'd look at a painting, know something was wrong, but she didn't know how to make it better. She'd plunge into new paintings without first working out the composition. She'd paint a woman in a chair next to the window, but the woman would be too large for the chair and the window too small. She'd paint another and the room would be so large in contrast to the woman, it would swallow her. She tried to joke about it. The Incredible Shrinking Woman, she called it.

Then she covered it over with white.

It would help if it weren't so cold all the time, if the house could hold a little warmth, but the old plaster walls and single-pane windows seemed no more shielding some days than cotton bedsheets. On windy days the glass rattled loudly in the old window frames; cold air sliced around the panes. They should do something about it, she thought. They would do something about it. Just like they would do something about the floors that sloped so badly they needed leveling blocks under the refrigerator and stove, and the unplaned doors they couldn't close, and the knocking in the attic that Anne feared was bats.

The bedroom especially had an altered disposition now. It was a place where he slept and she couldn't, not a place to make love, although they still occasionally did. She hadn't felt sexy for a while. She didn't feel unattractive so much as nonattractive, as if her senses had been diluted, and so Jack's desire seemed odd, and disconnected, an impersonal appetite.

How is it you want me? she thought. How can you want what's dead?

He wanted a different wife, she knew (and why shouldn't he have her?). One who looked and spoke like her, perhaps, but who would plan meals ahead, and shop more, fill the house with staples, and go running with him after work. Who'd always be in the mood.

She wasn't sad or angry or happy. Her emotions were fragmented. Refracted into chaotic particles. If she could only retrieve her concentration, she thought, then she could figure out what it was that had stopped her in her tracks.

HICKEY HAD SUGGESTED they all go out for drinks after the town meeting that week.

"After we share the good news with everyone," he said. "You and me, and the girls."

They would go to the Holiday Inn and order, if not the best bottle of champagne, "certainly an above-average one," and maybe Anne and Sarah could plan another lunch together.

One look at Anne when he arrived home told him it could never be that simple.

"Are you going to get dressed?"

"For what?"

"The big meeting."

It was clear she'd forgotten. "I'm sorry," she said. "I think I'm going to miss the big meeting, if that's okay."

"All right."

She could kill any good mood, if he allowed her to.

"Are you annoyed by that?"

"No," he said. "Actually . . . kind of. I thought you were coming to celebrate with me tonight."

She avoided his eyes now, stared at her feet.

"I'm not feeling so hot. Let me just rest a while and we'll see."

He went to the other room. Rest. From what? She'd stopped painting, as far as he could see. What did she have to rest from?

He put on a tie and the brown tweed jacket that had looked good in pictures. He hadn't liked the file photo of him the newspaper kept running. The light had been strange. It made him look like he had a skin condition.

He walked over to Anne, placed his arms around her shoulders.

"So what do you think?" he said warmly. "You coming?"

"Would you mind terribly if I didn't?" she said, and kissed his cheek.

"That's fine," he said.

THE MAYOR'S HARDY, CORNY PRAISE of Jack ("this great mind, a local mind at that, our best and our brightest local great mind, a rising superstar of the town-planning world") during the first minutes did little to douse Jack's rancor. He was, as of this moment, done worrying about her. He was too pissed off. What he was doing was important. Fuck, it was artistic. Architecture was the mother of all arts. Didn't she realize that? He made his decision. As soon as he did, he felt calmer, and rejoined the discussions in the meeting hall. There was no need for another fight.

"SO YOU'VE MADE UP YOUR MIND," she said when he told her.

"It's only a few days. It'll give us both a little space."

"Don't you think I might want to go too? That I might want to take a trip?"

He narrowed his eyes at her.

"Yes, Anne, I did. I figured we'd go again when I don't have to work every day. Besides, if you think it's cold here, it's about twenty degrees colder in Chicago."

Anne fidgeted with her sleeve.

"I don't think you'd be missing much. You can paint all day and night if you want with no disturbances. And anyhow, I'll be back before you know it. You won't even have a chance to miss me."

"I'll miss you," she said.

"Well, maybe that'll be a good thing." He walked into his study and closed the door.

AS A POINT OF pride Anne awoke before Jack the next morning and set right to work. She would show him she'd be fine, though in truth she didn't feel fine. Sleeplessness was wrecking her, steamrolling her thoughts thin as paper.

He quietly went about making his own breakfast.

"Do you want anything?" he asked politely, deferentially.

"I'm fine," she said.

"I'm sorry, Anne," he said. "You can come. I mean, if you want to."

It was an empty offer, and it further depressed her.

"No. It's better this way. I'll paint. I'll have a roomful by the time you get back."

"That's great," he said. "I know you will."

He told her again how talented she was, and said again that he was sorry. She said she was sorry she'd been so withdrawn. She asked him if he was still thinking of quitting.

"Not right now," he said. "You were right. We just got here, really. I think this time apart will be good for us, I really do."

"I do too," she said.

THE CLOUDS MOVED IN. The close white sky was pocked and jagged. It would be like this until May, everyone said. Frozen brown fields of cattails, aster, and goldenrod.

She dreamed in disturbing fragments. And when she was awake she felt washed out and restless.

Out of the blue, Sonja, her old boss, called. Anne wanted to tell her everything, how some days she was numb, and others a jangle of nerve endings, how her work had gone poorly, how she couldn't sleep and thought all the time of returning to New York, how three months after her grandfather died she was still convinced it was partly her fault. Instead she said that it was beautiful in Lakeland and that Sonja should visit.

"I will. I definitely will," Sonja said. "I didn't want to say it because I wanted you to stay, but secretly I knew this was perfect for you. I just knew it."

And it should have been perfect. She had time and space and free rent. That was all an artist was supposed to need. It was all Cézanne had needed. She was plagued by what she feared was unearned unhappiness. She couldn't concentrate enough to read now. It was like eating on a sick stomach; she couldn't hold the words down. She turned off the radio because the lyrics of three straight songs were disturbingly relevant. She felt as though she'd transformed into another species, one of those bats from the attic perhaps, poorly adapted to light and the presence of humans.

She could see humor in this. It was a prank some celestial engineer was playing on her. She almost laughed. She began obsessing about Chicago. Had Jack asked her to come, she might have chosen to stay. She didn't like him wanting her to stay. She wanted to have a choice. The wind screamed through the trees, pushed into the house.

AS THEY LAY IN bed the night before his trip, Jack began caressing his hand lightly along Anne's thigh. "It's just a week, sweetpea. That's all," he said. "I love you so much, did you know that?"

"Just a week," she said sadly, trying to sound otherwise and then, reading his signals over the next few minutes (and wanting to avoid an awful conversation), she allowed him to slowly but firmly push her nightgown above her hips, and slide beneath her, his hands circling her back in a way that used to send pleasurable chills across her skin, but that now felt crude and insistent.

Just go to sleep, she willed him, but he didn't. Without them kissing, she soon brought him inside of her—though neither her mind nor body was ready.

She tried to enjoy it, or to convince herself she was enjoying it. She should be enjoying it, shouldn't she? He seemed to. Anne, Annie, lover, he said afterward, That was amazing (*How?* she wondered. *Tell me so I can find a way to agree*), and he held her tight, with a force that seemed genuine. She thought maybe, after everything, they could still get somewhere. They could spend the night awake together, talking and touching, illuminating their interiors to the extent where she could feel instinctive and sexy again—like swimming together in the freezing lake, the way they had the night he'd proposed to her—and then she'd feel better about his trip and their time apart, but instead he vanished into slumber.

Eventually she took hold of his heedless arm and peeled it off. No talk. No walls broken down. She curled the other way, left out of his dreams, and in that moment it came to her what the trip to Chicago was; it was a way to get away from her, and he had no intention of returning. He'd get a job there. Maybe he'd send her money, come back to pick up his things, but he'd be gone. That fact gathered force, and then a horrible volume as the night wore on.

Next to her his breathing was slow and healthy. A man on a mission.

She wanted to confront him. She wondered if there was a woman there. Then decided no. That was one thing he wasn't.

She walked to the dresser, searched around and found his plane ticket. She held it in her hand. There was a return flight (although you weren't legally bound to take it, were you?). She carried it into the kitchen. She was wide awake and would be for hours. She sat at the table and looked at the ticket.

She looked at the time then. It was just past three A.M. A whole sleepless, horrible night ahead of her.

At some point, the noise of the heat stopped. Cold filled the house. The sort of cold that made your head hurt. Her breath made smoke. At daybreak the heat mysteriously returned. They moved about, nervously making breakfast and coffee, stomaching a perfunctory conversation about how much they'd miss each other.

Anne felt sick. Her whole head felt clogged, as if it were filled with thick water.

"I think there's something wrong with the heat," she said.

"Seems like it's working now."

"It went off for a while last night."

"I'll get someone in," he said, then corrected himself. "No one's up at this hour. I'll call from Chicago. Unless you want to call. I can give you a couple of numbers."

"I'll call this morning," she said.

She balled her hands for warmth and pulled them inside her sleeves.

"If it goes off again, call my mother. You can stay there," he said.

Her face must have revealed something, because his went sour.

"I'm just saying they'd be more than happy to have you. They really like you."

"I appreciate that."

His expression softened, disingenuously she believed, though she knew she wasn't a fair judge right now.

"You know it'll be strange without you," he said. "A lot of cold nights there with just Bill to keep me warm."

He kept chattering on like that, and she closed him out, because she couldn't stand to think of how thin and self-serving his endearments had become. It was an unexplainable paradox: She didn't want him to leave, and at the same time she couldn't wait for him to leave. She didn't know what she was feeling. If she could figure that out she'd know what to do.

"You can still come if you want," he said, as he put his dishes in the sink. But then he didn't wait for her response. He went back to the bedroom to retrieve his bags. She thought: Wasn't that a lot to take for a week?

It had begun to snow outside, in nasty, swirling pellets.

"You're going to get all the fun," he said.

"How so?"

"Looks like lake effect out there."

The Hickeys would pick him up. She thought about going to the airport, but she feared she'd make a scene, though she didn't know what sort.

"A week," he said, as though reading her thoughts. "Six days, really."

CHAPTER 27

Turner believed the lake effect needed a literature like the Sahara's—it was a tsunami, a freak of nature that in full storm painted every cubic inch of air white. The experts said it was colliding temperatures, air drawing moisture as it moved over the warm lake and then over the colder land mass, making sky-loads of white. Simple enough. But in the midst of lake effect, science and reason had no place. In its thickest squalls, it felt as if that whole huge lake had dropped down on the town. Every-thing and everyone got covered. It could take you a day to find where you left your car.

When he walked around some days Turner longed for a sound track to crescendo behind him. Lawrence of Siberia.

These storms created character, he thought, carved person-alities. Once you'd been through a winter up here, you'd never be the same. He spoke briefly about the snow into a tape re-corder he used for interviews, so he could be vivid and properly awestruck when he wrote about it.

He had an interview with the managing editor for the job downtown, ironed his shirt and trousers for it, and vowed to say nice things about Clark even if it took a bald-faced lie.

But Digby, a thoughtful, bearded man who didn't mince words, started on the attack.

"People say you're a prima donna," he said after only the most perfunctory of niceties had been gotten out of the way.

"Well, I'm working on that," Turner said, and then he remembered what every college guidance counselor had said. "Sometimes I guess I care too much about my stories."

"Hmm. Well, maybe you should just care a little less, then," Digby said.

"All right."

"You know what I mean. Pick your spots. No question you could be a star here, Turner," Digby said. "You're the only one getting in your way."

"I'm learning a lot every day," he said.

"You hate it," Digby said. "We all hated it. It's boot camp. Just get along a little better with Clark, okay? Decent editors are hard to come by."

They talked more about story ideas, and about Turner's journalistic philosophy, which Digby seemed to like, almost reluctantly.

There were two things Digby had said in parting. He said the next month or two would be crucial. They wouldn't fill the position until then. And he said God he wished Stewart would find himself another job. There wasn't a chance in the world he'd ever make it downtown. "You should see some of the things he's been sending in."

He shook his head, and then made the closed-eye smile of a parent who's watched a child bump into a couch in a home movie.

ON HIS WAY NORTH again to Lakeland, Turner watched the air thicken incrementally with snow, and the land grow wilder and whiter. Along the roadside, ragged cattails hunched beneath the snow's weight. The clumps of willow and dogwood had dried and wizened and seemed permanently severed from spring. Turner thought of Stewart readying for his interview, checking his hair in the mirror, straightening his tie, maybe even preparing that same line—*Sometimes I guess I care too much.* Then leaving full of hope, with the editors all shaking their heads like Digby and laughing at his expense. Turner had known they wouldn't promote Stewart, known it like he knew it would snow all weekend, or that the Knicks would lose to the Bulls. And yet hearing it said explicitly seemed like an awful violation of the man's precious dignity. It filled Turner with an empathetic sadness that bordered on despair. Digby'd encouraged him, given him a light at the end of the tunnel. But Turner knew not to take too much solace. If he didn't watch out this could happen to him. He could become Stewart, and no one would bother to tell him it had happened.

Two cars passed him going sixty. Anyplace else they'd be down to twenty, Turner thought, but here people knew better how to handle this. They checked their tires, or drove trucks.

They accepted and accommodated, which he was beginning to think he didn't want to do. I will not rot out here, no sir, he said to himself. No siree. He thought of Anne in the snow, throwing her arms up in the air, and was filled with such longing he nearly drove off the road. He had no comfortable place in his thoughts to put this. He would like to stop his car and, for safekeeping, place his desire gracefully and respectfully in his trunk.

Outside his window the sun set violet over hill-less white land. A flock of Canada geese flew in one long V, then in two of them over the distant wetlands. He turned the tape recorder on and tried to describe it. Then he turned the recorder off, because he couldn't.

THAT NIGHT ANNE WENT for a drive in the snowy dark and found herself at a pitched-roof country bar with neon Budweiser and Molson signs in the window. She sat at a back table and ordered a cheeseburger, and then drifted into so many pockets of sadness and dread thinking about Jack's being gone now and for good that when the thick, charred ketchupy burger arrived it looked improbable, someone's unkind idea of a joke. She took a few bites. It wasn't bad, really, but she couldn't stomach it. Someone sent a glass of red wine over.

The wine was nice. She could almost taste it.

She drank the glass down. And drank the second one that was sent to her.

A few of the men asked her to join them. She politely declined. The older woman bartender asked her in a concerned voice, Are you all right, honey? Do you need a place to stay tonight? They seemed all to be smiling at her, in a nice, caring way.

Then she started crying. Not about Jack, or about herself even. It was for her grandfather. For just a moment she'd thought she'd seen him among those men on the barstools.

She lost track of the hours. She shouldn't have drunk the glasses of wine. She was sick, heavy-headed on her drive home, and since she hadn't eaten more than a bite or two of anything, she had no stamina. Only her brain was active, but randomly so. Thoughts escaped before finding shape. Conversations crisscrossed in her head; a voice would say something nice, then another would scold her. It took her an hour to find the house. The car was making awful noises.

When she lay in bed, she was unable to sleep. Her mind raced through images of Chicago. Rooms full of nicely dressed people waiting for something to start. Al Capone, Carl Sandburg, she thought. Marc Chagall.

She dozed occasionally.

She thought about the word *brainstorm*. That was supposed to be a pleasant thing—*we're brainstorming here*—and yet that was what was happening inside her: a storm.

Only a few days, she told herself, and he'd be back. Would that be any better?

Problems are simply as big as you make them, he'd told her once. They exist in your mind more than anywhere else. *Minimize them, then deal with them. They'll only eat you up if you let them.*

Oh, if she could only think like that, like him. If she could just do that their lives might work out.

The house was no longer simply cold, it was unendurably so. She made fires. When she went to the shed for more wood, the roof there had caved in, and the wood was all wet. In desperation she broke one of the old ladder-back chairs for wood.

IT WAS TOO COLD to paint. Too cold to do anything but lie in bed under piles of covers. The furnace was frozen, and she felt panic in her limbs. "Is this all in my mind?" she asked aloud. "Is it my mind that's freezing me to death?"

In the morning, everywhere was white. White cars, white trees, white lake, white river, white buildings. She woke early and went walking, the sky a milky blue. It felt peaceful. She walked and walked without knowing where she was going; at some point she knew she would simply turn around and go back. When she tried to turn around she found she didn't like the light, and so she kept walking although she was freezing now. The wind howled around her ears, and she didn't think about hypothermia; she knew she was cold and she didn't care or know what to do about it; she had a terrific energy and then very little. She felt tired. She wanted to lie down in the snow and rest a while, but she had the presence of mind to know that might not be good, that she might sleep for too long and the cold would cover her over, and there was nothing out here, no stores, no restaurants, no gas stations, no homes. She had no idea how long she'd been walking, and then she began to see spots. The wind howled, a hard wind—she'd never really known what that meant, not really, but this was a hard wind. She realized she was crying. She hadn't generated the emotion, she'd simply dropped inside it. It was too late to turn around now. And when she thought she might pass out and give in to the storm, a truck came traveling up the road. She waved her arms like a semaphore.

She closed her eyes, and when she opened them again she was being walked into that cold house.

At some point Anne realized the ringing she was hearing wasn't a school bell from a dream. It was the phone. Jack, she thought expectantly, calling to tell her to join him, or to tell her he was rushing home, or was already home and would take her somewhere where the heat worked. Maybe they'd drive back to that hotel in Saranac Lake. They'd make big fires and sit on one of those handwoven carpets. And after they'd warmed up maybe they'd decide to ski or go ice-skating.

She pictured them there at that hotel. She liked the picture. She finally made it to her feet. Her legs felt shaky. Her joints ached. She'd aged in this house, gone from twenty-seven to fifty somehow. She wanted the years back. She felt tired, dizzy, and wound-up, but mostly tired. And very, very cold. The phone kept ringing. She crossed the room, lifted the receiver, dropped it to the floor, dropped herself to the floor to retrieve it. "Hello?" she said.

She pictured him in a crowded hotel lobby, people all around with name tags on their lapels, his hand over his other ear to keep out the noise so he could hear her. There was no other noise. "Just wanted to check on you," the voice said.

"Who is this?"

She couldn't hear him. It felt like she had snow in her ears.

"Who?"

"You don't sound good."

"I'm fine."

"Well, I was just making sure. It's Turner."

"Thank you. That was good of you. I guess I'll see you, then."

"Is that your teeth?"

She was shivering. "There's no heat."

"That's awful. You should get out of there."

"The car's not working." She felt like she might go to sleep now, that maybe now it would be a good idea. "I broke down. A truck took me here." She coughed. "I'm sick, I think."

"Try and stay warm, Anne. I'll come get you," he might have said.

He hung up anyhow; she dropped the phone down, and followed it to the floor. She curled into a ball as close as she could get herself to the embers that were dying blood red in the fireplace.

Snow blew wildly outside. It felt as if she'd been dropped inside a cloud, the whole damn house had been dropped in a downy white, white cloud.

She wondered what death would be like. She wouldn't kill herself, because she couldn't. She didn't have the strength that took. But she could be dead. There were worse things. She'd thought this before, a long time ago. After her father died and she stopped eating.

There were other things that stopped. Sleep, of course. Lucid thoughts. Quiet.

Quiet people were rarely ever quiet, Anne knew. Just on the outside.

Death would be quiet, she was certain of that.

CHAPTER 28

Chicago must have been where they invented all the phrases: *cold as a witch's teat, cold as hell, cold enough to freeze your nuts off, cold as ice.*

The wind lashed off the lake as it did in Lakeland, but here it was sharper. It gusted and funneled around buildings, reddened faces. *That's some windchill*, everyone kept saying (as though the words *wind* and *chill* couldn't exist apart). Jack and Hickey shared a two-room suite at the Drake. The suite had gold plush carpets, puffy, king-sized beds, and a wet bar Hickey was getting to know on a first-name basis. The cleanliness of Jack's room was a welcome reprieve from the clutter of the farmhouse.

The meetings went on downstairs, and it seemed wherever Jack walked there was someone else who'd just heard about the Lakeland harbor project and wanted to ask him questions. There were presentations, mixers and displays, trips around town. Jack recognized quite a few people from graduate school and from New York.

The second night he gave his talk about the Lakeland harbor plan to an audience of four hundred.

He talked extemporaneously to show that this came from the heart. And it did. What they were doing, he said, was reviving an American archetype, the classic old coastal town, and they were doing it on a Great Lake, within an afternoon's drive of Manhattan. He talked of the American longing for community, for a simpler, less lonely and alienating life, and how places like

Lakeland were facing extinction just as the country was waking up to their worth.

He went on for nearly an hour, spelling out the particulars, his vision not only for Lakeland but for the whole region, and he showed slides of the winter festival, of the new restaurants and the weekend markets, of Lake Street before and after.

It was a work of art, really, and at the end the applause was effusive if not thunderous.

As the evening wore on, and others gave their speeches, Jack felt almost giddy.

"Pinch me, so I know this is real," he whispered to Hickey. Discreetly, Hickey pinched him through his jacket.

"Thanks," Jack said.

IN THE EVENING JACK WALKED around downtown by himself. He allowed the scale of Chicago to awe him. Those buildings! Here was Burnham and Sullivan and Frank Lloyd Wright and Mies van der Rohe, Adler and Richardson. The great turn-of-the-century monuments. The Chicago School, the first modern city planners. Hell, the tallest building in Lakeland was the seven-story senior citizens' home.

Chicago was the Athens of modern architecture, a hall of fame, birthplace of the City Beautiful Movement. Maybe all it took was a fire. Then the stars of architecture would come.

He stopped at the Green Mill to hear some jazz, then took a quick look at Wrigley before the cold drove him into a taxi.

ON JACK'S WAY to the hotel, his mind traveled to a time he hadn't accessed in a while—his first days at Brown, when he'd felt overwhelmed but intensely happy, possessed of the belief that his life would now be different and better. His first night out drinking with his hallmates, he listened to their stories of high school girlfriends, drug experimentation, and exotic (to his ears) travel. When it was Jack's turn for beer-induced self-disclosure, he found himself editing out the dull parts, telling of days crewing on Great Lake charter boats or working the pit at the speedway or visiting his father at the woolen mill and seeing a man lose a finger. The stories transformed as he told them, becoming by turns more romantic, or rugged, or more appealingly oddball than they'd been when he'd lived them. His past, he understood, could be whatever he said it was. He could reinvent Lakeland as the place he *should* have come from and no one would know the difference. In truth he'd long ago discarded any affinity with upstate New York, was already directing his ambitions elsewhere. But it didn't mean he had to wear his past like a scar.

It was in those late night reminiscences that he'd begun to craft the image of Lakeland he was now bringing to life. If the past was a *flexible* thing, so might the future be, in the right hands.

BACK AT THE DRAKE he saw a couple in the lobby returning from a night out, and a group of friends around the hotel bar, the Coq d'Or. He treated himself to a nightcap. No one stared over at him, no night security guard asked him to show his room key. He could fit in here. He'd always been able. He had loved staying with Anne in places like this, watching the heads turn as she walked into a room.

He thought of when his high school girlfriend, Shauna, visited him at Brown. Jack had wanted to hide her. He told her he didn't fit in, but what he meant was she didn't.

"It's like I'm a step or two behind," he said.

But she didn't see it. She saw that a month into school he knew the location of two exclusive parties, knew the best Portuguese restaurant; that he smoked the occasional cigarette when he was out and that his haircut was different.

"I finally invested in a decent one," he said.

Her face grew sad and then he remembered that she had cut it the last time.

Still, there was nothing in that weekend that suggested it would be their last time together, that he would never see her again. At lunch the next day, a quiet, sexy woman he knew vaguely from his literature class smiled over at him from another table.

"You've slept with her, haven't you," Shauna said.

"Why do you say that?" he asked.

"Because of the way she's looking at you."

Until then he hadn't imagined someone like that might be interested in him.

"I don't even know her name," he said.

While that was true, he did in fact sleep with her the following weekend. Her name was Ursula. She was from San Francisco and he dated her for three months before he dated Rachel, and Stacy, and after that Sabine. He met Ursula at a party, and Shauna had been right. She'd been interested. Shauna was right about a lot of things that weekend. It was as though her speaking her worst fears had allowed Jack to live them. There was nothing more to hold him back. When she left that weekend, he watched her bus round the corner, then heard himself mouth the words: *Thank God.*

He went to sleep now in his puffy hotel bed in the middle of the country, wondering not about the next days when he and Hickey would be meeting with potential architects and developers, or about Anne, whom he resented for not being there, but about Shauna. He'd heard she was married, had moved to Ohio or Indiana, where she was a teacher and her husband a school administrator. If he saw her again he would apologize for not returning her letters.

He'd say it had had little to do with her, that it was himself he had been breaking up with, but he gathered she already knew that.

AT BREAKFAST HE MINGLED with two West Coast planners and an architect who'd been to his talk. They'd loved it, they said.

"All that untapped potential," one of them said, whispering as if the words might explode if spoken aloud.

He saw his old boss, Reefsnyder, right before lunch the following day.

"I told you this was your ticket," he said.

"Who would have known?" Jack said.

"I did. It's Americana is what it is."

"Yeah, it is," Hickey agreed. "What do you mean?"

"That's what the galleries are putting out in Soho. It's what people want. A trip to their past. Or what they think is their past. Lakeland is America's past."

"It's my past," Jack said.

THAT AFTERNOON JACK FOUND himself having drinks with a well-known shopping mall developer, Raymond "Shep" Showalter, who introduced himself as "a huge fan." He talked to Jack about the importance of culture, and how to use it as a marketing tool. There were two upstates people thought of, he said. One was Chattaqua and the Finger Lakes. The other was Roseanne.

"We're gonna leave Roseanne out of our marketing plans, if that's okay," he said.

Showalter had built malls all over the northeast and in Florida. What he lacked in tact he could make up tenfold in leverage, so his use of *we* was just a bit thrilling. Was he asking in?

"What we're putting across, Jack, is an old fishing village, right, with real fish. A romantic weekend spot too, concerts on a lakeside lawn, some repertory theater with Broadway names." (These were straight from Jack's speech.) He paused, having arrived at a thesis. "Culture's a hotter amenity these days than golf courses. It really is." He looked at Jack as though he'd said something unthinkable.

"I'm not that big on golf," Jack said.

"I just read how in Germany they're building a museum a

month. They see where the trends are pointing. You get more bang for your buck with culture."

Lakeland could be the meeting point for Canadians and Americans, Jack said. A French quarter might bring in tourists from Quebec, alongside downstaters who want an Old Quebec experience without the ten-hour drive.

What was crucial, Jack emphasized, was to build a first-rate harbor, not a tawdry outlet mall. And equally important was finding work for the unemployed Lakelanders. Showalter nodded as if his child had said something smart.

"I'm right with you on all this," he said. "A mix. I've got people ready to build yesterday if they get the nod. Maybe it's your winning narration back there, but I'm honestly beginning to believe these classic old coastal towns might be the next hot real estate—if we pitch 'em the right way. Places with a history, with a *community*, and a nice-sized body of water. A Great Lake."

He spread his hand across Jack's view as if demonstrating Lake Ontario's expanse.

"I'll bet your average New Yorker doesn't know how fast he can get up to a Great Lake. Four hours, you said?"

"Three and a half if you're really booking."

"Excellent. So all you need, then, is to get them up here for a weekend. That's where the entertainment comes in. The amphitheater. The Great Lakes Theater, we call it. Get people into town to see, oh, I don't know, Billy Joel or Janet Jackson. You need big names for starters. Once they're up there, then you can charm the pants off of them with all your old-fashioned American texture and fabric."

Jack nodded. He was cautiously excited, like a screenwriter might be talking to a producer who liked his script, but who might very well butcher it when push came to shove.

Showalter then lowered his glance and said, "Can I ask you something?"

"Sure."

"You weren't planning on ever returning there. Am I right?"

"What makes you say that?"

"Just a sense. I grew up in a town like yours. Western Pennsylvania. I was ashamed of it. I'd tell people in college I grew up outside New York. Everybody leaves where they came from, and they piss on it the rest of their lives. It's a sickness in our country. Now, I haven't done there what you're doing here. I built a small plaza with some nice restaurants, but there's no Great Lake there. Not even a decent-sized pond. You've got a chance to really do something for the place you sprung from. Give it some self-respect and pride, and maybe a little refinement they can take into the next century. That's a very big thing, Jack. If that's not the American dream, then we all ought to change our sleeping habits."

AS HE CLOSED THE door to his hotel room, Jack reflected on the last forty-eight hours. It was almost too much to assimilate. His work was evolving and unfurling in the way he'd hoped it would. A subtle change was happening within him. His voice sounded different to his ears. More self-assured. He'd said the right things not only in his talk, but in all his conversations.

He felt as though he'd arrived at the locus of something big, something distinctly American, and perhaps, finally, distinctly his own. It was *his* words they were all responding to, *his* vision, and *his* taste. He remembered what they'd said about him in his high school yearbook, that they'd be writing biographies about him someday. Ridiculous, he still thought, but perhaps he'd begun to close the gap between the man everyone believed him to be and the one he was.

AT THE END OF THE NIGHT, with a few beers in them, Hickey had talked again about Jack running for mayor.

"Always go political after you hit a home run."

Was it all that insane to think of a two-year stint, and someday a run for the governorship? What had Bubba done before he was elected governor?

He was happy, he thought. And he allowed himself to believe that all his decisions had been good ones.

IT WASN'T UNTIL HE READIED for bed that he felt Anne's absence. She'd been out when he'd tried her earlier, and by now she was certainly asleep. He thought how sad it was for her that she wasn't here for all this. If only she could appreciate him the way others did. If only she bothered to pay a little attention, she'd realize how gratifying all this could be. She could even have a role of some kind. She could be a cultural advisor, plan the art shows, and maybe some theater and dance. It might take the pressure off her painting.

He'd assumed they'd be together when all the good things happened, when good things happened to both of them. It was what they'd said in their hastily written vows. Now he wasn't so sure.

CHAPTER 29

The next thing Anne would remember was being on a bed in the corner of an unfamiliar room. The room was warm, and a lemony light streamed through the bedside window. Clouds floated inside her head, nuzzled at her cranium. She tried to lift her shoulders, then dropped back down onto pillows.

She couldn't recall anything about how she'd gotten here. There were a lot of books in the room. A blue Persian carpet. There was a note next to the bed.

Back before noon. There's juice and bagels in the fridge, fresh coffee on the stove.

Turner.

She thought of drinking some juice, but then she fell back asleep again.

She slept all day. When she awoke it was dark out. In his outstretched hands Turner held a bowl of chicken soup. She took the spoon from him and fed herself two sips.

"Good soup," she said. It tasted like childhood.

"Thanks. It's from a can."

"What day is it?"

"Friday."

"What happened to Thursday?"

"You slept through it."

"You're kidding."

"I'm not. You needed it. You weren't doing so hot. You had a pretty high fever."

He pulled out a thermometer.

"Say *ah*." He placed it under her tongue.

She started to ask him how he'd gotten her there, but he said, "Hold on. Can't speak yet."

In a minute he removed the thermometer, looked at it under the light. "A hundred and one. That's a good deal better."

"How high was it before?"

"You don't want to know. You were pretty sick."

"I was cold. It's not supposed to be cold inside."

"You have a landlord or a handyman who knows heating systems?"

"I don't know," she said. "You keep a *thermometer* at home." She said it like, You know four languages.

"I get sick a lot. I'll make some calls about the heat in your house."

"This is a nice room."

"Is it warm enough?"

"It's tropical."

"Good. Get some more sleep if you want. I'll be in the next room." He gathered some things and began walking out. "You can stay here if you want."

She laid her head back down on the pillow and fell asleep again.

Snow fell all day. She dreamed in blue, a blue tint everywhere, the farmhouse in blue, the snow slightly blue. A cold blue. The blue of lips, of frostbite and kicked shins. She saw herself in the kitchen painting something common, while something uncommon happened just outside her window. The woman who was her wasn't looking in that direction; things kept passing all in blue. A bit blatant, she thought. Were everyone's dreams this transparent?

But it was what she'd been thinking. Inspiration existed. It had simply passed her by. Until now.

It was light out when she awoke. He was fixing his tie at his dresser mirror.

It had been three days and she hadn't left the bed. She wondered if she could still walk. She didn't want to try.

"Are you leaving me again?" she asked.

"Only for the shortest of times," he said. "How do we feel?"

"We've got no idea."

"You certainly have been sleeping."

"I love to sleep. I don't think there's anything in the world I love more. Is it Sunday?"

"Saturday. I found some mangoes at the supermarket. What's up with *that*? Anyhow, I can slice one up for you, would you like that? And how 'bout some eggs?"

"Don't you have to go to work?"

"I do and I don't."

"What does that mean?"

"I have to get work done—at some time."

"I'll fix my own. I think it's time to check out the land legs." She pulled herself out from the covers.

She looked at what she was wearing. A T-shirt—*Property of New York Knickerbockers*.

"Did someone give me away?"

"It's a nice team. You'll like them."

She felt weak and dizzy when she stood, so she sat back down.

"How do you stop the room from spinning?"

He stamped his foot down.

"Thank you," she said.

Her dizziness actually seemed to fade.

He left and she made her own breakfast. It occurred to her he could be telling her anything. It could be Tuesday, or Friday still.

She didn't remember when Jack was supposed to return. She thought she remembered the hotel, the Drake.

She tried calling. Jack was out. She didn't leave a message.

"THINGS ARE GOING WELL in Chicago," Turner said when he got back.

"Did you talk to him?"

"No. Stewart talked to Hickey. They raked in the hardware. Jack made a big speech in front of a lot of people. The harbor's a comin' soon."

"Who's Stewart?"

"My colleague."

"He's the one Jack's always ticked about."

"He's probably been trying to call you. You should let him know you're okay."

"Stewart?"

"No, the man you live with. Although you could tell Stewart too, if you like."

She buried herself under the covers. "And do I tell him where I am?"

Turner stood thinking about this. "Tell him he left you in a freezing house and you almost died."

"I'll call him from home."

"You want to borrow my car?"

She poked her head out again. "I want you to come along."

THE SKY WAS FILLED with a windless squall. It was like driving through down, feathers scattering, then falling softly. Winter in Lakeland is unreal, so white, so quiet, so dreamlike, so completely otherworldly, that anything might happen, or nothing at all.

The heating had been fixed. It was livable again. But Anne didn't want to be there.

The blue tarp flapped in the wind like laundry.

"I feel like I won't sleep," she said. "It feels like I've fallen back into something I don't want to fall back into just yet."

She walked through the rooms, straightening things.

Turner walked alongside.

"Kind of a cool old house, if you don't look at the roof. I like the furniture too."

She liked that he didn't flip through the canvases.

She called Jack. Turner left the room.

"I don't want to stay here tonight," she told Turner afterward.

"Where do you want to go?"

"I want to go to your place," she said.

She took her box of paints and a pad of canvas paper.

SHE WOULD SLEEP WITH HIM. It surprised her that she understood this so completely and unreservedly—the way she knew that she felt better—because for weeks she'd been unable to understand anything. Now she rose with conviction out of bed. She sat in the chartreuse reading chair looking out at the black winter night, and she was amazed at how calm she felt, how in her head she heard no confusion of voices, only the one she wanted to hear, which meant she was all right again. She would be all right now, and maybe for a while. She wanted to tell this all to Turner, but there was no reason she needed to do that now. She thought of Jack, but now without concern for what he might decide to do, and also without self-reproach.

She'd accepted the notion of marital fidelity, bought into it the way you buy into a work ethic, or that six glasses of water a day was good for your skin, and to defy it was to bring guilt and shame and chaos, but what if it didn't? What if your life improved? What could you trust anymore?

She put music on lightly. She sat relaxing, eyes closed, arms folded.

I'm getting it back, she said softly. I'm reassembling.

A FEW MOMENTS AFTER Turner had settled onto the couch before going to sleep the next night, Anne crept out of the bedroom. He watched her walk barefoot toward the bathroom, still wearing his Knicks T-shirt.

"She walks by night," he said.

"Mothers, lock up your sons," she answered.

Since the day he'd brought her here, his house had felt cozier and sexier. It unnerved Turner how much he liked it. His indifference to company was rapidly falling by the wayside.

When the door closed he realized how intensely he'd been breathing.

She called from inside, "Can I use one of these toothbrushes?"

"Whichever one you like," he said. In a hopeful gesture he'd kept two toothbrushes. No one except Serena had used the other one. He hoped she was using his toothbrush.

On her way back across the living room she stopped by him and leaned down.

"You're good to me," she said.

She kissed him lightly on the mouth.

Snowdrifts tumbled; the lake shook.

She left him alone there on the couch, bewitched and stupefied, cocooned in his down sleeping bag. He smiled against his pillow, and kept that face deep into the night until sweet sleep finally claimed him.

When he woke up the next morning, they were kissing. She was next to him on the couch, beneath the sleeping bag. Their legs were twined, her hand was on his face.

Miraculous didn't describe this. Soul-subduing came close.

"Hi," he said finally, to see if he could speak.

"Good morning."

"I would say so."

She was kissing a circle around his mouth, then his neck.

"Should we be doing this?"

"Ssshhh," she said.

She was sliding out of her T-shirt.

"Is this what you want?"

"Yes," she said. "It's exactly what I want."

CHAPTER 30

Time floated. There was no demarcation—snow on everything, no beginning, no end, no borders. Hours might have passed, and then Turner left and wrote a story as quickly as he could. She was reading in bed when he returned.

It was as if her life with Jack had receded. By the second day, they were as familiar to each other as they were to the snow. Here was the soft inside of a thigh, here the smooth back of a neck, here coarse stubble on a cheek she would not have him shave in spite of the burn she felt on hers. There was less talking, because the days were quiet and sensuous, and they knew words could keep them from hearing, seeing, tasting. Better not to fill your mind with responses when it could be filled with the soft sounds of legs sliding through sheets, wine pouring into a wide glass, snow falling on a windowsill. They forgot to sleep, forgot to eat until they had to. Then they ate their meals on the floor. He brought back bread, cheese, and fruit. There were crumbs on the sheets, and a dampness from their skin. They traveled the landscape of each other's bodies.

"Do I know you?" she said, more than once, but she didn't want an answer, she was making a statement with the question—and in truth he couldn't answer her because he didn't know what was or had been anymore, everything was turned on its end, and he could no longer predict what he'd say or feel, could no longer turn his experience into sarcasm, into something light and disposable. All his best defenses had been disarmed.

It occurred to him at the center of the night, as she lay across his chest, her face open to the room, her eyes closed, that he did not care about anything outside of this apartment. Outside of this bed, outside of him and her. He left at eight or some morning hour; she read a book, made herself tea, walked around his apartment naked. He was back in an hour. They slept for much of the day. He thought he had nice dreams but he couldn't remember any of them.

It kept snowing. Cars were covered. Ice glazed the trees, wind blew comically high drifts, the few drivers out fishtailed down the street, people bundled like cream puffs, the sky looked pregnant, strained under the weight of what it would soon give birth to, what it would soon release. There was a smell to it, to its cold whiteness, some of it dirty, but so much of it clean and new, and it made you think of a blanket, or a covering, and who knew what was beneath; it could be paradise, it could be a cesspool, and under snow it was the same.

Snow blew horizontally. Eyelids froze. Parts of cars snapped off, it was so cold. But there was beauty too; the bruised sky drifted in rivery patterns over a frozen white lake. The same waves you could see in your scotch at night.

Everything was slower in winter. The joints squeaked.

He couldn't sit with his feelings for Anne. When they arrived he'd get up from his chair and take a walk. Strange, he thought. It was like drinking, you needed to pace yourself, walk it off, get a good night's sleep. If you simply sat there drinking you might drink yourself to death. He could see this killing him. He really could.

When he woke again, the windows were blue with dawn. His head hurt. He looked aside. She was talking in her sleep.

THE PILES OUTSIDE kept climbing. He wrote more about snow. He interviewed people about just how snowy it was. He thought only briefly about the barrels and the farms, but decided for now to leave them under the snow like everything else. He wrote about the lake effect instead. Outside the bedroom window he made a snowman while she slept and got healthy. He was happier than he ever remembered being. The snowman was small and fat, and Turner gave him cherry tomato eyes and a wine cork nose.

Her skin held heat; he could feel it inches away. He talked to a man once who'd been to a healer. He could feel heat from the healer's finger a foot away. If you touched his finger your hand would burn, he said.

Turner didn't burn when he touched Anne. And that's what kept surprising him.

SHE SLEPT ALL THE TIME. She said she was making up for the month in which she never slept. She felt better.

"Has he called?" Turner asked.

"He left one message."

"Just one?"

"It's only been two days."

"Is that all it's been?"

"Maybe two and a half."

He didn't tell her about the dream he had when he fell asleep at work, a frighteningly literal one of Jack driving a car over his legs. He asked instead if she had a birdcage.

"Why do you ask?"

"Matisse had them in his bedroom. He kept hummingbirds, Bengalis, and guittes. Blue budgerigars."

She laughed. "How do you know that?"

"He put Congolese tapestries up on the walls, panther skins, Persian rugs," Turner said. "He drew in bed and he posted whatever he was painting on the wall facing him so he'd see it when he woke up."

They had three more days. It kept snowing. They played a game they called Uncle. They'd take off their clothes and lie on the floor an inch apart, not touching until one of them said Uncle. The longest they made it to was ten minutes.

AT WORK HE CALLED snow experts (there were a half dozen about locally), learned about pyramids and columns, needles and sheaths. Squalls, dumpings, dustings, and pastings. He'd cornered the snow beat again. He'd also cornered the Things That Have Gotten Fucked Up Because of the Snow beat. Power lines were fucked up, the theater marquee had partially collapsed. A bread truck slid onto the lake, then got stuck there for six hours. Someone suggested Turner find out how many babies were conceived during the last big storm, and when he called the hospital they said there were nearly twice the normal number. He thought of the headline: FUCKING UP WHEN SNOW FUCKS THINGS UP.

IN LAKELAND THEY MEASURED snowfall by feet. The temperature was one degree. It froze the hair in your nostrils, and your piss before it could reach the earth.

On the street Turner ran into Serena, her body sheathed in Lycra.

"I'm still picking you up next Saturday, right?"

"Saturday." He tried to remember.

"Ten A.M. The soup kitchen?"

Turner remembered in the throes of it he'd agreed to help Serena serve food to the elderly and homeless. There were a lot of things he'd have agreed to in that position. Painting a mile of fence, swimming the width of the lake.

"All right, then."

"I'll come get you."

"Okay. But how about you pick me up at the office."

"What's up, Turner?"

"Nothing. I just want to go in early."

"Tar stuff."

"Something like that."

"Haven't seen you for a while."

"Busy informing the public."

"I've been reading."

"You wearing that?"

She looked down admiringly at herself.

"Nah." She winked. "Don't want to make 'em pop a pace-maker."

"Self-assured, aren't you?"

"Self-determined, Turner. There's a difference. I work at things."

AS THEY GAZED OUTSIDE the window, Turner told Anne fresh snow was cheap bread, puffed out with air, and you could pack five feet down to a few inches if you squeezed it enough. When it melts and freezes again it becomes corn snow, he told her, the kind that causes avalanches.

"You know a lot," she said.

He shook his head. "Smoke and mirrors."

"But you do."

"It's the job. At some point all those information snippets get out and run loose in your head. They hog space."

"Look out. Renegade information," she said.

"Contradiction. Keeps you from knowing anything."

"I don't believe it."

"My knowledge pool is ankle-deep."

She liked his home. She liked his voice. It was familiar to her. It was her father's, she thought once, but would never say that to him, and did not want to repeat it to herself. But she loved his voice.

MORE THAN ANYTHING she loved sleep, and the resumption of her dream life.

For a short while it cleared. Anne and Turner went walking under the early stars.

"I'm different around you," she said.

"How?"

"Lots of ways. I don't parcel myself. I mean there are so many things I don't tell Jack."

"Such as?"

"How about this: I was mugged right before I arrived here. I never told him that. That's pretty strange, isn't it?"

They were on a dirt path that skirted the high school and wound its way toward a series of bluffs over the lake.

"Were you hurt?"

"Not badly. They pushed me and I hit my head. It happened on the subway."

"Were you knocked out at all?"

She pulled closer to him, allowed his arm around her shoulders.

"How long?"

"Five stops. I don't know."

"Did you go to the hospital?"

"No."

"That's not good. Head injuries need to be checked out. I did a story on this once."

When they reached the lake he stopped and pushed her hair from her forehead. He looked at her scar. "You got cut too." He ran his finger across it.

She shrank from his touch, and then allowed him. "That was from something else."

"Playground accident?"

"Something like that."

CHAPTER 31

"Is this the part when the dam breaks and we tell all the horrible complicated things of our pasts?" she said.

They had moved to the wall side of the bed. "If we want. We can tell the good stuff."

She smiled.

"There are nice things," she said.

"Like what?"

"Like a trip we took to Portugal. Like sixth grade."

"Only sixth grade?"

"Tenth grade was good too."

And as she talked on she saw specific images: her Yamaha stereo, a bottle of suntan lotion, a tan suitcase, a row of scarves in her mother's closet.

WHAT WAS STRANGE WAS that Jack had become the affair. Turner's light had thrown darkness over Jack.

He had the right answers for whatever she said.

"I should buck up, roll with things better . . ."

"*I* certainly can't."

". . . and stop abstracting myself."

"What would we do sometimes if we couldn't jump out of a dull conversation into a nice abstraction? I'm a walking abstraction."

She laughed. "I'm stalled out, always."

"Most people die waiting for inspiration to descend. You went for it, that's the important thing. Now you're second-guessing, as if a little stalling isn't part of it."

"It's not the end of it?"

"No," he said. "Not even close."

CHAPTER 32

Midafternoon they went for a meal in the outside world. At a diner, Turner had waffles; Anne, a stack of hotcakes. And then they walked together down the street, brazenly, relaxed, a couple, Turner was beginning to believe. Here they were in this snow-bitten, time-lost town, on the brink of change, a town that would soon be filled with strangers, and strange new places, businessmen only a few notches above snake-oil salesmen.

What would they do about all the poor people? wondered Turner. What would they do with the welfare lines when the tourists came in?

"I need to go to the bank," Anne said.

"Want company?" he asked almost shyly.

"Of course," she said.

They walked right up Pine Street in the direction of the bank, and while he did not take her hand, or put his arm around her, or stop in the middle of the street to kiss her, Turner wanted to think he could and that it would be all right—or even, simply, right—and just as he was forming a tranquil belief that they could have all this without misgiving or a steep price, ahead Turner saw Jack Lambeau's stocky, square-jawed younger brother, Harris, sharply turning the corner and now on a collision course toward them. There was no polite way to avoid a meeting. Here he walked, and there they walked. If Turner abruptly peeled away it would look stranger than their walking down the street together. He and Anne had run into each other.

People ran into each other all the time in this town, after all; there wasn't anything suspicious about it.

And besides, he didn't want to run off.

The whole situation might have been a tiny forgettable blip if Turner had not at that moment seen Anne's face lose all color.

It was the face of a caught shoplifter, and it sent Turner's spirits tumbling.

Oh, Steven, you are a fool, he thought.

Harris didn't seem to recognize Turner right off. Perhaps in a moment he'd just go away.

"Sorry about the new look, Anne," he said. "But it stopped the leaking at least, didn't it?"

Anne looked positively spooked.

"The blue tarp?" he said. "I ripped out those rotted roof shingles. I'll take all those boards out too eventually."

She nodded slowly, as though deciphering a foreign language.

"Yes, the leak. Thanks, Harris."

"That house needs a lot of work. What have you been doing in that cold?"

"Using a lot of blankets."

Harris looked at her dubiously.

"Need a hell of a lot of blankets to get through a night there. You must have froze."

"I did."

Harris started to go, then recognized Turner.

"Turner," he said.

"How are you, Harris?"

"If you want the truth, I've been better. Marla won't let me live with her and my baby girl. But you don't want to know that." Harris began to look puzzled, as though trying to guess: Which one of these doesn't belong?

"You need a ride somewhere, Anne?"

"No thanks," she said.

"How about you, Turner my man?"

"I'm just going back to work now."

"Where's that?"

"Just three blocks away."

"C'mon in. I'll give you a ride."

Turner looked over at Anne, whose eyes said, *Please go ahead. Let's avoid a scene.*

"Know what you need?" Harris said to Anne in parting. "A nice warm room to do your painting in. When Jack gets back we'll do some Sheetrocking. We'll make you a real art studio, Anne."

"I would really love that," she said.

And then she vanished into the bank.

"QUITE A WOMAN," Harris said as they drove.

"Jack's lucky."

"I don't know if I'd say that. My hunch is she's a handful."

Turner didn't answer. He stared out the window at the dying day. And he was upset. Harris had thrown a disfiguring light over them. He stood as a reminder that in spite of this week, the matter was far from closed. They were not a couple; they were only lovers now, hidden like fugitives.

His concerns had been suspended, or, more aptly, hidden in snow. Harris had shoveled them clear.

"You gotta get right back to work?"

"Yup."

"Can't grab a drink?"

About six months ago, Harris, Jack, and Turner had gone out for drinks. They'd gotten themselves three sheets to the wind, Turner and Harris. Jack, of course, had known when to stop; as always, he'd played within his limits. That night Turner liked Harris more than Jack, who seemed to grow disgusted with the two of them. On the walk to their cars, Harris had told Turner what it was like growing up with a brother like Jack. He said he never felt competitive; there was never any point. It was like busting a gut when you were forty points behind in a football game. All you did was risk injury. His father said once, "You're better at fucking up, Harris; least you got that on him."

"You know I'd like to, Harris," Turner said now, "but I have a story to finish."

"By when?"

"By eight."

"But it's only three-thirty. Let's have a drink."

"Oh, I don't know."

"Relax," Harris said. "I'll get you back in time to write a Pulitzer."

THERE WAS NO INTERROGATION. All Harris wanted was advice. He wanted his wife back. And Turner wanted Harris's mind fixed to his own problems.

Bad food, dirty clothes, and on top of everything he was getting blue balls, he said. He added that Turner was beginning to look kind of good.

"I'll stay away from that one," Turner said.

He'd been getting wasted, spending way too much money. He hadn't cheated on her, not since the first months of their relationship anyhow, but he'd have to soon if nothing changed.

Then they talked about Jack. "Weird, them not going together to Chicago," Harris said.

"People do that. He's focusing on his work."

"That's what got me in trouble."

"Is it the reason she won't let you back?" Turner asked.

"Sort of," Harris said. He pushed his coaster back and forth on the counter.

"This is it, what I'm thinking now. When you take each thing you do apart—it should all add up to something decent," he said.

Turner couldn't get Anne's face out of his mind now. He wondered, was that it, was that the end of things between them? He knew it couldn't be. Nothing so sweet could die that fast.

He thought about Jack, *stupid fucking Jack*. Gone during all this. Leaving Anne freezing and alone like that. He'd as much as invited this on himself. Hail the new harbor; fail the wife to be.

"Got another question," Harris said.

"Shoot."

"You ever have a friend or a relative die on you?"

"Two different grandparents."

"What did you do? Cremate them?"

"Buried one, cremated the other."

"Do you think their souls lived on?"

"That's not a question, Harris. That's a philosophical inquiry. I'm not drunk enough."

"I'm serious."

Turner looked at him. He was serious.

"I do, actually."

"I want to make some changes. I think it was seeing my little girl being born. It's a bigger thing than I thought. It's like Marla was pregnant and now I am, you know? Filled up with it."

"You'll be a good dad, Harris."

He should be with Anne right now, driving back to his place (she was heading there now, he thought, he wanted so badly to believe). And here he was talking about mortality in this dingy bar with Jack's only brother and so would push back his time with her another two hours.

A poor trade-off.

He was tempted now to make a declaration, a public statement, to make them public and therefore tangible.

We've been sleeping together. We're falling in love, he would like to say, though he was pretty sure saying it here would be a bad idea.

"Everyone's got a soul," Harris said.

"You'll be a good soul."

Harris looked at his coaster, then looked up.

"I got more to say, but this little part of me keeps thinking you're gonna write all about me in the paper. You're not gonna write about me, are you?"

"Not unless you want me to."

"You're all right," Harris said.

Turner knew where this was heading. The alcohol would settle deeper into the crevices of their brains and in just a few short drinks he'd be no good for any story, and worse, he might not make it back to the office at all. With no forethought, just a grasp in the dark, Turner said, "You know anything about Harlan Stanyan dumping barrels of toxic waste around town?"

He saw Harris struggle with himself, like a man trying to force a boulder through the top of his head.

"No," he grumbled. "D'he say I did?"

CHAPTER 33

Stewart was asleep beneath his desk again, snoring, his story left out on his screen like unrefrigerated food. Turner nudged his leg just a bit and the volume dropped to a tolerable rumble. He wanted to think. His mind was working. If Harris Lambeau was actually in on any of the dumping, this whole situation would become extremely interesting. Here was the brother of the man in charge of the whole harbor project, making a mess out on the farms.

Turner wanted another brain. He wanted the sort of brain that would focus on this task and this task alone. He was no detective when you got down to it.

He'd never been one for really hunting down a story, digging through deeds and records, appearing unwanted on people's property, following them through their routines like an under-cover cop. He'd never had the patience to conduct thorough in-vestigations.

But a few facts remained.

Some sort of black chemical sludge, caustic enough to burn skin, had been dumped on at least one farm. Stanyan was prob-ably involved. Harris knew Stanyan. Harris cleared land for the harbor project. Jack had arranged Harris's job. Jack had never seemed particularly interested in talking about environmental problems, either on the harbor site or farms, had he?

Turner made notes in his computer.

What are you doing? he asked himself. Are you going to fuck him over in order to steal her away?

With the help of some reworked paragraphs from an old story he quickly pushed his daily into shape.

Before he left he walked over to Stewart's screen. He sat on a chair inches from his sleeping officemate, and in the strange green light of his screen he began to push paragraphs around, then words. He began to edit. Then to write. He wrote the hell out of the story, his fingers flying of their own accord over the keys. He read it back to himself quickly, and then sent it in.

It was a pretty damn good story, he thought.

Stewart then began to move.

"Huh . . . what the hell," he said.

"You're all done, Stewart," Turner said. "You can go home now."

OUTSIDE, IN THE ABSENCE OF SNOW, it was cold-cold. Wind ripped the night open. Ice floes drifted like gray bags of garbage down the river.

Turner would probably live if Anne wasn't at his apartment when he got there. It'd be just fine, he told himself, knowing it wouldn't be fine at all. They hadn't run their course yet. The week wasn't over and Jack wasn't home. At least Turner didn't think he was. Snow kept dumping on Chicago in historic depths. Planes were snowed in at O'Hare, his car radio said. And it was too close to how he would have prescribed it for Turner to think it was an accident. He'd willed it. If she's there, my will conquers all, he thought.

And then he wished he hadn't because of what the reverse would mean.

His car made strange rattling noises, like bouncing marbles. He would have to get it checked out because he couldn't have his transportation die on him. Not in winter, when it hurt to walk four blocks, much less the thirteen between his apartment and the office.

She'll be there, he thought.

But still the night felt very different, the air inside the car smelled foul.

When he opened the door of his apartment, Turner felt queasy. The living room was barren, and the bedroom too. No notes, no signs of her presence. He thought of the look she had when she saw Harris. Had she run for cover? His stomach knotted like an airplane passenger in a loss of altitude. He walked back to the kitchen, and as he looked into the room and saw her rummaging through his refrigerator, he wondered how he could have doubted anything.

"Took you long enough," she said, pulling out a stalk of celery.

She was comfortable here, he thought. She belonged. How very, very strange. He had never met anyone like her. Not by a long shot.

"You of all people should know art can't be rushed," he said.

"He left a message. He's coming back early tomorrow."

Turner stood and tried to appear unblenched.

She said, "I don't want him to come back. I don't want anything to change."

"It doesn't have to," Turner said, but the words felt like wax in his mouth.

THERE WAS NO TONE of finality in their lovemaking that night. There was continuity, the easy coupling of two people who knew each other well and would spend a life together, or at least a few months—that's how it felt to Turner. There was no urgency.

Before they went to sleep she talked about her father.

He was imaginative and resourceful, she said. He wrote songs for her on the piano. He was an advertising art director with one of the bigger agencies, and yet he almost never came home late. He was the one who came up with the family news shows at dinner. Anne and her sister as the anchors. He was the weatherman.

Lauren would begin by telling about what happened in her ninth-grade classroom in a newswoman's voice: "Today Mr. Gilde decided on a pop quiz as appropriate punishment for the class's recent behavior. Gilde said, 'This quiz will count as ten percent of your final grade. . . .'"

Anne would offer an editorial response on pop quizzes.

Then Anne's father would put his hand out the window and say "Cold today," or "Swampy," or "You know, Anne, I just can't tell. Back to you."

Anne's mother was the Nielsen audience.

Then Anne told Turner about the accident. They'd been walking down Broadway near Wolff's Delicatessen. "I remember because I thought it'd be nice to stop and have a pastrami on rye, the piled-on kind with lots of grainy mustard. Maybe he saw something across the street, or saw something on our side he wanted to avoid; at any rate, he stepped between two parked cars and I didn't. Usually I'd have just followed him. I don't know why I didn't this time. Maybe I wanted to wave at him once he'd crossed. You know, like, Hellooo, remember me?

"Well, he looked back then, and when he turned to get me—which was unnecessary, because I was following then—the taxi streaked in front of me and hit him. A Checker cab, which they don't even have anymore. It hit him full speed. I got knocked down too. But he took the brunt of it. He got knocked about twenty feet." She sounded unstirred by this, but wasn't, Turner knew. He certainly wasn't.

"That's about the most awful thing I've ever heard."

"It was pretty bad."

"You were a second from being killed yourself."

"I know. Wasn't I lucky?"

"How'd your mother take it?"

"Poorly. She had a boyfriend at the time. I'm fairly sure they were doing it that afternoon."

"Aw no."

"Aw yes. Maybe that made it harder on her. I hope so. Sometimes I think he walked in front of that cab to get back at her."

Turner pulled Anne against his body.

"It was pretty lousy for a long time. You know, bad sleep, no appetite, that sort of thing. I was crazy for a while. I mean certifiably. What it did was launch my disabling solipsism."

"What?"

"That's how the counselor put it. 'Possesses a disabling brand of solipsism, which may be a root cause of her disorder.' I read it on a piece of paper he left in view when he went to the bathroom. 'Believes it was her fault,' he'd written. Of course I did. If I crossed right away, it wouldn't have happened."

"You know that's ridiculous right?"

"I do and I don't. And it gets worse. The more time I spend alone and isolated, the more deaths I think I caused. You better not get too close to me."

"I'm glad you can joke about it."

"It's no joke."

"You need to get out of that house, Anne. Twenty-four hours a day in a spooky old farmhouse is a recipe for at least a little eccentricity."

"Do you think I'm crazy?"

"No."

"But I was. When you found me I was crazy. It never lasts long. Or it hasn't in the past. But two or three times in my life I've felt certifiably crazy. Panic, palpitations, the whole deal. I feel like I can't breathe. Then I get over it. I get a break for a few years and I feel like I'm past it."

"You had a very high fever, Anne. People feel crazy when they have a fever like that."

"Yes. And then you saved me, Dr. Turner."

"Please."

"You didn't even take advantage of me until I made you."

"You didn't make me."

"Oh, but I did."

They lay a few inches apart, hands on each other's shoulders.

"My god."

"What?"

"Here I am telling you about my mother fucking around—why to this day I can't really talk to her—and look at *me*."

It was an irony that hadn't escaped him.

"I'm glad you're talking about this with me."

"Yeah? Why?"

"It makes me feel close to you."

Her eyes looked frightened then, as they had when she'd seen Harris. It was disturbing to think how unbreakable his attachment to her was becoming; the weight of it at that moment seemed almost unbearable.

"It feels like we're on an airplane," she said absently.

Turner tried to figure out what this meant. He imagined them on an airplane, flying, looking down from the window, seeing the traces of things, specks of roads and houses, clouds. Did she mean the clouds?

"How do you mean?"

"You know how you meet someone nice on an airplane, and suddenly you've told them your life story?"

He felt insulted. "And then you never see them again."

"Sometimes you don't."

AT FOUR IN THE MORNING—the two of them lying against each other like spoons—Turner got a call from the overnight editor about a barn fire twenty minutes outside of Lakeland. He should take his camera.

"You're going out there now?" Anne said, as she watched him throw on his jeans and a shirt.

"Got no choice," he said.

This was the absurd part of his job—he couldn't say no. Nor, in the past, had he wanted to. He liked to be the one called upon—just not at this exact moment. "I'll be back in a couple hours. Keep sleeping."

The fire had mostly smoldered by the time he arrived; no one injured other than two guinea pigs, neither of which had died. But he'd still had to file a small story. As he wrote and filed it, he thought about how easy it would have been to have just let the phone ring and say later he'd been too sound asleep to hear it.

He was often surprised by his own professionalism, how he responded to these calls like a country doctor. Would that he could actually save something.

By the time he was done and returned to his apartment it was six A.M. and Anne was gone. He put a tape on so the apartment wouldn't feel so empty.

When he called over to the farmhouse she picked up on the first ring.

"Jack?" she said.

Turner let silence convey his mortification.

"No."

"I'm sorry, Turner. I'm waiting for Jack to call from his stopover."

"Back on the ground again, huh?" he said finally.

"No. I wouldn't say that."

No one said anything then.

"What should I do? Stay at your house and wait for him to figure it out, or wait for Harris to figure it out?"

"When will we see each other?"

"I don't know. Soon, I hope."

It wasn't an answer he could easily sit with, but it was the only one he'd get.

"I shouldn't have left then. I just figured you'd still be here asleep."

"You had to. It doesn't change anything. We had an amazing week together."

He felt something slipping away, but he didn't know how to stop it. "I think I . . . ."

"Don't say it, Turner. Please don't say it. Not now."

"I think I'm going to say good-bye," he said.

"I'll talk to you soon," she said, and she hung up.

It felt as though he'd been robbed; someone had broken in and emptied his apartment.

He started to call back and then put the phone down.

The snow had stopped and everything outside seemed still and bare.

Something was wrong with his tape player. The music had slowed to a warble. He turned it off, and when he pulled the tape out, he saw that it was caught and had begun to unravel.

CHAPTER 34

The wind whipped off the lake, then rattled the downtown shop windows, shook hanging signs, bent tree branches, swept snow and sleet across the deep lawns of Spruce Street, whirled up the cloverleaf of Italian, Irish, and Polish American neighborhoods on the near west side, barreled past the old clapboards and bars of Crate Hollow to the east where people left big things like cars and broken washing machines freezing on their front yards; this wild, swirling, damned haunting wind, as constant here as time. And so it should not have been a surprise to Jack that the wind off the lake could damage an aging farmhouse—it did—or that it could break a door down. It had.

It was only the back door to a pantry that was set off from the rest of the house, but it was an ominous sign. The heat had been fixed. But what good was that when it flew outside so unobstructed? The whole house could go down at once if it got any worse out.

"Oh, jeez. Was it like this the whole time, sweetie?" he asked Anne.

"Worse."

"You should have stayed with Belle and Frank."

"I was all right. But we can't live like this. We can't be constantly cold, inside and out. We're not Eskimos."

"We'll do something," he said.

"I guess your hotel room was good and warm," she said.

"It was, Anne. You would have liked it." He set his bags in

the bedroom, and then returned to the living room where Anne had seated herself under a pile of blankets. He told her about his trip and he tried to conceal his enthusiasm, but it was hard to do. He was pretty damned enthusiastic. He wanted to sound as though he'd missed her. The longer he spoke the more he got carried away and didn't just tell her about the meetings, but about Chicago, and Hickey, and the eager shopping mall developer, and even the hotel staff and the blues singer they'd seen on Rush Street, a woman named Big Sarah. He was giving too much detail, he realized, explaining too much. He could tell she wasn't listening.

"But who knows if all this will ever pan out," he said at the end. And he went back to saying how cold it was, how miserable it was.

And then they didn't talk for a while. Each read a book, Anne on the couch, Jack on the armchair across from her.

"How was your week?" he asked.

She shrugged.

"It was complicated, I suppose. The end was better than the beginning."

He pulled next to her.

"You look better. More relaxed."

"Yeah?"

"It's good to see."

He put his arms around her. He stroked her hair and she stiffened beneath his touch. "I'm sorry I was away for so long, Annie, but I'm back now. I'm back for good."

"Yes. But I'm not sure if I'm back just yet, if that's okay."

"I want things to be better," he said.

Wind battered the walls.

"Can we make it stop?" Anne said. "Just for a month or so. No wind for a month."

"I'll make it stop," he said.

LISTENING TO HIS STORIES exhausted Anne, and she passed out shortly after her head touched the pillow. But only a few hours later, she awakened thinking of Turner. She missed being in his apartment, and she resented Jack for keeping her from him.

She'd feared Jack's leaving, his staying in Chicago, and now it was hard to fathom that anxiety. In fact, she wished he'd fly back there and stay for a month or two. He was solicitous to her now, sufficiently contrite, and he told her how much he'd liked Chicago, how he wanted to take her there. But she felt absent from the conversations, as though she was across the room, watching a woman talk to her husband about his trip. He was so damn dull, so entirely wound up in his project, in his accomplishments.

He'd get wrapped up in his kingdom, her grandfather had said, lock her away.

He hadn't locked her away. She'd done that. She wouldn't any longer.

She rolled over to her side that night and didn't respond when twice he tried to wake her with kisses and soft declarations. She would have hated someone being this way, but there was nothing else she could do.

Before she fell asleep, she thought, *I have to tell him*, and she prepared to endure the fallout. But Jack left early the next morning and came home late and tired that night, with flowers and a whole case of good wine, and it was wrong to talk then. They drank wine instead, a bottle with dinner, and then another afterward.

She told him that she'd been afraid he wouldn't come back.

"That's a terrible thing to think." And he told her how he'd thought about them, how they needed to get back to how they used to be, did she remember the night they ordered four courses in four different restaurants and pretended each was a separate date? She did. And it was a nice memory, but she wasn't ready yet to roll the highlight film. It only made you realize how far away you'd gotten.

"We need to be imaginative. Let's take a weekend in Montreal or something like that. Go to some jazz clubs."

"That'd be nice," she said.

They talked of how she needed to get out of the house more. No one should spend all day and night in the same house. Exercise was key, he said. When he didn't run, his thinking went astray.

"I hate running," she said.

"What about swimming? Or yoga? They've got a great pool at the Y, and I've seen signs about a yoga class in town."

"I don't really understand yoga."

Whether it was the wine, or him, or the hopefulness of their discussion, she let him kiss her eventually, let him lead her to the couch. He kept saying softly, "Are you back yet?" And she said, "Not yet. But I'm in the vicinity."

He kissed her again. "I'm in the neighborhood," she said.

All this confused her, because he was no longer familiar—his body was unfamiliar now. When he told her good night and held her against the cold, he did so with so much pure affection she felt wretched and deceitful, though toward whom she wasn't sure.

PART IV

THE DEEPEST GRAY

CHAPTER 35

That Sunday morning Harris Lambeau found himself in church, looking for answers. He was not a terribly religious man, but Harris believed in the holy spirit, and believed too that there might be dangers in staying away from God's house for too long, especially when you lived the sort of suspect life he'd been living. You needed a spiritual framework, he knew, even if you chose to stray from it.

He'd been talking about this lately to whoever would listen and he'd received a variety of responses, mostly curious: *You doing okay, Harris?*

He had the misfortune one night of tuning the TV onto *Night of the Living Dead*. Dozens of bloated corpses roaming about. He found himself dreaming of them a few nights later and at least two of the corpses had Dieter Parkhurst's pasty face.

During his sermon, Father Branagh asked everyone to stop and meditate on the mysteries of the life of Christ.

Live in union with him, he said.

Let him soothe you, let him bring you close to everyone and everything.

He said a lot of other things Harris listened to. How life wasn't what got handed to you, it was a matter of the choices you made. Listen when you make your choices.

After the sermon, Harris watched the parishioners leave the pews to take communion: the razor-nicked men, the powdery old ladies, the angel-faced teenage girls, the boys reluctantly dressed in collared shirts and neckties, hair oiled, hungry for reverence, and all of them puffed up with God afterward as if they'd just left a big buffet.

How easily they carried their untroubled souls, Harris thought. And he was still carrying that foul-smelling green trunk. Burying it hadn't afforded him peace. It was strange, wasn't it, because no one gave a shit about Parkhurst when he was alive. Harris certainly hadn't. Not at all. Not one bit.

The congregation inched forward. Harris took to his feet, but his legs wobbled beneath him. Bile rose in his throat. All the others in church were people who'd take care of their dead when the time came, who'd arrange a proper funeral. They wouldn't deny a proper good-bye to a dead person's family. They wouldn't lie bald-faced to every living thing, man, or dog.

Someone was watching him. Seeing right through him.

Harris left the line, then the church. His steps quickened to a light run. He had had no right to be there, he knew now.

When he got to his truck, he rattled through the glove compartment, under old tickets, coupons, and bills. He found the piece of paper on which he'd scribbled the phone number.

He folded it up again and put it in his wallet. He walked to the pay phone at the 7-Eleven down the street and closed himself into the booth. He took the number out, then dialed.

A woman answered on the third ring.

"Mrs. Parkhurst?"

"Mrs. Who?"

"I'm looking for Mrs. Parkhurst."

"Mrs. Parkhurst? There's no Mrs. Parkhurst here."

"I'm sorry. I have the wrong number."

"Wait. Are you a friend of Dieter's?"

"Sort of."

"Kathleen Cullen lives here. She's Dieter's mother. I'm a friend of Kathleen's."

"Can I speak to her?"

"You can speak to me."

"I'd really rather speak to her."

"She won't talk back."

"Why not?"

"Because she can't talk back. She can't talk. She's lost her speech. She can hear perfectly and she's smart as a whip. She can't talk, though. That's why I'm here. I'm her roommate and her voice, until mine gives out. Do you want to talk to her?"

This was too weird, Harris thought. How could he talk to someone who didn't talk back, how could he tell something like this to a silence, to a silent phone?

"That's okay . . ."

"I'm putting her on," the friend said.

He heard the phone being exchanged.

"She's on right now."

This was Parkhurst's mother, her ear was to the phone. But how could he be sure? Maybe this was a prank they were playing on him. A woman with no voice, just like a dead man.

"Mrs. Parkhurst . . . I mean, Mrs. Cullen." He heard breathing from her end.

He'd feared her reaction and now he feared none at all. He wanted to hang up, but he was in a new phase now. He was going to face things. It was his choice. It had to do with the baby.

There were reasons you took care of the dead, that you honored them, he thought. The soul needed a send-off. He would want it.

"Mrs. Cullen, Dieter had an accident at work," he said. "He was a good worker."

And then, seated in that booth, a block from church, Harris confessed.

HARRIS'S FRIEND CLAUDE CALLED around to cemeteries. Turned out Claude knew the son of a cemetery owner from when he worked at the morgue. They could bury Parkhurst, he said, although he wouldn't bury him in any army trunk. They would have to spring for a coffin.

"Even with a pile of bones?"

"It's a professional thing," he said.

It was also the right thing.

Mrs. Cullen would arrive from Albany Sunday on a Greyhound bus, and Sunday night they'd bury whatever was left of Dieter in the Horace Parker Memorial Cemetery.

"It's not a top-of-the-line cemetery," Claude said.

"That's all right," Harris said.

"In fact, it's kind of a bottom-of-the-line one. But it's the only one who'll do it for us."

Harris could only imagine what a bottom-of-the-line cemetery would be like. "At least we'll get him buried," Harris said.

"And at least it'll be at night."

They dug the trunk up around three-thirty Sunday morning, when Harris was sure Jack and Anne were asleep. Without speaking, they slid it into the back of the ancient hearse Claude had borrowed for the next two nights. When they got to Claude's house they'd move what was left of Parkhurst into a coffin.

He had done pretty well, Claude said, due to the coldness of the earth. "Just moldy, that's all. He'd have looked a lot better if you'd have let me embalm him like I said I would," Claude said as they drove across town.

As they left downtown they drove past a Lakeland ambulance, and for the briefest of moments Harris caught his mother's eye.

"Oh shit," he said.

She did a double take and nearly rammed the sidewalk.

CHAPTER 36

There were four women in their sixties leaving the Greyhound bus from Albany that night, and not one of them looked terribly much like Dieter Parkhurst. A woman with well-preserved skin and a violet suede hat walked off first.

"Mrs. Cullen," Harris said.

"Who?"

"Cullen."

"Calling? Who's calling?"

"Cullen," Harris said, "I'm sorry." And he headed after the short, squat woman with wispy white hair.

"Kathleen Cullen?" he said, but then a thin old man in a red plaid hunting jacket moved ahead of him and took the woman's bag from her.

"No Kathleen here," he said peremptorily, as if Harris had been selling drugs.

Of the last two coming out of the bus together, Harris chose the one who wasn't talking.

"So nice to meet you," the other woman said in parting. "Is this the young man who killed your son?"

UNDERSTANDABLY ENOUGH, MRS. CULLEN SAID nothing on the ride to the hotel, but she wrote several notes. She wrote in childlike capital letters. The first said, CAN YOU TAKE ME TO WHERE HE LIVED?

"Sure," Harris said. "But they moved his stuff out. There's someone else living there by now."

WAS IT A HOVEL?

Dieter kept it nice, Harris said.

HE WAS ALWAYS A SLOB.

"But a lovable one."

She passed him another note. DID YOU LOVE HIM?

"Guess not."

THE KIDS WERE ALWAYS MAKING FUN OF HIM, OR THEY WERE FRIGHTENED OF HIM.

"When was the last time you saw him?"

IN MAY IT'LL BE FIVE YEARS.

He dropped Mrs. Cullen at the Laker Hotel, still mildewy in anticipation of an overhaul in the spring, but at fifteen dollars a night a decent deal. There were signs in the hallways reminding you not to clean your fish in the rooms, but still there was a constant fishy stench. There were a dozen of these cheap hotels that served as residences for construction workers during the building of the power plants, and now they served as cheap temporary homes for visiting fishermen.

Harris waited downstairs while Parkhurst's mother cleaned up, changed her clothes. When she came downstairs she looked refreshed, but she also looked solemn. She didn't write any notes for a while.

"We need to wait until after eleven," Harris said finally.

ELEVEN?

"That's when we have to go. They're letting us in special."

WHY CAN'T WE GO IN THE DAY?

"They won't let us on account of me holding him for so long."

WILL I BE ABEL TO SEE HIM?

"You mean his face and all that?"

She nodded.

"It's like I said. Some time has elapsed. He's not gonna look like what he looked like."

HE HAD HIS FATHER'S LOOKS UNFORTUNITLY.

"I can see a little of him in you. In the eyes," Harris said.

WHY ARE YOU DOING ALL THIS?

"Taking care of him and all?"

She nodded.

"Don't really know."

Harris looked at her as she straightened her dress. She was a surprisingly normal-sized woman, considering her son's enormity; even a little small. Her hair was white, short, and curly, and he imagined someone calling her cute when she was a teenager, though she wasn't at all cute now, even for an old lady. She was hardened, and right now it looked as though a lot was on her mind.

The strangeness of the situation began to strike him. Here he was in the lobby of the Laker, with the mother of dead Dieter Parkhurst, waiting to bury his bones in a third-class cemetery.

"I would understand if you wanted to call the police. I mean, you could do it if you want."

THEY'D WANT TO SEE HIM.

"Yeah. It'd be a hassle. But I wouldn't try to stop you."

She sighed.

THANK YOU, HARRIS, she wrote.

CLAUDE WAS RIGHT about it being a bottom-of-the-line cemetery. Even at night you could see the turf was full of weeds and dead leaves, the shutters were falling off one of the crypts, a few of the markers had fallen down and were crumbling.

It took them a while to find the plot. It was dug that morning, Claude said. "You can't do things too far in advance in the winter or you wind up with a gravesite full of snow."

The grave had a mechanical device that lowered Parkhurst's coffin in. Harris was glad for the coffin. It was the right touch.

Mrs. Cullen watched it all, and then the queerest thing happened. She just started bawling—a woman without a voice. She made loud whimpering sounds, like nothing Harris had ever heard.

She knelt then next to the grave. She put her hands together and prayed. Harris didn't know what to do so he knelt next to her, hands at his side, scratching at the ground.

There was a message he should take from all this, he knew, but he didn't know what it was.

Eventually Claude tapped Harris's shoulder.

"I think it's best if we get out of here," he said. "With all due respect."

CHAPTER 37

Three weeks went by and Anne told Jack nothing about Turner, about the week he was away. They woke up at different hours, and usually didn't see or talk to each other until the evening. Sometimes they cooked dinner together, and then sat around in the living room reading, but mostly they went their separate ways, he to his study, she to anywhere else; two people living unconnected lives beneath the same broken roof.

One night he practiced a speech on her, and she showed him the sketches she'd made toward a new painting. They drank more of that case of wine (would they always need to?), made love, and it felt almost like it had during their first months here. Maybe it's like he said, she thought—all behind us. She wanted to believe it. But it wasn't. Sober, they were strangers again. At least he was to her the next morning. She strained to return his good-bye kiss.

Soon work piled up on him and he began to arrive home too late for dinner, which was fine with her really, although she was quite lonely and would have welcomed uncomplicated company. She had always thought of marriage as a culmination. The end of the doubts and misunderstandings, the end of gutting it though an awkward evening. Marriage was peace. Inner and outer, she'd thought—it was profound and transformative, and it meant the end of loneliness, of longing. It wasn't small talk. It wasn't hoping against hope that the other would just go to sleep at night, without needing anything from you.

WINTER HELD ON, UNREMITTING, and gray as wood smoke. It snowed often. More than she could ever have imagined. Snowplows made head-high mazes (like roofless tunnels) of the sidewalks. And of course the snow made her think of Turner. He was writing about snow still. She read his stories in the morning newspaper. There was usually something funny in them, a subtle joke, a double meaning. She imagined that they were for her. She remembered stories he told her about glaciers in Greenland. How some of the snow there remained unmelted for over two hundred thousand years.

She thought he might call, but he didn't, or that she'd run into him, but that didn't happen either. She kept anticipating him, imagining she saw him or heard his voice, so her days were a series of disappointments. She thought she saw him once on the street. She followed through those snow mazes for two blocks, but when finally she caught up, it wasn't him. It was someone who looked nothing like him.

HARRIS AND A FRIEND fixed the back door and insulated two large rooms so Anne could more comfortably paint. They Sheetrocked; a painful process, as far as she could see. Lots of ripping and hammering, the whine of the screw gun, and then plaster dust everywhere from the sanding.

In her new surroundings she painted a lot. She was funneling her desire for him into her work, into her painting. Transference of passion, she could tell him later.

You just forgot me, he would say.

But she hadn't. She thought of him too often.

ONE NIGHT SHE AND JACK went to dinner with the Hickeys. The Hickeys talked about marriage, theirs and Jack's. They told the story of how they got together, on a double date with a couple who argued the entire night. They'd decided to leave early and the Hickeys stayed out all night getting to know each other.

They danced the peppermint twist. They ended up on Sarah Hickey's porch swing drinking tall glasses of Miller High Life.

"When's the big day, anyhow?" Sarah Hickey asked.

"I'm sorry?" Anne said.

"Dum dum dee dah, dum dum dee dah."

Jack said sometime next summer.

"Do you need any help planning?" she asked. "I love weddings."

They were sitting at La Riviera—Bill Hickey's new favorite restaurant—and Anne tried to avoid the attention of the waitress, who had served her and Turner.

Sarah Hickey talked about the drive-in movie they went to on their second date, Bill Hickey finally taking her hand at the end. Then Jack told the story of meeting Anne.

He'd been doing that a lot, bringing up old times to stir up new ones.

She thought of Turner while they spoke. And she wondered where he was. With another woman? A young one perhaps, from the college, or someone else's wife. He had several new girlfriends. She imagined him taking someone's hand the way he'd taken hers, saying something clever. The Hickeys were waiting for her answer to a question.

She smiled, and that seemed to be enough.

"See," Sarah Hickey said. "She's in love."

AS SHE GOT READY FOR BED, she thought first of Turner, and then of her husband and all the things that irritated her about him: the way he kept his clothes organized, how he perfectly squeezed and rolled the toothpaste tube (not only after he used it but after she used it too), how he always cleaned his dishes moments after he finished with them, as if he feared raccoons would descend if he waited half an hour. How even his affection in bed had a predictable order, first a kiss on the neck, then the cheek, then the mouth, then his hand brushing her breast (the left breast first, with his right hand), then the other hand strolling up her right thigh, and around to her backside. None of this was bad in and of itself. It was only that she could predict it. Intentionally, she violated this need for order. She'd leave dishes out, magazines, her clothes sometimes. She was baiting him into a fight. But he wasn't taking the bait.

She had begun to long for New York, even. It started with a phone call from her sister, who complained about traffic, and about going to a snotty restaurant where she'd had to wait an hour for a table.

Anne found herself longing for that wait—waiting in line for a movie or a restaurant and seeing the other people there and enjoying knowing that you were one of them. So much better than going to anything here, one of those awful family-style restaurants, or really truly greasy-spoon diners where you might actually see grease on the spoon (she was being an awful snob, she knew).

Or seeing the only dismal movie in town, and worse, having to listen to everyone afterward remark on how clever it was and how they might see it again next week.

Or going to the community theater, or a little bluegrass show to see the Old Time Fiddlers, or smiling your way through another boring dinner with the Hickeys. She saw herself at fifty, playing bingo and watching daytime TV, and she felt something like panic seize her.

She longed for a night at a steamy basement dance club, or simply walking around the Village or through Central Park, or riding the subway on a spring day up to the Cloisters, or going to a real party, where there might be seven or eight people you wanted to meet and where you could talk about modernism and postmodernism, or Robert Ryman and Eva Hesse and Ellsworth Kelly, or even Andy Warhol or Georgia O'Keeffe, without everyone thinking you were a terrible snob, and you could dress up without everyone staring over at you thinking, Who does she think she is?

Where she could simply fit in again. She wanted to fit in. Turner had understood what she'd been feeling and he had allowed her to complain. But with Jack these were sore subjects. She wouldn't bring them up because he would take it personally. Later he'd agree with her. And then she'd have to hear him attack the provinciality of his own town (which always sounded uglier, she thought, from his mouth, always like self-loathing, always a little pathetic).

One night, before she turned in, she wrote a letter to Turner. She told him how she was painting now. How he'd gotten her to start again.

It fills hours, keeps me from thinking of you too much.
I like how I don't really know what will happen next.
It doesn't feel random, just surprising.
One day I painted the accident. I painted on a large canvas and I included everything, the deli behind, a kid staring blankly out the glass, the girl on the street—me. The man lying facedown. The cab and the cab driver. I wasn't emotional while I painted. I simply watched it evolve, and I liked it. It was sort of beautiful.
I'm not always so morbid. I paint a lot of other things. Sometimes I paint a sound or a smell. Painting calms me. Makes me feel whole, even purposeful. It's the one thing no one can take away from me.

Love,
Anne

Writing the letter allowed her to be with him. And not sending it allowed her to be with her husband.

SHE PAINTED MORE: cab wheels spinning at the center of an asphalt-colored canvas. Then an overview of halted traffic, a girl weaving her way through, faceless, a smudge here and there to suggest features. She varied paint quality and textures. Then she painted the hospital room. It wasn't actually a hospital room per se, no tubes, and no bedpans, it was just a white room with a bed and people looking over at a sleeping man, but she caught the temperature of the place, the mood. She filled the canvas, and she resisted liking it, tried to resist any judgment at all.

She wrote another letter. A short one.

I wonder what you look like. I mean I know. But I wonder if I've changed you in your absence into some sort of idealized creation. I've been known to do that.

Anne

p.s.

Been swimming at the YMCA pool. I started with eight or nine slow, graceless laps, and then each time I raised the number. Now I'm up to thirty, which I think is my limit.
I like how afterwards, I feel springy and strong.
I like how the air feels on my face when I walk to my car.
I keep thinking you'll sneak up on me. I keep hoping.

Maybe it was true, she thought. The idea of Turner was more powerful than the actuality of him. If she could see him again, sleep with him, she could bring him back down to earth.

That seemed the best and only way to close him out of her thoughts.

CHAPTER 38

Turner kept vigilant. He called everyone he could, from soil experts to groundwater scientists.

A group called the Citizens for a Safer Lakeland had begun calling him with questions and requests for stories. CSL, headed by John and Jeanette Cornfeller, was holding its meetings at the Cornfellers' house.

He talked to Robiolio, the reporter who'd covered the closing of the incinerator.

"Yeah. I wrote about it. Total fuckin' disaster. Supposed to solve everyone's problems. That's how we first described it. It was post–Love Canal. Dante Pavio saves the day, offers to take the waste at a cost, sends notices out to all the bigs: He's got state-of-the-art furnaces. They cook the waste and leave only a little white puff of smoke.

"So you got the companies sending their unmentionables. Barrels got stored on site, right? You know the rest. They can't maintain eighteen hundred degrees. They can't maintain twelve hundred. Black soot pours from the smokestacks onto the cars outside.

"They knew they were fucked early on. The thing is, they kept burning that stuff anyhow, and accepting more barrels, 'cause they liked the money. Took them too long to take their lumps. That's how they screwed themselves. By staying in operation."

Turner knew all this. He told him his theory about the harbor sites.

"You gotta do a couple things. Get yourself some aerial shots. You can get those from the geological survey. See if you can see anything interesting. I'll bet you do."

"Like what?"

"Tanks. Stockpiled barrels. Then see if you can track down the old site engineer. And there's another guy too you should talk to who'd be perfect."

"Who's that?"

"Pavio had a partner. Sunk a heap of cash into that business. I'm not sharp on the details, but they had a big falling out when it failed. Guy took a bath. I think his name was Hadfield. I bet he'd have a bunch to say about all this."

HE CALLED THE SITE ENGINEERS and arranged to see old aerial photographs from 1981 to 1989. He filed a freedom of information request for the incinerator barrels.

Donaldson, his contact at the EPA, said Stewart was right—dumping on the farms was hard to document. If they could show the harbor was used as a stopover point, or the city was involved, then everything changed. He'd left several messages for Dante Pavio and Harlan Stanyan, and hadn't received a call back. One of the messages on the machine at the office said, "You better watch how you cross the street, Turner."

A little melodramatic, he thought. Like an old Edward G. Robinson movie. Next they'd be threatening that he'd be sleeping with the fishes.

HE SPOKE TO NATURALISTS, to environmental scientists. He wanted to get the story right, to see if this was as big a deal as he thought.

"We don't know," the scientist, a man named Victor Green, said. "We know what they've done to those farms. But no one knows how long it'll take to clean them up, or what the effects will be.

"Here's what you might want to do. Get out there and take your own soil sample. Then send it in to the EPA. Say it's from your lawn and you have concerns."

Turner drove to the harbor sites and then to one of the farms. He took soil samples, making sure to wear plastic gloves and to use plastic, sterilized shovels provided by Victor Green, to avoid any possibility of contamination. And as suggested, he shipped them in clean prescription bottles to a lab.

He began to write an opinion piece on the arrogance of Lakeland, and of his old pal, Jack Lambeau.

> Incinerator largest of Lakeland's mistakes.
> Begun with so much promise.
> Not so much that the incinerator failed so much as that it continued to operate after it failed; owners refused to shorten losses, kept trying to make more money. Arrogance—failure to accept inevitable (like harbor?)— ability to ignore a problem—is Lakeland making similar mistake with harbor? Lambeau like Stanyan? Focusing on profits they may never see?
> The town will fracture. That's for sure.

He underlined this. He scattered other notes.

FINALLY HE PHONED the three men in the Lakeland telephone directory who were named Hadfield. The familiar bristly voice on the last answering machine startled him so that he hung up.

Of course, of course, he thought, and a jolt of excitement rushed through him. It was like piecing a damn puzzle, wasn't it?

ON HIS WAY HOME that night Turner thought about Lambeau. It had been a long time since they'd played basketball, or gone running, or met for lunch. They'd had one telephone conversation since Jack had returned from Chicago. He'd been wound up about all the new interest in the harbor, about Showalter, his new developer. While confident, he sounded a bit unnerved at the pace of his ascendancy, and seemed to want to talk it out with Turner, the way they would have months back.

They would have joked about it over beers and a game of darts, and Turner would have kidded him about selling out, half-kidded him really, and then Jack would have sought his advice as to where to stand his ground. But Turner had ended the conversation early, saying he had an interview he couldn't put off. *Tell someone who cares*, he'd muttered to himself.

Turner recognized that his disdain for Jack was a convenience he was affording himself, a hedge against guilt. If he disliked him (and he didn't yet) then he could convince himself Jack had all this coming to him. You couldn't have it both ways, couldn't obsess over a man's fiancée and at the same time remain his confidant.

HE NOTICED NOW a pickup truck that had been behind him for several blocks. Just going the same direction, he told himself. Don't be paranoid.

But when he made a left turn, the truck made a left. After two blocks he made a right, and the truck followed. He picked up his speed slightly, then noticeably. The truck kept pace. Turner stopped at a light and the truck pulled up behind.

Go away, Turner whispered, but it didn't.

Turner saw the driver's door open and he got a bad feeling. He stepped on the gas and rushed through the still-red light. He sped down the road, hoping a cop might stop him, but there were no cars out. He was going fifty now, far too fast with a road this slick. But he wanted to put some space between his car and whoever this was who was making him nervous, wanted to get home and into a hot bath. Soon he saw the lights of the truck again. In his mind's eye he saw this ending badly, his body limp and bloody against the steering wheel. The truck pushed closer, flashing its high beams. The driver leaned out his window, motioning Turner to pull off the road.

The truck accelerated and pulled closer again, then crossed over to Turner's side, threatening the oncoming lane. The driver yelled at him, "Pull the fuck over!"

Turner drove faster. The truck kept pace.

"Pull over, asswipe! I want to talk to you!"

But Turner ignored him.

Asswipe? An unappealing thing to be, he thought, nearly amused, but then a car emerged from the other direction, fifty yards from the truck and headed straight for it. Turner's limbs tightened, and he bit hard into the inside of his cheek. Horns blared. Slush flew. His teeth broke flesh and he drove straight ahead, both hands on the wheel. The words passed his lips: *This is it.* A yard before a horrendous crash, the truck skidded into the thick brush off the side of the road. The other car stopped. Turner saw the scene in his rearview mirror. No explosions, screams, or metal crunching. But it was no place to be. Turner hightailed; he drove like a crazy man, would keep on driving until he reached home. His shirt was damp with sweat. His head roared and his mouth tasted of blood. He was laughing nervously, or maybe he was crying. They had nearly killed him, and someone else. And they'd be back, he knew. How awful, he thought, but then he thought, How fucking amazing.

He drove on edge all the way home, playing the near collision over in his mind, and feeling, absurdly, like an action hero, albeit an ill-groomed and unmuscular one. It occurred to him there were people out there, like this truck driver, who hated him, and who would stop at little to keep him from doing his job. They likely wanted to scare him more than anything, but he wouldn't scare; not now. He had a big one going, a prize salmon at the end of his line, and he would reel it on in. He considered driving by the police station, but he realized then that he didn't trust the police. He didn't trust the town right now. He had opened wounds, touched a nerve. It was an improbable position for an unsung and formerly indistinct Brooklyn boy to find himself in. The center of a movie plot with high-speed chases and anonymous voices on the phone. But here he was.

WHEN HE GOT TO HIS APARTMENT, he saw someone, a woman in a gray overcoat, leaving a note on his door. When she turned to leave, he saw it was Anne. Out in front of his apartment house at ten-thirty at night. He wouldn't hope for anything.

"He's not home," Turner said. "He left for Europe, didn't you hear? Rome. Our man at the Vatican."

"Tell him I stopped by, then."

"What are you doing here?"

"I want to stop thinking about you," she said, "and this was the only way I knew to do that."

"All right. You want to stop thinking about me inside my apartment?"

She nodded.

He let her in. The conflux of emotions nearly overwhelmed him, but he wanted to be here with her and leave everything else behind. He was relieved that his place was somewhat clean. He hadn't been around enough to make a mess.

"So you didn't forget me then," he said.

She looked everywhere in the room except at him. "What do you think?"

"I don't know what to think, Anne. I'm not sure I know what it is you want from me."

She stood fidgeting.

"Have a seat," he said.

"I want you to vanish," she said.

"Okay." He made a magician's disappearing motion. Then he shrugged.

They stood looking at each other. He wanted her more than he could stand.

"I want you to kiss me," she said.

It was like being offered a meal after a month without food. Your body needed it but you couldn't take too much too fast.

"Okay," he said. He kissed her.

"Can we go to your room?" she said once their lips had parted.

"Yes, Anne. But then can we talk a little?"

"I don't want to talk. Please don't make me talk."

"I won't make you do anything," he said and he led her to his moonlit room.

CHAPTER 39

Harbor fever was everywhere. Posters and placards in the windowsills: HARBORTOWN—CATCH THE SPIRIT. Aqua-and-yellow bunting fell across wires and from street lamps along the main streets. All told there would be fifteen new restaurants along the water and a dozen new shops. Every day something else was being built, or rebuilt and redecorated. Existing businesses were primping feverishly, altering their personalities to fit the new scheme. There was music in the streets and everyone wanted in on the festivities. The key was to have something going on every evening and on the weekends, activity, people moving through, and it seemed to Jack as though they were dressing and carrying themselves better. Each night the Syracuse news stations ran another update, which brought small crowds around the tavern TVs ("It's like they're watching the playoffs"). The sermons in the churches spoke of the harbor coming as "a time of great change." Clergymen asked people to think ahead to what they'd want for themselves and their families. They urged people to hold on to their values, which enticingly implied there might be a challenge to them.

On Jack's recommendation the city had signed on with Shep Showalter, who had promptly set up an office in town and got down to business.

For all his negative preconceptions about developers, it didn't take long for Jack to see the advantages of working with a mind like Showalter's. The man simply knew how to get things done. He had more connections, and knew better how to get sites ready for building, how to secure the larger, anchor tenants (Subsidize them, he said. They're like movie stars at a nightclub. You gonna make Bruce Willis pay for a drink?), and how to cut the right deals with contractors and subcontractors. How to shave design costs and pull strings. He would cover the costs for the sprinkler systems and the seismic improvements, with plenty left over to put toward the debt-service coverage.

It was impressive to see this kind of muscle at work. He was close to getting the whole project financed. He was making them look good. He was large and well capitalized, and he had staying power.

Showalter said he didn't need the credit. He only wanted to make sure it all happened. He would offer his ideas, but it would always be Jack who made the final decisions, and who took center stage.

"You can't buy the sort of excitement you've raised here," Showalter said. "But I'll be damned if I'm not going to try and stir up a little more."

For sure there were differences in their visions. Showalter wanted to keep away from the harborfront businesses he called marginal, ones like secondhand bookstores, pawn shops, and hardware stores (Jack wanted some of them). Shade trees and planter boxes (which Jack loved), he said, could block a passerby's view of a shop window. Victorian street lamps and expensive paving stones were a waste; all they did was draw attention away from the storefronts, he said.

Jack would disagree, and Showalter would answer politely, "I'm just giving you the businessman's perspective, right? You're the artist."

Benches and tables attracted loiterers and teenagers, he said. "Got to make sure there's a business behind them. A café owner to keep it classy."

You had to make some concessions to profits, he said. You couldn't build as either an act of art or an act of philanthropy. It simply never worked.

There would be some familiar names among the stores, a Pottery Barn, perhaps, and Saks, but no Gap or Guess Jeans, and there'd be an equal number of independent stores. The theme would be a living, breathing harborfront, with fresh food, good restaurants, and an exciting nightlife.

ALONG WITH IMPROVING THE LOOK of the town, Showalter urged them to spend equal time and money improving Lakeland's marketing.

He sat Jack and Hickey down in his office to go over the old pamphlets and posters put out by the Lakeland Chamber of Commerce.

"Beyond dismal," he said, and they were, yellowed photographs from the fifties of someone in a baseball cap tossing a softball to his daughter on a field, another of a blown-dry couple standing waist-deep in a kidney-shaped swimming pool at the city rec center.

"This is what you send out if you want to keep people away. Now look at this."

He showed him the marketing material his team had done for a river town in Louisiana.

There were stylish-looking couples holding hands as they stepped out of a nightclub, glossy pictures of men and women swimming and tanning, and others having intense conversations over salads at a cozy café. Everyone seemed fit and stylish, effortlessly so. There was a variety of ethnicities, and the subjects didn't all look like models. They looked like people you'd want at your next dinner party. Balancing these shots of bourgeois bliss were others of fishermen, chefs, craftsmen, and street musicians at a waterside gathering, and potbellied merchants peddling seafood and fresh produce at an outdoor stand.

It then dawned on Jack that some of the pictures were of people he recognized, and had been taken in Lakeland.

"I brought a pair of photographers up from New York. Told them I'd feed them and house them, and they could have a boat each day to take out and go salmon fishing on the Great Lakes."

"That's all it took?"

"I paid them too. But they came for the free fishing." He raised his eyebrows at the mayor.

"You need to think of Lakeland as a brand," he said, as though uttering unalloyed wisdom. "That's what all the forward-thinking towns and cities are doing. They're figuring out who they want to go after, and who it is they're competing with. They're tailoring their image.

"We're not after the NASCAR crowd—though naturally they're welcome. The couple we want is the one that shared a house with some friends in the Hamptons and found it fake and irritating, who want to go to the theater, play tennis, hike, and maybe pick wildflowers or apples in the fall. We'll do a big push in the fall about seeing the colors in the trees. A summer home in Lakeland should be part of your identity. Not just the red-barn look, but stone walls in the style of Tuscany or the Alps. We want people to feel they're getting in on the ground floor of the next new thing. Classic Great Lakes port towns. 'Live in a century-old farmhouse or a six-bedroom Victorian, see some theater, know your neighbors.'"

Within a week Showalter's design consultant, with Jack's help, had built a preliminary version of the Lakeland Web site, and Jack had to admit it was impressive.

Click on one link and you saw historical photographs of the port, packed with schooners and old fishing vessels. Click on another and you saw photos of the most beautiful farmhouses; click on a third, and you saw those stylized pictures of the crowded vegetable bins at the Lake Street Marketplace, and others of ruddy fisherman holding up or deboning prize-winning fish.

There were links to the charter boats, the shopping districts, and the town beach. A cruise boat where couples could dance and dine in style. There were links with information on mountain biking, water skiing, and wind surfing.

The press on all this was unvaryingly positive, including editorials from area papers that could just as well have been advertisements. But with all the hullabaloo, all the good news, Jack was still a bit uneasy. Partially because of the sheer momentum of all this, and partially because of Showalter's tendency to make ungenerous remarks about people he saw around, anyone who was a little overweight or wore ill-matching or outdated clothes. "Clear 'em out, Jack," he'd say, partly joking but mostly not. More than once he'd said things about people Jack knew (an old mill friend of Jack's father, and his wife). And the worst part about it was that Jack had had similar thoughts when he'd seen them; he'd simply had the sense to know how ugly they'd sound when spoken aloud.

DURING THESE WEEKS, he and Anne had been seeing each other sparingly, little more than an occasional dinner, breakfast, or late glass of wine. For a while he thought she understood the sort of pressures he was under, and that was why she hadn't been asking more of him, or insisting he stay up late talking as they used to do. She let him sleep, work, whatever he wanted to do. She'd say things like, "If you feel like working tonight, don't let me get in the way." She'd been cheerful and productive in her newly insulated studio. Sometimes she took drives into town and didn't come back for hours. She was swimming, as he'd suggested, and taking a yoga class. She loved it, she said. She'd met some nice people, some hippie types. He'd never told her there were hippies in Lakeland, she said, even though he had.

She was getting out of the house, which he'd said was important for her to do. When she was home she was painting. But she never showed him anything, never spoke of it, so who really knew?

There was a thin line, he recognized, between their respecting each other's needs to work and sleep, and their simply not needing each other. If it didn't matter when he got home at night, or what they'd done away from each other, what did matter?

He thought then, She's finding her independence, and she's happier. Wasn't that what you wanted?

CHAPTER 40

"April is the worst," Marla told Anne. "It's so much worse to get some nice days and then have it be awful all over again. It'll be nice and sunny and I still can't enjoy it."

"Because it can turn on you."

"Yes. And then you're snowed inside your house for a week."

The two young women had run into each other at the drugstore, and now they were walking together. Charlotte was bundled in pink and blue and seemed quite happy with the walk, with her life.

Marla talked about what good company Charlotte was, and she didn't say whether or not Harris was helping her out.

"I guess it's all pretty exhausting," Anne said.

"I'll get her back someday. You know, she'll be twenty-one and off in college somewhere, and I'll call her at three in the morning like she wakes me up now."

Anne laughed. "Yes, and you can say, I'm hungry, damn it. Can't you do something about it?" She pictured Charlotte in a poster-filled dorm room answering the phone, maybe a boyfriend asleep next to her. She wondered if Marla had taken any college classes, if she'd ever dreamed of getting out of here.

"Can I ask you something?" Marla said.

"Sure."

"How come you don't wear a ring?"

She allowed the question to take on too many dimensions, then she said, "A lot of people don't."

"Really?"

"Yes. How come you keep wearing yours?"

It was a testy response and she regretted making it.

"We're not split, you know."

"But you kicked him out."

"I'm sorry. I just thought it was kind of funny, not wearing a ring, and not having a date yet to get married, that's all."

"It is funny."

"He didn't give you a ring?"

"He did."

"And you just don't want to wear it."

"One of the stones fell out. It's being repaired."

"I bet it's beautiful. Anything you two would have would be beautiful, I bet. Sometimes I think of you two, and I try to imagine what it would be like if we were like you."

Anne looked again at the baby.

"It'd be terrible. You wouldn't have Charlotte."

"No. I guess you're right. Hmm."

They kept walking for a few more blocks. Anne thought of Turner and wondered if at that moment he was thinking of her. She hoped he was. She hoped she was making it difficult for him to work.

"How's your painting been going?"

"It's going all right now. Thanks for asking."

"Hey," Marla said, "I just had an idea. Would you like to paint us sometime? You could come by and I could make you lunch, and afterward if you wanted you could paint us."

As Anne thought about it she liked the idea. She saw how she might do it. Mother and daughter in winter. Defiant. Uncute. Marla had a pretty face. Anne could see why boys had lined up outside the movie-house ticket window.

"She'd be a good model. She can sleep an hour in my arms, easy."

"Sure," Anne said. "I'd love to."

SHE WROTE TO TURNER:

I am trying hard not to think of you. To paint.
But I'm feeling manic since the other night.
Wound up with this strange energy.
I am not myself, or maybe I'm more.
I can't really tell yet.
How did I get home? And why?
I am turning into my mother, of course.

She crossed out the last line.

Love,
Anne

CHAPTER 41

Stewart got sick. Stomach flu of some kind, so Turner was covering the common council meeting for him Monday. He arrived behind a group from the merchant's association, five minutes before the start. They were all wearing Harbortown T-shirts, one with a picture of a wave, which read: LAKELAND—WE'RE ABOUT TO MAKE A SPLASH!

Since the sleet storm, Turner had been watching his back, changing lanes and streets when he drove. Once he thought he'd seen the man from the truck only to find out it was someone he knew, the bearded, slightly brain-dead clerk from the 7-Eleven. The more time passed the more the whole evening seemed unreal—the chase, and then Anne staying over; and he wondered if he might have imagined it all, or simply made more of it than he should have.

The turnout at City Hall was inspiring. A year ago there were twenty people at a typical meeting. Now close to three hundred had crowded in. The ones not wearing T-shirts had dressed upscale—because of the television coverage, Turner guessed. Shep Showalter had hired a public relations firm to spread the word about Lakeland, and it was clear they'd done their job well.

Turner noticed a few new faces with reporter's pads, two guys in their midthirties and a woman around his age with a cool spiky haircut.

He sidled over to the woman.

"You covering this thing too?" he said.

"Yes," she said.

"For who?" he asked.

"*The Village Voice.*"

"Hunh. And the other guys?"

"One's from the *Times* and the other—you're going to laugh," she said.

"I doubt it."

"He's from *People*. He's doing a feature on the fishing mayor."

Turner laughed. He tried to picture it, Hickey sandwiched between Elton John and an Oprah weight-loss story.

The waterfront looked entirely different now. They'd finished the wooden esplanade and cleared out the old warehouses. There were a few new restaurants and bars, a couple new shops, and with the grain elevators and all that debris out of the way there were decent views of the lake from everywhere. It was a nice little story. But it was a town of eighteen thousand. Towns of eighteen thousand didn't get visits from *People* magazine.

The *Village Voice* woman told him how they'd been wanting a good upstate story, how she'd grown up in Poughkeepsie and had been thinking lately it might be nice to move back, and Turner stopped listening because he saw Jack Lambeau and Anne walk toward the doorway of the meeting room.

"Be still," he said softly to himself.

"Excuse me?" said the woman.

TURNER TOOK EVERYTHING IN. Presentations from the developers, what amounted to a pep talk from Marcia Causwell of the chamber of commerce, and then, of course, the Bill Hickey Show.

No amount of success could make Bill Hickey's speeches anything other than overblown nonsense, Turner thought. The mayor was dressed in his Kelly blazer and navy pants, and Turner marveled at how public opinion had turned in his favor. How after all the foolish decisions and feeble attempts at apologies this man had evidently made over the years, people seemed now to love him.

"Until now it's been a tale of two states," he said. "Downstate the market keeps climbing, apartment prices are soaring, everyone's cashing in, and up here home prices are falling through the bottom. Well, all that's about to change—it's going to change in a big way.

"People outside the county, outside upstate New York, want to know if it can be done," he said at the end of his spiel. "They want to know if the best designers, architects, and planners can save a dying town, and do it here in the industrial northeast, not in Florida or California or any warm place. It's the question of the late twentieth century."

He said the financial world of Wall Street was paying attention now. Hypo Bank from Germany, the Bank of Tokyo, and Goldman Sachs's municipal bond department.

"Ever hear of Goldman Sachs? Not the sort of guys to bounce a check." The gallery laughed. "We're getting a little buzz," Hickey said.

There was talk of building an old-style brick baseball stadium along the lines (though a third the size) of Camden Yards in Baltimore. What was better for the classic small-town image than a good ballpark?

"I know what you're still thinking. You're thinking, Here we go again. Even with all that's happened, you're keeping your doubts. How can we do this, Captain Mayor, you're thinking, when we lost twenty-three businesses in ten years' time? When we've got welfare lines going 'round the block? My simple answer to you is, That's what *was*."

He let the words sink in.

"It's not what *was*. It's what you want. What sort of town do you *want*?"

The crowd stood and cheered.

Hickey went about the hallway and stairwell reminding people about the ABC report on Lakeland that would air on Thursday.

The *People* guy asked him a few questions, then laughed loud and patronizingly at something Hickey said, and replied, "I love it. I love it."

Now Anne was walking in Turner's direction, but she didn't stop when she reached him, nor did she even look at him.

She slipped a piece of paper into his jacket pocket.

The meeting began again. Turner headed inside with everyone else, took his seat, telling himself she wasn't his priority here. He had a job to do.

He read the piece of paper. It said only:

The first-floor conference room.
I'll leave first.

As the meeting progressed she did not once look over.

Then, during a presentation by a citizen's committee, she left the room. Turner waited a moment, thinking he should stay and take notes, then followed, leaving his bag and jacket so it would look like he'd escaped to call an editor.

He stepped quickly down the marble stairs, his blood jumping. He tripped and nearly fell at the second-floor landing. He didn't remember where the conference room was, nor for that matter could he fathom how Anne might know. On the first floor he saw a door close. He walked over and opened it, then traveled the unlit corridor. What the hell am I doing? he wondered. He tried the three doorways at the end of the hallway. One opened, and there she was. In the dark, waiting. He saw her outline against the night-lit window.

"Anne?" he said.

"Yes."

"This is crazy. There are people upstairs."

"I wanted to kiss you."

"Let's go back upstairs," he said.

He heard a door opening then, and he pulled her into some kind of large supply closet. He heard chairs being arranged in the room, the windows closed. Then he heard steps leave the room.

He could feel her breath, her warmth. He felt light-headed, drunk. He might soon hallucinate or pass out. Her hands slid under his shirt across his ribs. He found her lips, and then they lowered themselves to the floor. It was crazy is what it was, like careening down a hill without brakes and with a blindfold on.

CHAPTER 42

"There was a lawyer here looking for you, Harris," Bazorcik said.

Harris was just waking up on the lumpy foldout couch.

"He's talking about you digging up bodies and barrels. I told him that was crazy. That I never heard anything about that. He somehow got a few of the other guys' names and addresses."

"A lawyer? Whose lawyer?"

"He's from Gloversville. His client's some lady who was here burying her son with you? I thought we already buried Parkhurst."

"We did."

"What'd you do, dig him up all over again?"

Harris said nothing.

"You're nuts. You're absolutely fucking nuts."

"It was the right thing."

"Well, it wasn't all that right, I guess, because she's suing now. She's gonna sue Harlan. And he's gonna be awful mad then, Harris. I don't even want to see that."

HARRIS GOT THE LETTER from Mrs. Cullen the next day.

The afternoon she'd returned to her home in Gloversville, she had found herself flipping through old photo albums, she wrote, and missing her youngest son. And from missing her son it wasn't a long leap toward being angry about what those people had done to him.

She appreciated their picking her up at the bus station and taking her to the cemetery. However, it wasn't enough.

It wasn't, was it? thought Harris.

At the heart of the letter she wrote:

WHAT I HAVE COME TO IS THAT MY SON SHOULD BE ALIVE STILL. HE'S BEEN TAKEN ADVANTAGE. AND THEN DISREGARDED. AND WHAT A HORRIBAL WAY TO DIE. MY OWN FLESH AND BLOOD. THE BOY I CARRIED ABOUT AND TOOK FIFTEEN HOURS TO BIRTH, DROPPING DEAD LIKE THAT BEFORE THE AGE OF 45, BEFORE TAKING A WIFE AND GIVING ME A GRAND-CHILD. I FOUND A PICTURE OF ME PREGNANT WITH DIETER AND WITH MY OTHER SON, ANTHONY, WHO IS NOW A PARK RANGER IN CALIFORNIA—

I TOLD THE WHOLE STORY TO MY ROOMMATE AND FRIEND DOROTHY CIURCAK WHO ASSURED ME I WAS RIGHT TO BE UPSET. SHE SAID THERE IS A LAW SUIT TO BE HAD HERE. THAT I SHOULD CALL A LAWYER.

I LET THAT PLAN SET IN MY MIND OVERNIGHT. IT WOULD MEAN I KNOW AN INVESTMENT OF MY TIME AND HEART. I HAVE BEEN FEELING EMPTY SINCE THAT NIGHT. DIETER WASN'T MUCH OF A SON, I KNOW, BUT HE WAS MINE.

WHEN I WOKE THE OTHER MORNING, I DECIDED TO DO THIS.

The letter then went on at length about discussions with Dorothy and then with the lawyer. Evidently, Dorothy had called a local lawyer, Glen Stapleton, who was a friend of her sister, and had handled her brother-in-law's father's estate.

Mrs. Cullen had not wanted to reveal the location of the body, but in order for the lawsuit to have a chance, she would have to, her lawyer advised. And she would have to tell them who had helped with the burial.

I NEED YOU IN ORDER TO HAVE A CASE, HARRIS.
THIS LAWYER SAID "YOU CAN'T JUST SAY, MY SON
IS DEAD. YOU NEED THAT BODY. AND YOU NEED
THE TESTIMONY OF THOSE MEN."
SO I NEED YOU, HARRIS. WILL YOU HELP?

SINCERELY,
KATHLEEN CULLEN

P.S. I AM SORRY TO BE MAKING MORE OF A MESS. I
APRECIATE ALL YOU DID FOR ME, HARRIS. I HOPE
YOU CAN SEE THAT I COULDN'T JUST LEAVE IT
LIKE THAT. TRY AND IMAGINE ITS YOUR CHILD
AND HOW YOU WOULD REACT.
YOU WILL BE ASKED QUESTIONS BY MR.
STAPLETON. I HAVE TOLD HIM HOW YOU HELPED
ME. HOW YOU DIDN'T HAVE TO, AND HOW YOU
ARE A GOOD MAN ALL IN ALL.

"THE MAIN QUESTION," Mrs. Cullen's lawyer was telling Harris, "is whether you all were adequately assessed of the dangers."

"Well, we knew it was illegal. And we knew it wasn't all that good for you."

"On the other hand you had a boss paying you money to do this."

"Yes."

"And you believed you were doing right by the Lakeland harbor."

"Yes."

"And by your brother, Jack."

"Yes." He realized he said the wrong thing. "What are you getting me to say?"

"Only that you had no idea of the risks involved in the work you were asked to do."

"You're trying to get me to say more than that. Jack didn't know anything about this."

"But he let you bury my client's son in his backyard."

"Who told you that?"

"A Mr. Terry Miller, I believe."

"Jack never let me do anything. I lied to him."

He wrote that down in his notes. "Your dog," he said.

"Quit writing."

"This is my job, Mr. Lambeau."

"I think I'll get my own lawyer."

"Be my guest. As it stands now you'll be named in the lawsuit. You will have to testify."

"I got nothing to hide."

"That sounds like a fairly naïve mindset."

"Just leave my brother out of this."

"I frankly don't know whether your brother's involved or not. This is what we will try to do—provided, of course, that you cooperate. We will try and put you in the same category as my client's son. We'll say you were unwitting participants, that you did not know the extent of the risks you were asked to take."

"And what about all the carrying and dumping?"

"We'll say you were under orders. And that then you tried to do right by Mrs. Cullen. We'll say you didn't know any better."

"Stupid rather than criminal."

"Those are certainly not my words."

"No, but you thought them, didn't you?"

Stapleton leaned across the table.

"I will admit freely that I am operating on my client's behalf first and foremost. If that seems unfair, then by all means seek your own representation. This is a serious matter."

"All right," Harris said. "There's another thing."

"What's that."

"My baby girl's got some growth problems."

"How's that?"

"Slow development. Low blood counts. The doctor said Marla might have been exposed to chemicals. He asked her what kind of work her husband did, and did she wash his clothes for him."

CHAPTER 43

It was fair to say that Walter Hadfield wasn't thrilled that Turner had uncovered his identity. He hung up on Turner and then wouldn't answer his phone. He finally called Turner himself.

"I call you, on my terms, okay? Never the other way around."

"Got it," Turner said.

"And you keep my name out of the paper."

"I will."

"If you do, I'll help you. If you don't, I will rearrange your facial features."

"And we don't want that."

"No, you don't."

Turner talked a bit more, reestablishing Hadfield's trust. "All right then, Scooper. Here's what you do," Hadfield said. He told Turner to do a search on the manifest records, the paper trail that companies had to keep regarding the waste they accepted.

"Check the numbers, Turner. Somewhere along the line they're not going to match up."

A LAWYER BY THE NAME OF GLEN STAPLETON put a call in to Turner that Thursday. He wanted to know the status of Turner's investigations, and if the state had conducted tests.

"What's your angle on this?" Turner asked.

"I can't tell you right now, but I might have something for you very soon."

"Can you give me the gist?"

"Yes. And you'll tell me what you have."

"Fair enough," Turner said.

"I've got a dead young man who was paid to drop that sludge," Glen Stapleton said.

The dead man, Turner learned, was an overweight loner by the name of Dieter Parkhurst. No kids or wife, few friends. The mother, interestingly enough, was dumb but not deaf. Dumb from birth.

The voice of outrage had been made by a silent woman.

TURNER CALLED CLARK.

"Oh, this is good, Turner. This is really good stuff. And they tried covering up the death? Perfect."

He asked Turner if he could try and get some of the others who dumped barrels to talk.

"Let's get a profile on him. Make him a symbol for the town that can't right itself. A town that'd risk health and welfare for a few more bucks."

"Maybe he was just a lonely old guy with a lot of bad breaks."

"That's half of Lakeland, isn't it?" Clark said.

With Hadfield's help he dug up more about Dante Pavio: Pavio, it seemed, had never sent those barrels to Buffalo as everyone thought, had never taken his lumps as he claimed, had never ceased accepting waste. The amounts were higher than anyone knew. Almost two million gallons of liquid chemicals. Enough to fill 150 backyard swimming pools, and it was still going on. A few years back he and a dozen men had indiscriminately dumped barrels of toxic waste throughout the town into ravines and creeks, into the lake and on farms, into sinkholes and lagoons. Pavio had compensated the farmers, but not enough for the sort of damage they were doing. No one knew the extent. Perhaps Pavio hadn't even known. The city bore some of the blame. They took too long acknowledging the situation, because they hadn't wanted to accept the fact that their maverick, entrepreneurial success had been a massive and environmentally criminal failure. They let Pavio bury whatever he needed to bury at a minimal fee, which Hickey had collected—maybe as a kickback.

It had paid for his first home, a retirement fund, two trips he took to the Virgin Islands, and his boat.

The last part was conjecture on the part of a few city employees who wouldn't go on the record. But when Turner investigated Hickey's financial records, the conjecture seemed accurate.

Not that kickbacks were anything new. Hell, the former mayor of Syracuse had rotted away in prison because of kickbacks, a sixteen-year policy. Caribbean bank accounts and the like. Now Harlan Stanyan and the city DPW had gotten involved.

Dumping all those chemicals had repercussions. He would be drinking bottled water from now on. The worst would happen when the sun came out. The barrels would thaw. Gases would explode, one of the scientists told him.

"It'll be nasty. You can't just leave rusting barrels out in nature like that."

WHEN HE CALLED STANYAN, he got Stanyan's young son on the phone. He told him he had to speak to his daddy about work.

His son yelled that it was someone who worked with him.

When he got Stanyan he asked him again about what had happened with all the barrels. He asked Stanyan if any of his men had turned up missing, or had sickened on the job.

"You accusing me of something here?" he asked.

"I'm just asking questions."

"You keep it up and we'll be talking about a slander-libel-type of situation."

"I'm only going on what my sources tell me."

"Yeah. I got a hunch who your source is, Turner. And I think that one's gonna dry up soon."

"I'm trying to give you a chance to set the record straight here," Turner said.

"Listen. You get *this* record straight. Leave me the fuck alone. Go write your stories on the ice-carving festival or the potholes, or whatever it is you fish-wrap hacks do, and leave alone the Watergate reporting, okay? We're a little town here, Turner. Going about our business, and trying to survive. Don't go saving what isn't asking to be saved," he said.

"Thanks for the advice."

"Oh, and Turner."

"Yes."

"Next time you talk to my boy, tell him who you are. I want him to get the habit of hanging up on wormy little shitbags."

TURNER WENT BY THE TRAILER PARK where DMV records showed Dieter Parkhurst had lived. He had just up and left one day, the trailer park manager said. He'd owed two months' rent.

"But that's not all that unusual. We get a lot of deadbeats. Not much money to be had in this town lately."

"Did you report him missing?"

"No. Just kept his deposit. I'd ask for a bigger deposit, but no one would take the place then. Not much demand right now. There might be more soon what with the construction and all. Had 'em all filled up when they built the nuke plants; had to turn folks away all the time. That's when the boss bought all those extra trailers. We were doing pretty damn good back then. Everyone was. Not now, though. Shitty market now."

"So you just threw his stuff out."

"Nothing in there worth anything. You want his TV? I got it in my kid's room. My kid's been watching too much of it."

"PEOPLE ARE GETTING ANTSY," Stewart said. "They know you got something big. They feel it. All over town they're bracing for the fallout."

"I know."

"You got the mayor in this. You got one of the mayor's best friends, Stanyan. You got some other city officials. This is big stuff. A lot of subpoenas coming, huh?"

"I'd say yes."

"Too bad they filled Rathaman's beat."

"What? With whom?"

"With Rathaman."

"He's back?"

"Got canned his third week on the job down in Florida."

"For what?"

"Sexual harassment. An intern said he touched her boob—at least that's what's going around the newsroom. He calls Digby, crying he's innocent—he's got a wife and kid and all that. So Digby takes him back. No more opening."

Turner was ticked. He had been counting on the northern suburbs opening. Clark had as much as promised it to him.

He tried to focus on pulling his notes together, but the truth remained: Rathaman was back, and there'd be no promotion. He would push on. He'd get some good clips and one way or the other he'd get out of here, and maybe he'd take Anne along with him.

"Ever find out who it was tried to pull you off the road?" Stewart asked.

"No."

"Exciting, huh? I mean, your professional and romantic life heating up at the same time."

"Who said that?"

Stewart held up a small silver hoop.

"Left your earring in here last night," Stewart said.

Turner didn't answer.

"And right here in the office? Jesus, Turner. We don't even have shades."

SINCE THE NIGHT THEY'D LEFT the meeting together, Turner and Anne had been making more of a habit of seeing each other. Anne would call when she saw she could get away and they'd meet somewhere and often wind up back at the office if it was empty, or at Turner's apartment. Even when Turner was sifting through documents or chasing leads around town, he couldn't pass an hour without thinking of her. Anne seemed fairly lighthearted for someone in her shoes, though Turner considered it might have to do with how well her painting was going. He could see it in the streaks on her skin, and he felt it in her need to explore and study, and sketch on a stray sheet of paper, the beautifully sad places—crumbling churches, abandoned Victorians—they passed on their walks. Anne was nearly manic some nights, her words racing, and Turner found that his own excitement, while just as real, was at a slightly lower pitch. Still, he liked seeing how different she was from the woman he'd pulled from that freezing house. He'd had a role in her transformation (it was no less than that); and that helped erase the guilt he might have felt for stealing her from Jack. He found it dispiriting still to watch her leave his bed and get dressed again a half hour after they'd made love, and to hear her mutter something about how insane it was they were doing this; but he found it less so lately because he'd begun to think it wouldn't always be this way, that soon they would be together, and for a long while. This was all new territory for him, not simply with Anne, but with anyone.

In his last years in New York, Turner had perfected the mode of detached indifference. At first it was only a pose, and then it became who he was. Something had died in him around the time of his twenty-sixth birthday. He had found himself inhabiting a person with no real interests. He'd done the right things, read the right books, lived in the right neighborhood, but he'd find himself at the end of evenings bored with his company, critical of everything. He'd kept his attachments limited because he feared seeping into them, that as soon as he gave of himself he'd give up his options. As long as he kept moving, kept his possessions to a minimum, then anything could be his. He felt as though he was holding out for something, but he didn't know what it was; he simply had the sense that he'd know it when he saw it, and then his life would begin—that would be that. And then he'd exiled himself here in Lakeland, and he'd begun to think, maybe this is it, maybe it won't get any better.

He became the jack-of-small-trades. Arcane subjects, pinball. He read voluminously, in part because he liked the company of a great mind; but then he worried he was wasting whatever brain space he had of his own.

He'd had girlfriends in New York, but he'd always reduced them to one or two irredeemable characteristics. He hadn't liked when they'd brought him to parties and expected him to like everyone and to participate generously in the scene around him. He would rather float around the room, watching and wandering, and leaving when *he* wanted to. He'd had a girlfriend who'd filled his weekends with plans, parties, and dinners with other couples. And afterward she'd been disturbed to hear how he'd dissected the evening, or mocked a close friend. Turner would pretend he hadn't known it was a friend or that he hadn't meant what he'd said, but he had. He couldn't keep himself from being cruel then. He was mean to people in subtle ways, and sometimes, when he'd had too much to drink or smoke, in not-so-subtle ways.

He'd light into people he thought had sold out or who thought they were great artists or great humanitarians. For a year he hated anyone in a suit, and then he hated any man with a ponytail or a goatee, or any woman who wore tennis shoes and stockings beneath a skirt or dress.

He'd hate the businessmen he saw ignoring homeless people on the subway, and then the ones who gave twenty dollars, or the ones who gave the leftovers they carried in doggie bags and then said "enjoy" as though they'd cooked it themselves. He hated people who bought houses in the suburbs, or who bought condo apartments in the city, or who tried to "rough it" out in the country and still managed to bring their cell phones and computers and DVDs, or the ones who roughed it out in the country and brought none of those because they thought a weekend of deprivation proved they were of simple, decent character. He hated people who spoke of the TV shows they watched and those who refused to watch any of it, and those who only watched some shows, and those who taped the shows and fast-forwarded through the commercials and then talked about it at dinner, as they compared TV-recording technology.

For a while Turner dated a psychology student who told him that he hated himself, that he was afraid to feel anything.

He wasn't afraid to feel; he simply didn't.

ALL THAT HAD CHANGED NOW. Anne came over to his apartment three times in four nights. There was no misreading that. They played games, took more walks, and twice cooked meals. She let herself be seen with him at the grocery store. He left a key for her, under a rock she'd picked out, in case he wasn't home. She told him more about her past, about her future and how she wanted to live, and she was allowing him to place himself in those imaginings. They didn't talk about Jack. Nor about her engagement.

Something good was happening, Turner permitted himself to believe. He heard it in her voice, and felt it in her touch. He wanted to call everyone he ever knew and tell them. He'd made someone's life better. And this was unmistakable: For the first time in his life, Steven Turner was in love.

CHAPTER 44

Anne was feeling increasingly conflicted. It wasn't so much about her nights with Turner as it was about her ability to get away with them so easily. Betraying her marriage had been as simple as breathing, and seemingly just as necessary. And yet, she wondered, if she was falling in love with Turner—and it certainly felt that way—why was it that she felt so relieved when she left his place and made it back to the quiet of her studio? Why was it that she hadn't told him she was married, and why was it that she'd told Jack nothing at all? For all their troubles, it meant something to her that she was married. She feared making a choice right now that might be irreversible. So she continued to test her heart: to wake up in one house and make love in another. And in between she worked in solitude as though nothing else mattered. She would understand soon what it was she should do. At least she hoped she would. Or maybe waiting too long would assure that she lost them both.

Jack was out at a hearing, a concert, or a restaurant opening nearly every night. Sometimes she went with him, and did her best to present herself well, but usually she took the opportunity to see Turner. Jack said he understood her absence, that most of those events were boring. But she knew he'd simply given up on her.

Worse in some ways than his finding out was that he still didn't know. At the end of the night he was so contrite about coming home late that it didn't occur to him to ask her where she'd been.

ON A SNOWY APRIL NIGHT, Anne and Turner were seated cross-legged on Turner's living room carpet, smoking pot and playing checkers. For the second straight night, Anne was trouncing him, and Turner was pretending to be crushed, mind and spirit. "Mother of God, not again!" he yelled. It was a wet snow outside and it wasn't sticking. It would be Anne's father's birthday over the weekend, and Anne had been thinking about him, and her mother, for days. She told Turner of a birthday party she and her sister had thrown for their father. They'd made him steak and eggs for brunch and taken him to the circus, not Ringling Brothers, but some artier one with lots of gymnasts and contortionists from Eastern-bloc countries, two little girls who could fold over backward like pocketknives. "How come *you* can't do that?" her father asked them.

Her mother was already cheating on him by then, Anne said, though they didn't know it yet.

"When did you first know?"

"First time? I remember pretty clearly," she said. "I was in ninth grade. I heard them fighting in their room. He was upset, in a . . . disturbing way. He didn't sound like himself. I remember him saying something about her 'invalidating' him. 'It's like you've completely invalidated us, Elaine,' he said. I didn't know what he meant by that, so I looked it up in the dictionary that night. It said 'to make invalid, to nullify.' Then I looked up nullify."

"Ever industrious."

"So one night about two months later my sister said she'd seen our mother walking with a man near Belvedere Castle, and holding hands. 'You're lying,' I said. But of course she wasn't."

Anne's sister, Lauren, had always been the courier of disturbing news. She'd been the one to tell Anne when John Lennon had been shot, or when a teacher they'd both had in third grade had been arrested for indecent exposure. *It's all so fucked*, Lauren liked to say, meaning everyone and everything.

Anne stopped her own story now and took a hit. She blew the smoke out cleanly.

"Wow. I'm usually quite the cougher," she said.

Turner nodded proudly. "The lake region's smoothest."

"Anyhow. The next day we cut our morning classes and walked up to Ninety-first and Central Park West. To the El Dorado. We waited on a bench like spies. I think we even wore sunglasses. Sure enough, ten A.M. comes around and there's my mother leaving the apartment building, holding hands with a man with wavy gray hair. 'He ain't the first, either,' my sister says. After that we made jokes about them. We called the man with the wavy gray hair the handburglar. 'She's off boffing the handburglar again,' Lauren said. I felt hollow. I thought: You're not supposed to talk this way about your mother. My father must have known, all that time . . . he must have known.

"After that I started noticing how often he looked distracted, and it was just about every evening. It was *her* fault, I kept thinking. He loved her, and she allowed herself to love someone else."

While she was speaking, she watched Turner's face grow serious. She thought of Jack for a moment and wondered if he was home now.

"What happened to him in the end?" Turner said.

"What do you mean, what happened to him? He died. I told you."

"I don't mean your father."

Poor Turner. He wanted to know what would happen to *him*. Anne was surprised by what she felt now. She felt like being mean.

"I guess he just disappeared," she said.

"Why?"

She was becoming quite stoned, and she regretted getting into this topic now, in this state. She wanted to get back to checkers.

"Who knows?" she said. "Maybe he found someone else's life to fuck up."

She meant it as a joke, but Turner didn't laugh. It wasn't all that funny, she supposed.

WITH JACK AT A LATE MEETING the next Monday night, Turner took Anne for a drive out to the nuclear power plant. Romantic landscapes, Turner said, were in the eye of the beholder. They drove past open fields and long stretches of snow-quilted pine trees. By the clearing Turner said, "All right now. Look out the window."

"Oh no."

"Amazing, isn't it?"

It was. A modern-day Taj Mahal.

"There's something both grotesque and sort of beautiful about it," Anne said.

"Five hundred and forty feet. Sixteen thousand, five hundred cubic yards of concrete. One thousand, two hundred and thirty tons of reinforced steel. It's my favorite spot in town."

Steam rose from the top. It was, in its own way, spectacular. Like being near a mountain, or a volcano.

"They'll block it off, the bastards," Turner said. "They're planning to build a big hotel with views away from the power plant. They'll landscape so you'll barely know who your neighbor is. And then when you look down the shoreline, rather than seeing the cooling tower you'll see a big new hotel and conference center. With maybe just a puff or two of steam rising up above."

"Will that work?"

"Not for me. They think so. They're counting on it. But there's something eerily beautiful about this, in a Fritz Lang kind of way."

BACK AT HIS APARTMENT, after they'd lit candles, drunk beer, and made love in Turner's bed, Turner asked how she could do this and continue to live with Jack.

She believed in sticking to things, she said.

"Forgive me, but this isn't exactly the height of loyalty."

"I know. But I made a vow."

He turned on his side, propped his head on his palm. "What kind of vow?"

"That kind."

"Your engagement? You can get out of that one."

She half-smiled, and then her face had the look of someone watching a bus pull away. "Not so easily."

"Why not?"

"We eloped."

"What? You're married?"

She nodded.

"When?"

"In September. Right before my grandfather died. We just didn't tell anyone."

He lay back down again, facing the ceiling. This was lousy news.

"Why didn't you tell anyone?"

"I can't really remember, to be honest. It had to do with our families."

"I don't believe it."

"It's true, Turner. We've got the license to prove it."

He felt the floor give out beneath him.

"I wish you'd told me this."

"Would it have made a difference?"

"That you're married? Yes."

"How's it different from my being engaged?"

"The difference is you were dishonest," he said.

"You wanted a more honest form of adultery?"

"Yes, Anne. I suppose I did."

She lowered her eyes. "I can't just walk out like that. You don't just walk out."

"The way your mother did."

She stared back at him.

"But she didn't walk out, right? She just cheated on him." He stopped himself from saying anything more.

"It so happens that I do love him."

"So what if you're happier with me."

She studied the fields of blanket around them. "Why is it people always think they're supposed to be happy, as though that's their birthright . . . as though it's something they could perpetually maintain?"

"A dangerous misnomer. By all means be miserable." He'd wanted to sound teasing, but he came off bitter instead.

"You sound just like Jack."

She was right, he thought.

"So what is this then, Anne? A little fling?"

"Would that be so bad?"

"Yes, it would."

"What do you see it as?"

He had things to say, but he was still reeling from her disclosure. The room felt cold around him. "Nothing. You're right. It's nothing."

And with that, they both began dressing. He walked her out.

The snow had stopped. The night outside was damp and clear. Stars poked through the moonless sky. He did not want her to leave. He stood there, stupidly proud.

"Of course it's more than a fling," she said as she got into her car. "That's why it's so screwed up. Let me clear my head a little, Turner. I'll come by soon."

IN THE MORNING, Turner saw broken glass around his Honda. He walked over to investigate. The back window was smashed; there was glass inside and out. There was a note on his dashboard in magic marker that read, "Next time it's your typing hand."

CHAPTER 45

Anne kept painting. She was surprised to find that she still could, that when she entered her studio, time vanished, and when she looked up again the day was through.

She painted a Thomas Hart Benton–esque painting of a cab driver standing over a dead cat, onlookers moving about in face-less chiaroscuro. She painted another of a boy in the delicates-sen with his face pressed to the window. Breath stained the window in a circle around his mouth. She painted a woman in the office building across the street, kissing a man, kissing the handburglar, the window huge behind them, streaked with flashes of yellow and red.

She painted a faceless cab driver hovering over the skeleton of her father, a crowd of skull faces all around it. The bones were translucent, the sky all around them thick and cobalt.

Some days she looked at photographs of paintings and she tried to reproduce the brushstrokes. She did her own Kandin-skys and Klees and Francesco Clementes, and she did a par-ticularly offensive de Kooning in wild greens and pinks, which looked more like something from John Waters.

Then she returned to her own work, allowing her lessons to sink in transparently.

She painted a simple painting of a man and a woman. The man was clearly Jack. The more she painted of the woman the less she liked it, so she slurred the colors by dragging her brush across sideways, and she liked the effect, how it left the woman undefined. That seemed right.

In two weeks' time she'd also made three trips over to Marla's to paint Marla and the baby, and to paint Marla by herself. Marla was a terrific subject. And Anne liked being with the two of them.

Her days alone were so different now. The sky didn't press down on her so heavily. The town seemed warmer, hers finally, which was something she hadn't counted on happening.

CHAPTER 46

"We have a theory," the long-haired, fortyish man seated in Jack's office said. "Want to hear it?"

Anne's yoga teachers, Jeanette and John Cornfeller, were Lakeland's vocal and ubiquitous environmentalists. They attended meetings and talked of asbestos levels in the schools, rusty drinking water, rampant use of pesticides, global warming, and they were always pursuing a conspiracy theory of some sort, drug running at the airport, poor hygiene among the volunteer servers at the local soup kitchen. They were bright and earnest, and often dressed alike in matching GORE-TEX and Thinsulate. They sat side by side now, concern on their handsome faces, notebooks and pencils in their hands.

"Sure."

"We think those lots were used as toxic dump sites."

"What makes you think that?"

"A number of things," Jeanette Cornfeller said. "We asked people in the neighborhood and they said they saw trucks coming and going in the middle of the night."

"So?"

"Why would they work in the middle of the night?" she asked.

"They're clearing the sites for construction."

"At three in the morning?" John Cornfeller said.

"Doesn't that seem a little late?" Jeanette Cornfeller said.

"So we went ahead and followed one of those trucks," John Cornfeller said.

"And?"

"And it stopped on a farm out near the county border. They drove right onto the farm. And then they dug their ditches and buried their barrels."

"You actually saw them do this?"

"No. But we went out there later on," John said.

"There's a lot of dead vegetation out there. And quite a few dead birds," Jeanette said. She showed him a photograph of dead birds on dead-looking land. "The chemical compounds tunnel into the body, into the cells, and they mimic estrogen."

"What would you like me to do?"

"Look into it."

"I am," he said.

"We think the city's been covering this up," John said.

"Thanks for coming by."

THEY WERE ON TO something, Jack knew. And they were going to follow up on this. They were nothing if not diligent. And there were more in their ranks.

Now those concerns had reached others in town.

He had said in an affidavit, given for purposes of the environmental impact statement, that the sites were ready for building, that he knew of no prior use that would make the site a hazard. But that had been a guess, or wishful thinking, or willful untruth. He had not looked into it far enough. He would have to now, he knew.

On his way home, he stopped at Terry Miller's house.

"Jogging again?" Terry Miller said.

"I had some questions. Concerning that discussion we had a while back."

"That crap they're dumping out there?"

"Yes. I want to know how much."

"What did Harris tell you?"

"I haven't asked him."

"You two are pretty tight, huh?"

"Are we talking dozens?"

"Try thousands."

"Christ almighty . . . just dumped like that."

"You know. Some were buried, some dumped, some piled up inside an old barn, some emptied out into creeks and the like. Choking the minnows. Poisoning puppies. Killing all those little deer. You read about it. Burning the tread off rubber tires. And there were oily tanks too, oozing and dripping. But they've covered over most of it. They'll end up growing vegetables again. Next summer you'll be eating the stuff in your salad."

"Well, thanks, then. I'm gonna get going."

Terry Miller started laughing and shaking his head. It was a mean, contemptuous laugh and it made Jack furious.

"You think this is funny?"

Terry stopped laughing. He made a stern face. "What's funny is . . ." he said, and then broke out laughing all over again. "What's funny," he said with great effort, "is Harris telling you his dog died. I think that's pretty funny. Don't you?"

"His dog did die."

"Jack, you're either the most gullible guy I ever met—or the cagiest."

"He loved that dog," Jack said, and he left.

JACK WAS SPOOKED. He would search for Harris and find out what all this meant, but there was an event he needed to be at, a party commemorating the hundredth anniversary of the Lakeland Moose Lodge. He and Hickey were to be the featured guests, and Jack had given his word he'd be there. The Moose Lodge was one of the first local groups to lobby in favor of the harbor plan, before the unions, before the town council. Jack liked the Moose Lodge as a result, and he couldn't stand them up.

When he arrived, the mayor was in the midst of a speech describing his "lifelong love affair with the Moose," to go along with his love affair with the Elks, and the Masons, and the Knights of Columbus, and the VFW, and the Lakeland Auxiliary Firefighter Association, and the Ladies' Bridge Club, and everyone else whose support he wanted.

Hickey said he practically grew up in the lodge and that he and Sarah had in the past five years visited both Mooseheart, a 120-acre campus in Illinois for poor sick children, and Moosehaven, a retirement village for elderly Moose in Florida.

"Like all of you, I'm Mostly Moose," he said. And then he cut the anniversary cake.

"It's great to have camaraderie," Hickey said as a server passed around the plates. "But to have a purpose such as care from the cradle to the grave is something very noble in this day and age." The diners applauded politely and then grabbed at pieces of the spongy white cake.

Later, as they stood alone in the corner holding cups of an orange punch that had been spiked with whiskey, Jack said, "Had a little visit from the Cornfellers."

"Banana Republic," Hickey said.

"What?"

"Charthouse, Rusty Scupper."

Hickey winked and waved at a fat man in a blue blazer across the room.

"They want to set up here. I like 'em all. But I'm partial to the Charthouse. Better cup of chowder. Fishier."

"People are catching on," Jack said. "They followed Stanyan's trucks."

"Hmmm. Later, okay?"

The Lakeland Moose president, Frank Seeley, stood then on a small platform across the room.

"I want to thank everyone for coming tonight, and I especially want to thank Mayor William Hickey and his brilliant—if tardy—protégé, Jack Lambeau."

The Moose members laughed and applauded. Jack faked a smile.

"Jack has been the vision behind the new Lakeland. The boy genius. America's foremost genius on the new old small town, quote unquote. I've assured both Jack and Bill—hey, that's sort of cute, isn't it, Jack and Bill went up the hill."

They laughed again.

"I've assured them both that the Moose wants to be an integral part of the new Lakeland. We're considering hosting a national Moose convention on the waterfront a year from this July." More applause.

"Nobody gave this part of the country a chance to come back. They said we'd up and died, bit the bullet. I'd say we've proved 'em wrong, wouldn't you?"

The applause grew louder.

"Viva Lakeland!" he said, and the group called out in echo, "Viva Lakeland!"

It would have cheered Jack a few days ago. Now it made him cringe. He felt like a pilot who knows his plane will crash but can't yet summon the nerve to tell his passengers.

Frank Seeley continued, "I want to also thank you for the wonderful turnout we had at the Mooselodge Valentine Sweetheart dinner. Forty-two couples. Eighty-four of you love-aholics raising money for kids. There's a lesson in that."

Hickey said sideways to Jack, "Don't listen to a bunch of whackos. Everything's going forward." He raised his eyebrows. "Pier One . . . The Nature Company."

THEY CONTINUED THE DISCUSSION in the Moose Lodge parking lot.

"It's not just the whackos, Bill. It's guys from Stanyan's team. I just talked to one of them."

Hickey winced. "The hell are you doing, Jack? You doing their legwork? You talk to Showalter? We're about to get the loan commitment from the banks. Don't go panicking now."

"I'm not panicking."

"You are. You're going out and investigating."

"We have to come clean on this, Bill."

"We're too far down the road for that."

"And we've got ourselves a sizable roadblock here."

"People won't listen, Jack. You can't underestimate the will of the town. You heard them in there. They want this. They want jobs. They want the future. Excavation starts the first nice day. You think anyone gives a damn about a few barrels left out in the middle of some farm they gave up on ten years ago? I don't think you get it, Jack. We've taken the necessary steps."

"And what are those?"

"They're never going to be able to prove anything."

"It's against the law."

"Yes, and your brother was one of the ones breaking that law, right?"

"And . . ."

"You don't want to see him in jail, do you?"

"Maybe he should be in jail."

"Let it go, Jack."

Jack shook his head in disgust.

"They'll name streets after us, just wait. And like you've been saying, other towns'll follow our lead. They already are. You see how many hits we got on our Web site last week? They've been having stories in the paper on how everyone wants to copy us."

"I'm quitting."

Hickey stared at the sky. "You *can't*."

"What's that supposed to mean?"

"Means you can't. Maybe before Chicago you could have."

"There's no choice."

"I hate saying this, Jack. But I've got your signature approving the dumping of barrels, and declaring the sites safe for building, sites they'll say you'd never bothered to properly check out."

"You told me it was all good to go. I trusted you."

"You didn't trust me. You called me a liar, remember? The truth is, you got swept up in all this, just like me. And I don't blame you, Jack. I really don't. We're human is what we are. But don't go acting high and mighty, because the clothes don't fit. You're as dirty as the rest of us here, right?"

"And that's what you'll testify to, huh?"

"It's not going to come to that. Come on, Jack. As far as the public's concerned you're a hero. You've got people eating from your palm. If you say panic, they'll panic. If you keep your cool, they'll keep theirs. Let's finish what we started."

Jack shook his head.

"We give up on this, Jack, and it'll kill this town. . . . Put a fork in us. . . . I won't be a party to that. We'll never have an opportunity like this. You might. But we won't. This town won't."

Jack felt trapped, and used. He would lose his good name, and with good reason. He had played into this. He'd left himself vulnerable.

"Listen, you goddamned weasel. You burned me here. I'm not going to sit around and do nothing."

"What are you going to do?"

"We're in trouble, Bill."

"It's nothing," Hickey said. "You been by the magazine rack? Our pictures are in *People* magazine. We have the governor coming in, and CNN for Chrissakes. We're a genuine American success story. What the hell more do you want?"

JACK SPENT THE NEXT hours searching for Harris. He went by Bazorcik's, then to a few bars where he thought his brother might be. No one had seen him.

"I hear he's back with the wife," someone said.

He stopped by Marla's to see if that was true.

"You just missed him," she said. "I sent him to the supermarket to get some juice and milk and some diapers and stuff."

"He's been around?"

"Just about every day. You'd be surprised. He's been such a sweetheart. I'm pretty close to letting him back."

THE P & C SUPERMARKET on Walnut Street was nearly empty, just a few tired-looking shoppers picking up beer and other late-night supplies under the bright fluorescent lights. Two bored clerks were slinging rubber bands at each other. There were March Madness displays, and signs that said GO ORANGE-MEN with a smiling picture of Jim Boeheim. Ordinarily Jack would have followed the college basketball tournament. This year he had no idea who was playing.

He found Harris in the cereal aisle comparing two boxes.

"Harris," he called out.

His brother looked like he'd been caught shoplifting. He dropped one of the boxes into his cart. "What are you doing here?" Harris asked.

"Tell me again how Sammy died."

"Why?"

"'Cause I want to know."

Harris closed his eyes, pained.

"He isn't dead, is he?" Jack said.

"Not so far as I know."

"So you lied."

"Yes," Harris said, softly but emphatically. "Yes, but I've stopped. Turned over a leaf. No more of that."

"What's buried in my yard, then?"

"Nothing."

"Bullshit nothing. Tell me what the fuck is buried there."

"We moved him."

"Him?"

Harris looked around. The aisle was completely empty.

"He's buried properly now."

"Who?"

"And we didn't kill him. I hope they didn't tell you that."

Jack felt ill. This was sounding disastrous.

"They didn't tell me anything. Who didn't you kill?"

"Parkhurst."

"Who the hell is Parkhurst?"

THEY PAID FOR THE GROCERIES and then walked out to the parking lot. Under the buzzing fluorescent lamps Harris began telling Jack about the night drops, about how bad he'd needed the money, about Harlan Stanyan's threats, and then about the lawsuit, about the questions the lawyer was asking about Jack. Everyone in town was going to need a lawyer, he said.

Harris had fucked up again. Story of his life. Only now as a result of his mistake, they were both fucked. His brother had buried a body in Jack's backyard. The body of a man who, it could be argued, had been working for Jack.

It was wrong to clear barrels of any kind from the harbor sites without reporting it. Wrong to dump sludge on all those farms. But a body was a whole different matter.

What possible spin could you put on a dead man paid to do your dirty work?

"What's this lawyer saying about me?"

"That you were in on all this."

"I wasn't."

"That's what I told him."

"What did he say to that?"

"He's looking into it all. He's going to talk to you and he's going to talk to Captain Mayor. Main thing is, we didn't kill him. He wasn't asked to do anything we weren't asked to do. What this lawyer says is that we come clean. Tell them all we did was our jobs. We're not to blame. Neither are you."

Jack wasn't sure about the law, but if you knew about a crime and didn't report it, or if you knowingly profited from it (as he had, in a sense), you were liable.

"How could you be so stupid, Harris?"

"Stupid? What was I gonna to do? He died. And then, yes, we all fucked up. I'm trying to make amends."

"What were you doing out there in the first place?"

"It was my job. You got it for me."

"Not doing that, Harris."

"Yes, doing that. That's exactly what my job was."

Jack shook his head.

"Wasn't like there were a lot of other options out there. You have any idea what it's like to go a year without a paycheck, Jack?"

No, Jack thought, but he might soon.

"You never did. You never had to stand on line waiting for what comes along. I cleaned bathrooms for a month. I've done worse too—stuff I definitely shouldn't have done. But I'm through with that, Jack. I'm on a new path. I'm ready to make my amends. It's the only way. I've been going to church again."

But it wasn't a way at all. If they all confessed, the project was dead. At the very least. The banks and Showalter would do what the banks and Showalters of the world always did, separate themselves from a sinking ship.

They'd be charged with crimes. Jack's hand was everywhere. Who would ever trust him with their money, with a town, again?

"I knew none of this," Jack said.

"But you do now, right? That lawyer fellow, he says the first to talk gets the best deal. I say, let's get ourselves a good deal, Jack."

CHAPTER 47

The house was empty when Jack arrived home that night. He checked for Anne upstairs in the bedroom, in the study, in the kitchen. Then, against their unwritten rule, he stepped inside her painting studio. In the cool, close dark, he took a few deep breaths. It smelled like paint and wood. He started to run a film in his mind of his brother digging up that body, and then he replayed a few lines of the mayor's unabashed venality. He tried to stop the tremors in his head then by turning on the light. As his eyes adjusted, Jack looked around the two rooms, and as he did so he felt as though he'd wandered into a stranger's home. Anne's studio wasn't at all what he'd been picturing. There was an order to this place; brushes put away, canvases hanging or neatly stacked. Before, her painting station, or stations, had been chaotic. This place made him want to paint. Then he began inspecting her work. The more he saw, the more amazed, and perplexed, he was.

The new paintings were nothing like the old ones. No more fruit bowls or simple landscapes. These ones were fever dreams. They were complex, and the colors were lush, at times mesmerizing. There were odd and disquieting details everywhere, and while he knew some of their derivations, he could only guess at others. It pained him then that she hadn't shown him any of this, that she'd arrived at this without him. It was as though she had a double life, an underworld of fixation and emotion he hadn't been granted access to.

And that had him thinking: It was after eleven. Where could she be after eleven on a Thursday night? On any night, for that matter.

She didn't know anyone in town. Not really. She had dinner occasionally with some of the women from the yoga class. Maybe she was with them. But eleven o'clock was pretty damn late for dinner, wasn't it? He left her studio and poured a scotch. When he finished that he poured another.

He sat in the living room a while mulling over his options, but it only made him feel more boxed in. The best thing to do, he thought, was to get royally fucked up and put the whole dreadful day and evening out of his mind.

He'd had three more drinks by the time Anne walked in. It was close to twelve-thirty.

He asked, "Where were you?"

"You weren't here, so I went for a drive."

"A *drive*?"

"Yes. Is that so strange?"

"Driving around at midnight?"

"Are you interrogating me? I had dinner made, Jack. I made lasagna and salad. We were supposed to have dinner together, did you forget?"

Christ. He had forgotten. They'd made plans to cook together that morning.

"If you're going to blow me off, at least have the courtesy to call and tell me, so I'm not sitting around waiting for you."

He felt terrible. "I'm sorry, Anne. You can't imagine what this day's been like."

"It's all right."

But he could tell from her voice it wasn't. Nothing was. He went to stand up, but when he did he knocked his glass to the floor, and it shattered.

They looked at it lying there as if it were a living thing that had just died.

None of it mattered, he thought then, not the barrels, or the body, or Hickey, or his career. Contempt had crept into his young marriage, had crept in a while back. They were strangers. He was sorry he had missed dinner, and he was sorry she'd needed to go out driving, if that was what she'd done.

"You okay, Jack?" she said.

"Yes," he said. But he wasn't. He began picking up shards of glass. Before he finished he slipped, and as he tried to break his fall he landed on a shard and cut himself deeply at the base of his palm.

THE PAIN WAS ENORMOUS. Anne pulled out a two-inch piece of glass, then wrapped a clean rag around the gash. She drove Jack to the hospital. It felt like a small creature was gnawing through his hand. They had to wait while two teenagers were admitted with broken bones and facial cuts from a drunken driving accident. You could learn a lot about a community from hanging around an emergency room, Anne said.

The doctor, a woman in her late twenties, gave Jack seven stitches. She anesthetized the area around the cut so that he didn't feel the stitching. Anne was there by his side through it all. The woman doctor recognized him, Jack could tell.

She told him to keep the stitches clean or he would risk infection. Maybe it was the blood, or maybe it was the three drinks Anne had when they got home, but they slept in each other's arms that night as they hadn't in months.

In the morning Jack decided he'd been paranoid. Anne had been driving by herself, and she had every right to. His hand still hurt, and blood stained a small portion of the sheet. And he had a nasty headache from the scotch. As he popped a few aspirin and drank a few glasses of water, he began to think about those paintings, about the large tan and black one that seemed to be about her father's accident.

They should share their work with each other, he thought.

Husbands shared problems with their wives, didn't they? It probably made them closer.

He climbed back into bed. "Anne," he said.

"Yes?"

"I guess I can tell you later."

"What is it?"

"You'll hear about it soon."

She rolled over and faced him.

"There'll be things said about me, about Hickey, and Harris."

"What sort of things?"

"It's about the project. We've got some problems."

He tried telling her, and he started out accurately enough but somehow he found himself altering the story so that it sounded like they'd done nothing improper. He told Anne they'd reported the barrels, which of course they hadn't. He added the part about Parkhurst dying from breathing caustic sulfates so the whole thing wouldn't seem like an out-and-out lie. He recognized that this wasn't for her. She didn't matter here. He was thinking aloud, and he was trying to convince himself he'd done nothing wrong.

"A human body."

"Yes."

"In our backyard?"

"Yes. He's been moved to a legitimate graveyard. As I said, the mother of the dead guy is suing us. This Mrs. Cullen. And there'll be other lawsuits. Dozens, maybe. But I think we can get them settled." His words had a stiff, press-release sound to them.

"It sounds awful. What are you going to do?"

He thought about Hickey saying this was their moment, and he knew that was right. They had momentum and if they lost it, they'd never get it back. They'd lose their tax credits and state aid, for one thing. Showalter would opt out, and then everything else they'd set in place would fall. So maybe they could settle out of court with Mrs. Cullen's lawyer, and with all those workers. And maybe they could find everyone good-paying steady jobs at the harborfront, enough pay to keep them quiet. Eventually they'd clean up those farms, as Hickey had said, and as he'd just told Anne, but in the meantime Lakeland would shine. And people would come to visit, or even settle down. And he'd have made his mark on the world. It could still happen that way, he told himself. But it had all started to sound thin; dangerously so.

He was waiting for a path to emerge, the way it had for Harris. But nothing came.

"I just don't know," he said.

Anne was studying him. He pushed his hair over his temples where it had begun to recede. Anne gently pushed it back. In different ways, she was exposing him.

"What do you think?" he said.

"What do I think?"

"Yes."

"I suppose I feel kind of bad for that man who died, and for his poor mother. Don't you, Jack?"

THE NEXT NIGHT Anne woke at around two and saw she was alone in bed. She looked around the house and then found Jack out on the empty road throwing rocks at the pale night sky, one after another. In a while he came back in the house holding his hand.

"Let me see that," she said. She took his hand in hers.

"It's nothing. Stupid shit rock."

He'd ripped several stitches open.

"We should go get those fixed up."

"I'm fine," he said, and he took his hand back and walked from the room.

She followed him into the kitchen where he was rinsing the cut.

He looked up at her. "'Course I care about someone dying, Anne," he said. "I'm sick about it. I'm sick about this whole thing."

"You'll do the right thing," she said.

"What does that mean?"

"It means you're the only one you have to answer to."

"You think so? You know what'll happen here, Anne? I'll tell you exactly what will happen. People are going to get scared. And there'll be protesters outside my office, and the mayor's. There'll be scientists running around calculating every inch of dirt around that harbor. And every case of emphysema, or hacking cough, or cancer, or the flu, at the Lakeland hospital will be our fault. And we'll trot out experts who'll say the cancer rates are normal and everything's fine, and they'll have their experts, and they'll say we're greedy liars, and maybe a few people will be on our side, but there'll be plenty others shouting me down at every meeting. And suddenly all the people who were against this to start with, they'll start holding press conferences. They'll have *credibility*. And the sum of it will be that we'll lose them, the banks and developers. Whether it's fair or not."

It sounded to Anne like a fair enough prediction.

"And Hickey's right on one thing. At the end of all this, someone's still going to have to pay for that cleanup."

They talked more over the next few nights. His tone shifted. If it came to it, he would cooperate with an investigation, he said, but he wouldn't hasten the end of this project, and he certainly wouldn't quit. He had convinced her that his choice was an impossible one; and so, she recognized, was hers. Maybe he sensed that. They were both at crossroads, and that made them closer. He would find a way out of this, or he wouldn't. She would tell him about Turner, or she wouldn't.

He told her about the heir to a real estate fortune, who decided to redevelop a twenty-four-acre decimated area in the heart of Brooklyn. "This one had everything going for it," he said.

A renowned San Francisco architect and planner wrote the master plan; a huge New York design firm drew up plans for the major buildings; Mayor Koch was behind it and said it would be a model for a nation full of bombed-out neighborhoods in need of renewal.

"Remind you of anyone? They went through all the hoops, just like us. Tons of office space and retail, and new apartments. It would have meant twenty-five hundred jobs, lots of tax revenue, changed the whole borough around."

"And . . ."

"What do you think? They killed it with lawsuits. They said rents would go up in the adjoining neighborhoods and poor people would have to move out."

"Wouldn't that make sense?"

"To sue a project because it improved a place? It's crazy, Anne. It's the sort of self-defeating bullshit that goes on everywhere, and it's why no one ever does anything like what we're doing here. They don't want to go near these places. It's why they go down to Florida and build on a swamp."

He took a deep breath, calmed his voice.

"Anyhow, this guy puts years and a good chunk of his fortune into fighting this, but eventually all his anchor tenants withdraw, and the whole thing unravels."

"Never got built?"

"Not a brick so far as I know."

"And they didn't even have anyone die."

He gave her an exasperated look.

"You're really going to ride me on this, aren't you."

"I'm not. I just get sick of hearing how the world's out to get you."

"It's funny," he said.

"What?"

"I'm just thinking of how I rode you when you were stuck. How rigid my expectations were, how little I was actually listening to you, seeing you."

She felt a twinge of guilt. She wondered how it was she'd gotten herself here, in the middle.

"We were both at fault," Anne said. "But thanks for saying that."

FOR A FEW NIGHTS they said nothing about any of his work, and that was a relief to them both. They read magazines, or they sat on the living room couch under the big violet quilt and watched police shows and courtroom dramas on TV. She was painting all day, every day. When she entered her studio the work took her over, like a sweet illness. She escaped into it, and the outside world did not intrude.

CHAPTER 48

Stanyan called Harris in a dither. "She wants eight hundred thousand dollars," he said. "Or her lawyer sues the department, i.e. me, for wrongful death."

"Whad'ya tell him?"

"I said nothing. I said leave me the hell alone."

"He's giving you a chance to settle, Harlan. I don't think you want to piss him off."

"Yeah. Well I don't know why we're eight hundred thousand bucks responsible for some fat dead fuck who didn't know how to do his job right. How many others of you dropped dead. None, right?"

"Not yet."

"If I call around maybe I can get her ten."

"It's her *son* you're talking about."

"Damn fucking damn," Stanyan said. Harris heard the phone drop, or maybe it was thrown.

"The deal was no one talked, right? We were all in on this so no one talked. No one called the police, no one called the state, no one called anyone's mother. You're the one who carried the body around, Harris. They're gonna throw you in jail, you know that?"

"I made a mistake. I'm ready to own up to it."

"Well, I sure as fuck am not. I don't have eight hundred thousand dollars," he said. "Here's what I want, for starters. I want a map of everywhere you dumped, all right? Then we'll try and figure a way out of this."

He was tired of Harlan, tired of his threats. "You gonna try and move them all?"

"Never mind."

"How much you going to pay me for the map?"

"Are you kidding? You should be paying me."

"You never paid me what you owed me," Harris said.

"He was good and buried, Harris."

"It's her son. She needed to say good-bye."

"Get me that map, Harris. And you keep your mouth closed, maybe nothing too bad'll happen to you, right? I get sued and I'm taking it out on your ass."

PART V

THE THAW

CHAPTER 49

Turner dug through the manifest records, the travel itineraries of the hundreds of thousands of barrels of toxic waste burned or not burned at the incinerator.

The law was set up around 1980, and it was designed for just this, "cradle-to-grave documentation of hazardous materials," Donaldson, his DEC source, told him.

When you're born, they start a file, and then a paper trail follows you the rest of your life.

Turner set himself up in the records room of the state DEC and sifted through each month, year after year, writing in his notebooks when the barrels were brought in, when they were burned, and if they weren't burned, then where they were sent. Twenty thousand in, twenty thousand out to a waste treatment site in Buffalo, and others in Niagara Falls and St. Louis.

It was tedious work, and not much fun. Then he hit pay dirt.

During the period from October 8 through November 1 of 1989, while the incinerator was closed for repairs, Northern Waste Alleviation still accepted barrels. From what Turner could tell nearly four thousand barrels of liquid chemical waste were accepted. None of those were ever sent out to any of the waste treatment sites. They weren't accounted for; there were no records.

"What does that prove?" Stewart asked him at lunch.

"I don't know if it proves anything. But it raises the question: Where did they go?"

"Dumped out on those farms, no?"

"I went to the old police reports, fall of 1989. A guy who lived near the old Davis Woolen Mills called in to say he'd seen trucks out there."

"Why shouldn't there be trucks out there?"

"Because it was dead land, foreclosed property. And it was the middle of the night. The man named in the report still lives there. He says there were men out there several times this past fall."

"What does he do, stay up all night waiting for them?"

"I guess so. Cops said they'd look into it, and they never did. Or maybe they did, and someone told them not to worry about it."

TURNER KNOCKED ON DOORS around the farms, interviewed families. Most people were aware of the barrels. Now with the snow melting, and the earth softening, there were smells drifting out into the roadways, and, on bad days, across into other people's property.

He'd been told this would happen, that the snow and frozen ground had kept a lid on this. At one of the houses he talked to two boys, twelve and sixteen, who told him they knew where one of the dump sites was located. They had to cover their noses whenever they rode their bikes by.

"We can show you where they are."

"It isn't all fenced off?"

"Hell no. You can walk right out there. I mean, not in the middle of the day. But when it gets dark you can, pretty easy."

"Can you show me?"

"Just come back at night."

THAT NIGHT TURNER STOPPED by the house again. Before he reached there he drove a few streets out of his way to Anne and Jack's farmhouse. He saw a light on in Anne's studio from where he parked a hundred yards or so down the road. He considered knocking on her door, because he was fairly sure Jack was out at a merchant's association meeting he had gotten Stewart to cover. There was no car in the driveway. But he couldn't be certain it wasn't parked around back. Turner drove on. He was out here for work, he reminded himself. It was probably best anyhow to stay away, he thought. He didn't know what he'd say, or how he'd be around her now. Sweat pooled around his collar, and down his back. The whole thing was starting to make him feel out of control. Let it rest, he said to himself. Although he wasn't at all convinced he could.

HE LEFT HIS CAR on a wide muddy shoulder and walked to the mailboxes where the kids told him they'd meet him. The parents were indoors watching television.

"They got four hours ahead of them. They won't even know we're gone," the younger boy said.

They were dressed like commandos in camouflage pants and black T-shirts. The older boy had a blond buzz cut and the first thin aura of a goatee. The younger boy had darker shoulder-length hair and big dark eyes that made Turner think of those awful velveteen paintings of dogs seated around a table.

"No one told me to dress up," Turner said.

"Just makes it easier," said the older boy. "Your shirt's a little too white."

He went back in the house and retrieved a large navy blue sweatshirt. Turner put it on.

"Kinda stinky, I know," the boy said.

In exchange Turner gave the boys the protective gloves he'd bought. They walked down a road jutted with potholes, and surrounded by weeds and the year's first wildflowers. In a month, it would be green again.

"Have you gone out here before?"

"Coupla times. It's nasty, though."

They walked out onto what he was fairly sure was the old Carter farm, a stretch of dirt and scrub surrounded by maple trees and bisected by a thin creek where the boys said they used to look for frogs. The creek was overrun with bulrushes and cattails, and there was some kind of slime in the water, like oil or sludge. Turner pointed his flashlight and it glistened.

When they reached a clearing they saw first some dead plants and dead trees. The air smelled zincy, metallic. He could taste it on his tongue. It reminded him of how a lawn smelled after it had been sprayed for aphids.

"Look here," the younger boy said. He pointed out the tire tracks, thick, the tracks of a truck. The ground had been disturbed.

The rusted rims of five or six barrels had made their way to the ground's surface. It was like finding the elephants' graveyard. He saw others, and when he poked with a stick he touched several more.

"Over here," the older one yelled. Behind a stand of trees there was an old shed, and behind the shed barrels had simply been dropped, above ground, and many were rusting, some obviously leaking.

It was no place to be. Turner shot two rolls of film.

When they made it back to the house the boys asked Turner was he hungry, or did he want a pop or a beer?

"I'll take a pop, thanks," he said.

They gave him a can of Sprite.

"I got some weed if you want," said the older boy, whose name was Gerard, and Turner understood then what had brought them out to an empty farm.

Turner raised his eyebrows. "No thanks," he said. "So you've actually seen them drive out there?"

"Sure. We seen them. I bet they just dump it out there sometimes, without even asking who owns the land."

"Do you remember what the trucks looked like?"

"Blue, and covered with a green tarp."

Turner retrieved from his notebook the photo he'd taken of the painted truck outside the DPW.

"That's it. They had a U-Haul out there too."

"Anyone ever approach your family?"

"Maybe. I don't know. It's not like my dad would say so if they did."

"I bet he didn't," the younger boy said.

"He might have," Gerard said.

Turner wrote the quote down, not to use it, but because it was so telling. No one knew what they were living near, and even family members were suspect.

"There's a real bad place about a mile east. But they closed it all off and put those skull-and-crossbone signs on it. The ones that say HAZARDOUS KEEP OUT," Gerard said. "They had dead animals all over it before they did that."

"What kind?"

"You know, ducks and raccoons and squirrels. I think a couple deer."

Turner wrote notes to himself. He wanted to be able to recall the whole night completely. "You know who's doing it?" Gerard asked him.

"Maybe."

"Who?"

"People who maybe didn't know what they were doing, paid by people who maybe did."

"My uncle says it's companies from Manhattan and Long Island."

"What do you think?" Turner asked.

"Petey thinks he knows."

Petey shot his brother a look.

"Who do you think it is, Petey?"

"You won't make fun?"

"No."

"I think it's Saddam Hussein."

CHAPTER 50

They ran Turner's photos and story on the bottom left corner of the front page. The image of these barrels, left leaking and leaching on open farmland, was disturbing, even in this town. His phone rang all day. One woman wanted to talk about destiny, how she'd seen this coming, and how the devil had played a majority role. Greed on the part of "the mayor and everyone else," had opened the door to evil.

Others blamed unknown forces from downstate. "We don't make any of this, and it all ends up here. Like we're some big sewer," said the teller at his bank when Turner made a deposit at lunchtime.

"Seems unfair," Turner said.

"Sure is," the teller said. Then he leaned forward so his fellow employees couldn't listen. "Corporate America takes a dump on the little guy," he whispered.

Turner had become a hack psychologist for the place, fielding fears, or justifications, or general disillusionment; people's philosophies, scatological or otherwise. Stewart said he was like an anthropologist who'd stumbled into an arcane culture. A world that might not exist in another ten years.

He continued to make himself an expert on all matters pertaining to toxic waste and the local soil. He called medical experts to find out what diseases could be expected, what symptoms people should watch out for. He published a story listing the symptoms and the next day the phone rang off the hook with people asking questions about their coughs and poor concentration, and the color of their urine—too white, too yellow, too green—occasional fatigue, odd fits of anger. And he continued his record searches, pouring over blue-and-red tax maps, and the ownership histories of the parcels along the waterfront. It was painstaking work.

He looked up all the inspection records. Phase 1 reports.

"That's where the cheating goes on," Carpenter told him.

"How so?"

"Any clown can do a Phase One for you. Doesn't even need to be an engineer. He can be a bureaucrat, and he can sign off on it from the comfort of his office. He says there's no reason for concern, and so there isn't."

Turner located the Phase 1 reports. Amazingly, they'd been signed off by Harlan Stanyan.

The Phase 2 report was done by an environmental engineer. Turner made a note to find the engineer.

THERE WAS NOTHING HERE with Jack's name on it. Nothing incriminating. It was simply unlikely that someone so bright and on top of everything could have missed this, could have missed what everyone else seemed to know, and with his own brother at the center of it. At the pace he was on, Turner felt certain he'd have proof soon that Jack knew about this, and knew early, and if he hadn't ordered it, he hadn't done anything to stop it. And then what would he do? Warn him? Give him a chance to talk his way out?

He would handle this without allegiance or malice, he thought, or else turn the whole thing over to someone who could.

CHAPTER 51

All across town there was gossip about the dead waste-hauler and the barrels; Anne had heard it at yoga and at the supermarket. She was returning from the pool one day, and she saw a group gathered on the sidewalk with placards. She asked one of the women about it and heard an elaborate conspiracy plot that involved the mayor, the developer, the head of the DPW, and Jack. The woman talked about articles in the paper and how more were going to follow "from that fellow Steven Turner."

"Turner?"

The woman gave her a newspaper to look at.

She thought of all those times they'd been together, how Turner had told her about the Old Time Fiddlers, the man with the country's biggest hubcap collection, every story he'd been working on but this one.

She wondered, Was he going to tell me? Or was he planning it as a surprise?

SHE WENT BY HIS OFFICE that afternoon. He was there alone, on the phone. "Tell me about this woman who's suing," she said.

He covered the phone.

"I'll be just a minute."

She waited outside in the hallway until he motioned her in. Her anger surprised her and she wasn't sure where it was issuing from.

"Where'd you hear about that?" he asked.

"Jack. He said you'd be writing a story."

"Her son died."

"I know that."

"So what would you like to know?"

"I want to know what you've found in all your digging around."

"We can't disclose that kind of stuff. Not until we publish the story."

"Don't panic, Turner. I won't tip off the TV stations."

He told her what he'd found, what he was still looking into, and where it concerned Jack.

"I was planning on telling you, Anne. The night after we went to the power plant. But then it seemed like it would be tit for tat, you know? You drop your bomb and I drop mine. I should have told you."

She nodded.

"Anyway, listen. This stuff happened long before Jack got into town. He's not behind it. But he didn't try to prevent it, either."

"What does that mean?"

"Means he got so caught up in saving this place, in being the big hero, that he ignored all the red flags. He got a little arrogant." He said more, and even if it was true, or maybe because it was true, she couldn't stand to listen. She began making her way out.

"You're just going to leave? This is crazy. Let's get lunch or something."

"I'll pass," she said.

His face turned to irritation.

"I'm sorry, Anne. I'm just doing my job. I don't relish this."

"Come on, Turner," she said from the doorway. "You're eating it up. You're having the time of your life."

He followed her downstairs, and then out to the parking lot.

"What do you want? You want me to drop the story for your sake?"

She didn't know what she wanted. She felt confused and pissed off.

"You should have told me about this," she said.

"Like you should have told me you were married?"

"I guess so."

"Maybe this isn't the best time to say it, Anne"—he inhaled and then deeply exhaled—"but I pretty much . . . love you. I have from the second I saw you there at Giovanni's, and ever since then, and I want to spend my life with you, have kids with you, grow old with you, clean each other's dentures."

There was no one around, but Anne was aware that it was a public parking lot, and someone could be watching.

"You're right. It wasn't the best time," she said.

"I mean it."

"Do you?" she said.

"I've put some thought to this, Anne. There's plenty of space in my apartment. I could clear out the dining room and you could use it as a small studio. I mean, I can't remember the last time I ate in the dining room."

"And I'd get a divorce."

"I know it'd be complicated, but yes."

"And we'd get married."

"If we want to, someday."

"And we'd live here in the same town as Jack and his family, and all their friends."

"Not for long, I hope."

"And then where would we move?"

"Anywhere we like."

How easy it was to be certain, she thought, when you had nothing to lose.

"Where would you live if you could live anywhere?" he asked.

She wouldn't answer. She thought of a few places, but she didn't want to continue this. You could agree on a destination, but that didn't mean you could get there. Could she see them together? Maybe. But he suddenly seemed slippery to her, and she wondered what other things about him she didn't know.

"You act as though it's all so easy, as though there aren't any consequences."

"I know there are, Anne."

She felt disarranged, as though she could either strike him, go home with him, or walk away and pretend he wasn't there. There were too many choices and she was frightened by the fact that at this moment none felt inevitable, the way she thought love was supposed to feel. She had brought herself here, she recognized; willfully divided her heart. It was her own fault.

"I've got to get out of here," she said, and she did, but she wasn't sure what she'd meant by *here*.

"I'm not just messing around," Turner said. "I've never said these things to anyone."

Anne sighed.

"I guess I don't get an award for that," he said.

ALL THIS TIME ANNE worked. From daybreak until three. She would not, when she was done for the day, be able to say much about what she'd done. Some nights when she looked at these images she was forming, she had the strange and slightly unnerving sense that they weren't hers, but that someone had sneaked in and painted them for her. They evoked the accident, still: variations of that afternoon, the way the air felt, the conclusive sound of the collision.

A WEEK AGO, Turner's words might have moved her, might have won her over and answered her doubts. Said as they were while she was feeling misled by him, and far better about Jack, they had no force. They'd simply dropped between them onto the ground of the parking lot. She couldn't definitively say whom she wanted to be with, and so being with neither of them seemed like the easiest choice. The best thing she could do was barricade herself in her studio, as one might hide from a war going on outside. Jack was deep inside his own problems. His confidence had been wounded, and he seemed lost, which was the last thing someone would say normally about Jack. He wanted to talk through his thoughts, and so she let him, and gave him her opinion. It was the least she could do. Whatever came of them ultimately, she'd be glad she helped him through this. It was a crisis, and she wouldn't quit someone in a crisis.

She tried to shake the thought of a dead man buried in her backyard; of Jack being involved in it somehow; of Turner exploiting it for his own purposes; of those pretty farms destroyed by someone's greed.

It was a town of opposites, at once sunny and hopeful and dark and criminal, religious and sacrilegious, neighborly and cruel, and just as she was starting to feel comfortable it seemed to be falling apart at the seams.

In her studio she could forget about all of this.

As she swam one afternoon, she sifted through potential futures, saw them ahead in the chlorinated water. A life with Jack (for seven laps), or a life with Turner (six). One night she dreamed she'd left them both and moved to New York on her own, and it was a good dream, she was surprised to realize. She saw herself riding subways, walking city streets, attending gallery openings and painting, and feeling strangely content. And in the days after she had that dream she began to think more about that as a possibility, of moving back to New York, and maybe living alone for a while, without either of them. Whether or not she would, she liked thinking that she *could*, that she could do just fine on her own. She could paint and swim, and make money *somehow*, and while Turner might have played a part in helping her onto her feet again, she liked thinking she didn't need him to stay on them.

She had made her own life here after all. She counted eleven people she knew by name, five homes she'd been invited to independent of Jack, six lunches she'd gone out to. Her world had expanded at the same time she felt capable of solitude. It was having the choice that suited her.

On an old teacher's suggestion, Anne shot slides of her work at various stages. Three weeks back, after she'd finished what she thought were some fairly good paintings, she had gone out to a photo store and had the slides developed, and then sent them down to a friend of hers who ran a small gallery in Soho. Immediately Anne wished she hadn't. What if she never responds? she thought. Or, What if she responds, and doesn't like them? Anne didn't really want to know that they weren't as good as she'd imagined, or that they were "an interesting start," for that matter.

The point was to keep painting, keep loose. She liked them well enough to keep at them, and that was all she needed. She decided to put the whole matter out of her mind.

Now, moments after Jack had left for work, the phone was ringing. It was her friend Anika.

"Anne," she said.

"Yes."

"I got your slides."

Her heart raced. She couldn't read Anika's voice. "Good," she tried.

Anika said nothing for a moment. Someone else was talking to her, giving her instructions, "I'm trying to set that up right now," she whispered. "I'm sorry, Anne," she said. "That was my boss."

"No problem."

"So anyhow . . . when can you make it down to New York?" Anika said.

CHAPTER 52

Charlton Carter, the farmer who owned the fields Turner had photographed, called Turner the day after the story ran. Initially he'd had no comment. Now he said he'd made a big mistake.

"I had no idea what it was," he said.

"Who paid you?"

"Who said someone paid me?"

"I'm assuming you didn't just volunteer."

"Didn't give his name."

"He paid in cash?"

"Let's just say he didn't give his name."

"Do you remember what he looked like?"

"Bony-looking guy."

"How old."

"I don't know. My age, I suppose."

"And how old is that?"

"Around fifty. Listen. They didn't tell me what it was. Not the truth, anyhow. You got me? It was construction debris. The barrels was supposed to be paint and the like."

"They didn't tell you it was toxic chemicals?"

"No, they didn't."

Turner called the DPW. He said to the receptionist that he'd been talking to an official, and he needed to follow up on a question.

"Can't remember his name. He's a pretty thin guy, around fifty, I'd say."

"Arthur Franks?"

"Yes. I think that's it. He works with Harlan Stanyan, doesn't he?"

"Yes, he does. Would you like to talk to him?"

"Is he there?"

"No, but I can leave a message and have him call you."

Turner left his name and office phone number.

He called the newspaper's library and asked if there were any photos on file of Arthur Franks. There was, a photo of him in a feature on the postcard club of Lakeland. Turner had a copy of the picture sent to him. He brought it out to show Charlton Carter.

"This the guy?"

"Oh yeah. That's him."

IT WAS ALMOST ALL there. Turner would talk to Hickey. He would try again to talk to Pavio and Stanyan. He would talk to Harris and the rest of the team. And he would talk to Jack. He had confirmed a member of the Department of Public Works paying off a farmer to dump barrels of hazardous chemicals.

The letters and calls kept coming in. The merchant's association, predictably enough, was furious.

"You have done the whole community a grave disservice," Philip Crisalino said in a letter. "Let's end this harmful and injurious invective."

It was the end of the cold war, said Herb McShain, his friend on the county legislature.

"How so?"

"Toxic Terror has replaced the Evil Red Empire."

Turner thought about that. He wasn't convinced.

"For decades we nearly bought the end of the world because of our delusional paranoia. We were deluded about the Russian military capacity. We're doing the same now."

"This isn't a delusion. It's a quantifiable problem, and there are people with very real symptoms."

"Yes, yes. The problem is that it's partially true. There are threats. But now people see them, sense the dangers even when they aren't real. They believe toxins are everywhere, underground and in their bloodstreams and in their children's bloodstreams. And anytime someone yells about it, it might as well be true. Guilty until proven innocent."

"Looks like there's proof of guilt."

"Yes. And the town'll bankrupt itself, and demonize one another in getting to the bottom of it."

There was truth in that. People called to ask about their neighbors, or to tell Turner they'd heard trucks, or might have seen trucks, or that they'd definitely seen trucks, or that they were worried trucks might come not only to their neighbor's house but to their own, at night, when they were sleeping, or they'd smelled something odd, or a strange cough had kicked in.

One of the council members said it was Jack Lambeau. That none of this had gone on before he came into town. He asked to remain anonymous. He said Lambeau had cut deals with the land inspectors. And that he'd tricked the mayor into going along. He was risking everyone's safety to build what amounted to a glorified shopping mall.

"I'm not going to put it in if I can't get attribution," Turner said. "I'm not going to simply print innuendo."

"Is that 'cause you're drilling his wife?"

"This conversation is over," Turner said.

MORE THAN ONCE, TURNER thought his car was being followed—by other trucks, and once by a beat-up old Cadillac. Each time he'd lost them, though he was fairly certain they could catch him if they wanted. It was a game of some sort and he was playing along. Maybe he was fatalistic; or maybe he was counting on Anne visiting his hospital room after he'd had his arm broken.

But he wasn't as terrified as he should have been. He was riding on adrenaline, caffeine, and an evolving sense of purpose. And likely he realized that if he ever took this for what it was, he would never make it out of bed. He would bolt himself in. Or else drive down to a motel in Mexico and take a room under a fake name.

CHAPTER 53

On a warm Tuesday morning, Turner drove down to Syracuse to meet with the newspaper's editorial staff: Ellis McCourt, the regional editor, Jerry Cass, the projects editor, Digby, Clark, and someone from the art department.

His stories were appearing not only on the local pages (all editions), but three times already on the front page. Now, with all the new material Turner had gathered, Clark was pushing for a four-day, front-page series. Turner was ecstatic. All his hard work had paid off in spades. He'd been relentless and resourceful. He didn't see how he could have done better with the limited time he had.

He walked quite proudly through the newspaper parking lot and up the stairs to the newsroom on the second floor. Before when he'd entered the newsroom he'd been an unwanted vagrant. Now Digby saw him coming, and urgently motioned him over.

Turner came armed with information. The soil samples taken from the farms, he told Digby, had come back with a long list of contaminants, a veritable spumoni: "PCBs, phenol, xylenes, methylene chloride, ethylbenzene, benzene, dichloroethane, arsenic, chromium, cadmium, toluene, and that's just a partial list."

The area near the farms was populated by several underground lakes known as aquifers. The earth was underlayed by bedrock, a similar formation to that of Love Canal. Turner had become learned on the contaminants, and on the composition of the earth in Lakeland—both subjects for lengthy sidebars.

Digby nodded, eyebrows knitted in thought.

Turner explained how they took soil samples from the harbor sites and the farms and were able to match the chemical fingerprints.

"Fingerprints. Hmm. Use that word," Clark said. "Makes it more like a true-crime story."

"It is a true-crime story," Turner said.

He told them the charges that would likely be filed, everything from reckless endangerment to involuntary manslaughter.

"Are you going to get an interview with the deaf lady?" Clark asked.

"She isn't deaf," Turner said.

"I'm sorry. The dumb lady. That sounds disrespectful."

"The correct term is mute."

"All the technical stuff, the chemicals they dumped, the poisoned aquifers, and kids drinking cancerous water. We've covered all that before," Clark said. "The news here is a man dying on the job, and this deaf lady's lawsuit."

"And what it's done to a town's dreams," Turner said.

"Have they exhumed the body?" Digby asked.

"By the end of the week."

"And it's Jack Lambeau's brother who did the burying," Clark said.

"It doesn't mean Lambeau knew anything about it," Turner said.

"No. But it's damn interesting, isn't it? And you've got a dirty mayor and a dirty DPW head, people paying off farmers with city tax money. Hoo boy."

Two photographers had been assigned, and the art department made maps of the polluted areas.

When the meeting was done, Digby told him to stick around.

"You hungry?" he asked.

"Sure."

"Good. I'm taking you to lunch."

AS HE WAITED FOR DIGBY he saw Rathaman returning from the snack room.

"Hey, Turner. Heard you got a good one going," he said.

"Every once in a decade."

Rathaman stood there. Turner had nothing more to say to him.

"I'm sorry Florida didn't work out," Turner said.

"It's a screwed-up world down there," Rathaman said.

Turner shrugged.

"It was a party. I was loaded. I tried to take her name tag off and put it on my shirt. No one's got a sense of humor anymore."

DIGBY TOOK TURNER TO lunch at Gigante's, one of those Syracuse landmarks where everything, even the food, had dust on it. Gigante's had been around since the 1920s, and four presidents had eaten there, Herbert Hoover being the first and Eisenhower the last.

Syracuse was another northeastern industrial city where the downtown had emptied and everyone had moved to the suburbs, most of which were formless and nondescript. They'd built a mall downtown, and filled it with all the right stores, and then no one came. The shops sat empty, employees were let go. Every place had a massive sale, and still no one came. They'd done a halfway decent job with it, Turner remembered Lambeau telling him. But the food court filled with vagrants. The cops dragged the vagrants away and then a homeless advocates' group picketed the mall, and then the few people who might have come to the mall on principle now opted against it. Now there was another larger mall on the city's northwestern outskirts.

Digby had started his career as a bureau reporter in Seneca Falls, he told Turner. It had been the model for the town in *It's a Wonderful Life*.

"That's how everyone sees, Lambeau right? As another George Bailey."

"They did."

"Listen, I like Clark's idea of doing a profile on that dead waste hauler. Such a symbol, isn't it? Poisoned land, poisoned body. Any idea how long they kept him before burying him?"

"No."

"We got a call from someone saying he was buried in Jack Lambeau's backyard."

Turner was beginning to see how this story might become misshapen by minds like Digby's and Clark's.

"That's all rumor for now."

Digby shook his head, and a smile came across his face, as if Turner had orchestrated the events. "It's too much is what it is. It's almost hard to believe. The guy that won't stay buried, just like the town that won't stay buried."

Turner said nothing.

"You still buddy-buddy with him?"

"With who?"

"Jack Lambeau."

"I wouldn't say buddy-buddy, but we're friends."

"Is that going to get in the way of your doing your job?"

"No. Of course not."

Digby said nothing. He was trying to read Turner's face.

"And everything's still going full steam for their big waterfest."

"The Lakefest celebration. Yes. They've lined up theater, and about fifteen different bands. They're trying to get Sheryl Crow."

"Sheryl Crow, huh? I like Sheryl Crow."

"The idea is they bring people in and then show them what life is like along the Great Lakes, show them a different upstate. An easy and culturally stimulating getaway from Manhattan. There'll be concerts, exotic food stalls, slideshows showing the old port and the best homes, and presentations by realtors and chamber of commerce folks. They're going to open up a section

of beach and allow people free windsurfing lessons, cocktail parties on a hundred-year-old schooner."

"You sound a little wistful there, Turner."

"I am, a little."

"And then there's your story with the pictures of all those
nasty barrels and tanks."

"Yes."

"That's not your problem."

"I realize that."

"It's just what happens to these towns. They're lost. Spiritually and economically. And then they grab whatever boondoggle
comes around. This thing was never going to come off, was it? I
mean, really?"

"I think it might have. They had it all lined up, public support,
private initiative, market research and advertising, cash."

"But it's upstate, Turner. Kind of like a cow. You can dress it
up, take it dancing and romancing, but at the end of the night
it's still upstate."

IT WAS A CONTINUOUS cycle, Turner thought on his drive
north. Towns desperate for a recovery without the means for
healthy skepticism, like poor old shut-ins who sign up for get-
rich-quick schemes that leave them heartbroken and broke. In
the past twenty years any plan mentioning growth or jobs stood
a good chance of making it through up here, be it a new prison,
an incinerator, an oil refinery, a military base, a landfill, or an
Indian casino.

The insidious part about Lakeland's renewal was the length
they'd gone to alter public perception, to prepare people for a
new life they were never really going to have. With all the new
businesses and the investment, you still couldn't turn a dead
factory town into a tourist town, not *really*, not without giving
the larger part of the population bus tickets and a few thousand
dollars to get out of town. People summered in the Hamptons,

Nantucket, Martha's Vineyard, and Bar Harbor to be with other people who summered there. What would they do when the first nasty bar fight broke out and someone put a broken bottle in another's face? Or when they took their Saab in for work and saw it being driven around town that night for kicks?

Turner remembered something they'd asked him when he'd signed up for his health insurance. Did he have any preexisting conditions? That's what Lakeland had, he thought, a whole host of preexisting conditions. Did that mean they weren't worthy of any benefits?

HE DROVE NOW by the cartoon strip malls and cookie-cutter housing complexes of Syracuse's northern suburbs, then past the dying towns of southern Lakeland County, Phoenix, and Fulton, by the former brewery site that a group of indie filmmakers from New York wanted to buy cheap and use as a studio plot. Turner pictured the films they'd make, hopeful and condescending ones about diner waitresses falling in love with handsome passers-through. Fulton made Lakeland look cheerful. Empty lots, barbed wire, potholed streets, broken sidewalks, everyone a little gray-complected, cigarettes hanging from their lips. Whenever he passed through Turner felt a small wave of panic that he'd find himself stuck up here in one of these lives.

Just north of Fulton he saw a man running ahead, and he knew from the fluid stride and the brown sweatshirt who it was. They were four miles from Lakeland, which meant a round trip Turner could never have managed—these days he couldn't run a mile. Jack was a driven runner, and on long distances he told Turner he entered into a narcotic state, his mind emptied like that of a Zen monk.

In the last month Turner had avoided thinking through his motivations, but he wanted to believe now that all these hours he'd been logging weren't about screwing Jack over, nor did they have much to do with Anne. They were about doing a job well.

Getting to the center of a story, and getting himself out of Lakeland. And yet it could be argued that in basic and unforgivable ways he'd betrayed a friendship, and been sneaky about it to boot. More than anything just then he wanted to be running alongside, or to insist that Jack climb in the car like any sane person, and they'd have a pitcher or two at a dive bar somewhere and talk this whole thing out. But of course he'd abdicated that right. They were no longer friends, and seeing Jack running alone, enclosed in his thoughts, underscored that.

Turner honked his horn as he passed, not knowing what else to do. Jack looked up and waved from behind, without affection, or perhaps even recognition.

CHAPTER 54

The weather got warmer and then it rained. Snow melted into brown slush. The ground squished. Mud splattered everywhere. Cars were covered in it, boots and pant legs too. The Lakeland High School football team played a spring scrimmage, and the pictures in the Lakeland Eagle were epic. Muddy pile-ups, jerseys and even faces unrecognizable. One boy was photographed after sliding headlong over the goal line; the ball, however, had slipped from his arms, and could be seen at the side of the frame. The caption read, "The One that Got Away."

The last rags of white clung to the roadsides even on a day when the mercury reached seventy, a reminder of what they'd been living in for months. The river swelled. Basements flooded. On one eastside street residents rode canoes from one house to the next. And then it would rain again. May showers were supposed to stir thoughts of June flowers (everything in Lakeland being a month behind). But the rains this year were too constant, and too corrosive. May felt like a hangover. There might be two nice days in a row, but never three, and what most people felt, inside or out, was damp. Damp shoes dragged over carpets, making puddles on hardwood floors, damp jackets hanging up, wet umbrellas standing in the corner of a room, wet hair, rain against the window.

Rain had no cleansing effect on the farms where Harris and Parkhurst and the rest had dumped all those barrels. It hastened the rust and leaking, the barrels' contents finding their way into soil and creeks. There were dead plants and quite a few dead animals. The extent of the damage grew hourly.

"In a dry climate this wouldn't have been half as bad," Donaldson, the DEC inspector, told Turner.

But it was as far from a dry climate as you could get. Even Seattle was drier in May, without a winter of snow to melt.

"You're gonna get some fishkills. I guarantee you. It's going to take a long, long time to even begin to clean those farms up."

The barrels had leached into streams. The smells along certain roads were overwhelming. Groups met regularly with a lawyer from Albany. There were two movements afloat in town—the movement to find out more, every last misstep and violation, and the movement to quiet what was being found out.

Clem Mullen from the merchant's association said it was hysteria drummed up by Turner and the media, for the purpose of selling newspapers and improving the TV news ratings, which is what they always said about reporters who did their jobs.

With all the bad weather, preparations continued for the Lakefest celebration. Shop owners painted their storefronts, city employees built soundstages for all the bands and variety acts coming in, and volunteers cleared trash from the side of the road. It was hard to find a store or bar without a poster in the window. The trucks rolled in with all the rides and food stands and games for the Lakefest carnival. They set up the tilt-a-whirl, the bumper cars, the rickety old roller coaster and Ferris wheel. Some other year they might have newer rides, but there was something charming about the old equipment, the excitement of knowing on a fast turn you might find yourself flying off into that big green lake.

"What do you think it is?" Stewart asked Turner. "Denial? Or do they just want to have a damn good party?"

"The latter," Turner said.

If the party was good enough, the thinking went, nothing else mattered. It filled Turner with admiration, and some repentance.

AS TURNER WALKED AROUND TOWN on his various rounds he kept looking for Anne. He finally tracked her down outside the YMCA on a Monday afternoon—the afternoon of her yoga class, he had remembered. As she walked out the front door she caught his eye, then ducked into her car.

"Anne," he called out.

"Oh hi, Turner. I'm kind of in a rush. How are you?"

"All right, I guess."

He felt the need to say something splendid, something profound that would make her rethink everything. But he'd lost this battle already, he realized. He'd stopped her on the way home and forced her to talk when she didn't want to. He felt earnest suddenly, and heavy, and he didn't trust his ability to do anything right now but fuck this up further.

"Is there something you need to tell me?" Her voice sounded exasperated and it deflated Turner.

"Not really. Not like this, I mean."

"Well, I've got to run then," she said. "You heading in to work out?"

"Yes," he said. "You know, got to work on that washboard stomach."

She smiled, and it gave him some relief.

"No, I'm not working out. I came by because I have no way to reach you."

She nodded.

"I feel cut off, Anne. You can reach me whenever you want, but I'm always waiting around for you."

"Well then, don't wait around for me."

He tried to read her face. It was unyielding.

"So what then . . . it's over?"

"No," she said. "I'm not saying that."

"What's going on with Jack?"

She paused and then said, "This isn't the place to talk about it."

"No. I guess not."

"I'll tell you what. I'll come over sometime and we'll talk."

He didn't like the sound of that. It sounded like what he'd say to someone he was planning to dump.

"I'd like that," he said.

"All right, then."

He tried to just leave then, to let her go, and to maintain his pride, perhaps show her just a touch of indifference, but the word came out of his mouth. "When?" Turner asked.

"I don't know."

"I'm sorry. Listen, this is ridiculous. You're married, and I'm getting strange here. Soon I'll be climbing trees and peering into your bedroom window."

Anne didn't laugh.

"Joke," Turner said.

"In the next four or five nights. I've got a painting I want to give you."

"What if I'm not there?"

"Then you're not there."

She started her engine.

"I'll probably be there," Turner said, but she'd already driven off.

BACK AT HIS APARTMENT that night, Turner spread out drafts of all his stories and he looked at them, his notes, and the photographs he'd taken. There was still so much to do, so much to organize, so much to cut. He worked well for about an hour, and then he started thinking about Anne. He was trying to put a positive spin on their exchange, but there wasn't much room for that. It was undoubtedly a complicated time for her, but he was pissed off regardless. She would bring him a *painting*, she said. Why did that sound like she was offering him the runner-up prize?

He put his work away, tried reading and then watching TV, but everything he read and every show he flipped through involved someone he could construe as Anne, someone with her hair color, someone with her voice, or close enough, someone female and desirable. He gave up and lay in bed staring at the ceiling. "Stop it, Turner," he said aloud. "Don't get maudlin." Then he got up, put his pants and shoes on, and took a long, rudderless walk around his neighborhood until he was too tired to stay awake anymore.

When he returned, he went to sleep wearing all his clothes—on his sofa, so there'd be no empty space next to him.

CHAPTER 55

It was not without hesitation that Jack agreed to drive with his father, for his father's birthday, to the Indian gaming casino in the next county. His mother had wanted a small dinner at home, followed by a game of Scrabble, or maybe Pictionary. He went because his father had been asking him for months, and because he knew his father would otherwise go alone, and being alone in a casino on your sixty-fourth birthday was something no one should have to endure.

"They're gonna be sorry they let us into that place," his father said.

On the drive, his father talked strategies, told him about picking the right table in blackjack, how to bet in roulette, the rules of craps. His father's health had declined over the winter. His eyesight was worse, as was his hearing. In January he'd sprained his shoulder slipping on the ice, and it had yet to heal entirely. But now, on a road trip with his son, he seemed rejuvenated. He'd even dressed nicely, in a pressed blue shirt and necktie.

"He's so excited," Jack's mother said before they left. She had no interest in gambling (which she called godless) but she wouldn't get in the way of Frank's going so long as he left his bank card at home this time.

WHEN THEY ARRIVED, Jack wanted to walk around to see what the Oneidas had put together since their long battle with the antigambling groups. The place was abundantly indistinct.

The typical layout of tables, the blue carpets, the outmoded lounges. There was no personality, nothing to differentiate it from the low-end joints of Atlantic City. The only Native American touches he detected were souvenirs in the gift shop, pictures of proud chiefs on T-shirts and the like. You could do a lot better with a place like this. He could do a lot better.

They walked by a room with around ninety tables, one after the other, with people sitting over cards. Bingo, Jack realized.

"You ever seen anything like it?" his father said, as though they were looking over the Grand Canyon. "Must be a thousand people in there."

Now they walked into the blackjack area, Frank surveying the tables for the right one.

"What are we looking for?"

"For integrity." He made sure Jack was following him here. "You look and see that people at the table are winning occasionally, having fun, laughing. Look and see that they're betting aggressively. That means things are going their way. It's a good sign."

"Makes sense," Jack said.

"And I always pick the women dealers. Not the young gorgeous ones. Someone with a little girth on her, and a gray hair or two."

"Why is that?"

"I had better luck with them."

In short time they found a happy table with a heavy-set dealer named Bonnie and one seat open. Frank sat down.

"Watch me here, boy; you'll learn something."

He bet ten and lost. Then bet fifteen and won.

"See what I just did? An even record, but I'm ahead."

He played on, pulling thirty up or ten down, but mostly staying ahead. He was talking to the others at the table, cracking jokes. They liked him. He liked himself. Indeed, Jack was somewhere between impressed and alarmed by how comfortable his father was here in this smoky, air-conditioned, blue-carpeted world, arranging his chips in neat stacks, tapping the table for another card, and in the next motion signaling the waitress for a drink. Slowly but surely, Frank's pile grew. The transformation in his father's personality made Jack uneasy. Frank overtipped the waitress. Laughed easily. He'd been so quiet these last months, Jack often felt as though he couldn't get more than a couple words from him, and then it was about whatever game or cop show was on TV, or about how proud he was of Jack. Now he was whispering tactics (*See, the reason I did that . . .*) after each hand. It had been a long while since his father had taught him anything, and Jack took the opportunity to appear interested, not simply disheartened by the thought of all the money his father had lost developing this strategy.

"I'm feeling it tonight," he said in the midst of a hot streak. He bet ten and lost; ten more and lost again.

"Uh-oh," Jack said. "The tides are turning."

"Nah, nah. It's like wasting the good pitches with a couple foul tips. Here we go." He bet eighty, got an eleven, and doubled down.

"You're crazy," Jack whispered.

But the dealer busted.

"Oh baby," Frank said, "it's over the right-field fence!"

"You must be three hundred ahead," Jack said.

"Two-eighty."

"That's a pretty good birthday, don't you think?"

His father grinned, then shifted to a glare.

"What are you telling me, you telling me to *cash out*?"

"No. I'm just saying it's a pretty good haul."

His father put down forty.

"You'd do that, wouldn't you?"

"Why not?"

"How would you know how high you could have gone?"

He lost the forty.

"You're making me nervous here, Jack. Play a few hands on your own somewhere, wouldya?"

Everyone at the table was all smiles. In fact, at that moment it looked to Jack like everyone in the casino was having fun except him. His father put a ten-dollar chip in the dealer's tip jar. This was the same man who wouldn't pay extra to put cheese on his hamburger.

"I'm gonna walk around," Jack said.

HE WANDERED THROUGH ROWS of slot machines to the craps tables and the roulette wheels, his ears full of bells, his eyes crowded with lights and garish clothing. He watched a group of people at the roulette wheel plunk chips down and shout their numbers over and over while the wheel spun; shouting as though it could make a difference, as though wanting something desperately enough could make it happen. He zeroed in on a man with a big white mustache and cowboy boots, chanting softly, "thirty-one, thirty-one, thirty-one . . . ," eyes closed tightly, hands together in prayer, while that little white ball dropped in one slot and out another. It pained him now, a sharp tug in his stomach, to perceive, as he glanced around at the eager faces of these high-stakes rollers in their sports jackets and stretch slacks, how closely their expressions resembled those of the audiences at his harbor meetings. Even now, with all that had been unearthed, they were counting on his pulling off a miracle, making it all better. They'd bet the house on it if they could. It made him angry, and a little crazy, that they'd expected so much. Or maybe it was just he who couldn't admit to failing.

He looked back at his father then, making pals with his whole pathetic table, the too-tan guy next to him and the big-haired woman with the plunging yellow sweater on the other side of the table. More than a family dinner, a talk with his sons, a visit with his granddaughter, *this* was the sort of moment his father lived for. A pile of cash. Someone waiting on him, strangers rooting for him. In his eyes, these people were his friends. Jack felt alone then, completely and utterly. He thought now that this trip might have been better with Harris, and he wondered why he hadn't tried harder to get him to come along. He'd worried Harris and his father would fight, he'd told himself, because they often did, and more frequently since Marla kicked Harris out. But that wasn't all of it, he knew. The truth was he feared a confrontation he'd been putting off, a clash with his brother's newfound moral clarity.

His father motioned him over. He wanted him to meet Leon, his new best friend. Leon was a hairdresser, owned his own salon in Rochester.

"But he's not a fruit," his father said. "I mean, he's married, got four kids."

"I could still be a fruit," Leon said.

His father laughed. "Isn't he a stitch?"

"Your father tells me you're an architect," Leon said.

"In a sense."

"He says you're a real trailblazer."

His father bet thirty and won.

"Thank you, ma'am," he said to the dealer. "That's right generous of you."

"Sit down with us, Jack," Leon said.

"Everything he does turns to gold," his father said. "Just like his brother turns it all to shit."

"That isn't fair," Jack said.

He shrugged. "Yeah, well. Are you going to bet or what?"

Jack bet ten and won.

"See," his father said to Leon.

Jack bet ten more and won again. He rolled the chips around in his hand. He felt dizzy suddenly, and panicked in the way of someone who realizes he left a burner on back home.

"I'm good to go whenever you are," Jack said and vacated his seat.

HE SAT HIMSELF AT THE CASINO BAR and watched the basketball play-offs on TV. Bucks and Pacers. Unlike his father and brother, and Steven Turner, he'd never been one to care about professional sports. The man next to him wore a Bucks jersey over a T-shirt. He looked to be in his midfifties. Jack drank two scotches and rooted loudly for the Pacers.

At one of the commercial breaks, his mind went to the questions he'd soon have to answer. Why, rather than going to the police as he should have months back, had he let himself fly to Chicago and get feted instead? They had him already, he sensed, the investigators he'd been ducking. Every day he stayed away it got worse. And yet he suspected the moment he told the truth the project would be dead, all those jobs lost, his brother headed for jail, and a whole town of people would hold him responsible for their shame. As if he hadn't risked everything for them; as if anyone would have given a damn about them if it wasn't for him. He had put them on the map again, brought them to the brink of a new life.

He began to consider the likelihood that he'd be jobless soon, perhaps for a while, and he might have to pay some hefty fines and lawyer fees. For all his hard work, he'd never saved up much. Anne had some money her father had left her, but he couldn't count on that; not for a lot of reasons. A flood of remorse overtook him then; the air left the room. He realized he'd been digging a quarter into the soft wood surface of the bar.

"How does it feel to know you're going down?" the man next to him asked him.

It took Jack a full ten seconds to understand he'd been talking about basketball.

HE ESCAPED out into the cool night to breathe a little. He stood flat against the building, like a kid cutting class to smoke a cigarette. *Think of something,* he told himself. *Come up with a plan.*

All he could come up with was this: If they could keep it together for another month, or better yet two, when the new buildings broke ground and the governor cut the ribbon and they'd had their festivals, then they might be able to push past this; it might be too late for most of the stores and restaurants to pull out. And they might not want to once they saw what this was. They'd all put too much into this, come too excruciatingly close to let it fall apart. It was even selfish to quit right now, he thought.

He could fight this.

He would double his hours, sweeten deals and hold hands, whatever it took (even stretch the truth, if need be); and he'd carry the whole damn town on his back if he had to.

WHEN HE RETURNED TO THE TABLE, his father's pile had halved.

"What happened?"

"Just a little bad luck."

"A *little* bad luck."

"His last bet was a hundred," Leon said.

"You shouldn't have left me here alone."

"The second you walked off he went in the tank," Leon said.

"But he did great last time."

"Root me on here, son."

"Let's go, you're still ahead." There was around $350 left.

"But I lost six in a row. I'm due," he said.

He plunked it all down, every last chip.

"Oh *my*," the yellow-sweatered woman said, her décolletage winking.

"Can you spell *balls*?" Leon said.

"That's a ridiculous amount of money," Jack said.

"Got to risk it to make it. I'm *due*. You nickel and dime and you never make any progress."

It was an insane sort of logic, because your odds got no better once you'd lost a dozen times. The next time out you were just as likely to lose, Jack knew.

His father hit eighteen, respectable enough.

But the dealer dealt herself twenty.

"You're a very evil woman," his father said.

"I'm sorry," she said. "It's not personal, you know."

His father stood then and gathered himself. His restraint was admirable. He didn't shout or curse or kick the table as Jack certainly would have done (Harris would have set the joint on fire). He shook hands with everyone at the table, pocketed Leon's card, and promised he'd get a haircut the next time he was in Rochester.

Then he walked out of the room with Jack at his side.

"You're handling it rather well," Jack said.

"I took my shot," he said. "D'you see the looks on their faces when they saw that *bet*?"

"No. I closed my eyes."

"Haven't felt like that in years."

"You lost everything."

"Not everything," he said. He pulled out two twenty-five-dollar chips.

"Got what I came with. Nice birthday. That's all I wanted. Didn't have to go home rich."

CHAPTER 56

It was a bit of a magic trick, but Jack had managed to keep the project relatively on course. An anchor store had pulled out, but another, on Jack's reassurances, had decided to move up their design date. He spoke to the owners of the Astros' minor league baseball team in Auburn, to see if they might want to move to Lakeland, and a New York director who had agreed to stage Chekov's *Three Sisters* at the Great Lakes Theater. Jack floated rumors a Broadway star was coming but he wouldn't reveal the name for fear of jinxing it. For everyone he secured there was someone else wavering. So he called from morning until afternoon, made trips and offers—free garbage pickup and sewer access, free water, beefed-up security. Guaranteed press coverage, a prominent spot on the Web site—whatever it took. One merchant asked for free membership for his family at the Lakeland Country Club, and Jack made it happen.

It wasn't only about Lakeland now, it was about the neighboring towns, and those along the Hudson, and through the Mohawk Valley all the way over to the Berkshires, whose hopes of renewal hinged on Lakeland's success. And there were the journalists who'd plugged the town, state officials who'd bent regulations and time constraints, and bankers in New York who'd placed their trust in him.

The news about the barrels kept appearing in the paper. Turner was hard at it, though Jack wasn't sure how much he knew, or how far he'd go to bring the town down. He found it slightly traitorous that Turner was doing all this without ever talking to him about it.

In the afternoons, he'd find himself staring at the wall in front of him sometimes, wishing he could be anywhere else; that he could take a week on a beach somewhere with Anne and forget all this, everything that had taken place since they got here. Never in his life had he felt so depended upon, responsible for so many. When he left to go home his eyes were tired, his back ached, and his voice was shot. He felt as though if he slept in one day, it would all collapse by the evening, like dominoes.

But he hadn't slept in, and each day his harborfront kept looking a little bit better.

THREE WEEKS BEFORE the start of Lakefest, Showalter told Jack he was leaving the project.

He didn't specifically blame the bad news in the papers, but he said it would be hard to build the way they'd wanted to under the circumstances.

He'd already told several of the merchants, who had indicated to him they were pulling out of Lakeland as well. Finally, he said he might sue, that his lawyers were on retainer, that he had better things to do than waste his time on a pack of small-town incompetents.

There wasn't much Jack could say to any of this.

"We've been trying to build a certain image here. The great old small town. Place to know your neighbors, and see a little Shakespeare. What's it going to do to that image when we've got guys in moon suits pulling drums off the ground by the truckload?"

"It's going to affect it."

"Damn right. I can't put anything more into this. It's a wounded horse. I'm going to cut my losses."

"Is that what you brought me out to tell me?"

"In part."

"What's the other part?"

"I want you to come with me."

"What do you mean?"

"I mean I like you. I like your intelligence, your enthusiasm, your way with people and the press. You've been damned impressive, whatever happens here."

"Thanks, I suppose."

"I want you to be my director of planning, and I want to triple your salary, for starters. How does that sound?"

"I don't know. Sounds a bit like jumping ship."

"That's exactly what it is. Leave this little crap town, Jack, you're too good for it."

THERE WERE PROTESTERS OUTSIDE Showalter's office. John and Jeanette Cornfeller and their posse. The signs said things like COME CLEAN NOW and IT ISN'T JUST DOGS ANYMORE.

Others were protesting on behalf of the project. Two people were shouting at each other. Jack managed to slip out a side door of the lobby undetected. He felt untethered and a little desperate.

He walked from Showalter's office through downtown. The weather had turned. It was warm now, and there were signs everywhere for the upcoming festival, bunting descending from the street lamps and balconies. The harborfront visitors' center was open now, with someone outside dispensing fliers and schedules. A team of senior citizens was painting a storefront across the street, a vision so hopeful, so *wholesome*, that he could scarcely imagine it wasn't assembled for the benefit of one of Showalter's photographers. There were no cameras around. One of the seniors, a man Jack had seen at church once, saw him and then called out to the others, and then someone else from a group near them heard. It was *Jack Lambeau*, they were saying. And for now that was still a good thing.

They waved over to Jack in unison.

He felt a warm rush through his scalp.

"Want to come paint?" someone yelled.

"Sure," he said, and he walked toward them.

THAT NIGHT AT DINNER Anne listened as Jack told her about his afternoon painting. He told her how the project had changed for him, how it had started as something to do on the way to doing something else, but that it had transformed along the way and became who he was. It had taken on so much meaning for him, he said, it had blinded him. It had become a receptacle for everything he wanted to say and do, like her painting, or like a symphony must be for a composer. "But being with these people today, seeing the hope in their eyes, and seeing everyone everywhere in the town getting excited about the big Lakefest weekend, about the governor coming in and about the fact that people will be looking at Lakeland, people from across the state and from elsewhere—it's just hard to give it all up, to suddenly shift gears."

And then he told her about Showalter's offer.

"Where would they be, these projects?"

"The first would be in Nevada."

"*Nevada.*"

"He wants me to help him come up with a concept."

"Is it a mall?"

"Sort of. It's more of a plaza. Shops and amusements, he said. And a couple of hotel casinos."

"And what would your concept be?"

"I don't know yet. Casablanca was what he came up with."

"Dealers in white dinner jackets. A piano player named Sam."

"Maybe."

"And you told him no, right?"

"He'd pay me three times what I'm making now. We could save enough to buy a house."

She stared at him blankly. "It sounds ridiculous. It sounds like everything you hate. Remember what you said the other night when you came home from blackjack? That stuff about preying on people's dreams?"

He remembered. What he'd actually said was they preyed on people's weaknesses.

"What am I supposed to do? I'm in a serious bind. I've got a chance here to salvage something of my career."

"But there are other ways of doing that."

"Like what?"

"You tell the truth, and you take the hits."

"I don't think you understand how this business works, how few second chances you get."

"Maybe not. But I just listened to what you had to say about your afternoon, and my hunch is that you don't want to go out to the neon desert and build some hokey Casablanca casino. I think you'd sooner shoot yourself."

"Thanks," he said.

"For stating the obvious?"

"Yes."

"So you're going to turn him down."

"I didn't say that. I don't know, to be honest. I don't like being poor. There's enough of it here to last a lifetime."

"There are worse things than being poor," she said.

He loved that she was here with him now; that they were talking this way. This was what mattered, he knew.

"I have a confession to make," he said.

"What's that?"

"You know the night I missed dinner, and then cut my hand?"

"Yeah?"

"I saw the new work you've been doing. I sneaked into your studio before you came home."

"You did? No tragedy, I suppose."

"I know now why you were so frustrated before."

"Why?"

"It must have been torture doing those still lifes if all that was stirring around."

"I thought you liked the still lifes."

"I did," he said, and he thought of how to phrase it. "But they were like paintings I'd seen before. The new ones aren't. But I'm sorry I invaded your privacy."

"Apology accepted," she said.

She surprised herself then by going to her studio and retrieving two new ones. She leaned them against the bookcase in the living room.

She wanted to see his response. He didn't just say *great*, the way he had in the past, and he didn't beam proudly either. He spent a while studying them, as though he were reading a poem and trying to understand each line. Then he told her what he saw, in words far more perceptive than she'd imagined him capable of. He talked about them as art, not simply as clues to her complicated past. She was relieved he didn't want explanations; he showed her where his eyes went, and where they moved to.

"They're not too morbid?"

"No, Anne. They're . . . significant."

It embarrassed her how good his praise made her feel.

He asked her how she'd broken through, and she told him about the day she'd been rubbing solvent over a finished piece she hadn't liked, and found something far more interesting in the underpainting, in what was less resolved.

"So you left it half done?"

"No. I just saw how I'd drained the life out of it."

THEY WENT FOR A short walk before turning in. She felt lightheaded, and a bit exposed, as though she'd read to him the pages of her diary. The sky was clear and the moonlight pitched shadows from the old barn and grain silo. She could forget how remote it was out here, how very quiet. There was only the wind, and it wasn't so cold now.

She thought of their year and a half together in New York, how they'd taken their time building their relationship because they knew that it was right, knew this was the one. They hadn't slept together until the seventh date. She remembered how nervous she'd felt during those first months, and how she couldn't stop thinking about him. Being with him made her realize how much more she wanted from her life than what she had. She'd been so bored of the men she was meeting, bored of her job, bored of her thoughts. He was the one who pushed her to paint again, who told her she should quit her job if she hated it so much.

She remembered the first weekend they took away together, in New Hampshire. How giddy she'd felt when they put their clothes away in the same bureau. She saw a thousand weekends away together, and there were plenty after that, and plenty of perfectly good weekends in his apartment or in hers.

IN BED LATER, SHE let Jack slowly undo her pajama top, let him kiss her stomach and the pale insides of her arms. Then he looked in her eyes and just stopped.

"It's not fair to sleep with someone night after night and never make love," he said, and turned away.

She wondered, Is this where it ends?

If she was going to tell him, now was the time. She could tell him everything, as he'd tried to tell her everything and afterward there'd be nothing to say anymore.

"Jack . . ."

But then something very strange happened. In the moment before Anne confessed, she saw looking watchfully at her the man she'd moved here for, the one she'd planned her life around. It was like seeing a photo of a time you'd forgotten about. She saw him replace, or rather replenish, the simplification that she'd created in her mind, that she'd been increasingly ready to leave. Her eyes had adjusted to the light enough so that she could see his strong, intelligent face, which was turned toward her now like an underpainting, and he looked at her not with resentment but with affectionate impatience. He'd said what he felt. It had been a lovely night, and he didn't want it to end just yet. It should have a better end, he was saying. She was flooded now with longing, not only of a sexual kind, but a longing for a better end, decades down the road, and any sort of leaving seemed suddenly impossible.

"Come here," she said. And she pulled him to her.

CHAPTER 57

Harris ate dinner the next night with Marla, their seventh meal together in the last two weeks. He'd gotten in a good two hours of peek-a-boo and pretending to be a dinosaur with his daughter, then he'd eaten with Marla, and they'd talked about themselves, their future. Marla wanted to take courses at the college. There was a chance she could go back to the theater as a manager. With all the development in town they were thinking of expanding, she said.

"I might be able to pick the movies."

"That's great," Harris said.

"I mean, it's not like it'd be entirely our choice. The studios have a lot of say, and the distributors. We'd have to figure out some child care."

"I'd stay home if I had to."

"You have to work, Harris, but maybe someday. If you're between things. You can do the Mr. Mom."

After he'd put Charlotte to bed and helped Marla with the dinner dishes and watched TV, Harris decided to play his hand. He had been through a lot. And he realized how much he didn't want to miss another day with them.

"I don't want to be a guest anymore," he said. "Not with my own wife and daughter. I want to move back in."

She nodded slowly in understanding. "All right, Harris," she said. "You really want to?"

"'Course I do."

"Because it isn't a part-time job thing, you know. Change a diaper or two and go out with the guys all night. Right?"

She studied his face. He did feel like a job applicant, but he didn't care.

"Right," he said.

"It's getting up in the middle of the night, three times maybe. And it's cleaning up her throw-up—"

"Haven't I done that?"

"—and taking her to the doctor if she needs it."

"I just got done doing that."

"And doing all that sterilizing, bottles and things."

"I know that. I want to do it all, every day and every night."

Then her face softened. She smiled. She was so pretty there in her little cutoff shorts and her pink-and-white checkered blouse, Harris thought. Not in a movie star way, but in his way. She was his last good chance.

"Then bring your things tomorrow night, and you can move back."

HE FELT SO COMPLETELY HAPPY on his way across town that night, and even better, he felt peaceful. The day before he'd met with the pediatrician and after a miserable, sweaty two hours of pacing and waiting, learned to his temporary relief that whatever negative effects his daughter had experienced were not life-threatening, or even health-threatening, *yet* (still a minefield of a word). Something—exposure to chemicals—might have caused her anemia and dropped her birth weight, but her red blood cell counts were up, and it no longer looked like the pre-stages of leukemia. They would have to keep tabs on her, but she was a normal baby girl, as far as the doctor could see. And now, despite Harris's missteps, she'd be his again.

He'd walked there and he was glad that he hadn't brought the truck, because he wanted to have a couple drinks and celebrate his good fortune without worrying about being stopped on his way home.

He stopped by the Colt 45 to play some pool. Harris was a great pool player. While Jack had been in college studying Roman architecture and de Tocqueville, Harris had been learning how to impart top spin and reverse to a cue ball. He was good at pinball and foosball and bowling and basketball and softball and darts and pretty fair at poker. These were not unimportant matters. He liked to win, and he liked being good at things.

Jameson was at the bar nursing a Labatt. "Harlan knows you met with the feds," he said.

"How?"

"I don't know, but he knows."

"Am I supposed to be sorry about that?"

"I think we all need to worry."

"That's the problem with you, Lew. I'm not gonna run scared. I'm not going to live my life like that."

"I'm just saying we all got to watch our backs, you know? I almost got hit crossing the street the other night. Maybe it was an accident, but it never happened that close to me before, you know. Just now, when I've been talking about the dumping."

"All right, then. I'll watch out," Harris said.

On this night Harris held the table for four games and three pints, and then he wandered out into the cool night, and he was thinking how there'd be fewer of these nights out at bars alone after tonight, and how that was all right. Maybe this was the last, in fact, the last night on his own, responsible for no one. He'd go out, but it'd feel different. It already felt different.

HE WAS THIRTY-ONE, and Harris felt himself crossing into a new life. And while it worried him that he couldn't be perfect, that he might slide into his old methods again, he had to take the chance. He would wake up every day under the same roof as Marla and Charlotte, and if he was ever lost again, he'd look at the two of them and he'd try and remember this walk, this moment when the answers seemed clear and within reach. He would work hard, he decided, at whatever job he had. He'd make it impossible for any boss to fire him. Maybe he could even take some classes at night. He would like someday to be a manager, he thought. He'd been pretty good with the limited authority they'd given him.

As he made his way down Bazorcik's street, thinking of his child again, her little hands and her smile and her little nose and the way she'd lit up that afternoon when he picked her up and the way her weight felt in his arms as he danced her around the room—so lost in his happiness was Harris that he failed to see or hear the men who sprinted out from the old white Buick behind him, threw a wool blanket over him, and clubbed him repeatedly in the head and legs and chest with what felt like a shovel.

CHAPTER 58

When Harris came to he was in what looked like a park. There were trees, and stretches of mustard-colored grass crested by asphalt paths. None of it was familiar. His head pounded, and he couldn't move his left arm. His vision was blurry in spots and his mouth tasted like pennies. Someone had whacked him in the legs—in the thigh, fortunately, and right below his hip, not his knees, so he could walk okay, though he was certainly in pain. His arm felt broken, and maybe his nose. He'd had his nose broken before. It was caked with dried blood, which he tried to wipe away with his dirty hands. He walked from the tree where he'd spent the night, out toward one of the asphalt paths. There was a woman in business clothes sitting on the bench, eating an expensive-looking pastry. Harris asked her where he was, or he tried, but the woman seemed frightened by the question, and probably by his appearance, and she stood and walked quickly away without her pastry, and without answering him. There were children in a playground, and a woman in a nurse's uniform watching them. Wherever he was there were electric street cars, tall buildings, and people busily walking to work, carrying attaché cases and leather handbags, walking little dogs, and there were nice cars, Volvos and a few BMWs and a Mercedes, even. It felt as if he were Rip van Winkle gone to sleep for twenty years, and here was Jack's plan now come completely to life. Prosperity. Activity. A snowbelt renaissance. A waterfront Main Street. It had all happened as he'd predicted, as he'd promised. And if Harris looked around town he'd find his brother, now fifty, and Harris would look at himself in the mirror and see he was the same age. He could see the waterfront in the distance, and all the hotels along Lake Ontario and the wooden boardwalk and the shops and the people all around. There were street performers on the street across from him, a violin and cello, and an artist painting portraits of what looked like tourists.

It was so lively! Lakeland. And it made him happy, and proud of his brother, though he felt groggy still, almost drunk, and he wondered how much he'd had to drink, and how was it that he'd wound up in a park, and how it was that twenty years had gone by.

He made his way from the park to a newspaper stand at the corner of two bustling streets, packed like Lakeland had never been. Such clothes and style. Money everywhere! He grabbed a newspaper and he looked at the date. Same month and year as the night before. And the paper was the *Globe and Mail.*

"Are you going to buy that?" a voice said.

All the magazines were Canadian.

"Is this Toronto? Is that what this is?" he asked the man behind the stand, although the question was silly. How could it possibly be?

"Of course," the man said. "What'd you think?"

HARRIS WANTED FIRST TO clean up and then find a phone. He walked into a restaurant toward what he thought was the bathroom, but wasn't. It was the kitchen, and the chef, who'd been cracking eggs, looked frightened.

Harris looked around for a bathroom and didn't find one. He saw a sink, at least, but it was over near the chef.

"You can't come back here," the chef said.

"I just want to clean myself up a little."

"You can't come back here. You have to leave," he said.

"Someone hit me," Harris said, "and they dragged me up here, and they left me in a park to die."

The chef was unmoved.

"All I want to do is clean up and use the phone. I need to get back home. My wife and my little daughter are waiting for me."

A woman poked her head in.

"Someone hit me!" Harris said. "A group of them hit me. They must have driven me up here. Why did they leave me here?" Harris said. "For Chrissakes, don't you have a bathroom, a *sink* or something? I just need some soap and water. Is it so much to ask for?"

The chef reached for his cutting knife, and then brandished it.

"Leave now," he said.

"You're gonna stab me? What the fuck?" Harris said. "For what? For wanting to wash up? Is that a crime in your country?"

"Leave," the chef said. "I won't ask again."

The head poked in again.

"We've called the police," the woman said.

"The police? For what? For trying to find a place to clean up? For getting beat up? Excuse me for getting beat up. It wasn't my plan. It wasn't what I set out to do."

He walked out of the kitchen. He would go somewhere else and clean up. The customers were all staring at him.

"What the hell. I'm just trying to find a bathroom," he said.

He saw two uniformed police officers at the front of the res-taurant waiting for him.

He turned straight around and, without thinking, ran through the kitchen and out the back door.

He ran and ran, down three alleyways, then across a parking lot, then down a busy street. He kept running and soon there was no one following him. And why would there be? It wasn't like he'd robbed the place.

Everything hurt. He sat on a bench for a while, then slept for an hour, or maybe it was three, or maybe it was ten minutes.

HE WANDERED FOR A WHILE around this strange town. As close as Albany, and he'd never made the trip. It was an entirely different world up here. So much of everything. So clean. And so many big buildings. The biggest building in Lakeland was the seven-story senior center. And the store windows in Lakeland were mostly filled with old things—not like this. These windows were bursting with new merchandise. It made Harris want to have money.

There were Indian people, and blacks, and Chinese, and Egyptians for all he knew. He liked that about this place, all these worlds packed together like this, like in New York City when he'd visited Jack. He wondered what he'd do if he lived here. Drive a cab, maybe, or work construction. From the looks of it they built things all the time.

It was a nice place to visit, but really it wasn't anywhere Harris could enjoy living. It was simply too big, too many people pressed on top of one another. And even with steady work he'd never have the money to do it right. He'd live in some one-room affair with Marla and Charlotte, and Samson when he got him back. And they wouldn't know anyone. Who would he play softball with, or go bowling with? In Lakeland he couldn't walk a block without running into someone he knew. He thought of Charlotte growing up here, in a town where they called the cops on you after you'd been beaten close to death. In Lakeland they'd have driven him to a doctor, or dressed his wounds themselves, or both. And then they'd have fed him whatever he wanted from the menu. And not only because they knew him; because of who they were. He'd had his share of free meals in Lakeland, in the years he'd been down on his luck and didn't have enough to pay. Once, on his twenty-seventh birthday at Puglia's Pizza, they'd even tossed in dessert. Surely that counted for something. Whatever came of it, Lakeland was *home*, he thought. This place wasn't, and could never be.

WHEN THE SUN RAN OUT, Harris walked into a McDonald's and cleaned himself up in the bathroom with his one good arm. He understood when he looked at himself why the woman in the park had been frightened of him. He looked like something from a horror movie. Blood on his face, his nose and lips puffy.

They'd taken his wallet, but he had a five-dollar bill crumpled in his rear jeans pocket.

He ordered a Big Mac.

"Can't give you a very good exchange rate," the man behind the counter said.

"The hell does that mean?" Harris said, and then he remembered. Going to McDonald's didn't necessarily put you back in America.

The server gave him two alien-looking dollars and fifty cents of change. Harris took a few ketchupy bites of the Big Mac, but his mouth hurt too much to continue. He went outside and called the operator. He made a collect call to Marla.

"Where are you, Harris?"

He could hardly fathom his answer.

"Canada," he said.

"Why are you in Canada?"

"I don't know."

"What's going on, Harris? The police were here looking for you. They said you were supposed to meet with them. They seemed kind of upset."

"It's a long story. I'll explain when I see you."

"Are you okay?"

"No. I want to come home."

"Then come home."

"They beat me up. I was walking back to Bazorcik's and they beat me up."

"Who did?"

"I don't know. I don't have any money. They took my money."

"And they took you to Canada?"

"Yes." There was silence on the other end. "You *believe* me, don't you?"

All the strain of the day—of waking up here, and the chase out of the restaurant, and not knowing who it was who'd done this—piled up in him.

"Of course I believe you," she said.

And then Harris did something very uncharacteristic. He started to cry, mightily.

"Can you get to a Western Union or something?"

"Yeah. Probably."

"I'm going to wire you money. I'm going to wire you a hundred dollars. Take the next bus home, Harris. Take the next bus home and we'll all meet you there."

CHAPTER 59

There was a special memorial service for Dieter Parkhurst at the First Baptist Church of Lakeland. More than two hundred mourners attended, almost none of whom had ever known Parkhurst. Several, however, gave speeches about his courage.

Parkhurst, the red-bearded minister said, was a hard-working, loyal man. A good friend. A good son. He'd worked on the construction of the power plant, and the rehabbing of the First Street Bridge, and he'd served two summers in the National Guard. He'd loved the Buffalo Bills and he'd loved his country. A fine man, a fine son. A fine citizen. A fine worker. He was repeating himself because there wasn't enough to say.

The reception and calling hours were at John and Jeanette Cornfeller's house on Sepulva Street.

"It's your stories that got everyone energized, Turner," John Cornfeller said. "It's a tragedy what these men were coerced into doing. They seared his capillaries. No goggles, no air mask."

When Turner followed the movers inside he was disturbed to find not just John and Jeanette Cornfeller, but a roomful of their compatriots drinking coffee and eating the same nasty carrots, celery, and dip they always had at their meetings. The conversations were all about toxic chemicals, the deals the town made, and the impending lawsuits. Turner stayed out of the conversations, but couldn't help listening to them.

Jeanette Cornfeller offered Turner a glass of lemonade.

"It's nice to know we've got someone like you on our side," she said.

"Thanks," he said. "But I'm really not on anyone's side."

"I getcha," she said, and she winked at him. They were secret partners in her mind.

He didn't disagree with the Cornfellers and their group; he simply couldn't join a crusade, and theirs was a crusade.

He sidled over to Mrs. Cullen and paid his respects. He asked how she'd met the Cornfellers.

THEY DROVE TO MY HOUSE, she wrote.

I'VE NEVER MET MORE GENEROUS PEOPLE.

Turner saw a stack of fliers on a table in the back, which read: *Don't Let This Man Die in Vain.* There was a younger picture of Dieter, at perhaps twenty-three, and already pudgy.

Cornfeller said that while he had never met Parkhurst, he'd gotten to know him over the last month.

The television stations were here, and reporters from the AP (one of whom kept talking about blue-collar rage) and from an Albany newspaper. A man unwanted in life. And everyone wanted him now.

They'd started a Dieter Parkhurst Memorial Fund, and they would hold a candlelight vigil outside City Hall that Sunday evening, the day the body was scheduled to be exhumed. Television was covering it. Would Turner be there? asked John Cornfeller.

"Maybe not," Turner said.

"You have to, Turner. We're getting close here."

"Close to what?"

"To nailing these assholes."

AFTERWARD TURNER WENT to the office to write a quick piece about the memorial service. When he was nearly finished, he heard his name spoken from the open doorway behind him, and he was startled to see it was Jack Lambeau standing there.

"You look like you just saw a ghost," Jack said, and indeed, pale and weary, Jack looked a bit ghostlike.

"I used to know someone who looked like you. I don't think he died, though."

Turner straightened the papers on his desk, like a news anchor who needed to do something with his hands. "Did you know it was me, passing you on the road the other day?"

"Yes."

Then neither of them could think of what to say for a while. Finally Jack said, "If you have questions about my character, Turner, you should ask me."

"I'm sorry," Turner said. "You want to grab a cup of coffee?"

THEY WENT TO THE donut shop across the street where they'd gone several times before. It seemed like another life.

"Here's what I do instead of running," Turner said. "I'm hoping if I eat enough I'll get my own squad car."

It was what Turner did when he felt awkward—make bad jokes. Jack laughed anyway. There were two people on the other side of the room who were staring ahead at the donut bins.

"You want to start?"

"All right. I feel like you've been tailing me, Turner. You've talked to everyone in town except me. You probably talked to Anne, for all I know."

"Just doing my job."

"But any time I've run into you you've got a question about the Lakefest or something nice to say. It's a bit disingenuous, wouldn't you say? It's like you're waiting around for us, for me, to screw up, to fail."

"I'm not taking sides. Something good happens, I report it."

"How wonderfully objective of you."

"If you want my opinion, Jack, this thing's a black hole. And as promising as it's been, I think you should get out of it right now. It's a huge mess from what I can see. They're going to try and blame it on you. Some of them are already doing that, telling me it's your doing, that you knew all about it."

"And you believe them?"

"No."

"Why not?"

"Because I know you."

"You do, huh?"

"I don't think you're entirely blameless, but I think you're mostly blameless."

"Listen, Turner. I just don't like the way you sneak around, that's all. Whatever you want to know, I'll tell you, all right? Just come at me straight."

"Like you've been coming at me straight?"

"And I'll try to do the same."

Turner nodded. "What do you want to know?"

"Everything you know."

"You got the rest of the night?"

"Start talking and we'll see."

"You know, I don't normally do this."

"Yeah? Well, what can I say, Turner? We're all on new ground these days."

"All right then, here we go. . . ." And he told Jack everything, all he knew and what he suspected.

When he was done Turner said, "The question is, how could you have possibly not known? This shit was going on right in front of you, or behind your back maybe, but not far away. Christ, and it was your own brother at the center of it."

"I knew. I didn't know everything. But I knew enough to say something about it. I knew enough to ask a lot more questions than I did."

"I appreciate your honesty."

"You going to use that?"

"No," Turner said. They shared a glance then that said they'd been friends and neither had entirely forgotten it.

"You know what we should do, Jack? We should get together this weekend and talk on the record. I mean, when you figure out what it is you want to say."

"Plan out my exit strategy."

"If that's what you want."

"Pretty sad that's what it comes down to."

"Maybe. Can I say something with the utmost respect?" Turner asked.

"I suppose."

"I know you're thinking your life depends on whether this thing comes off or not. But it doesn't. It *really* doesn't. You will get another job, a good one; someone's probably offered you one already. And the town will go on living and so will small-town America. And the great Lake Ontario. And peace and prosperity, and apple pie. Or maybe they won't. Or maybe some of them will and some of 'em won't but quite frankly, it's not all riding on your shoulders, Jack. Or mine, for that matter. There are real problems up here, and they weren't going to all go away just because you brought in a few nice restaurants and a Banana Republic."

Turner'd surprised himself with his candor, and he wondered what else he was about to say to Jack, whether he was about to tell him about Anne. He might have, if he thought there was anything left to tell.

"We don't have plans for a Banana Republic," Jack said.

"I didn't mean it as an insult."

"Of course you did, Turner, but I prefer it to your kissing my ass and then roasting me over the coals in the newspaper."

"There you go."

"You heard what they did to Harris, then?"

"No, what?"

"They nearly beat him to death. They clubbed him, broke his nose and his elbow, and they dragged him to some public park in Toronto. They called him yesterday and said it was a warning, that if he gave an honest deposition they'd do him worse."

Turner felt dizzy. They weren't fucking around. It could just as easily have been him, he knew.

"I've been getting warnings too," he said.

"And you're not afraid?"

"Sure I am."

"You want to stay with us?"

It was clear from his face that Jack meant the offer. He hadn't put the equation together.

"No, no," Turner answered. Too fast and too definitively, he thought, so he added, "but maybe, yes, if it gets really bad, maybe that'd be an option, thanks."

"Well. If you do, give us a call. No reason to risk your life."

CHAPTER 60

Jack came by to see Harris the next day. Harris held Charlotte with his good arm the entire time Jack was there. He had a light blue towel over his shoulder to catch her spit-up.

"Got my daddy license back," Harris said.

"Home for good," Marla said, and then she left the two of them to talk.

There were bruises around Harris's eyes, and his lips were puffy.

"Aw, Harris," Jack said. "You look awful."

"She makes the most amazing eye contact now," Harris said.

"I see."

"You should see her eat. She's getting on to solid foods now. We started with the sweet creamy things you're supposed to start with, you know, strained banana, strained carrots, apple-sauce. She didn't like the carrots. Book says to let her run the show, so I let her run the show. She doesn't want to eat, she doesn't have to."

He said he was learning to read parent-style, exaggerated and singsongy. Jack looked around the room. It was a warm, comfortable place, a few toys in the corner. A magazine on the coffee table.

"She's gonna be a smart one," he said. "Like you, I hope."

"I don't feel so smart these days. Listen, Harris, you don't remember anything?"

"No. But I have a pretty good idea."

"Did anyone threaten you?"

"Yeah."

"I need to know who."

"Hold on a sec." He called to the next room. "Honey!"

He called Marla *honey* now.

They walked into the next room. Before he handed Charlotte over to Marla, Harris did a slow waltz with his daughter twice around the room.

"Be nice if you took me dancing," Marla said in mock jealousy. She took Charlotte from Harris and walked out to the other room.

"Harlan," Harris said then.

"That's what I figured."

"I didn't want to jeopardize your project. I know what it is to you. And I wanted to tell you, Jack. I've been so proud of you. I want this to happen for you."

He looked at Jack.

"Listen, Jack. Come with me tonight out to one of these farms, and then tell me what you want to do in terms of Hickey and the feds."

THAT NIGHT, JACK AND Harris drove out to a part of the county Jack had never been to, a good fifteen miles outside of Lakeland proper, a place of old family farms that had long ago fallen into disuse. Jack wanted to see what Harris and his men had done. He wanted to know everything before he decided what to do. He wanted to know all the details, when and where the dumping took place, and to what extent. What sort of instructions they were given.

"First we were just clearing the normal stuff—bricks, cement, some machine parts and the like. And then Harlan tells us we can earn more by carting some barrels, double wages and overtime."

"And they never told you what was in them."

"No. I mean, we sort of knew. We knew it wasn't fruit cocktail. Jeez, Jack, it was extra money, that's all. Of course we knew it wasn't right dropping gunk like that out in some field. But you know, there's a lot of wasted land out there no one ever goes on. It's easy to make things disappear."

There was truth in that. Some of the homes out here were without phone lines or plumbing. Some without proper floors. This was the new American ghetto, the fouled and deserted heartland.

Harris said the farmers were paid between $100 and $500, but that not all of them knew what it was they were dumping. Some didn't even know there were men out on their property.

"How could you do that?"

"Easy. It was open land, and we had to get rid of the suckers. Out of sight, out of mind." He raised his eyebrows at Jack. "You can relate to that, can't you?"

They walked through farmland. Belle's mother and father had had a farm somewhere out here. Jack and Harris had spent much of the summer there when Jack was six and Harris four. Eventually it had gone under, like a hundred others. They'd milked cows and shucked corn. Memories hit Jack of long, mostly fun afternoons with Harris—out fishing, or playing catch or hoops. Harris was the better natural athlete, though Jack got more recognition. Harris's talents were dispersed. Jack had chosen two sports, baseball and then distance running, and managed to excel at both. Harris fucked up his knee in a wrestling match his senior year, a dreadful twisting that Jack could never fully forget. To this day when he saw an awful sports injury he thought of Harris's knee bending wretchedly under the weight of a crew-cut heavyweight from North Syracuse. It had kept him from finishing the semester. Harris fell two credits short of graduation, and then never came back. He talked of getting his GED, but he got his union card instead. He might have earned a wrestling scholarship to Oneonta or Plattsburgh, gotten himself out of Lakeland at least for a few years. Jack remembered something else. He remembered his brother trying to switch places the night they'd been fishing and Jack drove drunk into that ditch. It was crazy. Harris had just passed his driver's test the week before. How wrong was it that he valued Jack's future more than his own? Or maybe it was just a kind of love that Jack had never understood.

Harris was the one who volunteered for the National Guard. He asked Jack once if he'd serve his country in a war, and while Jack said yes, he knew it would never happen.

They walked through clumps of old snow and dried mud by what Jack guessed had once been a cornfield. Beyond that was cleared pasture surrounded by trees and brambles. When they got to a wire fence, Harris booted it down in one small spot so they could step over. There was no longer any doubt that they were trespassing. "Any chance someone's going to shoot at us?" Jack asked.

"Doubtful. Guy who owns it sleeps mainly at his girlfriend's in town."

The cool night sky was filled with stars, and a yellow quarter moon. Jack felt remote from all that had been his life the last fifteen years. Here he was in his workboots, tromping through a remote farm in a remote part of the state with his younger brother, looking for barrels, just as twenty years ago they might have searched the backyard for hidden Easter eggs.

They came over a hill to a stand of maples with a creek running through. They walked along the creek for a while until they found where all the barrels had been left. Jack reached in his pocket for his gloves, and his wallet fell out.

Harris picked it up. He opened it and held up a small picture of Jack and Anne in skis, on the top of a snow-covered mountain.

"Vermont?" Harris asked.

"Utah," Jack said, knowing how that might sound to someone who'd never been west of Ohio.

"Utah. You run into any of those guys with the sixteen wives?"

"I don't think the polygamists tend to ski much."

"Too many mouths to feed, huh?" Harris laughed.

"We didn't really see all that much of the local culture," Jack said. He put away the picture and wallet. He could see ten or fifteen barrels scattered about. "How much was left back here?"

"Maybe forty. There's a lot more I could show you, all around this area."

The air smelled tinny, unhealthy. Some of the drums looked partially buried, others were left lying about like litter. He thought of all the newspaper photos he'd seen of the incinerator cleanup. The men in their white suits.

"What'd you think, Harris? Did you think you'd come back someday and tidy up a little?"

Harris squeezed shut his eyes, as though he'd gotten soap in them, then he opened them again.

"Didn't think anyone would care. It was empty land, you know. Kind of place you'd dump a lot of things," Harris said. "We didn't respect it, is what it amounts to."

It was as good an answer as Jack could have hoped for.

He went farther, and he saw the heads of more barrels, dozens of them in various states of decay, some entirely rusted with metal flaking off, and he saw a pond not too far away, and some woods, and he saw three dead birds and a dead squirrel. As he walked about, Jack thought of the way people made choices, the worth of a piece of land, the worth of a life. Of all things, he thought then about that garbage barge from a few years back that kept floating around from country to country for month after wretched month with no takers until it reached the third world—Haiti, if he remembered right. There was money to be had, and so they took it. There was always someone who'd take your garbage out for you, who'd ruin his backyard for you, it seemed. It didn't make him evil or noble, just hungry enough.

"How many of these came from our sites?"

"Pretty much all of them."

Jack felt a growing pressure in his ears and in his chest, and he thought he might vomit too, not only from the smell, or the sight of the dead birds, but from an understanding of his role in all this. It was a terrible thing they'd done out here, and building within him was the realization that for all his talk about changing the landscape, and helping save the American small town, this would be his legacy. He had no confidence they could survive this, nor did he think they should, he and Hickey and whomever they could get to replace Showalter, but at the same time he couldn't turn off the part of his brain that kept thinking of what they might do, what they might have done, if this hadn't happened, or what he might do for the next town, and the one after that. He couldn't let go of any of this yet, though it was what he should have done a long while back. He had the sense that his whole life, every bit of it, was built on lies and half-truths, and that to give one up would bring the lot of them down on him, like a load of bricks.

It's over, he thought. Over and done.

And with that thought something powerful released in him, and soon something lighter, if also sadder, began to take its place. His mind felt clear.

"What do you think?" Harris said. "You seen enough?"

"I've seen enough," Jack said.

CHAPTER 61

In the days before Turner's series was to run, the Cornfellers were compiling additional information, requesting fences and large skull-and-crossbone signs warning of dangerous wastes in the contaminated areas, and they were conducting their own interviews and calling Turner with the results; the federal investigators had subpoenaed the mayor, Harlan Stanyan, Arthur Franks, and seven other city employees, and Dante Pavio, who'd said in an interview with Stewart that all they were doing was "digging up yesterday's business," without seeming to recognize the double meaning. Meanwhile plans for the Lakefest were going forward. It was like two trains bound for the same stretch of track. The hotels were booked up, and the campsites, and several of the restaurants; thirty thousand visitors were expected in all.

A total of twelve stories would run over four days. There were single articles about Hickey, Stanyan, and Pavio, and a history of the last cleanup, ten years back. In addition, they'd allowed Turner two different perspective pieces, in which he talked about the promise of the Lakefront plan and how everyone had been behind it, how they'd risked it all.

Jack was a great help. He'd let Turner look through records, told him what Hickey had said to him, and what he'd reported to the state police. There was a strong likelihood that Hickey would spend some time behind bars. Stanyan would, absolutely. And so might Harris and the others. The U.S. attorney's office was pushing for community service for Harris. Jack would escape with a slap on the wrist.

TURNER RAN INTO HARRIS in the midst of this, when he'd stopped to pump gas.

Turner paid inside and when he stepped outside again, Harris was leaning against his car.

"I saw you two in the parking lot," Harris said.

"Who?"

"The other day. I saw you in the parking lot with Anne."

"We were talking."

"It looked pretty intense."

"It wasn't."

"I don't know what it amounts to, but I'll tell you this. Don't go there, Turner. Or if you're there already, leave. Pronto."

"There's nothing to leave."

"Then what were you arguing about?"

"Nothing."

"She's my brother's fiancée."

"There's nothing between us."

Harris reached forward and softly patted Turner's face.

"Let's hope not," he said.

CHAPTER 62

"I'm glad you're coming," she said on their drive down to New York.

"Why's that?"

"For one thing, you're driving. And anyway, I've been thinking that for once I'll be the point of attention, and you can be the appropriately groomed appendage."

"Admiring you from the corner."

"You know it."

They were heading south now on Route 81. Anne told Jack three days before her big night that she was going downstate for a show of her paintings, and he surprised her by volunteering to drive her down. She had planned to go alone, but when he said he wanted to come she immediately agreed. It had been a hard time for him. Twice that week he'd awakened from bad dreams.

Now as they made their way past Binghamton and into the Catskills, she was feeling contented, happy even, and it wasn't merely because of her show, or Jack's presence; it was because of the decision she was making. Each mile she felt stronger, more clearheaded. She was deciding to leave Lakeland, the whole damn nightmare, if not this weekend, then soon.

She understood too that she had to tell Jack about Turner, that the untold had become a weight under which their recent renaissance could only feel precarious. She resolved to tell him not tonight but sometime in the next days, after the show. She watched him peel off his coat and place it in the backseat, his other hand still on the wheel, eyes fixed ahead through the windshield. He looked to her like a man escaping, although she might have been seeing within him her own urgency for flight.

MAYBE IT WAS THE STRANGE SURROUNDINGS, the noise of the traffic below, the puffy waist-high bed that dominated the hotel room, the absence of whatever it was upstate that had rendered them indifferent, or maybe it was the fear that they might soon part company and for good, but things were suddenly easy between them, and fun. They were instinctive again, and this surprised her; that something you thought you'd lost could return, worn and lovely, like glass from the sea.

She didn't want to return up there where everything was still so muddled. She wanted to pretend none of it had happened, not her affair, or his project, or all the mistakes everyone had made. In the middle of the night she awoke to see that his side of the bed was empty. He was having nightmares again, she knew. He was seated against the window, staring out.

Without glancing her way he said, "Parents gotta be away somewhere."

She walked over and she saw he was looking into the window of a party of teenagers in the apartment building across the street. She could hear the faint tremor of house music.

"Want to go crash?" she asked.

He considered it a moment. "What would we wear?" he asked.

"Good point," she said. "Come back to bed."

"In a bit."

"Call me if anything juicy starts to happen."

IT WAS A SHOW of emerging artists. Three painters; an abstract sculptor who worked in multicolored coils of rubber; a woman who used mixed media: film, video, and dance, all starring herself in a variety of disguises; and a photographer whose pictures were of houseflies and bees, crystal-clear closeups in which you could detect an expression, minute differences in the wrinkles on a wing. All of them were more entrenched in the New York scene than Anne, and they were all under thirty-five. The crowd was dressed in black, browns, and grays, a New York crowd. Anne's sister was there and a few of her old friends. Jack, crisp and pressed in jeans and a tab-collared linen shirt Anne had convinced him to buy, talked with them a while and then wandered off on his own. He stopped near a tall white-haired man in a lavender jacket and his skull-capped Japanese companion, whom Jack had been watching because they looked like luminaries. They were concluding their second trip around Anne's work. He sidled up next to them.

"Good, huh?" he said.

"Indeed," the tall white-haired man said.

"Are you her husband?" the Japanese man asked.

"No," Jack said.

"A friend?"

"Yes."

"She's got a few weak spots, sure, but she's a find, absolutely a find," the tall white-haired man said. "I love how she varies."

"Varies?"

"Between abstraction and figuration, and still remains the same artist."

"Yes," Jack said.

"There's a unified vision here," the man said.

Jack nodded. The white-haired man took Jack's arm and led him to his favorite, a particularly abstract one, and showed Jack how the azure light seemed first to bathe all the forms. "But you can see [and this Jack tried to memorize so he could tell Anne later] a *decisiveness* about tonal structure and the way sharp contrasts can be used both to hollow out the space of the painting, and to create a firm flat pattern."

Jack saw what he was saying, and it pleased him that he could do so. In front of another painting, the white-haired man spoke of the angles of an image, how beautifully *integrated* they were, how she seemed able in her work to explore all manner of nuances, shifts of tone, transparencies (yes, yes, yes, Jack thought, breathless with pride), and then something else Jack couldn't quite make out, and finally what he called an *exquisite sadness* to the narrative content. *Her father, I've heard.* And that was when Anne's friend, Anika, came over with Anne.

Turned out the man was an art collector and occasional critic. The Japanese man asked Anne if she had kept the drawings she'd done in advance of these paintings. She had.

Someone else, a frizzy-haired woman, was commenting in another part of the room on the *layering*, how like Matisse she'd left her paintings with the traces of their conceptions. The underpainting, Jack thought. The reworkings showed signs of curiosity, not indecision, she said. The colors were luminous.

Of course, the tall white-haired man said, she had some maturing to do; she had some areas of overindulgence, but who didn't at this stage?

Anne sold three paintings that first night, at prices Anika had set and that Anne had thought were amusingly high.

THAT WHOLE TRIUMPHAL NIGHT, as she moved about meeting people, shaking hands, holding forth, he remained in her periphery, around in case she wanted to introduce him. He let her negotiate the evening. He wondered for a moment what he'd think if he'd just stumbled into this show when he'd first moved to New York, and if he'd seen Anne, with her hair tied back, ochre silk shirt (which showed through to her black bra) and black suit, her slightly lazy walk, her tendency to touch the arm of the person she was talking to, her effortless command of the room, *her* room, full of *her* work. He wouldn't know what to say to her or to any of these people. It made him think of Anne up in Lakeland. Here was where she fit in. He'd kept her from this, expected her to adapt to a world he had never adapted to; expected her to care about what he cared about, to be his fan. Anne used to call him a chameleon because he fit so easily into either world, but he was wondering—not for the first time—if there was anywhere he could truthfully call home.

Before he could feel neglected she was beside him, hand laced in his.

"How're you doing?" she asked.

"A little in awe," he answered.

What he felt was unneeded. She could survive without him, and it scared him.

"Get us a couple more glasses of wine and we'll schmooze together."

"Schmoozing and boozing," he said.

"Exactly. Let's go check out the other artists."

IT WASN'T THAT NIGHT that she told him about Turner, what with the three bars they went to with Anika and the other artists. Nor was it the next day when they cruised around the Village drinking margaritas. It was that night after dinner, as they sat on a bench in Columbus Circle. She thought of him alone, without her. She had always thought that Jack would be better off alone or with another yet-to-be-determined woman, one of the attractive, athletic-looking women whose photos she made him remove from his albums, but now she didn't think so. She was *good* for him; or rather she could be. They could be good for each other. She could see that clearly now, as clearly as she could see his uncharacteristic three-day beard and the presence of something like bliss in his face. She thought, If this is the end, I'm happy for this weekend; I'm happy we had this.

Then, as a warm, light rain started to fall, and as she longed to forget their mistakes, she took a deep breath and told him about Turner, how it started, how it continued, sparing only hurtful details. She said everything she had to, and she hoped against logic and the new and frightening coolness in Jack's eyes that he could see it as she did. Not as an end, but as an imperfect and willful act of faith.

CHAPTER 63

You might have thought they'd pack it in, the people of Lakeland, the Boy Scouts and Elks Lodge, the Moose and the Masons, the steam fitters and pipe fitters and metal workers and
plumbers, the board of ed, the 4-H club, the merchants association, and all those churches, or that they'd go at preparing for
the Lakefest half-assed. They didn't. They were getting ready
for the governor, but even when they learned at the last moment that the governor had taken sick and wouldn't be able to
make it (sick, my ass, Councilman Bradshaw said), they still
prepped, still built the ten stages, still brought in the tall ships,
still practiced their routines, still stocked up on pizzas and kiel-
basa, Coke and Budweiser, and a few scattered, upscale items
like pesto chicken sandwiches, brandy-cured pork chops, apples
with brie, and wines from the nearby Finger Lakes.

"Pathetic is what it is," Stewart said. "Denial isn't just a river
in Egypt."

It was all a bit surreal, Turner thought. Television had jumped
in to give their obits, and then the newspapers, including one
that ran an editorial saying that there were two futures: "the
bright future of the rest of the country and the bleak future
of places like this, smokestack towns frozen in time, like old
athletes, their bodies too worn down, their hearts failing, their
spirits sagging." But Turner didn't see too many sagging spirits.
Even in the face of all the morbid news.

LAGOONS WERE DRAINED, drums carried away by moon-suited men with airpacks and respirators. Engineers from the state walked the fields, sampling soil, tracing point sources of the spills, placing barrels in larger overpack barrels, then dropping them into the back of green state DEC trucks. A spokesperson described the level of toxins on several farms as "beyond acceptable."

It had Turner thinking about the absurdity of that word, *acceptable*, when it came to poison. He was not a zealot in these matters, nothing like the Cornfellers anyhow, but still he wondered, how much was an acceptable level of mercury in your fish or lead in your water? What did that mean when you got down to it? That it wouldn't instantly kill you? Was that meant to be a comfort?

It was like designating an acceptable number of body hairs on a pizza you were eating. None was always best, wasn't it?

The talk around town was of lawyers and investigators, grand jury investigations, the various diseases and other ailments you could get from the toxic chemicals. The Cornfellers and their group were holding meetings every night, sometimes outdoors by bullhorn, twice on the steps of City Hall. They were calling for Hickey's head.

"I told you," McShain said. "Hysteria always wins."

The Occupational Safety Health Association was looking into Stanyan's orders, and his poor excuses for protective gear. Turner talked with three of the men, Jameson, Bazorcik, and Terry Miller. The more he looked into this, the more he found.

On a tip from Hadfield he found the old project engineer from the harbor sites.

A lagoon on one of the farms had burst, and the chemicals they'd emptied into it had seeped into a creek, and eventually into Lake Ontario. Fisherman called in fishkills. The Coast Guard was called in and they traced the plume of chemicals to farms like McBride's.

The justice department was involved now. Among the violations mentioned were reckless endangerment, manslaughter, polluting federal waterways, holding a body unreported, and obstructing justice. People were complaining of a host of diseases, from mysterious rashes and nosebleeds to infertility, memory loss, and cancer.

TURNER RECEIVED TWO MORE phone threats and a rock through his window. One night as he came home, Turner saw a stuffed animal in a shirt and tie, hanging from a noose on his porch. A pointless gag that he chose to ignore.

It wasn't until he returned home the following evening that he saw it wasn't a stuffed animal, but a real raccoon, and that real blood had been smeared on his windows. There was a hole in the back of the raccoon's head—a gunshot wound, it looked like.

Turner called the ASPCA to make arrangements for the body, and then the police, who told him they'd be by soon to investigate. But after another hour, when they hadn't come, Turner couldn't stand to leave the poor thing hanging like that. He cut the noose and wrapped the murdered animal in a soft blue bath towel. Blood soaked through the towel. It was cruel and grotesque, and if it made him feel less bad about wrecking the party, it also scared the hell out of him.

IT HAD BEEN TWO WEEKS since Anne said she'd come over to bring him a painting. And still Turner believed she would. The few times he tried to spend the evening out, he'd found himself wondering the entire time if he might be missing her, if he might be blowing his only chance, and so couldn't enjoy himself. Then he thought that he'd be better off. He should write his stories and find another woman, or better yet, no woman at all. Now was the time to see his investigation through. In earlier times Turner might have ridiculed someone lying awake at night over a woman, or claiming to feel the physical ache he felt, the *hole* inside him; but there it was. He could feel the breeze whistle through when he walked alone at night. Once when he thought he'd been thinking silently he discovered he was speaking aloud lines he might say to her: *I'm sorry I kept that from you. . . . I'm sorry I kept anything from you. . . . I'm sorry I was so damn bizarre when I ran into you. . . . Loneliness will do that to a guy. Love too. And long, unrelenting workdays. . . . I've been killing myself working, is the problem. . . . Though I wouldn't have it another way . . .*

What he wanted to talk to her about was the call he'd just received from an editor at the *Philadelphia Inquirer.* Turner had sent them his first stories on the harborfront and a few of his best features from the previous year. And now they wanted him to come in for an interview for their Montgomery County beat. Philadelphia. Four million people. Big-city culture, an hour and a half from New York, and unlike Manhattan you could afford a house. It would be a good place for him and Anne to move to. A fresh start for both of them. There was an art scene in Philadelphia. Wasn't it an art museum that Rocky ran to after he drank his five raw eggs?

He needed some time alone with her in his apartment to discuss all this. His apartment had been good to them. They had never *not* messed around here. And the more he thought of this, the calmer Turner felt. Just hang back, *be cool.*

"We will end up together," he said in the voice of someone reading a fortune cookie.

It occurred to him he was conducting the entire relationship alone. Each night brought a pattern of tension and reconciliation, followed by foolish optimism, and all this in his head. It was a depressing charade, but for now it was the best he could do.

ON A NIGHT when Turner was heavily caffeinated and committed to writing until three in the morning, on a night when his mind was focused, and he was poised to finish this series once and for all, he stopped home first to change clothes, and waiting there on his living room couch, looking awkward and beautiful, was Anne.

His first thought when he saw her through the window was: Not tonight. Too much to do. But when he walked in the door he felt as though this might turn out the way he'd wanted.

"The key was still there," she said. "Under the spotted rock."

"Yes."

"It made me happy."

Turner shrugged; tried a smile.

"I've been sitting here thinking about how much I loved this place," she said, "everything in it, your furniture, your books and tapes. The blue rug. I'd forgotten it all."

"Loved."

"Yes."

"Why the past tense?"

"I guess it feels like the past."

They were strained now. He'd been weird again, calling her on tenses. He kept trying to read her, her posture and facial expressions. There was something depressingly polite about the way she was talking, like someone tendering her resignation.

"I was in New York over the weekend. I had a show of my paintings."

"That's fantastic, Anne."

"It wasn't only me. There were six of us, *emerging* artists they called us. It was in a little gallery on Varick Street."

"You're a damn star. We should celebrate." Turner remembered the bottle of Moët he'd been keeping for when the series ran. He could finish his work later. He'd get up early, work all day, and turn in his series by early afternoon. Digby wouldn't know the difference. "Let's have some champagne."

"I can't really stay," she said.

"It won't take long," he answered. He retrieved the bottle from the kitchen. "Tell me about your show. Details, details."

She told him all about the night, the other artists, and what

New York was like. She told him about the feedback, great and good, and how she ended up selling four out of the ten paintings. Somehow, Jack's name found its way into the story.

"Must have been fun for him," Turner said, trying to hide his disappointment.

"I think it was," she said, and paused. "I told him."

"Told him?"

"About you and me."

There were far too many ways to interpret this.

"How'd he take it?"

"Not well."

"But you resolved things."

"In a sense."

The champagne was flattening in their glasses. Turner wanted to move to another topic.

"Well, I might have a new job," he tried. "I'm interviewing with the *Philadelphia Inquirer*."

"That's so exciting," she said.

"Not as exciting as a Soho art show, but it's not bad."

He tried inching closer to her on the couch. She didn't move away.

"Turns out the editor grew up a block away from me. Not that that should matter."

Somehow they were holding hands now, her thumb smoothing his wrist. His heart soared, and he felt lightheaded.

"Big city," he said. "Lots to do. An hour and a half from New York, but far more liveable." He paused before doing or saying anything else. Easy, boy, he told himself. But then, tentatively at first and then unabashedly, their mouths had come together. He hadn't known they were going to, and nor could he say who'd initiated it. Perhaps this was all they needed: a little good news to share. He started speaking softly between kisses about Philadelphia, as though it were Paris: ". . . cobblestone streets, the Liberty Bell. Come with me." And he was happy, and hopeful.

"Yes?" she said.

"Come with me," he whispered, "and we'll start our lives there." His hands were circling her ribs then, beneath her shirt, and he was imagining Philadelphia, a brick-walled loft apartment in an old warehouse building, their bed, sheets kicked to the floor. He was thinking of miracles and that his life would include them forever now, when he saw Anne had turned from him.

"Should we stop this?"

She nodded. They moved apart. She was trembling silently.

"This is wrong," she said, eyes averted.

"So why'd we start?"

"I wanted to see what happened."

"And what happened?"

"I learned I can't do this."

Turner's long-planned script had veered away.

"It's all right. We have time," he said.

"What do you mean?"

"I mean, no rush, right? We'll have time to hang out, figure this all out."

You don't get it, her look said. He felt a burst of anger then; not at her so much as at his own foolishness.

"Come on, Anne. Are you going tell me how you're *married* again? You had a little fly-by-night ceremony performed by some hack who probably sells snowshoes during the day? That's not a wedding."

Insulting her was pointless. But Turner didn't care.

"You're so damned sure of yourself, aren't you," Anne said, glowering at him. "You sit back and judge me, judge Jack. Judge the whole town. I can't wait to read about it, Turner. I can't wait to read every last little cynical nugget."

"That's not fair." He was thinking of their snowbound week. "We fell in love," he said.

She lowered her glance, a small girl told of something bad she'd done. He saw the scar on her forehead.

"It happened for a *reason*," he said, loathing the desperation in his voice.

"You were there for me," she said, with a look somewhere between love and pity. "You changed my life, Turner. I know that. And I *do* think of what it would be like to be with you. All the time. But I just need to be on my own for a while, can you understand? Find my own place in my own world. And maybe that sounds selfish or trite to you, but that's what I'm doing. I'm moving back to New York in a few days."

"And what about Jack?"

"I don't know. He's going to stay up here a while and finish whatever he needs to finish."

"And then he'll join you in New York."

"Maybe . . . I still love him, Turner."

"I know. You always said you did."

"But I never knew how much."

Turner nodded, hoping she wouldn't elaborate, but she did.

"I can't even tell you what it was. Maybe his falling down the way he did, losing some of his confidence, you know? Anyhow, it was like putting on glasses. I saw all our mistakes, our blind spots." She was speaking rapidly. "Maybe it's too late, probably it is . . . but I realized I blamed him for things that weren't his fault, that were my own creating. I saw in New York what we'd been, you know, before the move, when we first met, and everything was—"

"Please don't tell me how you rekindled your spark, how transcendent it was and all that, all right, Anne? Tell a girlfriend or your sister, because I'm not the best audience for that kind of crap right now."

"I'm sorry," she said, and looked terribly sad. "None of this is easy for me, you know. Sometimes I just want to escape to some island where I don't have to think about any of this anymore. It makes my head hurt."

"Well, send me a postcard when you get there."

She closed her eyes in exasperation.

"I'd better go," she said.

"All right," he said, hoping she wouldn't, that she'd spend the night, and the next and the one after that.

"I'm sorry," Anne said, and she left.

A HALF-HOUR AFTER ANNE LEFT his apartment, Turner could still smell her skin, still taste her breath on his lips. He felt empty. He had messed up, he thought. He shouldn't have kissed her, and he definitely shouldn't have pushed the Philadelphia idea. Still he wouldn't concede that anything had ended. Not yet anyhow. For now he had *work* to do, consequential work, and his mind was far from toxic barrels, shady officials, and blown development deals, where it needed to be. He wouldn't be able to sleep, he knew, and so he abandoned his plan of waking up early, slugged down two cups of coffee instead, and headed back to the office.

Stewart was there sleeping when he arrived, his computer screen displaying a half-finished piece on—who knows what, some other Lakefest preview, the fireworks extravaganza, or the two dozen Port-O-Potties they would put up along the lakeshore.

"You look like shit," Stewart said when Turner flicked his desk light on and his eyes had adjusted. "What happened? They gonna kill your series?"

"They'll run it, if I can finish it."

Turner gathered his thoughts, read through all his stories and Digby's suggestions, and then he worked straight until two. Stewart knocked off at one and then slept in his chair a while.

"Beer?" he asked when Turner switched off his computer for the night.

"Where would I get one?"

"Got a six stashed in the fridge."

There was a small refrigerator in the corner of the room under the bookshelves, where Stewart kept his sandwiches. Inside were six Mickey's Big Mouths.

"Sure," Turner said. "But then let's get the hell out of here."

He kept replaying the hour Anne was in his apartment, things he should have said, things he might still say. The streets were mostly silent but there were still a few men out building one of the performance sites, hammering. The place did look different, Turner thought. Gone were all the old tires and boards and farm equipment and dead tree limbs, and in their place a fine boardwalk now stretched clear down the shoreline, and the houses and lawns nearby looked better. The moon lay like chalk over the lake, where now two tall ships and a couple dozen sailboats were docked. You could do worse than to live here.

"Why does all this make me so sad?" he asked Stewart.

"Because instead of getting out of here you fell in love with this place in some sick way," Stewart said.

"Why?"

"I've got no idea. It's a little shithole. And in a year or two you'll forget all about it."

THEY WOULD HAVE HAD new amusements, the state fair rides, the rolling teacups and the flying elephants, but the company that would have paid for them backed out along with everyone else. So they had the same old rides they'd had every year for the last fifty. They walked by the carnival, by the rickety old roller coaster, the tilt-a-whirl, and the funhouse. Stewart said he'd worked at a carnival at the county fair the summer after high school. He'd hawked for a few games, ring toss and the one where you squirt water into the clown's mouth, and he'd worked the bumper cars. He had an uncle who was one of the concessions managers before he died in an accident involving a tractor.

"Talk about a bunch of miscreants," Stewart said. "It was fun anyhow. I met a lot of girls."

Turner raised his eyebrows.

"What? I was a lot thinner then."

They walked around and made it to the bumper cars.

"Your territory, huh?" Turner said.

Stewart smiled. "Go ahead, Turner, get in one of those babies."

"Why?"

"Just do it, okay?"

Turner stepped into one of the battered old cars. Stewart walked over to the control area and rifled through the drawers. "Whoa, Nellie! We're in business." He turned a key, then pulled a switch. "Give it the gas," he said.

"You're crazy," Turner said.

"Give it the *gas*."

Turner put his foot down, and the car started moving. "This is lunacy, Stewart. We're gonna get arrested."

"Anyone comes, we give 'em a few bucks," Stewart said.

Stewart jumped into another car and then began bumbling around the track.

"I think you need this, Turner," he yelled. "Clear your head, you know?"

He sped around the track. You never knew about a person's hidden resources, Turner thought. Stewart was a bona fide czar of the bumper car. And it was true, it *was* what he needed, or at least the next best thing. He built up speed over three laps, then crashed into a pile of twenty cars. He caromed off the side and then sideswiped Stewart like a turnpike drunk, one of those two A.M. wrecks he was too often writing about. Turner'd earned a reputation as being good with the bereaved, and so he was sent to every fatal. It was a reputation he'd be glad to lose. Stewart howled when hit, as though he'd been bludgeoned. They both kept switching cars so they could move the pile, then smash into it all over again, like kids. No one came; no one stopped them. Turner stepped out of himself a moment and observed the scene.

How had he gotten here, blasting about in an ancient bumper car ring in Lakeland, New York, a few hours before his biggest deadline, the same night he'd had his heart smashed harder than any of these cars? He asked himself then: *What if I lose her? Could he survive?* He wondered, if he brought Anne here, could he change her mind, show her you could break the rules and get away with it?

Let it go, he told himself, but that was like asking at dusk for morning to come.

As he shut down the ride, Stewart beamed like he'd won the Daytona 500, hair on end, shirt untucked and drenched with sweat. They said nothing walking out of the carnival grounds, Stewart chuckling at his own brazenness. There was a security station up front, but the guard was watching television at a loud volume. Slipping by was easy.

"Thanks," Turner said before heading to his car.

"Thank *you*," Stewart said. For the first time since he'd known him, Turner could picture Stewart as a teenager, before bitterness and disillusionment took root, when anything was possible.

"I don't want to get heavy here. But I really don't know what I'm going to do, Turner . . . I mean, when you leave. In some weird way you're family, you know?" He smiled strangely, a bit sadly. "You're my brother."

"I don't know what to say," Turner said, because he didn't. Stewart's affection had made him uncomfortable. "You're the man," he tried.

And then he walked off toward his car.

WHEN HE GOT TO HIS STREET Turner saw two men sitting in a dark blue Pinto down the block a few spaces. He thought of Harris Lambeau getting clubbed and dragged up to Toronto, left for dead, and he thought of that poor sad raccoon. He stopped and considered his options. They were waiting for him to make a move, he knew. If he tried to run, they'd chase after him. He would deal with this head on, he thought. He wouldn't let them intimidate him anymore, not on this night, not after all he'd gone through in the last months. All he wanted to do was to get some sleep. He needed it, and he *deserved* it: a little peace and quiet, damn it. Why couldn't these assholes stop pestering him, stop calling and hanging up, or firing rocks through his window, or following him home, or vandalizing his car?

He walked over to them, knocked on the driver's-side window.

"Now tell me," he heard himself saying, "what the fuck do you guys want, 'cause I'm really sick and tired of this."

The driver rolled the window down. Turner saw it wasn't two men, it was a man and a woman—an elderly woman. It was his landlady, Mrs. Willhillen, and her lumbering, overly friendly son.

"What kind of language is that to use?" Willis, her son, said.

"I'm sorry," Turner said. "I didn't know who you were."

"We just got back from the hospital. Mom's had some problems with her heart," he said.

"Is she all right?"

"For now. Yes. They say she'll be fine. We've got to change her diet a little."

"Hello, Steven," Mrs. Willhillen said.

"I hope you feel better," Turner said.

"Thank you, Steven. I'm sure I will."

He watched Willis walk his mother into their apartment, which was in the building to the right of Turner's.

He felt a little ill. And he wondered, what exactly he would he have done if it *was* two men in the car, thugs with guns or a baseball bat? Take them on with his bare fists? He pictured his mug in the paper over the caption: *Brokenhearted and broken faced.*

He whispered under his breath, "You can't break me, motherfuckers. No way, no how."

CHAPTER 64

When Jack heard the truth about Anne and Turner, he'd first felt more confused than angry, given where they were, sitting happily tipsy in the warm rain in New York City at the end of a good night, a pinnacle of sorts, and he wondered then what this whole weekend was for, the whole thing, the Soho art show and the lovemaking, and the talk of how right it all felt. If she was intending to unload a bomb like this, why had she taken him down to New York and then fed him full of drinks to do it? And why, *why* had it gone on as long as it had, *months*, she told him? It made him feel, well, like a jerk, like a pathetic fool, and he wondered while she apologized to him on that bench, her face soft from crying, rainwet and inappropriately lovely (he'd grown angry by now), how many people up in Lakeland knew, how many people had seen them slipping around town and wondered what that poor old chump Jack Lambeau must be thinking.

He wondered if when they gave him that somber, sympathetic face that he'd thought was because of the harbor fiasco, his faded and fated dream, whether it was really about this. How many times when she said she was going out to yoga or the swimming pool or out to dinner with a friend had she been with *him*, and how many times when he ran into Turner in town had he just finished screwing Anne? He pictured positions, the two of them doing everything someone in a porno movie might do. He could imagine killing him. He understood now the men who did such things.

SHE TOLD HIM ABOUT passing out in a fever in that cold house, when he was gone to Chicago.

"Why didn't you tell me that?" he said.

"You're joking, aren't you? Remember what you were like?"

"But I didn't know."

"Exactly."

They stayed another day in New York, figuring this out in that hotel room and in two neighborhood restaurants, crossing back and forth from hatred to love. He felt a little crazy, and increasingly aware of his own role in the desolation that had been their marriage. Everything had spoiled under his watch. All that he had worked for, that he had staked his life on. They had done everything wrong.

That night he'd decided to leave—he'd take the train and she could have the car—but she wouldn't let him, emptied his packed bag onto the hotel room floor. Later he yelled at her, broke a lamp. Later still she slammed the bathroom door in his face, cutting him on the forehead.

She was sorry for that. She cleaned his cut, found him a bandage.

In time he forgave her.

TURNER'S SERIES BEGAN the weekend before Lakefest. It wasn't that the stories and photographs were any great surprise, what with all the rumors, press conferences, and impending lawsuits. But all together as they were, and on the front page and on two inside pages, they had their impact. It was difficult to dismiss it as media-driven hysteria now with all the emergency cleanup crews in town and the investigators and inspectors searching records, walking between buildings in sports coats and dark slacks. Talk ran wild in town, facts and innuendo; everyone, it seemed, had an inside story to tell, a whistle to blow. The treatment of Hickey in the series had been harsh, and the subsequent scuttlebutt about him worse. One rumor had him owning an estate in the Caribbean, paid for with kickbacks. A letter to the editor compared the mayor (who continued to deny any wrongdoing and called his detractors traitors) to the captain of the Exxon *Valdez* in Alaska.

Jack was called in twice to talk to the assistant U.S. attorney who'd cut the deal with Harris. He'd asked, among other things, about Hickey, and Jack answered honestly (with his lawyer present), not vindictively. It felt good to do so, not simply to put a bright face on matters, as he'd been doing for so long. And anyhow he hadn't said anything they didn't already know; he just confirmed it all.

Stanyan, Hickey, Arthur Franks, and several men on Stanyan's team were all facing possible jail terms, one of the men said. And they'd likely nail Dante Pavio, once all the grand jury testimony and records were in. Jack felt bad about Hickey in some ways, but not in others.

He was convinced more than ever that the whole thing had been a mistake, his coming up here, and his bringing Anne. Even without the dumping and the scandal, it was never going to happen the way he wanted. The way Showalter was going, it would have been everything he hated, he was telling Anne, "and I would have allowed it all, pushed it through just to get something built."

"No, you wouldn't have."

"I might have."

"Well, you won't the next time."

EACH DAY there were more men in white moon suits clearing barrels, and others building chain-link fences around farms and fields and a few stretches of woods deemed hazardous. The cleanup would take years, and the court battles longer. The only ones thriving in Lakeland, the line went, were the lawyers.

The sermons in the churches were about faith and the need to keep it. Clarence Easterman gave more talks about toxic poisoning, and citizens' groups continued to amass around City Hall and around Jack's offices. The American Planning Association wrote to say they were disappointed and embarrassed by the turn of events in Lakeland. Jack should have alerted them to the potential problems. They were now considering taking disciplinary action against Jack, and they'd run an article on the scandal in the next issue of their magazine.

The TV reporters covered the demonstrations, then did short eulogies. Jack counted the times the words *broken dream* were used in voice-overs, invariably with a backdrop of the boardwalk and the rebuilt wharves, and then some half-built storefronts and the dead factories. A documentary film team came to town. They'd covered the brewery and lampshade and soda ash factory closings a few years ago and called the area the new Appalachia. Now they were updating the story.

Towns like Lakeland were like endangered species, the filmmaker said. Once they were gone we would never again see the like.

WITH ALL THIS, they were still going forward with the Lakefest. They'd shelled out a whole lot of money already, everything was booked and paid for. And with all the media attention, Councilman McHale said, "Why not give them something other than doom and gloom? Leave them with a different story than what they were expecting—one of resilience, honor, and pride in the face of all their brutal luck?"

"Why not leave them with the truth?" said an old man Jack didn't know. "That for the hundredth time we've been kicked in the teeth, and left out to rot."

ONE NIGHT LATER THAT WEEK, Hickey arrived on Jack's doorstep, drunk and desperate. After some strong words about how Jack had betrayed him and the whole town, he collared Jack in the ear, and Jack had to wrestle him to the ground, talk him through, and then drive him home.

The mayor said little on the way back. He was ashamed, and his nose was bleeding from where Jack had accidentally struck him with his forearm. Jack got him some napkins and cleaned him up outside a convenience store. Hickey finally said, "I'm sorry. I'm sorry, Jack. You're like a son to me. I love you like a son."

When they got to his house Sarah Hickey was waiting at the door.

"Thank heavens you found him. I was worried he'd crashed somewhere."

"I've got his car. He'll probably forget where he left it. I'll drive it by the house tomorrow."

"Thanks, Jack."

"Good night."

"Jack," she said.

"Yes."

"He isn't a bad man, you know. And whatever he said, he didn't mean."

"I know."

"You can't believe the things he says to me sometimes."

Jack nodded.

"He resigned today. Did he tell you that?"

"No. No, he didn't."

"At five he turned his letter in to the city clerk. We're going in over the weekend to clear out his office."

"Before the Lakefest?"

"Yes. A few of the council members told him it would be best. I guess they wanted to separate the festivities from Bill's name."

"I'm sorry."

"I am too. It's his own fault, of course. But he loved being mayor. It's all he wanted to be. That and a fisherman. But he loved being mayor. Especially lately."

"I'm sorry. This must be hard on you."

"Oh, I guess it's going to get worse before it gets better. Anyway, you're tired, I'm sure. You better get on the road. Thanks for bringing my boy home."

"You're welcome," Jack said. "I'll come by tomorrow with the car."

She closed the door. Jack felt heavy, and sad. He thought of the council members asking Hickey to step aside a few days before the big event. It was the right move in a lot of ways; he could certainly understand their reasoning, not wanting a soon-to-be criminal as master of ceremonies. He thought of the protesters outside city hall with the nasty signs demanding Hickey resign. He thought of how it must have felt. William James Hickey III, son of former mayor William Hickey Jr., and grandson of Mayor William Hickey, resigning in disgrace, amidst piles of lawsuits, then coming home drunk in the middle of the night with a bloody nose.

He didn't even like Hickey anymore, had no feelings for him whatsoever, but he thought that the least they could have done was to let the man have his party. What would have been so awful about that?

The door opened then.

"You'll need his car key," she said, and threw it across the lawn to where Jack was standing.

He picked it up and gave her the thumbs-up sign. She gave it back to him.

"Go home to that pretty girl of yours," she said, and then walked back inside.

HIS EAR STUNG on the way home. He thought for a while about those men asking Hickey to quit, about the town dividing, and how it would only get worse. Then he thought about that pretty girl of his. Things had been better since they returned, especially considering how low he'd felt in that New York hotel room. But it didn't change the fact that she was leaving in a few days, and they hadn't yet spelled out their plans, when he'd come down or where they'd live.

She would house-sit for a friend for the short term, until the end of the summer. The story they told people was that he'd follow her soon once everything died down up here. But in truth he hadn't figured it out yet. It had to do with his not having a job lined up, and New York being a tough place to be unemployed, and a worse place to be poor. But it had to do with them too, with all that had happened. He would have preferred a month or two of them getting their bearings again before moving anywhere, before throwing their lives into an upheaval again. If everything in her life was coming together, everything in his seemed unclear and off-balance—where he was going and who he'd be when he got there. It was an uneasy, untethered feeling, and he felt much too old to be having it.

HE SHOWERED under soapy hot water when he got home, and crawled into bed.

"What happened?" Anne asked. "Where were you?"

"Bill and I had a bit of a tussle. I carried him home."

"A tussle?"

"They made him resign today."

She looked at him, read his dolor.

"It's sad," Anne said, sounding tired but sympathetic. "The whole thing is sad. I can't wait to be out of it."

"You will be soon enough," he said, and he almost asked her then what would become of them, whether New York was such a good idea, or whether they were falling into the same sort of trap they'd fallen into here. But it was almost five in the morning now, and anyhow she was already asleep.

CHAPTER 65

Everything bloomed, the maple and oak, dogwood and sumac, lupine and purple loosestrife, the Queen Anne's lace. The sun broke over Lake Ontario and painted the water a sumptuous blue. Lakeland was lush and green again, as unsuited to the town's mood as a sundress at a wake. The mayor had resigned and then taken his boat out all night later in the week. His wife had called the Coast Guard, and they'd found him and the *Sea Queen* beached somewhere near Alexandria Bay. He was ordered to stay in his house until after the grand jury had convened.

TURNER RAN INTO JACK several times in the course of that week. The hardest thing about Jack's reaction was that there didn't seem to be any. He was treating Turner like a reporter, talking to him (within a group of other reporters) about the matters at hand and nothing else. There was no overt enmity, and it spooked Turner.

Finally he caught up to him outside a luncheonette where Jack had been eating alone. Turner had seen him through the window paying his bill, and he'd waited until he walked outside.

"Jack," he said.

"I've got no time, Turner."

Turner tried to gather the right words.

"I'm sure there's nothing I can say here other than that I'm sorry for what happened."

Jack smirked. "You mean you're sorry about how things turned out."

"That too."

"You can't help it, Turner. You're an *opportunist*. You see people in trouble and you try to turn it to your advantage. It isn't all that interesting."

It was what people always said about reporters, that they were nothing more than bottom-feeders or vultures, and it pissed Turner off. Jack started to walk away, but Turner blocked his path.

"That's not how it was."

"No? You got a new job out of this, didn't you?"

"Maybe. We'll see. I lost something too."

Jack glared at him. "Forgive me if I don't cry for you."

"Okay," Turner said. He nodded. And there was nothing more to say. He stood there regardless. "I . . . I should have said something earlier, about the barrels and the harbor and all that. I meant to. I really did."

"Yes, and what happened then, Turner? What the hell happened to that plan, when did you move from wanting to help me to screwing my wife?" The veins in his head pulsed.

"It just happened," Turner said. "You left her in that goddamn house. She was freezing. And you were off collecting your medals. Romancing a shopping mall developer. So who's the opportunist? Huh? You were in the wrong place, you just didn't know it because you were so wrapped up—"

"Please," Jack said acidly. "You want me to thank you for *filling in*? Or for lying to me, and using me to pad your clip file?"

"You had a *dead body* buried in your backyard, Jack, buried by your own brother. Did I make much of that? You *let* them bury those barrels. Maybe you didn't know the numbers but you knew something bad was going on. You didn't ask questions. You kept your head in the sand. Legally they can't nail you, but you and I know you fucked up big time. I took it easy on you. That's why you can still walk around town."

"Who asked you to do that? Did I ever ask for special treatment?"

"Not in so many words, but you expected it."

"I guess you can read minds now."

"What do you want from me?" Turner asked. He meant that he was the one left out in the cold, but he hadn't the temerity to say as much.

"Absolutely nothing."

Turner thought then of when he and Jack had first hung out, the nights playing pool or shooting hoops and theorizing about everything. He'd thought of him as the best part of Lakeland, an oasis of erudition and idealism, and a fairly good scotch drinker to boot. There was no way to heal this. And the more they spoke, the more they'd hate each other. That was clear now. He felt bad for his little speech, because the gist of it wasn't true. If Jack had deserved to be nailed, Turner would have done it. He hadn't spared him as a gift. He'd treated him fairly, like anyone else.

"I'm sorry," he said. "If I were you I'd feel the same way."

"That right?"

"Yes."

"We were friends," Jack said.

It was the first time in this exchange he didn't seem angry. He was disillusioned, and Turner was sorry for that.

"I guess I messed that up."

"Mind if I cut this little talk short, Turner? I'd like to get home, if that's all right by you."

TURNER STOPPED AT GIOVANNI'S on the Saturday night of the festival. It had been warm during the day but now it had dropped into the low fifties. No one seemed to care.

Two third-tier country musicians had made the trip north along with some formerly famous rock performers, Three Dog Night for one, and the stands had been packed. Along the shoreline and on the boardwalk, they were playing up the Great Lakes theme. There were monuments to the lakes' history. Stories of shipwrecks and battles, and all those staggering statistics: *Spread evenly over the continental U.S. the Great Lakes would submerge the country under about nine feet of water.* There were simula-crums of the old fish stalls and counting-houses. And people shouting out to one another in the husky voices of the imagined old port town.

They hadn't yet taken down all the models, and the pamphlets and posters that spoke of what the harborfront would bring, Shep Showalter's grand plan, though Showalter had left days ago. A sign above it all read, THE JEWEL OF ONTARIO. And next to it was a homemade headline, printed at the Lakeland Eagle, which read, LAKELAND'S HARBORFRONT: AN AMERICAN SUCCESS STORY.

SERENA WAS RACING AROUND serving drinks. She was wearing a tight-fitting aqua-and-yellow Harbortown T-shirt. The one with the wave.

"Must be a few thousand people in town," she said. "It's fuck-you-Turner weekend."

"What does that mean?"

"Means they're having their party anyhow."

Turner shook his head.

"I'm just joshing you."

"I'm glad it's still on. It's what I wanted. I didn't want to ruin everything. I just did my job."

"Of course you did. Listen, Turner. It's sick shit they were doing. I saw those pictures, the birds and the squirrels, and that kid with his weird rashes." She shook her head in disgust. "You're a hero. Don't forget that. I'm proud of you."

"How's Garrett?" Turner asked.

"Who knows?"

"What do you mean?"

"Means you haven't been around in a while. I moved out."

"What happened?"

"It just occurred to me when I woke up one morning that I really didn't like him."

"And that was it?"

"Isn't that enough?"

"Of course it is. I just thought you two had overcome that liking thing."

She gave him a look.

"Is it so bad that I wanted a little security? Don't you ever want it?"

"Yes."

"Anyhow I'm dating someone else now. He's there at the end of the bar."

Turner glanced down the bar where two young men were talking.

"Both of them?"

"No. The good-looking one."

It was difficult to make the distinction being that they looked like twins. Hip sideburns and muscles, like teen TV stars.

"Is it serious?"

"Nah. It's just sex for now." She winked at him, then walked down the bar and joined the two men.

When she came back he said, "I'm leaving here in a week. Philadelphia. I got a new job."

Serena smiled and nodded. "I knew you would. I knew good things would happen for you," she said. Turner realized he'd missed Serena, and he wondered if he might have been better off, healthier anyhow, with her all this time.

"When it happened—when I split, I mean—I kept wanting you to come in here again, isn't that crazy? I kept thinking you would, and then of course you didn't."

"What would have happened?" Turner asked.

"I don't know. I was open to the possibilities."

"My loss, certainly."

"You got that right."

AS HE WALKED OUT he saw groups walking in and others out on the street filling the restaurants and bars. The air had cooled, but the sky was clear and no one seemed to be heading home. What Jack said was true. He was sorry about how things turned out. He was sorry for a lot of things, but not for what he'd done. He'd acted from a place deep down in him, a place he'd never been before, and he could live with the results. The loss of a friend, the loss of love even. Maybe he *was* an opportunist, but he wasn't a vulture. There was a difference.

A foursome strode by, arm in arm, and they were singing happily, oblivious to him. He couldn't fathom what they could be celebrating. Survival; or perhaps the existence of beer. He stopped there on the sidewalk and he felt a calmness rush over him. In a month he'd be gone, living in another city, making a new group of friends, and he'd have an entirely different life, but Turner wanted to hold on to the feeling he had just then; it was an almost exquisite feeling of loneliness, of being alone against the world, and unafraid. It felt a little like heroism, or maybe just defiance.

And if he hurt badly, he also felt alive, as he hadn't in years. Conscious and receptive. The breeze felt cold against his skin. He braced himself and walked toward downtown, toward the lights and the noise.

CHAPTER 66

That same night, her last night in town, Anne and Jack rode the carnival rides together. They bought hot dogs and corn on the cob and fried dough, and they rode the bumper cars two times and the rusted-out roller coaster there. They played the games: hooking the bottle, shooting water in the clown's mouth, tossing softballs into a basket, and Anne won Jack a stuffed dragon.

He was telling her between activities about the trip he and Harris had made to pick up Harris's dog. Harris had worried alternately that Sammy wouldn't recognize him, or that Sammy would be near death. The dog looked exactly the same, only a little dirtier, and quite a bit thinner. He recognized Harris all right, nearly knocked him to the ground with what energy he had left.

"There's something perfect about that, I mean along Harris's road to redemption. He goes to rescue the dog he buried."

"I guess so."

In exchange for his exhaustive testimony Harris was rewarded with probation and three hundred hours of public service, during which he would paint houses and Sheetrock for the county's community development office. He was trying with Jack's help to get a bank loan to start his own business.

"It's sort of inspiring to see him with Charlotte, don't you think? I mean to see a person change like that," Anne said.

"He wasn't all bad before."

"He was a criminal."

They bought tall beers and talked about what Jack had and
had not accomplished here. He'd done a lot, Anne was saying.

"I failed myself and everyone here," he said. The line had
been an internal mantra since his night on the farm with Harris.

"I know you don't believe that."

"But I do."

"You only half-failed."

"What's the difference?"

"Look at your brother."

"What do you mean? I'm part of why he got in trouble."

"You're a good example, whether you know it or not. You make
people want to do better. To *be* better. It's not always easy is the
problem, and that's when we end up resenting you."

"I'm self-righteous, you're saying."

"Only sometimes."

Talk turned then to her painting, and the studio she'd be using in New York. She'd share a four-room space with one other
artist. The studio was in Tribeca, down the block from two hip
restaurants.

"Makes me a little nervous," Anne said.

"How so?"

"I wonder if it'll be gone in New York. I'll try and paint and I
won't be able to see anything."

"It won't happen."

"But it could."

"Then at least you'll have a swanky place to be blocked in."

She smiled. She talked on about New York, how she realized
she'd missed it—the intensity, and maybe more than anything,
the *food*, and he kept waiting to hear where he fit in, but he
didn't hear it. He heard her talk of a course she might teach, and
some people Anika wanted to introduce her to. He pictured all
the men she'd meet within her new circle, painters and sculp-
tors and writers, coffee-shop denizens who spoke in supercilious

voices about the books they loved and the movies they hated. He remembered meeting her friends for drinks one night shortly after he and Anne had met and making the mistake of saying he'd liked *Apollo 13*, and even found it inspiring. He'd felt a little like Harris must have felt with his friends, and then Anne had admitted that she'd liked it too.

THEY RODE THE OLD FERRIS WHEEL, and when the ride was over Anne asked if they could go around again.

"Why not," he said.

At the top they could see across the entire fairgrounds and out to the esplanade where there were performers and food stalls and more crowds. They talked and looked around. He looked out over the harborfront and let his mind travel.

He thought about all the reimaginings along the forgotten lakes and rivers and oceanfronts in the northeast, in Boston and Baltimore and Mystic and Manhattan, the elaborate tableaux of brick and limestone, festival marketplaces and rebuilt waterfront piers meant to bring back better times. They were stage props, Jack thought, all of them, drummed up to satisfy an incurable yearning, and they were as necessary as they were ineffectual. Everyone invents his own past, shapes it into what he needs, emphasizes one thing, forgets another, searches for a coherent narrative, when in truth the past is almost always a collage of contradictions even in the happiest of lives. With all his glossing stripped away, Jack was haunted again by his adolescent perceptions, the claustrophobia and longing of a precocious kid in a dying town, but he was filled with other things too. Allegiance and hope, a lingering urgency to make things better, though there wasn't much left for him to do. Through all this, he would find a way somehow.

It was clear something was wrong with the ride, though neither spoke of it. Five minutes passed, then ten. There were people gathering far below them at the control station.

"It's really quite lovely, isn't it?" she said, looking out over the fairgrounds and the lake, the two tall ships.

"Once you know you're leaving?"

He was surprised that he'd said this.

"Perhaps."

He said nothing. The ride moved a few yards, ungracefully, making disturbing creaking noises along the way. She would leave soon and put all of this behind her. She took his hand then, as if reading his thoughts. She whispered, "I love you more than you could possibly know."

"You're leaving," he said.

"We *both* are. Leave with me."

"I have to stay until all this is done."

"All right, then don't make it seem like I'm doing the leaving."

He did not say then that a lot could happen, because so much already had, and here they were anyhow. She squeezed his hand tighter as the ride moved upward, and then stopped once again. The breeze picked up, and they could barely hear the music on the ground.

"Something's wrong with this," Jack said. "It's not supposed to do this."

"But it's fun, don't you think? Not knowing what'll happen."

"It's dangerous."

"It isn't dangerous. It's not like a roller coaster. And anyhow we're in the best spot, right? Way above everyone."

He looked around. She was right. They were.

"Let's stay up here," she said. "Never come down."

"All right."

The ride lurched. She fell onto him and let out a small gasp. The entire ride bucked again and they dropped another five feet. She stayed pinned to him. He looked down to the ground and drew in his breath. A child in a car below them was crying.

"Scared?" Anne said.

"A bit."

"Me too. But it's okay, isn't it? To be scared."

"Yes, of course."

"If I die, I want it to happen with you. Is that strange? I just figured that out."

"I'm trying to find that reassuring," he said.

"Here we go," she said.

And then, with Anne leaning out, they dropped downward again, safely this time, to the crowds and the music.

ACKNOWLEDGMENTS

There are many people whose friendship and counsel I have relied on over the many years of writing this book. I want to thank Ray Isle, Ellen Levine, Frederic Stowt, Naeem Murr, Peter Rock, Keith Scribner, Ryan Harty, Tobias Wolff, Elizabeth Tallent, John L'Heureux, Nancy Packer, Erik Huber, David MacDonald, Jim Sullivan, Jonathan Franzen, Dan Chaon, David Relin, W. S. Di Piero, Christian Wiman, Tom Deller, Jim Mazuka, James Howard Kunstler, Craig Benedict, Richard Reinhard, David Berman, John Swomley, Caroline Killefer (for her tremendous generosity), Fred Pierce, Ronna Tannenbaum, Ilisa Barbash, Joy Boyum, Tim Craighead, Caroline Stechschulte, Joshua Ravitz, and Tom Bissell. Many thanks to Joshua Kendall, the MacDowell Colony, the San Francisco Writers' Grotto, James Michener, and the Copernicus Society of America. Special thanks to Carol Lamberg and Mark Weiner (for countless hours of moral support and advice).

In memory of Joseph Barbash and Heather Livingston Barbash.